## *SHE HAD THE WHITEST, FINEST-TEXTURED COMPLEXION HE HAD EVER SEEN . . .*

Her breasts rose gently with each breath, and his heart began beating heavily as he watched them move. Finally, inexorably, his gaze settled on her lips. The trickle of strawberry juice adorning one side of her mouth was the last inducement he needed. He dropped down beside her and placed his mouth over hers.

Magdalena stirred after her pleasant dream. Strong arms protected her, supported her, pleasured her. But when she felt a warm, imperative tongue flick within her mouth with shocking intimacy, her eyes flew open.

The man she had dreamed of now leaned over her in the flesh. . . .

*Books by Colleen Shannon
from Charter*

WILD HEART TAMED
THE TENDER DEVIL
THE HAWK'S LADY
MIDNIGHT RIDER

# Midnight Rider

## Colleen Shannon

CHARTER BOOKS, NEW YORK

MIDNIGHT RIDER

A Charter Book / published by arrangement with
the author

PRINTING HISTORY
Charter edition / October 1989

ISBN: 1-55773-265-5

Charter Books are published by The Berkley Publishing Group,
200 Madison Avenue, New York, New York 10016.
The name "CHARTER" and the "C" logo
are trademarks belonging to Charter Communications, Inc.

PRINTED IN THE UNITED STATES OF AMERICA

10  9  8  7  6  5  4  3  2  1

*To Richard Jeske: husband, lover, and friend.*
*May your sunny smile always shine upon me, your*
*stubbornness always make me mad, and your*
*laughter always make me glad.*
*I love you, my own Clint.*

# *ACKNOWLEDGMENT*

With the deepest affection and respect for a fine
writer and a dear friend:
To Maria José Reddick Wright, for editing my Spanish,
with thanks for our enduring,
special friendship.

# Chapter 1

"This air is clear, yet it is full of shadows that with each
breath strike inward to my heart, and haunt her
chambers with disastered shades of nameless fears,
presaging death and ruin . . ."

**Act I, DON JUAN TENORIO,**
Zorilla y Moral

The California sun heaved its dying gasps down on the two
fencers, silhouetting their macabre dance on the canyon
walls behind them. Cordovans shaded each face. Only the
clang of steel kissing steel and the gritting of teeth were
audible as the duelists engaged, their blades entangled,
grinding together at the hand guards. The deadlock broke
when the tall, red-jacketed fencer flexed his powerful arm
and shoved his smaller opponent away.

The slim figure in the white shirt stumbled. Only the
striated cliffs and one grim man bore witness as the large
fencer lunged at his off-balance adversary. Red Jacket's
blade gleamed like polished carnelian as it arrowed toward
White Shirt's chest. Instead of flailing for balance, the slim
fencer obeyed gravity's command and dove toward the
ground in a controlled roll beneath the arcing rapier.
Catlike, White Shirt rebounded before Red Jacket recovered

1

from his lunge. Red Jacket had to parry while still off-balance, but he rapidly regained his equilibrium.

With a circular motion of his forearm, Red Jacket feinted to his opponent's left, then quickly struck to the right. The tactic seemed successful as the right side of White Shirt's chest was briefly exposed. But when Red Jacket attempted the coup de grace on that vulnerable area, he found his blade enveloped with a supple, rotating motion and batted away.

The slight man who stood aside, watching narrowly, didn't appear surprised at the smaller fencer's adroitness. A satisfied smile curved his thin lips as he watched White Shirt take the initiative with an innovative series of feints and thrusts that forced Red Jacket to retreat.

Red Jacket did not seem concerned, however. Backing away, he jeered, "So fierce, *mi oponente*. Are you not tired? Such enthusiasm is wearing on the nerves and body."

Ignoring the taunts, the slim challenger maintained the attack. Still, White Shirt was unprepared when Red Jacket sprang backward, then lunged viciously. White Shirt shook with the force of the blow and barely countered in time. As they disengaged, both fencers gasped with their exertions.

White Shirt stumbled with weariness. Red Jacket took advantage of the sagging blade and leaped forward with a powerful, straight-armed lunge that seemed impossible to deflect. He was shocked to find his weapon entangled in a dazzling counterattack made with such steady blade control he could not disengage in time to divert the steel that winged to his heart. He stumbled before the force of the blow and crumpled to the ground.

Gasping, the slim victor jerked off the cordovan. Jubilant features beamed down at the vanquished. Waist-length hair fell free to ripple as buoyantly as the deep but feminine voice that mocked, "So tired, *mi oponente*? Or merely disgusted by your defeat at the hands of a mere female?" She slipped the button off her rapier as she spoke and dropped it in the pocket of her tight pants.

The man on the ground opened one wry eye and mourned,

2

"I can never hold my head proudly again. What shall abuelo say when I tell him, Magdalena, *hermana*?"

Magdalena Inez Flanagan de Sarria glared at her brother. She nudged him in the ribs with her dusty boot. Arms akimbo, she scolded, "You are impossible, Carlos. Each bout we fence you taunt me with my weakness and clumsiness, yet the first time I emerge as victor you immediately cry coward and threaten me. Bah, men!"

With a disdainful flick of her hand at his nose, she turned away, but Carlos leaped to his feet and caught her around the waist to swing her high in the air. He shed his injured look, and his eyes twinkled up at her disgruntled face. "You should know I am but teasing, *pequena*. In truth, I am so proud of you I could burst. Who would have thought a woman could defeat the most skilled swordsman in California?"

Carlos set Magdalena down and turned to the dark man who had silently watched their argument. "Is she not as graceful and cunning as a lioness, Joaquin?"

Both men surveyed Magdalena from head to toe. In her flaring pants, boots and loose shirt, she could have passed for a boy from the neck down—until the wind flattened her blouse and exposed small, rounded breasts. To be sure, though, no one looking at her countenance could ever mistake her for a man. Triangular in shape, with a widow's peak that gave her a naughty, sultry look, her face had the milky whiteness and fine texture of young ivory. Her nose was too long for her features to be perfect, but her full, stubborn mouth and direct gold eyes bespoke a character more arresting than perfection.

Indeed, when she narrowed her long-lashed eyes at Joaquin as she awaited his verdict, he was truly reminded of a lioness. Then he looked at her hair streaming in the wind and the illusion was dispelled. Not black, not brown, not red, it seemed the Creator had been uncertain which hair color to endow her with and had finally blessed Magdalena with the finest hues of each. Her sable brown locks rippled with streaks of fire in defiance of the encroaching night.

Joaquin delayed his answer to brood on the girl he'd

3

helped raise and now loved as his own. She was, at seventeen, already a woman—a woman at war with herself who didn't even know it. Many a man would long to be enriched by her alchemy of iron will and feminine fire. One, he feared, in particular.

Her grandfather had good reason to worry. However, Ramon's clumsy attempts to protect Magdalena only incited her. Joaquin dreaded the imminent confrontation. It had been building between them for years. Magdalena's volatile blend of Irish hot-headedness and Latin passion was not calmed by Ramon's Spanish bromides.

Past tragedy further complicated the situation. Magdalena was truly her mother's daughter, Ramon had groaned to Joaquin recently; if she persisted in these wild roamings, she could well end as her mother had. Magdalena had defied the poor relation Ramon had summoned from Spain to guide the girl upon his daughter's death until, defeated, the poor woman had fled back to Madrid. Now, no one remained to teach her to be a proper lady but himself. And teach her he would, Ramon had warned Joaquin last night. With or without her cooperation. There was only one way to keep her safe. When he'd confided his decision to Joaquin, Joaquin had tried to dissuade him, to no avail. Ramon insisted: Magdalena was a woman; she must finally learn her proper role.

Looking at her now, Joaquin knew Ramon was only partly right. Though vulnerably magnetic as only a lovely woman can be, Magdalena was also deeper, stronger, than many men. She would never be happy with the hacienda as her only province. Magdalena's spirit knew no boundaries but the wind and the night, and she'd fight any man who tried to chain her to hearth and home. Ramon had no understanding of Magdalena's fierce self-determination. Unless he learned it, Joaquin feared great conflict awaited the household. Indeed, it had already begun. And when Magdalena lost her temper, she seldom considered the cost of her actions.

Despite his worries, Joaquin's face was calm when he finally grunted a dissent to Carlos's question. "A lioness?

**4**

No. Playful as a lion cub, perhaps, but at least she doesn't have the arrogance of her brother, the strutting peacock." Stiff-backed, the little man walked toward the horses and saddled his mount.

Carlos cocked a rueful eye at his amused sister. "We are rising in his esteem, *hermana*. Soon we shall reach the level of dogs, no?" Laughing, the pair locked arms and joined their master. Though Joaquin was now the *caporal* of their grandfather's ranch, he was a Spaniard who had once been one of Europe's greatest fencing masters.

Many times Magdalena had wondered what tragedy made him sign on with a Spanish merchantman and desert Spain's cultured adulation. Joaquin was evasive about the matter. When questioned, he would only admit that he stayed at the ranch to help raise his friend's children as he would have wanted.

After their parents' deaths, Magdalena and Carlos depended greatly on his calm good sense and love. He was a desperately needed contrast to their abuelo's autocratic youth-rearing beliefs. However, Magdalena suspected Joaquin remained for other reasons as well.

The peaceful ride back to the hacienda became tense as they neared Rancho El Paraiso. Their hearts grew heavy with emotions that varied from disgust, to longing, to regret as they thought of the two men who awaited them.

"*Chica*," Carlos asked suddenly, "has Roberto asked you to marry him yet?"

Joaquin started. He turned in his saddle to watch Magdalena's reaction.

Magdalena's slim hands jerked on the reins. Her mouth twisted as though she'd bitten into a lemon. "Yes, how did you know?"

When they topped the rise overlooking the hacienda, the three halted and surveyed the scene below. The brightness of the moon bathed the sprawling, adobe ranch house in a flattering light that silvered the graceful arches and red tile roof. One-storied, with thick, white-washed walls that kept the inhabitants cool in summer and warm in winter, the

5

building seemed to slumber peacefully under the moon's luminous blanket.

In the distance a bull lowed. As though it were daylight, Magdalena could see in her mind's eye the rolling hills and lush valleys dotted with cattle for thousands of leagues.

Carlos stirred and flung a hand at the idyllic scene. "This," he answered simply. "Cousin Roberto will stop at nothing to gain the lands he covets. Now that he has blackened me in abuelo's eyes, his next task will naturally be to win you for his wife. And, I fear, our dear abuelo will make no objection."

Magdalena sighed at his bitterness, but she knew he was right. As *mayordomo*, Roberto had skillfully alienated Carlos from ranch affairs and then hinted to Ramon that Carlos was interested only in frivolous pursuits, such as fiestas, fencing and flirting. Since playful Carlos and his stern abuelo had never seen eye to eye, Ramon tended to believe the worst of his grandson. His pride hurt, Carlos further strained relations by escaping the hacienda as much as possible, thus appearing to confirm Ramon's suspicions.

And she herself stood little higher in her grandfather's esteem, Magdalena reflected wryly. Ramon Xavier de Sarria was a Californio to his toes, but he ruled his lands like a Spanish patriarch. He believed women were to be flattered, cared for, cherished and protected; in return they must never step out of their place as the natural consorts, comforters and companions of their men. Magdalena's refusal, like her mother's before her, to accept such a role both puzzled and infuriated him.

So she had to sneak in and out of the house during her escapades with Carlos. These blessed hours of freedom were the only times she felt happy and alive. Inez and Patrick, her parents, had never restricted her activities. To the contrary, they had encouraged her interest in such unfeminine pursuits as horse training, fencing and practice with the reata. Oh, for those days again, she thought, tears of longing in her eyes.

Joaquin cleared his throat. "Come, little ones, brooding accomplishes nothing. Let us return and fight for your

6

heritage. Your cousin's influence is great, but he will betray himself in the end. Ramon is stubborn as a mule, but he is not stupid. He will discover Roberto's greed sooner or later, and the rancho will be yours, as your mother wished."

Joaquin's voice softened with tenderness. "You love El Paraiso as you do each other, whether you admit it or not. Your mother went through much to save your heritage, and you must let no one take it away from you. Ramon loves you both deeply. Be patient with him, and he will show it."

The trio spurred their horses down the slope. After caring for their stallions, they walked to the house. Carlos strode to the front and Magdalena slipped to the back, intending to climb in her window. She tossed her sword into the room and levered one leg over the sill, but large, ungentle hands caught her waist and hauled her back down.

Angrily, she tried to shrug off her cousin Roberto's hands, her mouth already starting to form her angry words. But when she caught sight of the tall man with erect bearing and a gray goatee and moustache who stood behind him, she swallowed the abuse she longed to voice.

Roberto's dark eyes flared with a triumph she could see even in the moonlight as he trumpeted, "It's as I told you, *tio*. She has once more been fencing with Carlos. She needs a man to tame her spirit." Roberto caught her chin in his hand and turned her face from side to side, examining her features as he would a horse he contemplated buying.

Her dislike open, she glared at his austerely handsome face with its high, broad cheekbones, thick-lashed eyes and thin lips. Her stare jabbed like an icicle when she ordered glacially, "Release me."

When he did so, she stood unwavering under her grandfather's condemnation. His dark eyes razored over her from head to foot. His mouth curled in distaste. Grasping her wrist, he dragged her behind him into the house. Their footsteps clicking on the red tile floors echoed in the silence.

The two maids setting the long table scurried out of the enormous living area at Ramon's command. He shoved Magdalena into a straight-backed chair and stood over her, trembling with emotion. She looked away from his fury, and only Roberto saw him drag a shaky hand over sagging features.

Magdalena stared at the room, tamping down her own anger. The oak, hide and mahogany furnishings were plain and practical. The only colors in the monastic room glowed from a huge tapestry engulfing the wall behind the dining table. Rag rugs added rainbow hues to the somber ambience.

Inhaling deeply, Ramon leaned against the massive stone fireplace. When he was calm, he uttered with cold finality, "I have been too lenient with you. No longer will you be allowed to help about the rancho. You will stay in the hacienda and learn your place. Galloping around the countryside dressed as a man! You shame me and my name, Magdalena, and endanger yourself needlessly. Who will care for El Paraiso after I'm gone unless you do?" Ramon took several agitated strides across the room, then he turned and delivered his ultimatum.

"That is the last time you will display yourself so. You will marry Roberto at the end of the month, whether you wish it or not. When you have a proper husband and children, you will no longer want to behave so recklessly. You will thank me one day, *nieta*. I will not let you end as your mother did. Have you forgotten how she died?"

Magdalena sat silent throughout his decree, but at his last comment she sprang to her feet and cried, "My mother would still be alive were it not for your cruelty. You did everything you could to drive my father away. You'd not have his Irish blood polluting your Castilian . . ."

"Enough!" His voice stung like a whiplash. "Go to your room. Tomorrow, after the fiesta, you begin working with Sarita to learn the household. And, if you try to run away, I will have you locked in your room and guarded."

Magdalena curled her fingers into fists to keep herself from hurling insults at his arrogant head. She straightened proudly and said through her teeth, "I will never marry Roberto, or any other man, against my will. He has had my final word and so have you." His face colored with rage.

She turned on her heel and exited, her commanding but graceful strides emphasizing her attributes.

Roberto's eyes flared with more than triumph as he watched the gentle sway of her hips. His lids lowered, hiding the gleam.

When she reached her room, however, Magdalena's precarious control toppled. She flung herself face down on the brightly covered bed, and clawed at the soft cotton. "*Madre de Dios*, Mama, Papa, I can stand no more. Why did you have to die?" The two beloved faces she wished desperately she could see again wavered before her eyes. For once, she let the stories and memories claim her . . .

Her mother, Inez, was a high-spirited woman of twenty-five when she met the dashing Irish sailor Patrick Flanagan. She was independent, stubborn and indescribably lovely—irresistible to Patrick, frustrating to Ramon, whose repeated attempts to marry her off had been defied by his only child.

Her father believed she was too independent to give herself to a man, and Inez had come to believe it of herself—until she met the tall ship's surgeon. He was ashore on leave on his first voyage to California when he stumbled across Inez bathing in a frothy stream. When she rose from the water, she was as sensual as a fallen angel, raven hair plastered over pearly breasts.

Water curling about her ankles, Inez looked up and saw a red-headed, blue-eyed giant, standing as though carved in stone. She shrank in fear. Stammering an apology, he had handed over her clothes and turned his back, thus igniting the first spark of the love that would consume them. Before the day was out they were lovers, Inez's first, Patrick's last.

They spent a blissful two days together before Patrick had to sail away, but he returned as often as he could until the time of his service had expired. He wanted to marry her on his second visit, but Inez knew what her father's reaction would be, and she evaded him. On his next visit, Patrick insisted they confront Ramon. Ramon reacted exactly as Inez had feared: He forbade the match and ordered his daughter not to see the Irish *picaro* again. However, when

Inez discovered she was pregnant, Ramon was forced to give grudging, bitter consent to the marriage.

Patrick did all he could to gain stature in Ramon's eyes, to no avail. His attempts to help with the rancho were not successful, for Patrick was a magnificent sailor, soldier and doctor, but a ranchero he would never be. For the first few years after Magdalena's birth, Patrick tried to stifle his restlessness for Inez's sake. As is the Spanish way, she loved and respected her father and would have felt a deserter had she left him alone. She also loved El Paraiso, and she wanted her children to inherit. To distract himself, Patrick became involved in California's chaotic politics.

In 1822 California came under Mexican rule, ending the long, lazy years of Spanish neglect. Unfortunately, Mexico took little more interest in the remotest part of its new republic except to send an endless series of mostly incompetent, arrogant governors who were often hounded out of office by the independent Californios. Patrick had left Ireland because of the political repression shown to Catholics and did all he could to combat that ugliness in the new home he'd grown to love. His verve and determination supplied badly needed leadership in the fledgling land. Against Ramon's wishes, Patrick became a member of the territory's *diputacion*. At last, with the legislature as occupation he was happier, and Ramon's never-ending barbs ceased to bother him.

These happy years shone brightest in Magdalena's memory. Years of raillery and tenderness between her mother and father had filled the house with such gaiety that even Ramon's sour face could not stifle it. Years of roundups, rodeos, fandangos and horse races.

Even Roberto's arrival from Spain as a gangling orphan of twelve seemed cause for celebration in those days. His quick usurpation of her brother's rightful place in her grandfather's affections was a matter she barely noticed in the shadow of the adoration she felt for her father and her love for her high-spirited mother.

Then, four years ago, in 1831, came the man who would change all their lives . . .

Patrick had been appalled by the powerful Franciscans' treatment of the neophytes of California. The Indians' ceaseless work had made the church powerful and prosperous, but they were not allowed to share in the fruits of their labor. The good padres ruled their missions like despots. When one of their flock strayed from the path of work, obedience and prayer, the fathers often used such correctional methods as stocks, irons and whipping posts.

Patrick was helpless to combat the authoritarian power of the church, so he tried to change the Indians' lot by political means and had helped convince the former governor, Echeandia, to initiate plans for secularization of the missions. However, in 1831, Mexico summarily appointed a new governor of Alta California—Manuel Victoria. He soon became known as *El Gobernador Negro*, both because of his dark skin color and the blackness of his deeds.

Magdalena's hatred almost choked her as she reached this point in her thoughts, and her tears dried under its intensity. Deep in bitter memories, she didn't hear the door open or even notice Carlos until he startled her by sitting on the edge of the bed.

Comfortingly, he clasped her trembling shoulder. "*Hermanita*, what has happened? I go to dinner and see a fuming abuelo, a triumphant Roberto and your empty chair. Was our fencing match discovered?"

Bolting upright, Magdalena yanked off her boots. Her voice was muffled when she replied, "Yes, our dear cousin alerted abuelo to our absence." She flung her boots across the room, one after the other, but the violence did not assuage her fury.

Carlos cursed under his breath. He turned her to face him. "*Niña*, I have been thinking it might be best if we left El Paraiso. It is not the only paradise on earth, and perhaps we can find another place that doesn't harbor such a large serpent."

Magdalena shook her head before he finished. "I shall not leave. Our parents both died for love of us and this land. If they had left El Paraiso years ago, they would both still be alive."

"You don't know that, Magdalena. Papa would still have taken an interest in the political situation, even if we had lived elsewhere."

She answered stubbornly, "No. Papa would have opened an office or found some other occupation to keep him busy, and that *desgraciado* could never have murdered him."

"Come, Magdalena, even I admit Victoria's soldier killed him accidentally. The political situation being what it was, it's no wonder the governor feared for his life." Carlos sighed. "If only Papa had not been so furious about the execution of his little Indio friend for theft, he would have seemed less threatening . . ."

But Magdalena hotly interrupted her brother's reasonable reiteration of the facts. "He was *murdered*! They just used fear he pulled a weapon instead of the petition for Victoria's resignation as an excuse." She flung up a silencing hand when Carlos would have replied. "You know the soldiers are scoundrels. Convicts, thieves, murderers, all. The *cholos* commit more crimes than they prevent, led, no doubt, by our illustrious *comandante*, Luis. Why doesn't abuelo use his influence to get rid of him?"

The frenetic hatred in her eyes troubled Carlos. His own bitterness toward Victoria had faded with the governor's ignominious departure, but Magdalena's grief had evolved into an ugly loathing that lay like a blight on her passionate soul. He was at a loss how to comfort her, so his response was slow.

"You know Luis and Roberto are friends and that abuelo won't involve himself in politics. Besides, the comandante wasn't even present when Papa was killed. There is no reason to blame him."

"Bah! He is Mexican, that is reason enough."

Carlos was amused at that. "You are Mexican also, *amorcito*," he teased.

Jumping to her feet, she stood poker-straight. "Never call me that again! I am Californian first, a Flanagan second and a woman last. If I had my way, we'd declare ourselves independent of the glorious Republic of Mexico."

Carlos smiled, straight teeth gleaming under his rakish

moustache. "I know a number of men who would differ with your priorities, *chiquita*. They would consider you a woman above all."

Magdalena flushed and looked torn between pleasure and embarrassment, but she tossed her head and issued her favorite retort, "Bah! They are more interested in Angelina than I. She has curves where I have none and her smiles are always sweet."

His best friend's sister was indeed an armful, Carlos thought appreciatively. But, catching the note of envy behind Magdalena's bravado, he moved to comfort her as he always did. He pulled her close to tease, "You have curves enough to fill any man's hand, *muchachita*, and Angelina will go to fat as she gets older. Whereas you . . ."—he cocked his head to the side while he studied her—"will always be as slender, beautiful and true as one of our sequoia trees, and you will age just as gracefully."

Carlos's loving smile succored Magdalena. Ah, what a brother he was. She still had him, at least. She loved him too much to argue any longer. She slumped against him, relinquishing her bitter memories to the dark corners of her mind.

The close family circle of children, mother and father had been shattered by tragedy. That broken circlet of love had reforged into a stronger chain of only two links: Magdalena and Carlos. Their opposite personalities—she, intense and brooding; he, friendly and gay—but made their devotion more fervent. Even as Carlos coaxed Magdalena out of her melancholy, Magdalena gave Carlos perceptions beyond the obvious and temporal. The love they felt for one another was the primary stability in their world. They were devoted to Joaquin and respectful of their grandfather, but their sibling loyalty was the center of their existence. Now, they huddled in a fierce embrace, seeking reassurance that this last rudder that kept them from drifting uncharted seas would not also be forfeit. Without each other's guidance they would be lost, homeless, hopeless.

Since Magdalena had resolved to stay, Carlos made no

more attempt to dissuade her. He respected her and her reasons too much. Yet he would never leave without her.

Eventually, Magdalena pulled away and brushed back her hair, nerving herself to tell Carlos the rest of the bad news. She yanked a bone brush through her snarled mane as she reluctantly opened her mouth to speak. However, before she could say a word, a harsh rap sounded at the door. Roberto strutted into the room.

She and Carlos both stiffened, but Roberto ignored their anger and lounged against the bedpost. "I've come for my goodnight kiss, *querida*," he taunted Magdalena.

Magdalena eyed him contemptuously. "I'd as soon kiss a *cerdo*, but I'll not wallow with you," she rejoined, her nose wrinkling as if he stank.

Roberto's eyes narrowed to slits. He grabbed her by the shoulders and sneered into her defiant face, "Those pretty lips will be speaking differently on a night one month hence, *corazon*." His eyes lowered to her full mouth. He purred, "But of course, you wish me to show my devotion, no?"

Ignoring Carlos's puzzled expression, Roberto swooped down on Magdalena like a ravenous vulture. Their lips barely grazed before Carlos jerked him away and hurled him across the room. Roberto fell onto Magdalena's dressing table, knocking over her looking glass. The little mirror teetered uncertainly on the edge of the dresser, then it fell to the floor and shattered into bits. Magdalena would remember the unimportant incident later as an omen of what her life would become, but at the time she felt only fury when Roberto deliberately ground the fragments under his heel.

Her eyes locked on her brother and glowed with pride as his trim, muscular figure braced with determination. Pulling her to his side, Carlos ordered Roberto, "You are never to touch her again. You are not fit to look at her so. You may have abuelo fooled, but not me. You are slavering with greed and ambition. I will kill you before I let you wed her."

Roberto tensed to attack, but an arctic voice blasted from the doorway and froze him in his tracks. "Hold!" Ramon walked into the room with his usual dignity. The look he shot at Carlos locked Magdalena's throat with dread, but Carlos met it calmly.

"How dare you threaten your own cousin with murder and set yourself up as my judge? He at least shows respect for me and my land. You have made your indifference obvious."

Carlos protested, "I am not indifferent, but you reject my ideas. The old ways are not necessarily the best ways."

"You are not experienced enough to make suggestions. You are reckless, Carlos, dragging your sister into these dangerous escapades."

"She is not in danger. I would protect her with my life. I love her more than anything in the world. It is you who threaten her—and your relationship with her—by trying to keep her bound. She needs freedom like our mother!"

"Need I remind you that were it not for your mother's rebellion she might well be alive today?" When Carlos would have argued further, his grandfather held up an imperative hand. "Enough! I am master here, and no longer will I tolerate your impudence. Only because you are of my blood will I give you one last chance . . ." But he spoke to empty air, for Carlos had brushed past him and left. Magdalena watched Ramon and Roberto with equal hostility as the sound of a horse galloping away shattered the night stillness.

Magdalena braced herself to challenge her grandfather, "Why must you always condemn him unheard? It is his right to defend me."

Ramon's erect bearing wilted, as, briefly, he bowed his head. Magdalena searched his face, trying to understand this man who should have been closest to them, but his features were expressionless.

Perhaps tragedy could have been averted had Ramon not believed it weak to show emotion. But he was a strong man, with an even stronger pride, and his voice was cool when he lifted his head and responded. "He has no right to keep you from your novio."

Magdalena spun around and walked to the window,

15

seeking peace, but the serene hills and gentle wind made her own agitation more troubling. "Carlos will never allow me to marry Roberto, Grandfather, even if I agree. Which I won't."

"You will do as you are told. Seventeen and unwed! Do you want to be a spinster? No, my mind is made up. I'll have no more arguments. As long as you live on my land, you will obey my rules. Understood?" Magdalena didn't dignify his threat with a response.

Groaning with an equal mixture of worry, anger and frustration, Ramon stalked out.

When hard lips kissed the side of her neck, Magdalena started. She twirled away from Roberto, swiping at his reaching hands. "You don't own me yet, cousin. Claim again rights that are not yours and I won't wait for Carlos's protection. I'll deal with you myself."

Roberto followed her stare across the room to where her sword lay under the window. He jeered, "If it's swords you want, *amorcito*, I'll be delighted to oblige. I've a weapon of my own that begs for sheathing." His eyes dropped to her hips.

Magdalena whitened, lifting her hand to slap him, but he ducked, blew her a mocking kiss and exited. She jammed a fist against the wall, wishing it were Roberto's face. She would never marry that venal *cerdo*, never! She'd leave El Paraiso first! Magdalena paced her small room, avoiding the glass on the floor.

Yes, she loved this land and, she admitted, she even loved the stubborn old man who ruled it. How could she and Carlos leave Ramon with no one to depend on but Roberto? That one cared for nothing but himself. Somehow they had to change Ramon's mind about this marriage. She muttered a brief prayer for guidance, rubbing her aching temples.

Her fingers paused as her eyes narrowed. She rushed to the large trunk across from her bed, threw open the lid and shuffled through the layers of clothes and childhood mementos. She carefully pulled out a paper-wrapped dress. She held it against her, smiling as the old lace seemed to cling its approval.

Since Ramon wanted her to be more of a woman, he shouldn't be disturbed if she used a woman's weapons against him . . .

The love play of guitars and violins married with the flirty winds in perfect union. Lanterns flickered in the trees, illuminating the lively dancers with harlequin shades of light and darkness. The men were dressed in traditional California attire: breeches fastened at the knee above deerskin boots, embroidered waistcoats open at the waist to show a red silk sash. Many of the young men wore their long hair queued, covered by a silk scarf and wide-brimmed black hat. The girls wore short-sleeved, embroidered blouses, full skirts and silken hose and rebozos. A few of the wealthiest young women wore expensive English dresses imported from Europe.

Lovely as the señoritas were, one girl stood out from them like an exotic tiger lily amid a rose bouquet: Magdalena. She whirled with Jose Rivas in time to the waltz, laughing into his face. Her ruby-red dress brought out the carnelian highlights in her long hair, worn in a sweep of satin to her small waist. An exquisite ivory haircomb set with garnets swept her hair up on one side. Old, delicate lace, tiers upon tiers of it, hugged her slim curves as she glided in the dance.

"You do everything gracefully, Magdalena. Perhaps that's why you fence so well. Carlos told me you defeated him fairly. Would that I could claim the same."

Magdalena lowered her eyes demurely, but her smile glinted with mischief. "Would you like me to give you lessons, then?"

Bending his head, Jose whispered, "Only if you'll allow me to give you lessons in return." They had always bantered so, to Ramon's displeasure, but never had their flirting seemed more fun than tonight.

Magdalena pretended shock at his boldness. "Sir! If you speak so to me again, I'll have to fetch my duenna."

Jose rejoined dryly, "What duenna could keep up with you? You forget, I was here when you sent your last one

17

away. She was too sore to follow you around the mountains for another two days."

"Bloodless creature." Magdalena sniffed.

Jose teased, "No one can say the same of you. Who is the real Magdalena—this sultry creature who stuns me with her femininity, or the little rogue who bested me several days ago with her reata?"

Looking up fondly at her brother's best friend, Magdalena realized with surprise how handsome he was, with his regular features and wide, luminous dark eyes. "They are one and the same, Jose. Because I like to ride, rope and fence, am I any less of a woman?"

Jose's smile faded. He pulled her a little closer. "Not to me, chiquita. But I fear your grandfather does not feel the same."

The music climaxed to a stop with his words. Magdalena searched the crowd for Ramon. When she spied him leaning against the hacienda wall talking to Jose's father, Tomas Rivas, she excused herself. Her glowing face gave no hint of her nervousness. Would her actions this night allow her the time she hoped for? Ramon could not claim she'd shamed him this time. She'd been partnered for every dance, complimented on her dress by even the strictest duennas. If she asked for time to pick her own novio, surely Ramon would grant it now?

Magdalena spared a concerned look at Carlos as she passed him. He was surrounded, as usual, by the prettiest girls, Angelina Rivas among them. And, as usual, he was laughing. But when he glanced at her, she caught the sadness in the depths of his dark eyes. He'd returned only as the dance began, so she'd not had time to tell him of Ramon's decree. She prayed now she'd have no need to tell him.

Her eyes dismissed Roberto where he stood talking to another ranchero. Even dressed in the elegant attire that showed his muscular form to advantage, he reminded Magdalena of nothing more than the snake in paradise Carlos had so aptly named him. Magdalena swung her head around and advanced on her grandfather with renewed determination.

She smiled at Ramon in what she hoped was a pretty, womanly manner. Such artifice was new to her, but she found her role surprisingly easy. In fact, it was rather pleasant to fight so subtly for what she wanted. She'd never before realized how powerful the weapons of a woman were.

"May I be so bold as to request this dance, abuelo?" she asked gayly.

Clicking his heels together, Ramon bowed and extended his arm. "I shall be delighted, señorita. Excuse us, please, Tomas."

He whirled her away. For a moment, as he looked down at her, Magdalena fancied she saw a tear, but he glanced away and cleared his throat. "Have I told you how much you remind me of your grandmother in that dress? I well remember the first time I saw her in it in Madrid . . ."

Magdalena's heart lurched at the emotion in his voice. There would never be a better time than now. "You loved her deeply, didn't you?"

"With all my heart. I will go to my grave missing her."

"Then please, please, abuelo, allow me the same chance. Give me time to choose my own novio. I have enjoyed myself tonight. I promise I will try to be more of a lady. . . ."

But Ramon was shaking his head. "No, Magdalena, it's too late. I have given my word to Roberto. If I didn't think it a good match, I never would have agreed. But you need a strong man, and Roberto will make you happy. You'll see . . ."

Shattered hopes goaded her to rashness. She jerked away, crying, "What do you know of me and my happiness? You, a man who puts a scoundrel above your own grandson . . ."

"Enough! You only prove my decision right. I was going to wait, but perhaps if you're forced to make a commitment, you will see I am right. El Paraiso must be kept safe, and since your brother shows no interest in it, it's up to you."

19

And he whirled, striding to the small platform that had been set up for the musicians.

The other dancers had slowed almost to a stop as they observed the confrontation. They watched agog as Ramon gestured for silence, for Ramon's problems with his two spirited grandchildren were well known. Jose eyed Magdalena's white face with a frown. Carlos pushed his way through the buzzing crowd to touch her shoulder.

"What is it, *hermanita*?" he asked in concern.

Magdalena felt trapped in an obscene play of which she wanted no part. She opened her mouth to answer, but Ramon spoke first.

"It gives me great pleasure to make an announcement that is long overdue. This is not just a fiesta for friends. It is a celebration of a match that has been long in the making. Share with me, amigos, my delight in announcing the engagement of my nephew Roberto and my granddaughter Magdalena."

There were surprised gasps, claps and murmurs of congratulations, but Magdalena heard none of them. She was aware only of Carlos's shock as he stood rigid beside her. When Roberto pushed through to them and put a possessive hand on Magdalena's shoulder, however, Carlos came to life.

He flung off Roberto's encroaching touch. "You will never have her. I warned you of what would happen should you touch her again . . ." Carlos's hands doubled into powerful fists. Roberto put his hands on his hips, his very stance daring Carlos to carry through on his threat.

Magdalena put a staying hand on her brother's arm. "No, not here, Carlos. You will anger abuelo," she whispered frantically. If Carlos infuriated Ramon again, especially so publicly . . .

Jose, too, tried to stop him, but Carlos shook them off. Roberto advanced to meet him, but a stern, coldly furious voice blasted them apart.

"Carlos! You will get a grip on yourself immediately or leave. This is no place for brawling!" Roberto's fists dropped, but Carlos clenched his own tighter.

"You precipitated this, abuelo. Now watch the consequences of your own tyranny," Carlos spat, for once goaded beyond his patience. He rounded on Roberto again, determined to settle the scores that had been increasing between them for years.

Roberto appraised Ramon's ashen face. Magdalena saw him smile a fraction before Carlos's fist smashed into his nose. Roberto made no attempt to protect himself. Groaning loudly, he stumbled backward and fell, cupping his nose.

Magdalena longed to scream in fury at his ploy—as usual, he had brilliantly vilified Carlos. And, as usual, Ramon seemed blind to his nephew's craftiness.

Ramon's face was apoplectic as he leaped down from the platform and clutched his grandson's raised arm. The words he spoke then silenced the whispering crowd; they formed Magdalena's worst nightmare.

"You've had your last chance," he said, his soft voice shaking but resolute. "You are shallow, vain and worthless, as your father was. As you've no love for me or my land, you will no longer enjoy its profits." Ramon stepped aside and flung his hand out toward the mountains. "Be gone. If you set foot on El Paraiso again, I will have you horse-whipped."

The anguish in Ramon's heart didn't show in his steady eyes, and he looked away from Carlos as if he couldn't bear the sight of him. Other faces, too, averted from a moment they should never have witnessed. More than one woman wiped her tears away, for Carlos was as well liked as Ramon was respected.

Carlos looked at Magdalena's tormented features and hesitated. Then, without a word, he moved toward the corral, not even bothering to pack his things. Suddenly he longed to escape the cloying dust of this land that had exacted such a dear price for its bounty. He would soon be back for the only thing of worth remaining on it.

Sluggishly Magdalena moved to follow, but Roberto caught her from behind. "No!" she screamed, clawing at Roberto's hands, but he would not release her.

Carlos paused halfway to the corral, turning to look at his

sister. Magdalena returned his look pleadingly, her heart pounding a warning. He must not leave . . . She struggled for words to say it, but Roberto's cruel grip tightened until she could barely breathe, much less speak. All she could do was watch the moon bathe Carlos in golden light, making him precious, irreplaceable. Never had he been more dear to her, more representative of all that was good in her life.

"Fear not, *hermanita*, I will be back for you." He gave her a jerky little salute and a loving smile. Then he was gone. Hoofbeats faded into the night, leaving his image and voice burned indelibly into her mind and heart.

Magdalena struggled weakly to follow, but she could not break Roberto's iron grip. He crushed her about the waist until the breath left her laboring lungs. Her heard whirled with despair. "Carlos, wait," she croaked. Then she slumped in Roberto's arms. The world went black.

When Magdalena awoke, she was alone in her room. For a moment, she lay still, but when memory returned, she leaped to her feet and ran to the door. Julio, one of Roberto's favorite *vaqueros*, curled a mocking lip when she opened the door. He held one brawny arm over the lintel when she would have exited.

"No, señorita, you may not leave the room. Is there anything you wish?" The unctuous tone of his voice made her stomach churn. She slammed the door in his face.

She saw the dark outline of another man outside her window. Taking a deep breath, she went to the chest where she kept her sword. She had never killed a living thing before, but if that was the only way she could obtain her release, then so be it. She had not entered into this contest willingly, so surely Roberto and Ramon could not object if she followed their ruthless example.

Magdalena's hands trembled only slightly when she realized her sword was gone. She made a complete, methodic search of the room, but Roberto had been thorough. The rapier was not to be found. Her throat aching with the tears she refused to shed, Magdalena sat down on the bed, fingering her rosary as she tried to control her impulse to scream with helplessness and rage. The need built until her skull rang with the repressed sound. Unable to bear it, she threw her head back and emitted such a wail of despair and fury that Ramon shivered when he heard it. He paused in his pacing, back and forth, back and forth, but Roberto merely smiled.

Out in the chaparral-covered mountains, Carlos reined his tiring horse to a stop and whirled to face his three pursuers. They, too, halted. One by one, they pulled their swords. In other circumstances, Carlos would have accepted their challenge, but he was too frantic to get back to ease Magdalena's mind.

He'd pulled his purse and drawn back his arm to throw it at their feet when his eyes settled on the lead bandit. He'd seen that face before . . . He shoved his purse back in his cloak, dismounted and pulled his own sword from the saddle scabbard.

"So, as in everything else, your masters know nothing of fair play. But three against one are odds I relish . . ." Keeping his eyes on them, he wrapped his cloak over one arm. If he used the heavy velvet to help deflect their blades, in the old Spanish manner, he had little fear of being so outnumbered. But another fear ate at him. If he was hated so, what would be Magdalena's fate?

The men dismounted, two circling him warily, one standing to the side. The leader mocked, "Come, caballero, I'm a fighting man who will give you a fighting chance!" He made a lightning strike on the words. Carlos parried with insulting ease, whipping his cloak about the other man's wickedly jabbing blade. And so it went for five eternal minutes, Carlos holding both would-be murderers at bay with skill, strategy and strength.

When he slashed the leader's arm, the man's eyes lost their boldness and grew haunted. "So, the rumors are true," he gasped, his body quivering as his wounded arm took the impact of Carlos's thrust. "You are skillful indeed."

The other man stumbled under a savage blow, dropping

23

his sword. Carlos moved in to deliver the death strike, but the leader screamed, "Now, Raul!"

Carlos's nerves prickled a warning at the movement behind him. He started to turn—and the knife buried to the hilt in his side rather than his back. His sword fell from his numbed hand. Raul drew the knife out and struck again, this time in the chest. Blood spurted warmly over Carlos's clutching hands as he fell to the ground. The star-studded sky whirled above him, pulling his soul upward. He struggled against its lure, one thought on his heart and mind. Coughing up blood, he labored to give it voice, for he knew it was the last time he would.

The three murderers stood over him a moment longer, then they left him, leading his confused horse away. Only the moon remained to grieve. It shed glistening tears, illuminating the wetness saturating Carlos's heavy, ornate jacket. His eyes fluttered and closed as the stars took him and made him one of their own. Somehow, he found strength to whisper that last word before he died. The wind carried the sound away and dispersed it over the serene countryside like a blessing: Magdalena.

Magdalena dropped into a fitful doze as the sun appeared on the horizon. She was sleeping heavily some hours later, and she didn't hear the knock on her door or see Ramon enter the room. He shut the door and slumped against it. When he realized she was asleep, he no longer tried to shield the agony and guilt he felt to his soul. His head bowed in grief for several minutes. If tears appeared in his dark eyes, no one saw them.

Stirring, Magdalena muttered in her sleep. With an effort, Ramon pulled his weary old bones erect and walked to the bed. He shook her softly awake, then sat down on the edge of the bed and took her hand. She was still half-asleep, but something in the unusual gentleness of her grandfather's manner alerted her. She jerked upright, her heart pounding.

His thin, beautifully molded mouth tremored for a bare instant, then he said gently, "*Hija mia*, it pains me greatly to have to tell you this but—Carlos is dead. Julio discovered him this morning when he went to collect some strays. A knife of the kind used by the Indian renegades was found in his chest and his horse was gone."

His voice got huskier as he spoke, and he grew alarmed by Magdalena's lack of response. She stared blankly at him as though he spoke a foreign language. She slowly shook her head.

"He is not dead. I won't allow it. This is a trick to break my spirit."

Color returned to Ramon's cheeks, and his voice was strong again when he rebuked, "Whatever you think of me, I would not lie about such a matter. He is dead, my child. You must accept the fact."

Magdalena clamped down on the panic that threatened to engulf her, shaking her head again. "I will never believe you unless I see for myself." *Dios*, make it a lie, she prayed.

The pity in Ramon's eyes brought nausea to her stomach and a frantic pounding to her heart, but she steadily followed his lead. He opened the door to Carlos's room. There, on the bed, lay the form that had once contained the vibrant life of her brother. His shiny black hair was dirty and his clothes were rumpled, but she noticed only the rusty red that stained his still form from neck to knee. The color filled her world until she saw nothing but blood bubbling before her eyes; she smelled nothing but its sickly sweet smell. She was sucked down the maw of a red whirlpool, choking on the lifeblood of her brother. The sickness in her stomach boiled to her throat and she vomited.

Ramon supported her heaving body. Wiping her mouth, he half-led, half-dragged her from the room. He lowered her onto the hide settee next to the fireplace and rubbed her chilled fingers. There were several people in the room, but Magdalena saw nothing but the image of her brother as he had looked when he said, "I will be back for you."

Ramon had to pry open her jaw to get the brandy past her lips, but she refused to swallow, and it dribbled down her dress. He was further alarmed when she still stared straight ahead, as white as the wall behind her. When his urgent

*25*

entreaties brought no response, he shook her gently, then harder when she still wouldn't move. Her unfocused eyes finally settled on him. Last night's agonized wail was a whisper compared to the cry that now rent the air. It raised the hair on the back of the neck of each listener, even Roberto.

Crazed by grief, her only response was a primal urge to strike out or go mad. And before her, his strong features suddenly old, was the man who had sent her brother away.

She leaped to her feet and turned on Ramon like a wild animal, guttural sounds spitting from her throat as she went for his eyes. He turned his head and her sharp nails grazed his cheeks, two glistening, red trails appearing on each side of his face.

Roberto and Luis, the comandante of the presidio of Santa Barbara, pulled her away. "Murderer!" she screeched. "It's your fault! You sent him away!" She struggled so wildly the two men lost their grips. She dove for the knife that had been drawn from Carlos and set on a table next to the settee.

Clutching it in her shaking hand, she sprang at Ramon's chest, but Roberto and Luis ripped her away. Biting, kicking, scratching, she struggled to retain her hold, but Luis wrenched the knife out of her hand. Vicious curses filled the room with her agony, and even Joaquin was unable to calm her when he tried to pull her into his arms. She shoved him away and tried to bolt, but Roberto grabbed her and held her in a chair while an Indian maid stepped forward and broke pungent herbs under her nose. The acrid scent filled her already swimming head until merciful oblivion blotted out her agony.

The violence that erupted from her on that black day drained her spirit. For weeks afterward, Magdalena drifted about the house like a shadow, eating only when commanded to. She was haunted by guilt, both at her attack on her grandfather and at the knowledge that she, too, was partly responsible for Carlos's death. If she'd refused to wed Roberto instead of trying to fight it in that cowardly manner, perhaps her brother would still be alive. Never again would she let the woman rule her, she vowed in those dark days.

She refused to look at her grandfather, even when he tried to force a confrontation. When he raised her chin to make her look at him, she shut her eyes and ignored his words first of apology and sympathy and eventually of impatience and anger.

The only activity she would partake of was the training of her foal, Fuego, a beautiful animal of Spanish descent. Ramon had purchased his sire from a neighboring ranchero who had brought the stallion when he immigrated from the Andalusian plains of Spain. Fuego was as black as the grief filling her heart, but he had a white blaze on his forehead and three white anklets on his legs that relieved his darkness. Magdalena had no such solace in her stygian night.

Three weeks after Carlos's death, Joaquin watched her run beside the colt as she urged him over small jumps on a leading rein. Her unbound hair flowed behind her in the bright sunlight, sparkling with the vitality that seemed drained from her still face. She ran as fleetly as the horse, coaxing him over the jumps until Joaquin thought she must collapse from exhaustion. Worried, he jumped over the corral to force her to halt when she reined in the steaming animal and stood still, gasping for air.

He walked to her side and praised, "You make great progress. Soon he will be ready for the bit." She said nothing. He sighed and pulled her to the shade of a nearby willow.

She went obediently, lay back and stared up at the leaves drooping in somber sympathy. Joaquin nibbled on a leaf, then he folded his slim, muscular legs and braced his hands on them.

"You must put off this terrible grief, Magdalena. Carlos would not have wanted you to feel such desolation. Try to think of him as joyfully partaking of the nectar of heaven in the company of your mother and father. He is happier than we poor lonely souls here on earth, I am certain of that."

Magdalena trembled at the mention of her parents, and

her wooden mask cracked a little. Joaquin almost cried himself at the agony he saw in her face. He reached out a tender hand to stroke her hair. She buried her head in his lap and at last shook with sobs that racked every inch of her slim frame. Joaquin let her weep, stroking her back, shoulders and hair, offering the little comfort he could.

Almost half an hour later, she sat up. Her eyes were red, her features twisted with pain, but the lifelessness was gone. Heaving a relieved sigh, Joaquin smiled.

"Have I ever told you how much you remind me of your mother?" She shook her head, and the faraway look on his face ignited a half-forgotten curiosity. He glanced at her sidelong, continuing, "She was not as tall, or as stubborn, but she had your eyes and mouth and a serene loveliness that still makes me ache with longing when I remember it."

He had her full attention now, but he didn't notice because he was deep in memories. "You have always suspected I stayed here for more than love of your father. You were right. I loved him like a brother, but I loved your mother more." He didn't hear her surprised gasp. "Oh, there was never anything between us, and I never approached her in any way, but I think she knew. She used to look at me with a gentle sympathy that touched me and made me love her more. There was no man in the world for her but your father. I knew that, but still I loved her."

Turning to Magdalena, he asked softly, "Do you remember the night she was brought back from the mountains?"

Magdalena's eyes darkened in rejection of a memory she still shrank from. "I will never forget. The only solace she could find for her grief after Papa died were her nightly rides. If only she hadn't strayed so high in the mountains and come upon that band of trappers. For those filthy Americanos to use her as they did . . . but then to push her down the ravine and leave her for dead! How unfortunate for them she was not the poor girl they took her for. I am glad abuelo had each and every one of them tracked down and killed. I wish they were here so I could kill them myself!"

She clenched her hands. Her voice was low and piercing

as she finished, "Sometimes I don't know who I hate most, Mexicans, Americans or abuelo." But her voice shook on the mention of her grandfather. They both knew she didn't mean that part of her declaration, at least.

Sighing, Joaquin shook his head. "I reminded you of that night only to tell you what her last words to me were. 'Joaquin,' she pleaded, 'take care of my children. Don't let *mi padre* stifle Magdalena's spirit. Guide them, make them strong and above all, help them retain their heritage.' Her voice faded away and I thought she was gone, then she whispered to herself, 'I lost Patrick for my children's sake, and they must inherit El Paraiso or he will have died in vain.'"

Joaquin wiped away the tears that trickled down Magdalena's face. "That is why you must put aside your bitterness. Ramon spoke in the heat of the moment, and he would have invited Carlos back when his anger cooled. He loved the boy, just as he loves you, chiquita, as he loved your mother. He is just not a man to show it. He has been harsh with you out of worry. He doesn't want you galloping about the country, as your mother did to escape her grief. Surely you can understand his fears?"

Magdalena hung her head and he waited, holding his breath. When she looked at him with a flicker of her old stubbornness, he slumped with relief.

"I'm not certain I can ever forgive abuelo, but I will try to put aside my bitterness. I love El Paraiso and I will not leave it. It is all I have, now."

Joaquin helped her up and walked by her side back to the hacienda. The next days saw a melting of the ice that had encased her. She became warmer to Ramon, responding courteously to his conversation and accepting his touch. She was even polite to Roberto. When she asked to assist in running the rancho again, Roberto refused, but when her grandfather insisted, he had to agree. She threw herself into learning each detail of the rancho's affairs until she earned Ramon's respect by her hard work and even Roberto had to admit she made a good *ranchera*.

Ramon made no more mention of marriage. Magdalena

was all he had now of his daughter. He would cherish her and try to understand her better. He must, or lose her, as he had lost Carlos. He no longer tried to force Magdalena into the feminine mold that fit his notions. He grieved night and day for the loss of his impetuous grandson. He had never even told him how he loved him! The mistakes he'd made with Carlos made him determined to be wiser with Magdalena.

Thus, when he found her fencing with Joaquin one day, he didn't protest. He stopped to watch, lowering his eyes to hide a gleam of pride when she made an athletic leap and scored off Joaquin's shoulder.

With Ramon's new understanding of her individuality came a greater acceptance. He finally saw that, like her mother before her, her devotion could not be forced. It could only be earned.

Slowly, Magdalena grew closer to her grandfather than ever before. Consequently, the final tragedy in her young life hit her harder than it would have had they never reconciled.

Several months after Carlos's death, Magdalena went into Ramon's study to investigate the strange noises she had heard as she prepared for bed. The room was quiet and dark save for the light glowing from a candle. She heard running steps retreating outside. She rushed to the window, but the night was dark and she could see nothing. She turned back and headed for the door. A strange smell wafted to her nostrils as she neared the desk.

Magdalena froze as that unmistakable odor filled her head. It was a scent she had not smelled since Carlos died. Her eyes made a frantic search of the room. "Abuelo?" she quavered.

A faint moan drifted from behind his desk. She ran around it, then stopped in horror. Her grandfather writhed weakly on the floor. His shaking hands clasped the bloody hilt of the knife embedded in his chest—the same knife that had killed Carlos.

Her lips white with shock, Magdalena dropped to her knees beside him and tried to staunch the flooding wound with the hem of her nightgown. His eyes flickered, then opened.

His bloody hand covered hers and she had to bend to hear his tortured words. "Roberto . . . told him . . . changed will . . . all to you . . . not force you to wed." He coughed. Bright red, bubbling blood trickled from his mouth.

Tears came to her eyes as she watched him force the words out. "He . . . and Luis . . . partners . . . gold . . . Luis's men killed Carlos. Knew he would not . . . let you wed . . . Forgive . . ." He coughed again, harder, until blood overflowed their clasped hands. She had to bend closer to hear his wheeze, "Love you . . . always . . . forgive . . . will . . . in . . ."

He tried to force the words out, but his eyes went blank. His breath stopped. His hand slackened and dropped.

Trembling with shock, grief and guilt that she had never truly forgiven him, Magdalena bowed her head. Painfully, inevitably, her blurred gaze fastened on the knife—the knife that had drained Carlos's life away just so. Her eyes clouded with black fury. Hardly aware of what she was doing, she yanked the knife from Ramon's chest.

She ignored the blood that spurted on her gown and turned to the door, her face murderous. When the door burst open she didn't notice the comandante and his men, or see her grandfather's friend, Tomas Rivas. She only saw the dark, detested visage of Roberto as she leaped for his heart. Without an instant's hesitation, Luis rapped her jaw with the hilt of his sword. Hatred exploded in her head as she slumped, unconscious, to the floor.

Her arms and legs were tied to the bed when she came back to throbbing awareness. She heard voices raised in argument. She was wondering bitterly what lies Roberto was telling about her when a silent shadow slipped in her window and slunk to the bed. She stiffened in alarm, but relaxed when she picked out Joaquin's features in the gloom.

He was boiling with a fury that almost matched her own.

He mouthed a coarse oath that would have shocked her had she not been so beyond shock. He slashed her bonds, hissing, "Roberto has convinced everyone you murdered Ramon. If Tomas Rivas saw what he said he did, how could you have been so stupid? Especially when you had already tried to kill Ramon once with that knife?"

Rubbing her tingling wrists, she shook her head numbly. "Roberto killed abuelo and Carlos. I knew only that he must die, so I took the knife from abuelo's chest. Did you expect me to let him get away with the murder of my only remaining family?"

Joaquin was packing a small bundle of necessities as he spoke. "I could beat you for your stupidity if there were time. You should have called for help immediately. Dress quickly. We must hurry."

Magdalena jerked on black breeches, shirt and boots while Joaquin finished packing. He shoved her out the window, and she stumbled over the two unconscious men who had been on guard. They slipped to the corral farthest from the house, saddling two horses at random. Magdalena insisted on tying Fuego behind her mount, despite Joaquin's protests. They were galloping away when a thought struck her. She reined in.

"Joaquin, if you leave, you will be guilty too."

He smiled grimly. "I am already guilty. The guards saw my face before I knocked them out. It is too late, Magdalena. I would never let you go alone, even though it's improper for us to be unchaperoned. Survival must come first."

With the wind at their back, they made good progress, and soon reached the rise overlooking El Paraiso. Magdalena drew to a halt, ignoring Joaquin's urgings as she paused for one last look at her heritage. For a moment the moonlit scene glowed wetly, like the blood of her family. Then her vision cleared and she saw only the sumptuous valley. Roberto was to blame, not El Paraiso, and he would pay long and dearly for his treachery.

She was too deep in shock for full grief to engulf her.

That would come later. But hatred flooded her being with each throbbing heartbeat. Her teeth gritted with resolve.

Joaquin heard her words with a combination of dread and approval.

"You have won, but only for the moment, Roberto. My family's blood shall be avenged. You will die slowly, screaming in agony for the death of each of my loved ones. May *Dios* have mercy on you, for I'll have none. I will return when you least expect it and snuff your life as you have snuffed mine, or I will die in the attempt."

With one last glittering look at the rancho, she spurred her mount into the darkness. Joaquin followed, and the hoofbeats slowly retreated until the only noise in the yawning blackness of the night was the sad sigh of the wind.

# Chapter 2

"Satan with a suit of flesh upon him. No one except
the devil would attempt what he bears off."

**Act I, DON JUAN TENORIO**

## 1837—TWO YEARS LATER

Clinton James Browning, III, stretched and wiped his
sweaty brow. He sneaked a glance at the three men riding
ahead of him, then he eased one hand between the saddle
and his posterior to massage his sore buttocks. Blast Uncle
Charles anyway! And blast his own stupidity in agreeing to
this role his uncle had referred to so innocently as "scout."
He grunted in disgust as he thought back to their conversation.

"All I want you to do, dear boy, is to keep your ears and
eyes open as you trade. Rumors of California's potential
have even reached us here in the Chesapeake. If we are to
expand from sea to sea as is our destiny, we must have a
good port in California. Pay particular attention to each
settlement's presidio. Apparently, Mexico has been no more
generous to California than Spain was. It's rumored their

defenses are in a sad state. Any information you can glean on the customs of the people would also be helpful."

Earlier, while on a Mexican assignment, Clint's uncle had visited California and had become convinced that annexation of the territory would be in the best interests of both the United States and California. He had concluded that Mexico had too many problems of its own to make an effective administrator for the large, uncivilized land on the rim of its domain.

Clinton was extremely fond of his uncle, but he did not agree with his politics. Although Charles's business achievements were matched by his effectiveness as a diplomat, Clinton knew better than most that his uncle's successes resulted as much from his ruthlessness as from his acumen. Especially, Clinton had never agreed with his uncle's contention that the end justified the means. On the subject of annexation, they had had more than one argument on the philosophical question of the right of each country to decide its own destiny. Clinton viewed the debate as a moral issue; Charles viewed it as a practical one. No matter how eloquently each man argued his case, he could never make the other budge an inch.

Thus, Clinton had not liked the sound of his uncle's recent suggestion, and he did not hesitate to say so—curtly and succinctly. "I'm a sailor, not a spy. Get someone else to do your dirty work." He had then turned to walk away with his loose-hipped, sailor's stride.

Charles's smooth voice halted him in midstep. "I am most adamant about this, dear boy. If you won't humor me, I'm afraid I may have to call in that note on our little agreement."

After his father's death, Clinton had expanded the family trading enterprise; when he had needed money to purchase new ships, his mother's brother had been glad to assist for a share in the business. Now, five years later, Clint had almost enough money to pay back the loan, but he could not afford for Charles to call in the note yet. Bitterly, grudgingly, *stupidly,* he thought now, he had agreed.

The task had been easy and surprisingly enjoyable. He

spoke Spanish with the fluency painstakingly instilled in him by his childhood tutor. Most Californios were hospitable and charming to the man they took for a Swede. They were pleased to share their homes with the tall, handsome stranger. They appreciated him as a ship's captain who had brought much-needed goods to their land, they appreciated him as an honorable man. However, when his nationality was discovered, Clint was met with near universal wariness. First the Americanos had taken Florida, and only last year, they had stolen Texas. Would California be next?

Nevertheless, Californios were vociferous when questioned about their nascent land. Up and down the coast, Clint received the same reaction from everyone, whether they be *vaquero, padre* or *don:* Californios were tired of being second-class citizens of far away republics. They were not Mexicans, they were not Spanish. They were Californios—and proud of it.

He winced as his mount stumbled over a rock. He narrowed a jaundiced stare on the three Californians who swayed easily over the uneven trail that shook his bones. Give him a skiff, give him a dingy—no, dammit, give him a canoe—but save him from this four-legged walking torture chamber.

As though the horse sensed his discomfort, the stallion turned a sleek neck and whickered at him mockingly. Clinton glared at the animal and bit off a curse when it pranced sideways, bumping him into the rocky wall of the canyon.

His host, Roberto de Sarria, reined his bay in and waited, with ill-concealed contempt, for the gringo to catch up. Luis might be right that it was important to curry favor with this Yankee captain. True, they would soon need an unsuspecting exporter, but surely they could find more hombre than this pretty bear who couldn't even ride?

Luis pulled up beside Roberto, shooting him a quelling stare. As Clint drew even, he said smoothly, "It is not much farther, Captain Browning. As soon as we leave the Gaviota, as we call this pass, we shall be in the Santa Ynez valley. Roberto's rancho lies there and you will be able to visit one of the largest properties in California. You can see for yourself how we make our hides and tallow. You will be surprised, I think, at how self-sufficient our ranchos are." When Clint made no response, Luis rode on, Julio at his heels.

Clint urged his mount to follow, but the contrary beast ignored him, cropping at a swatch of grass growing in a cleft. A snort of contempt reached Clint's ears. He glanced up.

Even in the gathering dusk, Roberto's disdain was obvious. Clint was tired, sore and disgruntled, and his hackles rose. The two men glared at one another, Clinton suddenly upright, Roberto resting his forearms on the pommel of his richly caparisoned saddle in a pose so indolent it smacked of insult.

"You ride like a woman, gringo. Do you sail as poorly?"

Clint's teeth ground together, but he answered pleasantly. "This is the second time I've ridden a horse. I sailed across the James River alone when I was six. Can you claim the same?"

Roberto shrugged. "Sailing skills are of little use in these mountains. If you remain long in California, I suggest you learn to ride. Or be laughed at."

"By none more loudly than you, caballero?" Clint challenged softly. "But we Americans don't enjoy being laughed at. Santa Ana mocked the Texans' pitiful force, too. Until the Alamo. Until San Jacinto."

It was Roberto's turn to straighten at the razor-sharp glint in the gringo's eyes. Dislike was sent and returned in equal measure in the locked stares, and only Luis's return to see what kept them averted a confrontation.

Outwardly cool, Luis insinuated his mount between them, smiling at Clint. "Come, amigo, let us continue. I shall tell you the history of El Camino Real as we ride."

With a last appraising glance at Roberto, Clint rode beside the capitan, listening half-heartedly as Luis commenced his tale.

"Spain realized in the 1700s that without a land artery linking Alta and Baja California together, she could never hold her colony from the interests of the Russians, the English and the French. It was in 1769 that Don Gaspar de Portola was appointed as first governor of California. He was ordered to blaze a trail into the wilderness of Alta California that would link new settlements, colonize the area and civilize the Indians. That first trail he traveled is the road we are now on."

Luis paused and concentrated on his riding as they emerged from the pass, for the track was rocky. Luis and Clint rode in front while Roberto and Julio brought up the rear. Dusk was deepening, so Luis and Clint were slow to notice the two horsemen blocking their path. They were distracted by the chillingly close screech of a bird of prey. They heard the flap of powerful wings so near that the swoosh of disturbed air ruffled their hair. Instinctively, both men reined in and ducked. Luis withdrew his pistol and craned his neck, searching the midnight blue sky for the offending creature.

A deep whistling noise split the night. Clint looked up, spying two horsemen angling their mounts across the narrow path in a bold challenge. The taller of the two twirled a reata above his head with such effortless skill that Clint was struck by it, even in the surprise of the moment. The rope snaked out of the dusk. The pistol Luis gripped was jerked away with such strength that he moaned and cradled his sprained wrist.

Clint heard Roberto snarl behind him, but before he could pull his pistol there came the click of a gun being cocked at their rear. Clint and Roberto turned as one. Another, even larger, rider blocked their retreat. He held a pistol in each huge paw. The black mask shielding his eyes turned that bearded, genial smile into a nightmarish grimace.

A deep Irish brogue mocked, "It's yer purses or yer lives, gents. Be glad to fight if that's yer pleasure. It's been too long since me darlins' had practice. 'Tis a shame to get too rusty, right, Black Jack?"

The man who had thrown the reata rasped a sinister, deep-chested laugh that sent an involuntary shiver up Clint's spine. "Right, Mick." He fingered the hilt of his sword with a loving hand and added, "My beauty is eager for practice, also. Well, gentlemen, what's it to be? Shall you throw down your weapons, or do you prefer to fight?"

The hoarse voice was even-pitched, almost bored, but Clint caught a tremor in the hand that gripped the sword hilt as though to force itself to calm. There was another swoosh of air, and the stranger held up his heavily gloved left hand. A fierce-looking falcon lit on his wrist, its tether jingling.

Clint eyed the man in disbelief. He seemed a figure stepped straight from a nightmare, his goal more sinister than mere larceny. He was garbed from head to toe in rich black. Velvet breeches hugged slim thighs, flaring at the knee in a pleat decorated by jet buttons. A full, black velvet cloak shrouded his shoulders, and Clint caught the gleam of silk at his breast. His wide-brimmed hat was lined with black silk and decorated with black braid. His head was hooded, a black silk scarf holding the hood down at his neck.

He had one leg wrapped about his pommel. He held the falcon on one hand and stroked its preening feathers with the other. He appeared indifferent to their response as he looked at the bird, but Clint caught the glitter behind his eye slits. Instinct warned Clint that the cloaked figure was striving to muffle strong emotions.

The shock had worn off Roberto. He urged his mount forward, shoving Clinton's aside. "How dare you? Do you know who you assault? I am Roberto . . ."

The pose of indolence was gone. Black Jack straightened and leaned forward in his saddle to interrupt. "It matters little who you are, Don Roberto. Your flesh is as vulnerable as any other man's. You will bleed just as well—and die just as easily." The husky voice held a quiet certainty that shocked Roberto out of his braggadocio.

Black Jack relaxed again. He flipped his leg back over his saddle, adding, "But it need not come to that. We desire only your possessions. We have no need of your souls." He arrowed a glance at Roberto and whispered, "Yet."

Ever prudent in the face of strong opposition, Julio threw down his pistol and tossed his slim purse at the feet of Jack's

**40**

enormous black stallion. Tight-lipped, Luis did the same. Roberto choked on his fury, but when Luis hissed, "We cannot risk all for such a paltry sum. Give him your purse," Roberto flung his pouch at the leader's head and threw his pistol down.

Jack ducked easily. He straightened and mocked, "Such a temper. It will be the death of you one day."

The hooded head turned in Clint's direction. The hoarse voice prompted, "Well, señor? We most courteously request your purse."

Staring straight into the slitted eyes, Clint drawled, "Come and get it."

The man went still. Clint had the impression he was nonplussed. Then he shrugged gracefully. "As you wish."

The falcon launched in Clint's direction and the reata again whirled like a dervish. Clint barely had time to whip his pistol out of his coat before the hawk's talons bit cruelly into the back of his hand. Wincing, he dropped the weapon. A second later, the rope snagged neatly around his waist. He found himself jerked to the ground in an ignominious heap of long arms and legs.

To his fury, the three bandits chuckled, but when he tried to struggle to his feet, the hawk swooped at his head, forcing him to duck back to the ground. The small man beside Black Jack slipped off his mount and moved to fetch his purse. Clinton swiped at him. He stared through a red haze at Jack's mocking figure, so he didn't hear the small man give an exasperated sigh as he rapped him on the skull with his pistol. Black Jack's image expanded and enveloped Clint until the velvet cloak filled his throat and strangled him. His last sight before darkness claimed him was the leader's eye slits. They glittered with demonic satisfaction as Clint was drawn, struggling, into the realms of darkness.

Purses gathered, the small man mounted again. The huge thief ordered the three Californians to dismount. When they hesitated, he tapped Julio's arm with one pistol and warned, "Me darlins' be more eager than ever. Dismount, or I'll let them have their way."

He herded the men back into the canyon, gathered their

weapons and whacked each horse's rump until the animals bolted into the darkness. Then he joined his comrades. Roberto, Julio and Luis stared up at the trio of robbers with varying degrees of hatred.

Black Jack tipped his hat in taunting civility. "Gracias, amigos. I hope your walk is not too uncomfortable." He wheeled away, but when Roberto shouted a curse at him, he turned back and cocked his head to listen politely.

Roberto vowed, "You won't get away with this, *demonio*. I will hunt you down like a dog. We shall meet again."

The hooded face contemplated him for a long moment. Jack nodded his head in gentle agreement. "Indeed, we will meet again. I'll see to it." He saluted, two fingers to his hat. "Wait, and wonder, Don Roberto. When you least expect it, I'll be there. Ah, what fun I shall have discovering if you bleed blood or water."

The bandit laughed at Roberto's stunned look. He turned his stallion so sharply that the animal reared, then, his cloak flapping in the breeze like the grim reaper's robes, he galloped down El Camino Real, hoarse chuckles trailing behind him.

Magdalena stirred her frijoles with a spoon and took an absent-minded bite of her tortilla. She chewed methodically, swallowed, then forced a spoon of beans to her mouth. She was so tired of the monotonous meals. Beans, jerky, tortillas for lunch, then jerky, tortillas and beans for dinner. It was becoming harder and harder to force herself to eat. Ah, what wouldn't she give for just one cup of the morning chocolate she used to take for granted!

When she had emptied her tin plate, she rinsed it in the barrel of water kept for such purposes, dried it, and set it carefully on the rock ledge where they stored their meager provisions. She looked around the dim chamber. Joaquin paused in his never-ending task of grating corn with the *metall* to watch her examine the cave.

She found it incredible that this cold, rough cavern had been the only home she had known for two years. Three hide mats covered the dirt floor in opposite corners of the cave; a line strung from one stalactite to another served as their closet. In the rear of the cavern, their horses munched contentedly on the fresh, spring grass they had gathered. They cleaned their makeshift stable daily, but it was impossible to obliterate the odor. However, Magdalena had become so accustomed to the smell that it no longer bothered her.

Magdalena propped her back against the wall and picked up her guitar. The instrument had been stolen, as had almost all of their few comforts. She strummed it, concentrating on the mournful sounds, looking about the cavern, watching Joaquin, but she finally had to acknowledge the futility of trying to escape her conscience. She could not stifle her guilt. What would Papa say if he knew what had become of her? she wondered. His only daughter, a bandit.

Then she remembered the sneer on Roberto's face and the remorse melted under familiar heat. Everything they had stolen to date had been taken from arrogant, wealthy dons. The guitar she held and the clothes on her back had come from El Paraiso and were rightfully hers. Julio and Luis were Roberto's accomplices, so she had no need to feel guilty about taking their ill-gotten gains.

But another image swam before her eyes, an image she was finding strangely hard to banish. She beheld a huge figure with hair of spun gold and piercing, fearless eyes. His immense shoulders tapered to a slim waist and muscular thighs. She wondered for the dozenth time what color his eyes were. The dusk had shielded their hue, but it could not hide the blazing contempt and defiance. A smile stretched her weary face as she remembered again his dumbfounded expression when she yanked him from the saddle. She hoped his head didn't ache too badly from the blow Joaquin had given him.

She wondered what his nationality was. With such fair hair, surely he must be Swedish or Dutch. She sighed and tried to put him out of her mind, but again she was not successful.

Closing her eyes didn't help, for the insidious vision of herself cradled in those strong arms betrayed her will. She

*43*

had never been physically attracted to a man before, and her cheeks burned as she realized she was curious to feel that hard male mouth on hers. For the first time in two years, she missed the woman's ways she had cast off ever since that disastrous fiesta. She looked down at herself and sighed. Such as he would never be attracted to a woman who wore breeches and fenced like a man.

She looked at Joaquin guiltily, afraid her thoughts were visible on her hot face, but he was busy with the corn. Agitated at her unusual longings, she jarred a twangy chorus and exorcised the stranger's ghost by thinking of her arch-enemy.

She set aside the guitar and rested her cheek on upraised knees. Why had he been with Roberto? He was a gringo, and Magdalena knew well the contempt her cousin had for all things alien. So he must be of some use to Roberto and Luis. But how? She chewed her lip as she worried over the question; she did not even notice when Joaquin scraped the meal into a skin bag and sat down next to her.

He examined her tenderly in the dim light. She was wearing her usual attire: white shirt, brown pants and high boots, but Joaquin was seeing her as she had looked on the evening of their debut as robbers. There was nothing in the sinister appearance of Black Jack to remind one of the girl Magdalena. Further, he did not think Roberto had recognized Fuego because the sleek, muscular stallion had lost the blaze on his legs. Only a small white star on his forehead remained of the foal he had once been.

However, when Magdalena removed her hood and cloak, she metamorphosed with shocking rapidity from a suave caballero to a beautiful woman masquerading as a man. He was torn between amazement, pride and fear as he thought back to her performance on the Royal Highway. Who would have thought a woman could show such indomitable courage?

Ah, what a rough, lonely life they had led. Survival had been their only concern for the first year, and that had been a formidable task indeed. Magdalena had refused to travel to Monterey, San Franciso or anywhere far from Roberto. If

44

she was ever to redeem her name and reclaim her rights, she must both find her grandfather's will and prove her innocence. She could do neither of those things if she fled. So they stayed in the mountains between El Paraiso and Santa Barbara. The series of hot springs and caverns in the area made a natural hiding place that was almost never frequented by anyone save a few stray Indians.

Magdalena, too, was remembering those times. As the caves became more like home and less like banishment and as they gradually accrued the rudiments of survival, Magdalena's thoughts returned to vengeance. She remembered an Irish folk story that had been a childhood favorite. Her father's lilting voice rang in her ears as he regaled her with the tale of Black Francis.

"Maggie, me darlin', he was a highwayman the likes o' which ye've ne'er seen. He took to the hills with his gang and robbed the rich to give to the poor. Ah, he was a gallant lad. They were to rob Lisgoole Abbey one fine night to save some poor folk who couldn't pay their accounts. They would have got away free except that one of his gang insulted a girl in the house. He was chastisin' the fellow for his bad manners when the military came upon them. Black Francis was hanged, aye, him and all but one o' his gang. Corrigan, his name was, and this fellow leaped the Sillees River and got clean away. He dressed up like a woman and went to the hangin' and then he went to America."

The story had appealed to Magdalena's sense of adventure as a girl; as a woman who lived for naught but vengeance, the story of Black Francis spoke to her through dreary days and dark nights. What better way to humble Roberto than for a bandit to prove the respected ranchero's infamy? Disguised as a man, she could leave the mountain and travel freely, if stealthily, about the countryside. Further, she was convinced Roberto must be engaged in something illegal from abuelo's whisper about gold. If her charade was successful, she could eventually recruit a band who could help her investigate his activities. Perhaps they could even raid El Paraiso and look for abuelo's will.

Joaquin was aghast at her idea, but no amount of

persuasion, coercion or pleading would dissuade her. When he reminded her that her parents would be ashamed of her if they knew, she whitened for a moment, then she straightened proudly.

"I see nothing wrong with trying to redeem my honor. Would you prefer that I leave my name besmirched? No, Joaquin. A woman I may be, but no one but I remains to redeem the name de Sarria. My reputation is already ruined. I ask you, which is worse—to be thought a thief or a murderess?" When Joaquin spread his hands at the truth of that, she went on. "I will keep only a portion and give the rest to the poor indios. If I am successful in proving Roberto's viciousness, then it matters not if I am hanged as a thief afterward. My father died because he cared about the indios. I ask no better fate for myself."

When he still protested, she retorted, "I can bear this inactivity no longer. It is only a matter of time before we are discovered, and without disguise we cannot leave the mountains safely. All California believes Magdalena de Sarria is a murderess, but they will never recognize her in a gallant bandido who robs from the rich and gives to the poor. What's more, if I know my countrymen, many Californios will assist us rather than turn us over to Luis and his *cholos*."

Her arguments were persuasive. However, the first few times they had ventured down from the mountains, they had almost been caught. Once, as they tried to rustle a steer from El Paraiso's vast herd, Julio and several other *vaqueros* had given chase. Magdalena's hat fell off and her hair whipped behind her, but apparently it was too dark for the men to see. Only their superior equestrian abilities and their intimate knowledge of every crack and crevice of the mountains had allowed their escape.

A final time, Joaquin pleaded, "There is another way, Magdalena. Let me go to Father Franco. He has known you since you were a niña, and I am unconvinced he believes you capable of murder, whether all California believes it or not. He can plead your case with the governor." Magdalena looked at him with a sad honesty that brought acidity to his throat.

"Ah, but I *am* capable of murder, amigo. I did not kill abuelo, true, but I would have if Luis and Roberto hadn't pulled me away. And when I kill Roberto, I honestly don't think I will feel a twinge of remorse." Her golden eyes stared over his head with such a dark, brooding expression that Joaquin was alarmed.

She pushed the hatred back into the chasm of misery that was her soul and looked at Joaquin expressionlessly. "I must do this, Joaquin. If you won't go with me, I'll go alone."

Faced with such chilling determination, Joaquin could do nothing but agree. However, he insisted they hone their athletic skills to the finest edge possible. The odds against them were astronomical, so they must use the only advantages they had: anonymity and fiendish talent with sword, horse and reata. They spent months practicing. Magdalena never complained about the grueling schedule of ride, fence, run and train the horses. And when she found a weak fledgling falcon and nursed it back to health, Joaquin showed her the venerable European art of falconry.

Joaquin had deemed them as ready as they would ever be when, during the rainy season, he fell ill of the ague. Magdalena wrapped him in their blankets and serapes, bathed him and held him. Finally his burning fever went down, but his deep, watery cough frightened her and his chest shuddered with each rasping breath. When she could no longer bear his agony and her own helplessness, she rode like a Valkyrie down the mountain to the fragrant herb patch she had planted on El Paraiso to pick the sweet herb *yerba santa* that was so good for respiratory ailments. She was returning to the cave when, in her careless haste, a branch tangled in her hair and jerked her from Fuego. She landed awkwardly and broke her leg. The rains came again, and she was semiconscious when huge, warm hands skimmed over her as a lilting voice encouraged, "There, lassie, I'll have ye out o' this rain as quick as the twinkle of St. Patrick's eye."

47

Thus did Sean O'Malley enter their lives.

Too frantic with fear for Joaquin to be afraid of the huge man, she ignored her own pain and directed him back to the cave. Joaquin was already breathing easier, and the poultice Sean prepared under her instructions drained the last of the fluid from his lungs. Then Sean set her leg with his huge, amazingly dexterous hands, but still she passed out under the gentle pressure. Sean stayed with them through the night, tending to their wounds and igniting a flame of friendship that would flare into a bonfire and warm their lonely struggle.

Joaquin had sized up the enormous Irishman with his usual shrewdness. Seeing the way he looked at Magdalena, Joaquin didn't hesitate to take advantage of the man's gallantry. The next morning, Magdalena awoke to his explanation of her "hare-brained scheme." She sent as piercing a glare as she could manage at Joaquin's satisfied expression. She looked at the huge Irishman's startled face, and for a moment tears flooded her eyes at his likeness to her father. He was tall, red-headed, and he had the same vital spark in his blue eyes. However, she merely thanked him coolly and begged him not to mention their presence. When she politely suggested though that he be on his way, he looked at her with a wry amusement that made Joaquin's lips twitch.

"Sure, and the colleen might look like a madonna, but I've ne'er seen a madonna with such proud stubbornness in her eyes. If ye'd demanded me help, I would ha' been slow to offer it, but as it's so plain ye think yerself invincible, I must stay and watch ye get yer comeuppence. I was goin' to the mountains to try me luck at trappin'. I've had enough o' the sea, but methinks this mountain air will set well with me lungs."

And stay he did, despite Magdalena's initial hostility. Now, as she looked about the cavern, she wondered how they had ever managed without him. Her eyes went to Sean, then to Joaquin. Despair overcame her as she wondered what she had begun. What right had she to drag two such fine men into the mire of her deceit?

Joaquin and Sean were watching her. When that bleak, desolate expression both men hated to see contorted her features, they moved as one to comfort her. Crouching beside her, Joaquin stroked her hair, but she refused to lift her downcast face.

Sean took one of her slim hands in his and cradled it as tenderly as a butterfly in the hollow of his big, callused palm. "And what's troublin' me bonnie lass now? If yer havin' second thoughts, darlin', we can leave these old mountains and go to Mexico, or even to New Orleans."

When Magdalena still wouldn't look at him, he lifted her chin. The guilt and pain in her shimmering eyes set his features to quivering with a like hurt.

She mumbled, "I feel so ashamed. I will never forgive myself if you and Joaquin are taken or harmed because of me. Perhaps it would be best if both of you left me to fight alone. At least then my mind would not be clouded with worry."

Joaquin had been looking troubled, but at these words his dark eyes lit with a wrath Magdalena had never seen before. He swung her to face him and stuck his nose in her stunned face. "Sometimes I wonder if you want to avenge your family honor or if you're too much of a coward to take the risk of living. It would be easier to martyr yourself in a useless, quixotic gesture than to take the responsibility for what you have begun. Well, it's too late, do you hear? You insisted on this insane masquerade. We're committed now. Roberto will not rest until he finds the men who humiliated him. I suggest you remember what Carlos looked like the night he died and quit feeling sorry for yourself."

His voice had risen in volume until he was almost hoarse, but the fire of his rage had consumed itself. He reached out a pleading hand toward her, letting it drop when she ignored it.

Magdalena sprang up like a crouched lioness and roared, "I'll never forget that sight! I have not given up the struggle; I was only worried about both of you. Well, no more. If I am a martyr, you are a braying ass who thinks himself a stallion leading a herd of defenseless mares."

Joaquin rose slowly and listened, quite imperviously, to her tirade. His calm expression infuriated her more. She towered over him, for she had grown several inches in the last two years beyond her already above-average height. She shook her fist at him and would have looked comical had her face not been so white with rage.

"I am not defenseless, I do not need your protection and I am not afraid of living, if you can call this existence we have endured the last two years living. I *will* avenge my honor and prove my innocence, but I will do it *alone*. Now step out of my way before I push you out of it."

Joaquin stayed firmly planted in front of her long enough to state, "You will not do it alone if I have to tie you down and sit on you. You are an excellent rider and an incomparable fencer, but you do not know how to shoot, nor do you have skill enough to evade a bullet. We stay, Magdalena." He moved aside and returned to his *metall*, ignoring her.

Mouth agape, Sean watched the confrontation. He had seen many a brawl between vicious, drunken sailors, but he'd never seen or heard such raw fury unleashed between two people who supposedly loved one another. He looked down at his brawny arms, half-expecting the red hairs to be singed, but all was normal.

Stalking to the back of the cave, Magdalena saddled Fuego with jerky, frustrated movements. Her face was still dark with rage when she ignored Sean's sharp "Wait!" and galloped down the steep trail.

Sean moved to stand in grim disapproval over Joaquin's placid figure. "Why did ye turn on the lassie like that? She was but concerned about us."

Joaquin snorted his disagreement. "She was guilty and feeling sorry for herself. It's time she learned she must take responsibility for her own actions. She too often acts first and reasons about the consequences later. The time to worry about whether we would be endangered in her wild scheme was *before* we robbed Roberto. Now, it's too late. She must learn patience and strive to keep a cool head, or we are all doomed."

Sean frowned at the words, but he could find no flaw in

their logic. Sighing, he sought the uncomplicated company of his huge bay. Holy Mither, what had he done by throwin' in his lot with these two Latin fireballs?

Magdalena's rage cooled gradually, but she had urged Fuego to the foothills of the mountains before she realized where she was. Without her disguise, it was too risky to be this close to El Camino Real. She turned Fuego about to ride to a higher elevation, but bright specks of red amidst deep, lush green caught her eye. She scanned the rough track. It was deserted, so she rode closer to the ground-hugging cover.

The field of wild strawberries beckoned in the sunlight. Her mouth watered as their sweet, seductive scent tickled her nostrils. She looked one more time at the Royal Highway, then she leaped off Fuego, ground-reined him and launched herself at the bushes.

It had been so long since she'd eaten fresh fruits or vegetables. It would almost be worth it even if she were seen. She would only eat a few . . . Besides, she needed something to wash away the bitter taste of Joaquin's words. They held more truth than she wanted to admit.

She plucked a huge, ripe berry off a bush and stuffed it whole into her mouth. She closed her eyes in ecstasy as the cool, sweet taste bathed her parched tongue. One after another, she popped the succulents into her mouth, quickly forgetting her promise to eat but a few.

She was enthralled, unaware of where she was or the danger she was in. The emotive argument with Joaquin and the sweet taste of the berries erased all else. When she was so stuffed that she couldn't force another bite into her mouth, she plopped back on the thick, spring grass next to the berry patch and stared dreamily at the sky. In a minute she'd pick more to take back to Joaquin and Sean, but first she'd rest.

She couldn't remember feeling so relaxed and happy in over two years. In truth, she had forgotten what it was like to enjoy life. She watched the huge, fluffy clouds drift by overhead as she savored her brief peace. The warm sunlight, the gentle breeze, the scent of the berries and the contentment of her full stomach all combined to lull her. She'd barely slept last night. Surely it would be all right to close her eyes an instant?

Clint was preoccupied as he began the long, uncomfortable ride back to Santa Barbara. His visit to El Paraiso had indeed been most instructive. The ranch was a small city in itself, able to satisfy virtually every need for survival. The orchard provided pears and peaches; small plots yielded vegetables. Sheep, goats and hogs were abundant, but the sheer number of cows was mind-boggling. When Julio gave Clint a tour of the rancho, Clint was astounded to see cattle covering the verdant hills and valleys like a brown blanket. The animals were allowed to run free and forage as they would until the twice-yearly roundups.

The servants on the estate were usually Indian, but a good many of the *vaqueros* were of Mexican descent. Clint had witnessed an Indian woman making the ever-present "California bank note," the dried hide. The process was simple and rather crude. Hides were stretched in the sun and allowed to dry, then were scraped free of any remaining fat and meat and flailed to rid them of dust and insects.

Tallow was obtained simply by rendering the beef fat in huge iron kettles. It was then poured into *botas*, large rawhide bags. Clint had been surprised to find that dairies were not utilized. In fact, even upper-class Californios seemed to prefer pork lard to butter.

El Paraiso was impressive indeed, but its owner was not. Roberto had been sullen before the robbery; after it, he was impossible. When Clint recovered consciousness, he helped the others round up the horses, and the short distance to the rancho was covered in brooding silence. When they arrived at the graceful adobe homestead, Roberto curtly introduced his housekeeper, Sarita, and retreated with Luis to his study.

Clint's head still ached from the blow he had received, but his pride hurt more. He thought back to that fiendish figure, and he seethed. He would have been delighted to participate in whatever plans Roberto was making to catch the arrogant scoundrel, but he was not invited to lend his assistance. He shrugged to himself. Invited or not, he'd help apprehend that bandit even it if meant delaying his trip up the coast. He could find hides and tallow aplenty to fill his hold, and few of the goods he carried for trade were perishable.

The one time he saw his host, at dinner, the meeting had not been cordial. Roberto passed a slow-cooked steak flavored with spices and onions down to him, almost reluctantly. Clint didn't miss the resigned look he shot at Luis before saying, "We were wondering, captain, if you would be interested in trading for more tallow. My herds have proliferated in the past year, so I'll have much to sell."

Under other circumstances Clint would have agreed. He had come here to trade, after all, and Roberto's rancho was a large one. However, there was something about the man, aside from his abrasive personality, that troubled Clint. His long years of trading with men of many different stamps had given him an instinct that seldom failed him. And that instinct screamed Roberto was not to be trusted.

So he responded blandly, "I regret to say my hold is getting rather full, and I've still a ways to go up the coast. Another trip, perhaps . . ."

Clint selected a choice piece of meat, seeming not to notice Roberto's angry face or Luis's disappointment. Their parting the next day was brusque, with relief on each side. As he was packing his saddlebags, Clint overheard an intriguing argument between Sarita and a maid in the next room. He unabashedly paused to listen.

"Where do you suppose the senorita Magdalena is? Do you really think she murdered *el patron*?"

"No," Sarita's voice replied impatiently. "She was hot-headed, but no killer. I still say, no matter if she had his blood on her gown, I cannot believe she did it."

"Then who did? And why has she not come forward to prove her innocence?"

The older woman scolded, "If you turned as much attention to your duties as to the affairs of your betters, you could clean the casa in an hour."

Clint finished packing, ruminating on what he'd overheard. Before he left, he tried to question Sarita, but he was met with a sullen wall of silence. He was a gringo who had no business nosing into hacienda affairs. She wasn't so rude as to say the words, but her manner made it plain nonetheless.

Clint thought about the complexities of this proud territory, as he rode back. By its tranquil appearance, California was as peaceful and simple as its people. Yet only a few days in Santa Barbara proved much unrest lurked behind that facade: murder, larceny, hatred. Perhaps the mystery of the murderess was not his affair, but the bandit was another matter. By stealing his purse and knocking him senseless, Black Jack had made more than one implacable enemy. Roberto and the bandit both deserved a lesson in American mettle.

Clint smiled wryly to himself as he realized how much he sounded like his uncle. Their ideas of patriotism still differed vastly, however, and he found his uncle's blackmail as hard to stomach as ever. Anything that would delay his spying was a welcome diversion. He had nothing to rush back for. It would do Charles good to stew for a while. So why not set up a shop on his ship?

It would be good to return to the *Arabella*. He had a deal of goods yet to sell and, despite his words to Roberto, more room in his hold for hides and tallow. Santa Barbara's spring tides were calming now, and it was safe for him to lie in. If he found little profit here, he could always move on—after he'd bested Roberto by being first to catch the man who had humiliated them.

As Clint neared the Gaviota Pass where the robbery had occurred, he spied a riderless horse not far from the road. He scanned the area about the animal and caught a flash of white on the ground. Fearing someone had been hurt, he urged his mount off El Camino Real toward the motionless object.

He leaped down and went to stand over what he had thought at first was a man. He went stock-still when he saw the figure's face. The whitest, finest-textured complexion he had ever seen enticed him. Even the brilliant light could find no flaw. Dense, curling lashes brushed the pale rose of her cheeks. A long, straight nose was as regal as a queen's. Her nostrils flared with her breathing. Clint realized she was asleep.

He continued his leisurely survey down her slim body. She reminded him of a thoroughbred, all arms and legs and long throat, but her breeches cupped the vee between her thighs and reminded him potently that she was very much a woman. Small breasts rose gently with each breath, and his heart began beating heavily as he watched them move. It had been too long since he'd had a woman. Why was this one dressed as a man? She must be of the lower class, for she was alone. It had not taken long for Clint to realize how zealously the *gente de razon* guarded its females.

Finally, inexorably, his gaze settled on her lips. Her mouth was wide and full. The lower lip was indented in the middle, implying a sensual invitation that made his knees weak. Her mouth was an unnatural, bright red, and he realized she must have gorged herself on the berries around them. The trickle of juice adorning one side of her mouth was the last inducement he needed. He dropped down beside her and placed his mouth over hers. She was redolent of strawberries, and when her warm lips opened, he couldn't resist investigating the interior of her mouth to see if it tasted as heavenly.

Magdalena stirred after her pleasant dream. It was almost as though the embrace she had longed for still held her. Strong arms protected her, supported her, pleasured her. The man who held her was faceless, but gold hair glittered in the sunlight. The heated movement of his lips over hers barely impinged on her consciousness, at first, so enthralled was she by the novel experience of feeling safe and secure.

When she felt a warm, imperative tongue venture within her mouth with shocking intimacy, however, her eyes flew open—to stare straight into the bluest, clearest eyes she had ever seen. When she pushed at his wide shoulders, Clint reluctantly released her mouth. He drew his head back the barest distance and let his gaze roam her body with such admiration that her cheeks flamed to match the color of her lips.

She was so stunned both from her recognition of him and from his effrontery that the only rational thought she could grasp was, "Blue! His eyes are blue!" Her color deepened as she realized the man she had dreamed of now leaned over her in the flesh. Guilt, shock and embarrassment overwhelmed her. When she met those wicked, appreciative blue eyes her hair-trigger temper was jolted.

She squirmed under him furiously. When he smiled and leaned closer, her nails curved into claws under his pinioning hands as she tried to free a knee. He read her intent and subdued her with such effortless strength she could only open her mouth to blister him with curses.

Grinning now, he silenced her by the simple method of putting his mouth over hers again. He held her arms above her head and teased her mouth, but she bit him with sharp, white teeth. He grunted in surprise and lifted his head.

"Why so temperamental, girl? You've surely been kissed before. I'll ask nothing else unless you wish it, I promise." He lowered his shining head and confided in an intimate whisper that sent a chill down her spine, "I've always had an inordinate fondness for strawberries. Especially when they're packaged so . . ."—he drew back to look at her in a way that left no doubt about his meaning—"delectably." To punctuate his words he licked the trickle at the corner of her lips with a delicate tongue she felt like a lightning flash.

Color washed into her cheeks again, and when he noticed the appealing contrast of rose and ivory, she spat, "Unhand me, you *bellaco*!"

She struggled even more fiercely, but he cocked his head and looked thoughtful. "My, my. Beautiful and the tongue of an angel!" He shook his head as if in amazement. Molten gold eyes glittered at him, but when he looked meaningfully down at where her breasts were crushed against his chest, then back up at her with a flame kindling in his own eyes, she gave a frustrated groan and lay still.

He smiled in gentle approval, drawing her gaze to the corner of his mouth where a dimple winked at her like a sly eye. He had a beautiful mouth. His lips were generous but finely sculpted. The laugh lines at the corners emphasized the curves that seemed naturally made for mirth and gaiety. There was no threat in his long-lashed blue eyes. He looked at her with a combination of admiration and humor that muted her anger. She knew she was in no danger from him. Enjoy the beautiful day, his twinkling eyes seemed to tell her. Laugh with me, I'm but teasing you.

Against her will, a twinge of envy pierced her at his aura of total confidence and contentment. Here was a man who knew who he was and what he wanted. More important, he enjoyed to the fullest the life he had carved for himself as he looked forward to the challenge of tomorrow. Bands of pain, longing for what had been and regret for what she had become, tightened her chest, smothering the vestiges of her wrath. Her eyelids drooped to hide the shimmer of tears.

He was astounded at her transformation from spitting fury to despondency. What had he said? He had been unable to resist teasing her just to see if her eyes really were that incredible gold or if they darkened to brown with her moods. He sighed in regret and released her. He pulled her up and dusted the blades of grass from her breeches, ignoring the reflexive tensing of his hands at her soft warmth.

"Have I hurt you?" he asked anxiously when she still refused to look at him.

She shook her head. She turned toward her mount. When she raised a foot to the stirrup he put a gentle hand on her shoulder and turned her to face him. He had never seen such a tall woman. He was well over six feet, yet he topped her only by a head. She stood docilely before him, but she still refused to lift her eyes.

They stood so close a lock of her flowing hair brushed his face, and he couldn't resist reaching up to rub it against his appreciative cheek. It was soft but warm, like living silk. He wrapped it around his brown hand and turned it this way and that. He was amazed at the way the lock changed from sable, to brown, to red as it caught the sun's rays. She had a rare beauty, this strange, fiery girl, and he sensed a rare despair in her that aroused his chivalry.

"Forgive my discourtesy. You were lying like a sleeping princess, and I couldn't resist awakening you. What's wrong? Is there anything I can do to help?" When she looked at him, he was aghast at the despair he glimpsed before her long lashes went down again.

"You were very wrong to kiss me against my will, but it matters little. There was no one to see."

There was no one to care. She didn't say the words, but they both heard them. They lingered in the air like foul smoke, stinking and pervasive. He frowned until his straight golden brows met in an unbroken line above his bold Roman nose.

A slim finger covered his lips when he would have spoken. "Please, what's done is done. I must leave now, and if you truly want to help me, you must forget we have ever met. Tell no one you saw me." She looked at him wistfully, her teeth biting the lip that was still moist from his playful kiss.

Her eyes dropped to his mouth. His heart quickened again at the look in them. She shut her eyes, drew a deep breath and moved jerkily, like an unwilling puppet, to her horse. She clenched Fuego's mane in her hands. He saw her teeter back and forth as though he exerted some strange, magnetic pull on her.

Quickly, impulsively, she whirled. She launched herself at him with such startling swiftness he barely had time to catch her around the waist before she dragged his head down and fastened her lips over his.

The shock at her action was quick to wear off under the hungry movements of her lips. She seemed awkward and inexperienced as she tentatively followed the side to side motion of his mouth, but when her tongue licked him gently at the corner of his lips where his dimple lay in hiding, he shuddered and hauled her so close her feet left the ground. For a moment out of time, a moment out of Magdalena's reality and Clint's experience, all thoughts, all values, all emotions were superseded by a physical pleasure so intense they quivered with it.

Their mouths moved more passionately as self-awareness escaped them. When Clint hesitantly explored the crevice of her mouth, she eagerly allowed him entrance. The stabbing movements of his tongue were evocative of an act she had little knowledge of but both longed for and feared with every passing moment. His chest heaved with the thunderous pounding of his heart, but her bosom shook with a like tempest as they stood so close they might have been glued together.

Breast to breast, thigh to thigh and heart to heart, they clung until they could barely breathe. Magdalena's lips melded to his with the desperation of a woman enjoying a last drink before her execution. Her wildness incited his already inflamed desires until the urgency of his kiss deepened to a passion that bruised her lips. They parted to breathe, but he allowed her only a moment before he returned to her lips to nibble the reddened contours gently. He lowered his mouth to the pulsating cord in her neck and followed the smooth line with a series of hot, eager stabs of his tongue.

Free of the drugging pressure of his lips on hers, a modicum of sanity returned to her. She pushed at his arms. He laid his forehead against hers, gasping for breath. When he had won control, he lowered her back to her feet. With the quicksilver grace so characteristic of her movements, she vaulted on Fuego and fled at a full gallop.

She heard and ignored his desperate cry of "Wait!" Tears trailed into her hairline from the force of her ride, but she didn't notice. All she felt, all she saw, was the sensation and look of him. He had brought home to her as nothing else had what an outcast she was. He appealed to her as she had never conceived a man could. His strength, his humor, the goodness she instinctively sensed in him were qualities she had known only in her father and brother. She thought fate must be laughing again at its cruelty to her. Why allow her to meet such a man now, when she was a leper, a reject of society? Such as he was not for her. They must not meet again.

Luckily for Magdalena's peace of mind, she did not know Clint had resolved exactly the opposite. He had enjoyed and made love to many women, many more beautiful than Magdalena. But he had never felt so shattered, so enraptured, by a single kiss. As he rounded up the horse he had not taken time to hitch, there was a look on his face his sisters would have dreaded. It was the exact expression he wore when he had determined they would attend boarding school or they should not see a certain suitor again. His crew would have recognized it as the face he presented to the elements when he raced a storm to beat his rivals to port and thus win the best price for his goods.

And finally, it was the look he wore when he worked for weeks trying to solve the riddle of the jade, ivory and gold puzzle box he brought back from one of his voyages to China. The girl he had just met was as rare, as complicated, as that puzzle box. He was determined to find her, to unravel the mystery she presented. He must see if her allure stayed as strong once her riddle was solved. He suspected the triumph he enjoyed when he finally found the jewel inside the last box was mild compared to the pleasure they would bring one another. No matter what it took, he would find her.

# Chapter 3

"This is a matter I myself must probe and get the truth of."

Act I, DON JUAN TENORIO

Magdalena's meeting with Clint so distressed her that she forgot her anger at Joaquin. Thus, when she returned, she voiced a dull hello and led Fuego to the back of the cavern to curry him.

Joaquin raised an eyebrow. Magdalena's volatile nature could explode with alarming violence, but the smoke of her wrath did not linger for she seldom bore a grudge. She must be angry with him indeed to treat him to this fit of sulks. Sighing, he decided to let her brood longer on his words, for he had meant every syllable. He picked up one of his shirts to mend the sleeve.

Though Magdalena brushed Fuego's coat with steady hands, her thoughts were focused inward as she relived the stranger's embrace. She'd never responded physically to a man in this way before, but the odd heat he ignited in her body disturbed her less than the rejuvenation of emotional needs she had thought never to feel again.

She had almost forgotten how enticing it was to feel sheltered and cherished, for those feelings had died with her brother. Despite life's lessons, the remnants of that weak woman had been vulnerable to a stranger she'd probably never see again. For one raw second, she'd longed to pour out her story and plead for his help. She had hesitated because she didn't want his admiring look to change to disdain or contempt. Now, back in the cold cavern, insulated from his seductive vitality, she was glad vanity had kept her silent.

However, the resolve of Job couldn't have cheated her of that last wild embrace. The first times he kissed her she had been too startled and angry to respond. But ah, that last kiss . . . Her cheeks flamed as she remembered the way she had ground herself into his hard contours. She pressed her face against Fuego's neck to still her tremors, reliving the hunger of his lips.

That impulse she didn't regret, for at least she'd had a sample of the joy her mother had partaken of with her father. If she was not fated to sup at that banquet, then so be it. The taste of his lips was sweet enough to linger for a long, long time. No, crazy or not, she didn't regret the brief triumph of feminine instinct. She'd glimpsed how it could have been had she been the noble señorita of her birth instead of the outlaw she'd made herself. Sighing, she straightened her shoulders and locked the sweet vision away. Later, she would savor it again, for it would be all she'd have of him.

It wasn't that she didn't trust the stranger. She would have staked Fuego that his unwavering gaze reflected his honor. No, she admitted with grim candor, it was herself she didn't trust when she was around him. Above all, she could afford no distractions if she was to safely exit the treacherous maze Roberto had set her in. That golden-haired giant was distraction personified . . .

She must not be diverted by eyes of so clear a blue they glowed like crystalline jewels with lapis lazuli insets radiating from the pupils. They were strangely magnetic, those eyes, but no matter how she might long to blurt out the confidence they encouraged, she could not. She resumed grooming Fuego's mane, swallowing the bitter realization that, for the first time, she resented the harshness of her taskmaster—revenge.

Magdalena's brows knit together as she speculated about the stranger's identity and his purpose in Santa Barbara. She prayed, for his sake, that he was not in business with Roberto. Yet why else would he travel to El Paraiso? It was certain Roberto would not invite him on a social call, for her cousin despised all gringos.

Stuck in the emotional morass of her own making, she missed Sean's step. She jumped when he rumbled, "We be low on supplies. I thought I'd go into Santa Barbara and purchase some flour, corn and mayhap a few vegetables. What think ye o' the idea?"

Magdalena's mouth watered at the thought of fresh food, but her concern was greater than her hunger. "It's not safe, Sean. What if you should meet Luis or Roberto?"

In reply, Sean grinned, held up Joaquin's razor and rubbed his thick, red beard with his other hand. "Methinks it's time I shaved this forest. It was dark and I was masked, so 'tis not likely I'd be recognized even if I do see the scoundrels."

Still worried, Magdalena frowned, but it suddenly struck her he could do no more while he was in town than just purchase supplies. She nodded slowly. "Very well, Sean, but avoid the presidio area."

Sean turned to prepare himself, but Magdalena halted him. "One other thing. Could you please make inquiries as to the identity of the stranger who was with Roberto?"

When Sean cocked his head and looked at her curiously, she blurted, "I am wondering what interest Roberto has in him. If my cousin hopes to use him in his gold scheme, then perhaps we can warn the man and thwart his plans."

It was a logical concern, but Sean wondered why Magdalena refused to meet his eyes. He shrugged. "Very well, lass. I'll do me best."

After Magdalena fed Fuego and her falcon, she absently strummed her guitar while she watched Sean shave. The thick pile of hair at his feet grew with each measured stroke of that huge hand. When he wiped the last of the lather away and turned to face Magdalena with a sheepish grin, her eyes widened in astonishment.

The uncouth, menacing bandit had disappeared. A giant leprechaun stood in his stead. Without the thicket of coarse hair, Sean's face had a puckish look enhanced by his pug nose, dimpled chin and chubby cheeks. The paradox of that cute, boyish face atop the Herculean mountain of muscle was an appealing one that brought a delighted smile to Magdalena's lips. Her sense of mischief, submerged under a two-year weight of sorrow, surged to the surface with a joyous bound.

She rose and moved in front of him to catch his cheeks in her hands. Squeezing gently, she crooned in a thick Irish brogue, "Ah, 'tis a handsome lad he is, to me way 'o thinkin'. Why would ye shield such a God-gifted face from the light o' day, me boyo?"

Sean scowled fiercely, looking so like a disgruntled boy that Magdalena's bottled mirth bubbled merrily over. It was the first time Sean had heard her laugh, and the deep, melodic chuckles were so infectious that his ruffled pride was smoothed. A reluctant grin stretched his cheeks. Two more deep dimples appeared, adding to his cherubic look. He winked at Joaquin, who had also approached in curiosity.

He deepened his own brogue. "And why reck ye I keep these saintly features covered, ye devil's spawn? Sure, and 'tis many a battle I've fought o'er this cursed face. Instead o' showin' proper thanks fer me sacrifice, all ye do is laugh." He caught Magdalena's shoulders in his hands and added huskily, "But I'll let ye kiss the blarney stone as often as ye like, me manly pride be damned, if ye'll only bless us with that pretty laugh more often."

Touched, Magdalena sobered abruptly. Her shining golden eyes dimmed into dusky solemnity. "I do thank you for everything you've done for us, Sean. I don't know how we would have managed without you." She kissed his cheek, her lips quirking when his round face crimsoned to a shade that clashed with his hair. She stepped back and watched as he saddled his horse.

When he was mounted, she covered his hand with her own long, slender one. "Be careful, dear friend. Be as inconspicuous as possible, and for God's sake, don't get in any fights."

He saluted her jauntily and rode away. She called after him, "And I like that pretty face, me handsome boyo. See ye bring it back with no marks on it."

Joaquin put his arm around her shoulders as they watched him ride away. "Don't worry, Magdalena, Sean will be all right. He's shrewder than he looks, that's for certain. Who would suspect that face of belonging to Black Jack's meanest hombre?" Joaquin returned to his shirt, chuckling.

When, hours later, Sean reappeared, Magdalena and Joaquin rushed to help unload his burdened horse, Magdalena firing questions all the while. "Were you recognized? Were you able to get fresh vegetables? Did you see Luis or Roberto? What did you find out about the stranger?"

Sean staggered back as though she showered him with a hail of bullets. "Saints preserve us, give me a chance to catch me breath," he chided with a self-satisfied grin. He helped them put away the pears, potatoes, corn, squash, flour, coffee and beans, his movements slow and deliberate while he ignored Magdalena's increasingly impatient glances.

Joaquin smiled at this subtle revenge for her teasing and waited calmly.

Magdalena grabbed up a pear and sank famished teeth into it, her eyes smoldering as she watched Sean stretch out his long legs and begin to peel potatoes. He smiled at her angelically.

"Now then, did ye have somethin' ye wanted to ask?"

She opened her mouth to retort, but Joaquin recognized the glint in her eye and forestalled her. "Enough teasing, Sean. What did you find out?"

"Little enough." Sean's mocking grin disappeared. "I didn't see Luis or Roberto, but I met Roberto's *vaquero*,

Julio, I believe his name be." Magdalena gasped with alarm, but Sean hastily reassured her, "He didn't recognize me, lass. I bought him a bottle and plied him with so much *aguardiente* I don't think he'd have recognized his own mither. He seemed to know little o' Roberto's plans, because the fellow is such a braggart I believe he would've told all. What I did discover is that the man they were with the night we robbed them is an American named Clinton Browning."

Sean was watching the potatoes he was peeling, but Joaquin's eyes snapped to Magdalena when she started. He continued to watch her as Sean spoke.

"The fellow be an American ship captain who has come to Santa Barbara to trade for hides and tallow. Julio hinted that he be involved in some kind o' business with Luis and Roberto, and from the rascal's caginess, I'd bet me rosary it's beyond the pale o' the law."

Joaquin saw Magdalena clench her hands in her lap so hard her knuckles gleamed whitely, and his surprise at her reaction grew to alarm. Why was she so upset over Sean's revelation about the stranger?

"Not much else to tell. It was easy gettin' the supplies we needed. I didn't want to arouse suspicion by usin' the silver we stole, so I traded our last hides." He added almost as an afterthought, "Oh, I also heard the American is settin' up a shop in his ship. He's lookin' for a maid."

Magdalena rose unsteadily and croaked, "Thank you, Sean. You did very well." She walked outside with a heaviness far removed from her usual light grace.

Frowning, Joaquin watched her go. His protective instincts urged him to follow, but he sensed her need to be alone, so he forced himself to remain seated. He would question her when she seemed less upset.

Outside, Magdalena sat on a boulder and stared blindly at the crimson horizon. Her fingers and lips felt numb, as though she had ingested poison. Now her thoughts were not just unsettling; they made her stomach churn with bitter disgust. *Dios*, how could she have been so wrong about the stranger? How could she have believed he, an American,

66

typified every virtue she admired in a man? For one bare moment, she wondered if she could be wrong. She'd been so certain he was honorable . . . But Julio would have had no reason to lie. Her face hardened again. No, it was so. She just didn't want to believe it.

Like too many feeble women before her, she had been fooled by a handsome face and form that hid the true ugliness of the nature underneath. She recoiled partly because of the Americano's nationality, but far worse was his involvement with Roberto. Nothing could excuse his partnership with her cousin. If the American was Roberto's accomplice, it was all the proof Magdalena needed of the avarice and cruelty in his character.

Her sickened disappointment retreated, only to be over-taken by more dangerous emotions. Revulsion shook her as she faced the fact that she had actually kissed the scoundrel. Worse, she had been enthralled by his embrace! From revulsion, her outraged feelings took one short step and fell headlong into rage.

How dare he accost her, Magdalena Inez Flanagan de Sarria, granddaughter of one of California's noblest ranche-ros, and treat her like a harlot? The tender concern she'd felt in his arms and seen in his eyes had been a sham, a ploy he'd used to deceive her into submission. Submission? Her cackle was an ugly sound. She'd been aching, eager and responsive in her own humiliation.

Her proud nature revolted as she admitted she had been tricked by a pretty face. The tender, yearning shoots of femininity she had allowed to surface once more were scorched into ash by her fiery rage. No man had a place in her life in any capacity except as friend and partner. The realization that she'd almost been seduced into regretting her sole reason for living the last two years increased her fury. He would pay, along with Roberto. Inhaling, she closed her eyes and willed herself to calm.

When she opened her eyes, only a flicker of wrath was visible. She remained staring into the gathering dusk for a long time; then, her step as firm as the set of her chin, she entered the cave. If that glimmer of feral rage still burned in

*67*

the depths of her eyes, it was too dark for Joaquin and Sean to notice.

It was vital to keep her tone offhand. When Sean and Joaquin discovered her plans, the cave would reverberate with their objections. "Well, *mis queridos bandidos*, I think it's time Black Jack made his second appearance. Since we have charted our course, delay can only hurt us. We must make our first donation to the *indios*. Shall we prepare for our raid?"

Joaquin searched her expression. He was relieved the shattered look was gone, but he was disturbed at the indomitable set of her patrician jaw. Magdalena enraged was a formidable opponent; Magdalena icily determined was as dangerous and wily as a prowling tigress. When Sean went to saddle his horse, Joaquin stood waiting, watching her closely.

Magdalena forced herself to remain still under his narrow scrutiny. That level, assessing stare always made her long to shield her head, for she felt certain it must be made of glass and he could read her every thought. This time, however, her grim determination gave her the poise to stare coolly back.

"And why have you picked this night for us to break the seventh commandment, hmm, *niña*?"

Magdalena winced at his straight talk, for her conscience was still troubled by what they were doing, but she shrugged casually enough. "Why not tonight? The more we pursue our calling, the sooner our goal will be reached. Why, have you any objections?"

"None that I have not already stated, endlessly. But I am curious about one thing. Why did you react so strongly to Sean's news about the American?"

The steady gold eyes flickered. Magdalena blustered, "You imagine things, Joaquin. I was merely relieved Sean returned safely." When Joaquin quirked a brow at this blatant lie, Magdalena exploded. "What difference does it make? I should think you'd be relieved I am cool and rational. This decision to ride again tonight is not an impulsive one. I have a very good reason, but I am not ready to share it with you yet. Are you not pleased I heeded your advice, amigo?"

The note of mockery in her last question angered Joaquin. His snort was eloquent of disbelief. "It will be the first time, if you have, which I doubt. I don't know what your purpose is, but I feel it will lead us to disaster. Still, I expect you to pay me no more heed than you usually do."

He poked his sharp face into hers with a look that could only be termed pugnacious. "Just remember this, *mu cha cha*: When the young fail to heed the advice of those older and wiser that the fire is too hot, the only way they learn is *after* they've been singed. I am merely trying to spare you some of the mistakes I made in my youth; but if you are hell-bent and determined to get burned, all I can do is stay close and keep the bandages ready."

After this little homily had echoed with the uncomfortable ring of truth in Magdalena's ears, Joaquin also moved to saddle his horse.

Sean, mounted and ready, watched and listened to the byplay with rueful amusement. It was a thrust and retreat he'd become accustomed to over the months, yet he was still a little in awe of this frequent class of wills. That Magdalena usually emerged the victor surprised him no longer.

In Sean's experience, women did not wear breeches, wield swords and pursue such a physically arduous path of honor. But then, he mused as he shifted in his saddle, in his experience women did not ride like Indians, fence like wizards and merely breathe heavily at the exertions that sometimes made him gasp for breath.

When he'd first joined Magdalena's crusade, he'd been shocked and dismayed to find she was the brains and spirit behind their quest. He had watched doubtfully as Magdalena planned their first raid while Joaquin nodded his head in agreement. He'd believed Joaquin deferred to her out of respect for her former station, but after the success of that first robbery he realized it was Magdalena, not Joaquin, who had the best chance of leading them to victory. Sean knew of no man who could have led them more brilliantly.

69

Joaquin was a wiry, shrewd, mature man. However, he was also a loner, an introspective man lacking the aggression, energy or keen intelligence necessary to triumph against such overwhelming odds. Magdalena possessed all these qualities; most importantly, all her fiercely stubborn nature was channeled into a desire to win. No matter the cost to herself and even, if necessary, to her friends, Magdalena would defeat Roberto. With her last breath, if need be, she would fight.

Now Sean understood that she was their best, perhaps their only, hope for success. Thus, when they picked their way carefully down the mountain trail, Sean hooded this time, he felt little concern for their safety because he trusted their leader.

Once they reached El Camino Real, it was some time before a traveler appeared, for it was late and few were venturesome enough to ride the sometimes treacherous highway at night. When a lone rider came into view, Sean sighed with relief. He tightened his hands on the reins to urge his horse out of their shelter of laurel trees. Magdalena grasped his pommel before he could do so and shook her head.

Joaquin looked at her askance, for the approaching rider wore the plush, heavily braided velvet cloak of a wealthy man. They waited silently after he passed. Magdalena ignored Joaquin's piercing stare and patted Fuego's mane when he grew restive at the idleness. It was but a short time later that a carriage appeared, traveling slowly, one outrider attending.

Magdalena craned her neck around the thicket of trunks to get a better look at the conveyance. Her eyes narrowed in recognition. Quickly, before Joaquin could closely examine the looming vehicle, she wheeled Fuego out of the trees, gesturing for the two men to follow.

When they reached the road they separated, as planned. Sean galloped up to confront the outrider, relieving him of pistol and sword before the poor fellow had time to do more than fumble at his belt.

Joaquin held his pistol on the terrified driver and ordered

him to halt, but if his voice was calm, his spirit was not. He now recognized the carriage they were holding up. Was Magdalena mad? Angelina and Jose Rivas were only slightly less likely to recognize them than was Roberto.

Meanwhile, Magdalena rode up even with the now crawling carriage. She pivoted in her saddle and drew up a long leg over Fuego's side to ease her length through the small window. She plopped onto a plush seat next to a voluptuous señorita who wore a silk rebozo and a horrified grimace.

The girl shrank away, screaming "Jose!" in a terrified voice.

Magdalena threw a quick, satisfied look at the cowering maid across from them, then she soothed in Black Jack's hoarse tones, "Fear not, *niña*, I have no designs on your person."

The words relaxed Angelina only slightly. Her voice trembled when she croaked, "What have you done to my brother?"

"He is safe and unharmed."

When the carriage rolled to a stop, Magdalena stepped down. She held the door with a flourish as she gestured for the occupants to descend. Angelina picked her way daintily down the steps, her tall young maid following.

Jose Rivas, Sean's pistol prodding his back, could only watch with impotent rage as the bandit strutted up and down in front of the two girls. His eyes were points of menace as though he debated whom to shoot first.

When the tension in the little scene was screaming in the night air, Magdalena leaned into Angelina and purred, "It was foolish to drive so late, señorita. There are bandits on these roads." Sean guffawed at the boldness, but Jose stiffened with rage and Joaquin winced.

When some of the color had returned to Angelina's face at the barb, Magdalena drew a gloved finger down the warm cheek. "That's better, chiquita. Desperado I may be, but I would not harm such a fragile flower." Her husky voice grew brisk. "Now, we have need of your baggage, if you please. You there, get down and strap those valises on one

*71*

of the carriage horses." Magdalena swatted Jose's horse sharply on the rump. It bolted into the darkness.

While the driver obeyed, fumbling with nervousness, Magdalena turned to Jose. She walked up to him with a boldness she didn't feel, wondering wryly if he'd still praise her grace and womanliness if he knew her identity. It pained her to rob Carlos's best friend, but she had no choice. It would look odd indeed if they took only the luggage. She flipped his cloak back and quickly relieved him of his purse. She hefted the bag from one hand to the other, then she opened it and poured half the contents into Jose's jacket pocket.

She nodded at the furious man cordially. "It would never do to be too greedy. I leave funds enough to purchase another horse."

When the bags were strapped on one of the carriage horses, Magdalena turned again to Angelina. Bowing deeply, she took the girl's hand and examined the elegant fingers decorated by even more elegant jewels. She felt Angelina's hand tense and she knew the girl expected her rings to be ripped off.

Magdalena waited a full minute to let the suspense build, then, with her mischievous glint hidden under her hood, she gently, gallantly kissed the small hand in hers, patted it and let it drop back to Angelina's side. "Keep your sparklers, little one. I cannot bear to rob the beautiful señorita of the baubles that adorn her so prettily."

Vaulting nimbly back into her saddle, Magdalena drew her sword. With an adroit flick, she sliced through the carriage leads. Forcing Fuego into a flashy rear, Magdalena saluted with her sword. "Farewell, *amorcito*. *Vaya con Dios!*" She wheeled her mount into the darkness, Joaquin on her haunches and Sean bringing up the rear, leading the packhorse.

Helpless to do more, Jose yelled with fury reverberating in his voice, "*Vayan con El Diablo, puercos!*" He kicked at the carriage wheel and won only an aching toe to add to his rage.

Angelina, however, touched the back of the hand that still

tingled from the bandit's soft, warm mask and softer, gentler kiss. She stared after the retreating figures even after they had disappeared. The face stiff with fear a short time ago was now illuminated by a soft glow.

The next morning, Joaquin woke early. He had tossed on his hard bed even more than usual. How much longer could they get away with robbing people who knew them intimately without being recognized? He turned in Magdalena's direction to continue the lecture he had begun last night. He froze in dread. Her pallet was empty and the sun was barely up! Where would she go so early?

He sprang to his feet and went to shake Sean awake. The two men were frantically saddling their horses when a scuffling sound at the cave entrance alerted them. They turned, gasping in horror at the apparition that greeted them.

A poor Indian girl, braided hair black and lank, shoulders stooped with sorrow, squinted back at them. One side of her dark face was twisted with a long, ugly scar. As she stepped nearer, she limped on her left leg. She wore the tattered skirt and short-sleeved chemise of the lower classes. Her coarse wool rebozo radiated virulent colors that augmented the pitifulnesss of its wearer. Sean and Joaquin stared at her, looked at each other, then turned disbelieving eyes back to Magdalena.

As usual, Joaquin found his voice first. "So! This is why you wanted to rob the Rivases. You cared nothing about their money or jewels. You endangered our lives, our quest, everything, because you wanted to steal the maid's clothes!"

Joaquin sounded so outraged that Sean's sense of humor was tickled. Indeed, it was an odd twist of affairs. To think, it was the maid Magdalena had wanted to rob! Sean chuckled, then laughed, then roared while Joaquin fumed and Magdalena smiled weakly.

"What foolishness do you plan now?" Joaquin demanded. When Magdalena shifted her feet guiltily, his eyes narrowed, for he'd known her too long. "You've only one reason to disguise yourself—you're going where you're known . . . *Ay Dios mio*, Magdalena, you can't go into Santa Barbara!"

Joaquin slapped Sean between the shoulder blades, choking off the Irishman's laughter. "Hush! You fool, don't you understand what she's planning? She's disguised herself so she can go into Santa Barbara and apply as the American's maid."

That sobered Sean quickly enough. He shook his head at Magdalena. "Lass, this time I know ye've lost yer senses. Do ye really think ye can go about freely? Yer scar is slippin' already."

Magdalena felt the wax she had applied over the berry stain; indeed, it had slipped a little. Muttering, she went to her tiny mirror, warmed the wax with her hands and molded it more closely to her cheek.

When she turned around to face them, Joaquin groaned at the slant of her jaw. "I'll be very careful. I'll stay on the ship until dark, and then I'll wear my own clothes. Don't you see? I'll have easy access to the presidio. Who would suspect a poor, scarred maid of raiding the fortress? We must have more information about Roberto and Luis's plans, and how else are we to get it? It's far more dangerous to search El Paraiso where so many know me. You know how lax security is at the garrison. I promise I'll be careful."

Joaquin and Sean stared back at her, stone-faced with rejection. Magdalena lost her temper. "I don't ask your permission. If you disapprove, then you're welcome to pull out, the both of you. I'll go on alone." She spun around to stuff a sack with clothes, ignoring them.

The sound of Joaquin's gritting teeth was audible in the dank cave. "That's your answer for everything, eh, *mi salvajita*? You get your way or you go alone. You are selfish, Magdalena. We are concerned only for you, but you view us as interfering, presumptuous. I, for one, have had enough. I will wait here until I hear of your capture or death, and then I leave. My bones are getting too old to live in this cave much longer. They long for the sunlight."

Without another word, Joaquin marched to the back of the cave.

Sean watched Magdalena's stiff face for a moment before he put a comforting arm around her shoulders. "Ye know he doesn't mean it, lass. 'Tis worried sick about you, he is. Are ye certain ye must do this?"

At Magdalena's jerky nod, Sean hugged her, then put her from him. When she flicked a guilty look at the back of the cave, Sean encouraged, "Ye can't leave with such words between ye. If somethin' happened, he'd ne'er forgive himself. Why don't ye talk to him?" He gave her a gentle push.

Magdalena's steps dragged as she approached Joaquin. She was hurt at his words, but she knew she had pushed him too far. It wasn't fair to threaten him with rejection whenever he tried to caution her.

"Joaquin," she whispered, "please forgive me. I just can't bear this any longer. I, too, am tired of this cave. We must take the initiative if we are to win. I will be careful as a cat, I swear."

The poker-straight back relaxed. Joaquin swung around to jerk her into his arms. "Ah, niña, niña, forgive me as well. I will never leave you, you know that. But I fear for your life. How will this all end?"

Since Magdalena could not answer that, they took what comfort they could from the loving embrace. Joaquin stroked her hair. "Your beautiful hair. What have you done to it?"

"It's but a plant dye. It will wear off after a few washings."

Joaquin hid his worry with a determined smile. "You must at least promise to keep us informed of your progress. Come back to the cave every Friday evening and tell us how things are going. Yes?"

At her nod, he asked, "Do you take the carreta?" They had found an old abandoned cart, and Sean had recently fixed the broken axle.

"Si," she replied. "The carriage horse we took last night should not look too strange, but I'm worried about taking

Fuego with me. He is too distinctive and I want no connection between the raider and the maid. Can you or Sean bring him to the beach late tonight? I have somewhere in mind to hide him."

"Of course. I will bring him myself."

After Magdalena finished her packing, the two men escorted her outside to the hidden cart. Sean hitched the carriage horse to the wagon and lifted Magdalena inside. Joaquin handed her a wrapped sword, which she shoved under her seat.

She absorbed the two tense faces watching her, her mouth suddenly dry. She would be truly on her own in Santa Barbara. She'd either prove she could take care of herself or she'd be killed or captured in the attempt. Briefly, she was tempted to change her mind. But then an image flashed before her eyes: an image that lured like a jeweled idol, shiny, golden, but inwardly it was nothing but base metal. Her mouth tightened, blood rushed to her cheeks and eagerness for battle made her skin tingle.

She flashed a bold smile that clashed with her appearance. *"Hasta luego!"*

The two men watched her until she was out of sight, then Joaquin muttered, "If anything happens to that child I'll never forgive myself."

Sean smiled. It was a strange, confident smile of pride, a grin of anticipation. "Don't worry about Magdalena. It's the American you should pity!" And patting Joaquin on the shoulder, Sean began his daily chores.

Clint was not surprised he'd received no response to his posted ad for a maid. As soon as his identity was known, the friendliness everyone had formerly displayed changed to wariness. Oh, the townpeople took advantage of his ship. They needed the goods he stocked too much to be that wary, but they made their purchases quickly and left with barely a word exchanged. Not a one of them would allow their daughters to work for the gringo.

Leaving his cabin, Clint went to the crew mess where he had set up the shop. He smiled at Pritikin, the single crew member he had kept to help him. The rest of his crew had taken sadly needed shore leave.

"Pritikin, it's time for lunch. Do you suppose between the two of us we can fry a steak without charring it?"

Pritikin, a sandy-haired lad of eighteen, grinned impudently back, revealing crooked but white teeth. "As I reckon, it's yer turn, cap'n. Ain't my fault you give cook shore leave." The boy stroked his pride and joy, his nascent moustache. "'Course, the way cook is sometimes, yer cookin' ain't much worse."

Clint punched Pritikin on the shoulder with a teasing fist. "None of your lip, boy. Captains aren't supposed to cook." Clint's stomach rumbled angrily at this strategic moment. Pritikin grinned.

Grimacing, Clint joked, "Of course, if we have to survive like this for much longer, the point will be moot. I'll waste away and won't have to worry about cooking, or anything else, again."

Pritikin was no longer listening. His eyes had gone past Clint to the companionway. They widened with such an odd expression of mingled horror and pity that Clint whirled to look. A tall Indian girl was limping clumsily down the stairs, one leg dragging down each step. She stumbled at the bottom. Clint instinctively walked out to catch her, but she shrank away from his helping hand.

"Can I help you, señorita?" Clint asked politely. She left the shadowy companionway, and, as she entered the cabin, the light shining through the portholes illuminated her features. Clint strangled a gasp at the sight of her poor, twisted face. A terrible scar slashed down one temple and cheek, crinkling the corner of one eye and the edge of her mouth. She kept her eyes lowered. Though she was tall, her carriage was not proud. She seemed spiritless, defeated, hopeless. Clint's throat clogged with sympathy.

"You have a position open for a maid?" she asked huskily. Incongruously, her voice was as deep and mellow as a Stradivarius played by a virtuoso.

Clint started at the sound issuing from that twisted mouth. "Yes, I do. Are you interested in it?" Intrigued, he

77

moved a step nearer to try to see the color of her eyes, but her gaze dropped.

"*Si.* I have much experience. I was maid at one of the ranchos but my . . . leg made it difficult for me to perform my duties. I need an easier job, caring for fewer people," Magdalena lied.

Clint had already made up his mind to hire her, but only partly because he was in such dire need. Something about her roused his protective instincts. He wanted to help her, but he discerned the fierce pride beneath her fragile frame. Such a spirit would resent sympathy. His tone was brisk and businesslike.

"Your duties here would be relatively light. You'd need to keep only my cabin and shop clean, and prepare meals for me and my salesman here, Pritikin."

Pritikin nodded his head. "How do ye do, miss." Giving his captain a doubtful look, Pritikin went back to straightening the shop. Despite her height, the girl didn't look strong enough to perform even those light duties.

"Very well, you're hired." Clint named her wages, a generous sum, but she kept her eyes down and didn't seem surprised, or even grateful. What an odd girl. Her scar must have given her a hellish time of it. He appraised her again, thinking how pretty she must have been before her accident. Oddly, the thought made him uneasy, so he turned and led the way down the corridor to a small cabin.

It held one bunk, a sea chest and a chair that sat beneath the porthole. "This is your cabin. I like my meals served promptly at seven, one and six." He watched her look around, offering, "I'll bring your things down for you, if you like."

For the first time, he caught a glimmer of emotion in her face as she darted a look at him. Alarm? Why would she be alarmed? And what strange eyes she had. He had assumed they were brown, but they were a paler hue. Clint bent his head, trying to get a better look at them, but as he lowered his chin, she lowered hers. When they were both uncomfortably slumped, Clint straightened with a snap, feeling ridiculous.

She edged past him to the door. "I'll get my things and then I'll prepare lunch," she announced abruptly.

Frowning, Clint watched her limp back up the companionway. Something about this girl didn't fit, but Clint was at a loss to define what it was. Besides, he needed a cook too badly to worry about whether the girl seemed mysterious or not. His stomach growled again, reminding him that at the moment he didn't care if she was a thief as long as she could cook. Unaware of the irony of the thought, he returned to the shop.

Ashore again, Magdalena stabled the carreta and horse in the shed Clint had indicated. She caught her bundle under one arm and shoved the sword further under the seat before walking back up the gangplank. Tonight, she would hide the sword with Fuego after she met Joaquin.

Magdalena was careful to limp consistently as she returned to face her enemy. She had done it! She'd fooled the American. Her heart pounded with a mixture of elation, anger and excitement. She longed to mock him with her true identity. How would he react when he learned who she really was? He'd made a fool of her only once; she'd made a fool of him twice. She would do so again before she was finished with him.

The advantage was now hers because she knew him for what he was. Greedy. Ruthless. Very well, then so would she be. But even as she threw herself into the role fate had forced upon her, Magdalena was unsettled as much by the feelings she couldn't control as by fear of what she'd begun. This hollow sickness in the pit of her stomach was fear, she told herself firmly. But somehow she knew, even then, that the sickness was caused as much by sadness and a sense of betrayal. Why, oh why, was the only man she had ever been attracted to so handsome to look at but so ugly within? Why couldn't he have been the honorable man of her dreams? Dreams were poor substitutes for reality, but dreams were all she had to give her strength to go on. That one encounter with him had invigorated her, shown her how sweet it could be to throw off her man's role and become a woman again.

And then this same man had shown how foolish were such thoughts . . .

Magdalena glanced around the ship as she stepped on the main deck. She'd never set foot on any type of ship before, and the sheer size of the *Arabella* awed her. She looked around at the forest of masts and tightly furled sails. The heavy lines securing the canvas seemed coiled like great snakes, and the crow's nest far above her head was a spy tower. Did he bring such a ship for simple trading, or was his purpose more sinister? What did this gringo want of them? Had he come to scout out their land with the hope of stealing it, like others before him?

"Would you like a tour of the *Arabella*?" the subject of her thoughts inquired courteously, making her jump.

She smoothed her speculative look into reserve and looked down at the oak planking to avoid his eyes. "No, I think I should begin your lunch. Perhaps you'll show me the galley after I put away my things?"

Now how would a poor, uneducated Indian girl know the ship terminology for a kitchen? Puzzled, Clint nodded. "Certainly."

He followed her to her cabin, watched her place the sack in the sea chest, then led the way to the small galley. Contrary to Magdalena's inexperienced eyes, the *Arabella* was not a large ship. She was built compactly, lightly, for speed, so the crew's quarters, even the captain's cabin, were small to allow more room for the hold. The galley, too, was tiny, and Clint had to stoop to show Magdalena where the supplies were kept.

"Excuse these heavy dishes, but glass is simply not practical," Clint apologized as he removed several pewter plates and serving dishes from the built-in cupboards.

Magdalena was staring at the loaded larder. Sugar, lard, grains, fresh fruits and vegetables of every kind and, glory of glories, a squat jar of chocolate! After the last two years, the galley seemed stocked for royalty.

Setting the fresh steak out for her to cook, Clint turned to face her. He got a glimpse of the hunger in her face before he bumped into her accidentally. He reached out to steady her, only to find air where her arm should have been. He blinked. How was it possible for a crippled girl to move so quickly?

Magdalena shielded her expression by bending to kindle a fire in the small stove. *Dios*, is this how it would be? Was she to be constantly on edge, awaiting, fearing his touch? When he brushed against her, it was as though flame singed her arm. She must avoid him when possible. If she shied away every time he neared, he would grow suspicious.

Frowning, Clint peered at the averted back, then he shrugged. His hunger was making him light-headed. She was but a maid, strange or not. And a maid he decidedly needed. "Cook enough for me and Pritikin, and yourself, if you're hungry, then bring a tray to the shop."

Magdalena sagged with relief when he was gone. Her hands trembled as she set the thick steak on to grill. When she went to take down potatoes and onions, the chocolate drew her eyes. Unable to resist, she took down the jar and put some water on to heat. She peeled the potatoes, deciding this distasteful masquerade would have a few consolations. It would be nice to sleep in a real bed for a change. Even a bunk would seem a feather cloud after what she was used to sleeping on.

After she put the potatoes and onions on to grill, she took down a cup to prepare her chocolate. She mashed some crushed cacao beans to a paste, generously added sugar and poured boiling water over both. With a spoon, she stirred the concoction to a froth, then, slowly, she took a small taste and rolled the delicious flavor over her tongue. Sensuously, she savored each sip. She was so entranced with the aroma that she failed to notice another, less pleasant, scent filling the cabin.

The acrid smoke weaved its insidious way down the companionway, reaching Clint's nostrils. He and Pritikin glanced at one another. Clint jumped to his feet. "What the devil . . ." Clint dashed out of the cabin.

He burst into the galley too hastily and bumped his head.

Magdalena glanced up, her face dreamily content, to meet shocked blue eyes. She froze, the cup halfway to her lips. She slammed it down on the small table and leaped to the grill to rescue the smoking food. She was too mortified to remember to limp, but luckily Clint didn't notice.

He was stiff with surprise at the look he'd caught on her face. She'd been sitting in profile to him, her scarred cheek turned away. She had seemed vaguely familiar, but that wasn't what had shocked him. No, the sensuality she'd displayed as she licked her moist lips had given her a powerful attractiveness that had stunned him. He'd felt an impulse to grab her and lick the sticky fluid from her mouth. When she turned to face him, he watched that mouth.

"I'm sorry. I can fry another steak if you wish."

Clint shuddered when she licked her lips, but when he looked up at her scarred face, his pounding heart slowed. What was the matter with him? Was he truly attracted to her? Certainly her shamed, downcast face seemed as homely as ever. Bewildered at his own reactions, he reached out blindly to take the two plates from her.

"No, this will be fine." Without another word, he retreated. It wasn't until he'd reached the shop that he looked down at the charred contents of the plates. He and Pritikin looked at the blackened, wizened steak, the coallike lumps of potatoes and the seared onions.

Pritikin said dryly, "If it's all the same to you, cap'n, I'll wait until dinner to eat." Giving his captain a confused look, Pritikin went to stand in front of the porthole and breathe deeply of the clean air.

His nose wrinkled with disgust, Clint walked to the opposite porthole and tossed the unpalatable mess to the fish. Then, without a word, he went to his cabin to write his daily entry in the log. The familiar task soothed his unease away. He'd merely been without a woman for too long, that was all. His encounter with the strawberry girl had incited needs that now sought any outlet. His stomach growled, reminding him of an even more basic urge. He slapped the logbook closed, thinking irritably that the girl's cooking had better improve or she'd find herself without a job, sympathy or no sympathy.

And in the galley, Magdalena scrubbed the grill in an attempt to get rid of the charred odor, without much success. When she was finished, she made herself another cup of chocolate, but this time she drank it quickly. She'd had a lucky escape. By the time she realized she'd forgotten to limp, it was too late. However, Browning hadn't seemed to notice. The look on his face as she turned to face him had unsettled her.

He'd appeared almost . . . attracted to her. But surely no man would be drawn to the figure she presented. Magdalena was taking the last sip of chocolate before an explanation occurred to her. She sputtered as the brew went down the wrong way. When she recovered from her coughing fit, her eyes were as hard as gold agates. Was he cultivating her favor for some sinister purpose of his own? Perhaps he was so accustomed to using everyone that he never passed up an opportunity to ingratiate himself.

Very well, she was forewarned. Even disguised as she was, she was not safe from his wiles. Her hands clenched with rage as she tried to stifle the pain in her heart. Why did she feel such regret? He owed her nothing, after all. She was the foolish one for weaving such golden dreams around him. No man could be the knight in shining armor she had made of him. But no matter how hard she scolded herself for foolishness, a part of her cried out with pain. Was she destined always to be betrayed by those who should have been closest to her?

Closing her eyes, Magdalena tried to black out the memory that stole into her mind: being held by a tall, golden-haired man who seemed both a rock to lean on and a foundation to build on. But if that image were the mirage it seemed, why did she have to struggle so to remember the cold, hard facts? She was the servant of the man who was a partner to her enemy. No doubt he'd betray her, given the chance. She'd have to be constantly on guard.

Even more worrisome, how was she to bear living with herself? Despite knowing him for what he was, she could no longer escape the knowledge that he still attracted her as no man ever had. Dropping her head on her folded arms, Magdalena screwed her eyes shut to suppress the incipient tears.

# Chapter 4

"There's no risk (s)he fears, nor any
grim impediment that makes (her)
give ground a moment; the only hand
(s)he looks to hangs at (her) right
arm's end . . ."

**Act I, DON JUAN TENORIO**

Silence, of a kind, fell at last. Magdalena rose to change.
Clint and Pritikin had long since retired to their bunks, but
the sea's incessant murmur was nerve-racking to one used to
the quiet of a cave. Timbers creaked as the ship rocked to
the sea's lullabye; waves patted the *Arabella*'s hull. Magdalena almost dropped her boots when a wave slapped the
side of the ship, but she took a deep breath and forced her
fingers to steadiness. This would not do. Her first excursion
was no time to lose her nerve. Joaquin would be waiting.

She drew her loose-fitting skirt and blouse on over her
black breeches and shirt. She wrapped her cloak about her
boots, hood and hat and stuck the bundle under her arm.
She eased her door open and listened, then stole out on
deck. The strange sea noises, splash-suck as tide met shore,
accompanied her pattering heartbeat as she inched down the
gangplank and darted to the shed. She paused to listen

again, then stripped off her outer garments and stuffed them behind the carreta seat. She strapped on her sword.

The individual who swaggered out of the shed a minute later bore no resemblance to the maid who entered it. Boldly, her cloak flapping in the brisk sea breeze, Magdalena strode up the coarse sand and paused to look about. Ah, it was good to be here again, even in such a guise. If only Carlos were here to share it . . .

Swallowing the lump in her throat, Magdalena made a sharp appraisal of the wide, crescent-shaped bay that was formed by two points, the westward low and sandy, the San Buenaventura point rocky and wooded. It was to the latter she turned after assuring herself that she was the sole human occupant of the beach. She had ample company, however.

Sandpipers darted in and out of waves in their eternal search for food. A pelican, his shadow imposing against the moonglow, dozed atop a stump, capacious bill tucked into his breast. Sea lions slept on a rocky outcropping, several waking to waddle away in alarm at her approach. When she reached the San Buenaventura point, she skirted it to the thick brush growing at its far side.

She whistled softly. A gentle whicker answered. Satisfied, Magdalena walked through the brush to be greeted by a surly Joaquin.

"It's past time you got here. I was beginning to worry."

"They stayed up longer than I expected. Were you seen?" Magdalena stroked Fuego's soft muzzle.

"No. Did the American hire you?"

Magdalena sighed beneath her hood. She appreciated his concern, but she didn't hesitate to dash the hopeful note in his voice. "*Si,* as with all his kind, he thinks only of his own selfish needs. No one else will work for him. His belly makes him desperate, so he sees what he wants to see." She said nothing of the odd looks the American had given her or that part of her persisted in believing the best of him.

"And if his belly sharpens his vision after he samples your cooking? What then?"

"I will learn. Tonight he said nothing when I scorched the meat a little."

Joaquin snorted. "A little?"

A sheepish shrug was Magdalena's only answer. *Dios,* if Joaquin knew she'd met the Americano as herself, he'd be livid. Magdalena hastily changed the subject. "Do you go back now, or do you ride with me tonight?"

Joaquin frowned. "Tonight? Surely you should settle in . . ."

"Delay only increases the danger. I intend only to survey the presidio for this evening."

"But you've seen it many times before. Surely it can wait."

"I've never looked at it before as a bastion I must scale. My life depends on my caution. No matter what you may think, I do not risk it heedlessly."

Joaquin flushed at the gentle reproach. He took his mask from his cloak pocket and tied it behind his head. "Lead on, Black Jack."

The flash of white teeth was visible in Magdalena's mouth slit. She adopted Jack's hoarse tones. "Ah, *companero de armas,* such spirit will lead us to victory yet." She turned to mount the saddled Fuego.

Or disaster all the faster, Joaquin thought. But he didn't say it.

They rode the half mile into Santa Barbara at a quiet walk. The dirt paths were deserted. The white-washed adobe houses were dark and silent. Some had red tile roofs, others were capped by black bitumen. The largest town-houses of wealthy landowners had painted balconies and verandas and real glass windows instead of the grates on the smaller houses. Magdalena averted her head when they passed her own townhouse with its deep red veranda and balcony.

How many times had she sat on its patio with her parents and brother, listening to the cool tinkle of the fountain? But those days would never be again. Even if she succeeded in clearing her name and redeeming her lands, nothing would ever be the same. For a moment, she slumped in her saddle under the weight of a sorrow so great she thought her back would break. But then the presidio came in sight, and the anger that now dwelt always in her heart stiffened her spine. Yes, those happy times were gone forever. But she had a proud legacy to live up to. Somewhere, perhaps, her loved ones watched her struggle. She would make them proud. She would make herself proud again. Or die. For it was certain she had nothing else to live for.

Coolly, Magdalena reined Fuego in to survey the first of the many obstacles she must surmount to attain victory. She knew its history as well as she knew her own. The presidio was not the impregnable fortress envisioned when it was established in 1782. It had been damaged by two earthquakes, one in 1806 and another in 1812. Many buildings were repaired, but there was too little money and even less interest by first Spanish, then Mexican, authorities for the fortress to be the intended vigorous social and military artery for the scattered populace from north of Santa Barbara south to Los Angeles.

The outer defense walls, thick adobe almost ten feet tall, guarded the inner quadrangle. Cannon bastions abutted two corners: one, the southeast side facing the sea; the other, the northwest side facing any landward threat. The entrance, in the middle of the southern wall facing the ocean, was the one well-guarded spot. Inside, Magdalena knew, the fortress buildings formed another line of defense from which soldiers could shoot at enemies. Barracks and family quarters formed most sides of the quadrangle. The chapel and the comandante's quarters faced the entrance.

Magdalena and Joaquin hitched their stallions to a crumbling gate a street away, then walked back to the presidio. They circled it, looking for a break in the walls. There were deep cracks in a number of places and the wall was crumbling, but it was still formidable. The second defense wall behind the chapel had gaps enough for them to slip through, but inside, the first defense wall was unbroken. If they scaled it, they'd still have to go through or over the soldiers' quarters to get inside the central grounds. Their footsteps on the red tile roofs would scrape enough to wake anyone sleeping inside. They knew for certain of only two buildings that were unoccupied. The chapel, which was seldom used by the soldiers, and the warehouses, which were preceded by a corral. Magdalena craned her neck to look at the chapel roof two stories above. It would not be easy to scale, but it offered the best hope of stealthiness.

By tacit agreement, Magdalena and Joaquin left as quietly as they'd come. Only when they'd reached the beach again did they speak.

"It will not be easy getting in, Magdalena. Even if you do, how can you hope to search Luis's quarters without waking him?"

"I've but to wait until he goes to see Roberto. He leaves Leon in charge. And we both know his stupidity is exceeded only by his laziness."

"And how will you know when that is? With your new duties, you can hardly spend all your time spying on the presidio."

"I cannot. But Sean can. He settled here to trap. Let him trap. And bring furs in to trade."

Joaquin's voice lost its edge as he conceded, "This, at least, I can approve of. That way you will not have to enter the presidio alone."

"*Si*," Magdalena agreed humbly.

Joaquin ripped off his mask to fix her with a glare. "I mean it, Magdalena. You are not to attempt the presidio alone."

"*Si*." Magdalena changed the subject before Joaquin could realize her assent could be taken either way—yes, I will not; or yes, I will.

"Does Sean have traps?"

"No, he had not yet purchased them when he found you in the mountains."

"I know where I can get some. Let me put Fuego away and I will fetch them. Follow me."

She dismounted and led Fuego around the point and through the brush at the side. One moment there was movement through the brush, then nothing but stillness. Astounded, he watched as Magdalena emerged a few moments later, without the horse.

"But where . . . how . . ."

Magdalena interrupted his sputtering. "It's a grotto Carlos and I discovered when we were children. A cleft in the point, shielded by brush, leads to a cavern. There's plenty of room for Fuego."

"How do you know no one else knows of it?"

"It's impossible to see even close up because it's covered by grass and weeds. I only know of it because I fell inside when Carlos and I were playing *escondite*."

"This hide and seek is no game, Magdalena. If you're discovered this time, it will mean your life. Are you sure it's safe? If Fuego is found, it won't take long for Luis or Roberto to recognize him."

They'll know I'm here soon enough, Magdalena thought grimly. She snapped, "*Madre de Dios*, If you know of somewhere better, spit it out."

When he gnawed at his lip, she relaxed. She took off her hood to cup his cheek in her palm. "Ah, Joaquin, everything I do has its dangers. But most dangerous of all is inaction. Please don't fight me every step of the way. We need to save our energies for other things."

Joaquin squeezed her ribs in a fierce hug, then he set her from him. "As usual, you are right, *gatita montes*. What do you want me to do?"

A soft kiss on the cheek rewarded him before Magdalena said briskly, "If you'll gather some grass for Fuego, I'll fetch water and the traps."

She melted into the night. It was a good thirty minutes before she returned in her Indian guise, lugging a bucket in one hand and two small traps under her other arm. Panting, she set her burdens down and wiped her brow. When she'd regained her breath, she picked them up and led Joaquin through the brush. He carried an armful of lush spring grass.

He followed cautiously through weeds and shrubs as tall as his head. Blinded by them and the darkness, he was disoriented when he felt a tug on his arm. He fell forward, dropping the grass to keep himself from cracking his head on the rocky wall. Instead, he felt the scrape of vines against his palms, then dank air and velvety darkness.

Magdalena drew a candle from her pocket and lit it. Fuego had already found the pile of grass and was munching contentedly.

At least he was used to such quarters, Joaquin thought. He looked doubtfully around. From the salty rush of air, he deduced that the cave was not solid all around. He felt the walls and found several cracks barely covered by brush. This was more a hollowed-out earthen crevice than a cave. In an earthquake it would not be stable.

When he said as much to Magdalena, she shrugged. "Fuego would be no safer in a shed. And the cracks allow light in during the day. He'll be content enough."

She led the horse to the bucket of water. After he'd drunk his fill, she unsaddled him and brushed him down with the currycomb Joaquin had brought. When he was settled for the night, she gave him a fond pat on his powerful hindquarters, blew out the candle and led the way out.

When they reached the palm where Joaquin had tied up his Rojo, they stopped. Joaquin mounted and slung the traps on the saddle before him. He knew better than to ask where she'd gotten them. He was afraid to have his suspicions confirmed.

He covered her hand when she gave his stallion a pat. "Be careful, Magdalena. What, by the way, am I to do while you and Sean risk life and limb?"

"Amigo, I would be lost without your wisdom and guidance. I'll have need of you soon enough. Be patient."

Joaquin grunted. "Patient as you will be, no doubt. I'll send Sean as soon as he has skins enough to trade. Friday you are to come give us a report, no matter what."

When Magdalena nodded and stepped back, he dug his heels into his stallion. Magdalena watched until he was out of sight, then she turned back to the *Arabella*.

Clint was sleeping restlessly when the stealthy footsteps, passing for a third time, finally woke him. His eyes snapped open to stare about his shadowed cabin. His fuzzy head cleared when a door opened. He leapt out of bed, not even pausing to cover his nakedness, and peered into the companionway in time to see his new maid's door closing. He fetched his pocketwatch and carried it to the porthole to read the time by moonlight. Two in the morning! What the devil was she up to?

Frowning, he stared at the closed door. The uneasy feeling that she was more than she seemed returned, but he dismissed it. Perhaps she merely walked the beach because she couldn't sleep. When all was silent, he went back to his narrow bunk. His dreams were even more restless this time. Somehow his new maid became a siren, beckoning him with golden eyes and strawberry-flavored lips. When he awoke the next morning, he couldn't remember the dreams, but the ache in his groin testified to their eroticism.

He was in the shop before Pritikin, arranging the already neat shelves and tables of shoes and clothing, jewelry, scarves and shawls. The dry goods were kept on one side of the shop, including such items as cutlery, hardware, and crockery, while the foodstuffs sat in neat rows opposite. Teas from China, coffee from South America, molasses, sugar and spices from the Indies and dried fruits from the eastern seaboard added their tempting scents to the casks of spirits.

He paused in the hardware section. He counted the traps twice to be sure. When Pritikin entered, yawning, he turned to ask, "Did you sell two traps yesterday?"

"No, sir."

"That's odd. Two are . . ." Clint broke off. His nose twitched. The door opened and in limped their new maid.

She set the tray down with a bang on the table they kept clear to transact business. After one look, Pritikin turned away and busied himself.

Clint was not so fortunate. He looked from the congealing mess of porridge, barely cooked, to the charred slices of bread, to the mangled slices of pear. They, at least, seemed edible, if poorly peeled. His stomach growled hungrily, reminding him he'd not eaten last night. That, combined with lack of sleep, made him irritable. Why the hell hadn't the girl told him she couldn't cook before he hired her? He bent a stern look upon her, but the way she twisted her hands and kept her face averted, as if fearing verbal, if not physical, abuse aborted his scold stillborn.

Wearily, he sank into a chair at the table and poked a bite of pear into his mouth. After chewing and swallowing, he took an experimental sip of coffee. He sighed and took a deeper swallow. This, at least, she could do. He waved a hand toward the door. "Thank you, er . . . I'm sorry, I forgot to ask your name."

"Carlotta," issued the rich, husky voice that clashed so with her appearance.

"Thank you, Carlotta. For lunch, just make something simple. Slices of cheese and bread, perhaps. Until then, I'd appreciate it if you'd clean my cabin."

Nodding, she turned and limped away. She'd not deliberately spoiled the meal and had in fact feared he'd reprimand her. Was she judging him too harshly? His kindness, his patience, did not suit the monster she'd made him in her mind. She'd never liked or trusted Julio. What if he'd been boasting of his patron's influence? Magdalena's heart beat faster with both hope and fear. Hope that the *yanqui* was, after all, the man she'd been so attracted to in the strawberry patch; fear that, if he were, he was an even bigger threat. As a scoundrel, he menaced only her safety and pride. As the man of honor she'd dreamed of, he threatened her peace of mind and . . . yes, even her heart. Whatever his character, he was a threat she'd do well to guard against. She repeated the words to herself over and over, but her heart still beat a little faster as, for the first time, she entered his cabin.

It, too, was a surprise. If he'd been the selfish man she believed him to be, his cabin would be spacious and luxurious, leaving only crannies for his men. Yet it was barely larger than her own. It held the same type of sea chest, a smaller chest near the headboard, a spartan table, two chairs bolted to the floor and a small case in the corner for nautical instruments. The only concession to comfort was the size of the bunk. Though narrow, it was long and comfortably padded. Magdalena nibbled at her lip, uncertain any longer of what to believe.

93

Some instinct she refused to acknowledge drew her to the bunk. She sat down gingerly, then bounced. Her mind wandered . . . She leaped to her feet, prodded by her wayward thoughts. She tried to quell them by reminding herself that she couldn't afford to be weakened by a handsome face and body. Yet her eyes strayed back to the bunk. What wide shoulders the American had . . .

Magdalena grabbed a rag from the top of the chest and began dusting with a vengeance. She rubbed hard enough to take the finish off until she reached the bunk. Once more her eyes and thoughts wandered. Furious at herself, she threw the rag across the room. It slapped against the bulkhead above the table and chairs. Something fell with a clatter. Magdalena walked over to investigate. Her eyes widened. She looked from the floor, to the bulkhead above the table, back to the floor. She reached out to pick up the fallen object, handling it reverently. The distraction was so welcome, the object so enticing, that she forgot where she was. Forgot, too, the open door—and that her life depended on caution.

In the store, Clint swallowed the last bite of porridge he could stomach. When he shoved the bowl away, it slid off the table into his lap. Grunting in disgust, he rose, swiped as much of the gooey mess away as he could manage, then stomped out to change. It never occurred to him to knock as he entered his own cabin. He went still at the sight that met his eyes. His mouth gaped.

His new maid was holding one of his prized rapiers. As he watched, she bent the blade to test its resiliency; then she stepped back and took fluid slices out of the air, slashing one way, then the other. She turned to give herself more room and caught sight of him. She gasped and froze, her arm in midair.

Clint peered at her in the shadowy cabin, trying to read the expressions chasing across her face. Shock, fear, chagrin, then pride and . . . nothing. Her arm dropped. She swiped the blade with her rag, dusted off the other one still hanging above the table, then crossed its mate back were it belonged.

94

"They are fine blades," she said colorlessly. Had he seen enough to know that she didn't limp? He stared at her oddly, as well he might. Her resentment roused again as she realized that she'd been so confused at the feelings he stirred that she'd been reckless. Never, in her right mind, would she have dared to test the sword. In his own cabin, with the door open! Think, she scolded herself. How could a poor india maid be so familiar with such a weapon? When she found no reasonable explanation, she fell back on the truth.

"My brother taught me how to fence. Before . . ." she indicated her twisted leg.

Clint blinked back to awareness as she limped across to the bunk to begin making it. Despite the limp, she moved with an ease that was arresting and somehow familiar. The feeling that he'd seen her before gnawed at him. When she bent to pull the covers tight at the end, her bottom thrust against her loose skirt, displaying its shapeliness. He clenched his hands on the need to trace those curves, reminding himself that this girl was only his servant. He was foolish to get so worked up over her.

"I had a Spanish tutor when I was a boy. He's since moved back to Toledo. He sent me the blades. They are one of my most prized possessions," Clint explained. Her back straightened with a suppleness once more at odds with her appearance, once more familiar. Dammit, had he seen her before, or did she remind him of someone?

He watched her glance across the room to the crossed swords. She eyed the gold inlay on the hilt and handguard, the tensile, polished blade with an expression that could only be termed covetous. Then her face went carefully blank. She turned back to the bed.

Clint walked to his sea chest and rooted around, his thoughts on the woman across from him. Her face was expressive, when she wasn't cultivating that blank, cowed look. As if she played a role. A role that irked her and was far removed from the woman she really was. His mind went back to the astonishing sight she'd made while testing his sword. No slumped spine then or shuffling movements.

Only a flashing grace and . . . His word search yielded only one that was appropriate: power. A strength of will, purpose and body that would not be defeated. So, if she played a role—why? If she had some secret purpose of her own—what? And, if he was part of that plan—how?

He took out clean clothes, stood and faced her. "Why did you come to work for me, Carlotta, when no one else would?"

She paused in straightening the thin spread, then continued the task hurriedly. "I needed the work," she said in a strained tone.

His nose twitched as he scented a lie. Grimly, he planted his feet. "You needed it so badly that you'd work for the despised *yanqui?*" he needled in his flawless Spanish. She thumped the pillow. His lips quirked as he got the distinct impression she wished it were his head.

"The hungry don't have the luxury of choice." She finished the bed with a final vicious tug. She straightened and advanced to the door.

"Is that why you're so slim?" Casually, he closed the open portal and propped his shoulders against it. "Yet some men don't enjoy fleshy women." She froze as he eyed her from neck to heels. "Your lean and hungry look is uncommonly attractive. Yet are you dangerous, too, I wonder?"

"Do you accuse me of conspiracy?" she countered, unnerved by his masculine, assessing look. When his eyes kindled at her response, she groaned inwardly. She'd walked neatly into his verbal trap. What would an uneducated Indian know of Shakespeare? Why did she always react so strongly to him?

"I'm no Caesar, my dear, to be betrayed by those I should trust. Servants should be loyal, don't you agree?"

That damnable dimple winked at her again, but his smile was a bold challenge she had to rise to. Foolish or not, she was determined to best him in this verbal battle of wills. "I agree, señor, that you are no Caesar." When he looked inquiring, she mimicked his own gesture by looking him up and down. "A colossus you're not." Her risk was rewarded by his angry flush.

"How do you know? Would you like to measure me?" He levered himself away from the door and sauntered toward her.

Before she could stop herself, she backed a step. His cocky grin returned. A bare two paces away, he paused, appraising her closed expression. He tipped her chin up. She stood still, but when he reached up to caress her scarred cheek, she jerked away, into the pool of light pouring through the porthole.

Clint blinked, then looked again. No, he wasn't imagining it. The sun, which had hidden behind lowering clouds all morning, now filled the cabin with light. It struck the huge eyes staring at him with such a strange expression, giving him his first clear glimpse of their color. Gold. How odd, to meet two women in the space of a week with gold eyes when he'd never met anyone with them before. His eyes went to her hair, to the slim body lost in the baggy garments, to the scar on her face. No, it couldn't be . . . He'd only seen her that one time, but she'd been no Indian, that was certain. She'd had the cultured speech of the aristocracy. Yet why was she alone if she came from a wealthy family? That temptress, too, had been a woman of contradictions . . .

Impossible as it seemed, he had to test the theory. He tossed the clean clothes on the bed and casually unbuttoned his shirt. Holding those huge eyes, he shrugged out of the garment and stood bare-chested before her in that patch of light. "Tell me, Carlotta, do you like strawberries?"

Her gaze lifted from his chest to meet his. She blinked, looking a bit dazed, but then she straightened and said colorlessly, "Indeed, señor. Doesn't everyone?" She didn't look away this time, even when he licked the corner of his mouth. "If that will be all, I must start lunch." Her limp seemed worse than usual as she started for the door. When he moved to block it again, she stopped and stood waiting, head bowed, hands clasped, for him to move.

"I'll not beat you if lunch is a bit late," he snapped. When she seemed to shrink even more within herself, he stood aside. "Go. But this conversation isn't finished."

She scurried out as fast as her limp allowed. Magdalena trembled as she almost ran to the relative safety of the galley. Ah, had there ever been a more handsome man? Without his shirt, Clint seemed more mythological god than mortal, for surely no mere male could be so perfect. Powerful arms and immense shoulders tapering to slim waist and taut belly, a light golden dusting of hair at all points in between . . . In short, *hombre*, as if he, and he alone, defined the word. She felt as if her conflicting emotions would tear her in half. He'd proven his cunning yet again by setting that verbal trap. Yet could she blame him for acting upon his suspicions? Wasn't she doing the same? Until she had proof one way or another, she must not step out of her role again. Grimly, she set about preparing lunch.

In his cabin, as he changed his clothes, Clint contemplated what had passed between them. Could it be? Both women were changeable, graceful, and had gold-colored eyes, but the other girl had been attracted to him, even admiring. This girl had seemed more alarmed than pleased by his flirting. He turned to look at the bunk. It was wadded at the foot, elevating the mattress. The covers were crooked, and a ridge ran down the middle of the bed. Hell, she couldn't even make a bed right. Yes, indeed, there was something most odd about his maid. Because of her familiarity with Shakespeare and the rapier, she bore watching. Perhaps she was an illegitimate sister to the other and would lead him to her. His heart beat faster at the thought of seeing the strawberry girl again. Somehow, these two women were linked. If he observed her, perhaps he could figure out how.

In the days that followed, the food improved—slightly. Sometimes their meat was overdone, sometimes too rare, but at least it was edible. Her cleaning also improved. It was as if she'd never performed such duties before and now learned them. Clint's feeling that she was no more a maid than he grew to certainty. But he came no closer to figuring out who she really was or what she really wanted. She was evasive when he questioned her.

To his query of where she was from, she answered, "North." To his question of her age, she answered, "Growing older every day." And to his inquiry of why she'd left her last post, she answered, "It was time."

When he gritted his teeth over a sharp retort, he got the strangest feeling she rejoiced at his frustration. Yet her face betrayed nothing. No matter how outrageous he was, she no longer responded to his sallies. Indeed, she might have been the maid she wanted him to take her for. Two, he decided, could play bait and switch. It would be interesting to see how cool she remained then. Besides, he wanted to see if progress had been made in finding that cursed bandit.

She'd been here several days, but had not ventured into town. He had seen her disappear up the beach between her duties, but she avoided Santa Barbara. Discovering why could give him a clue as to her purpose.

The next morning, he put his plan into effect. After he and Pritikin had finished their breakfast of fried eggs and sliced bread, he took the tray to the galley. He found Carlotta standing before the counter sipping her usual morning chocolate, her eyes closed as she swirled the liquid on her tongue. Despite the scar, the twisted mouth, her utter sensual enjoyment made his skin prickle with sexual awareness.

Disconcerted, he banged his tray down on the counter before her. "Here, I brought it to save you a trip."

Her eyes snapped open. For a moment, their gazes locked. The masculine appraisal he made no attempt to disguise seemed to alarm her, for she took a hasty step back. Whirling, she set her cup down and picked up the dishes to dump them in the bucket of soapy water. "*Gracias,*" she muttered, scrubbing vigorously.

When he didn't leave, Magdalena peeked over her shoulder at him. Arms crossed over that imposing chest, one booted ankle propped over the other, he casually suggested, "I've a desire to see more of the town and wondered if you'd accompany me. You obviously know more of Santa Barbara than I."

She turned back around, biting her lip in consternation.

The gaze that bored into her back was far from casual. She could feel it, palpable as an accusing, prodding finger. He definitely had suspicions about her. She'd known it for days, but had hoped he'd wait longer to act upon them. She must have more time. If Sean didn't arrive soon, she'd have to take action herself.

"It is tiring for me to walk so far . . ." she demurred.

But he interrupted, "We don't have to walk. We can take your carriage, if you've no objection. I'll even drive."

Yes, and what if Jose's carriage horse were recognized or, worse still, she was? Again, she tried to decline. "I had intended to clean the store today. Perhaps another time . . ."

"Today. Now." The tone was gentle—dangerously so.

Magdalena stiffened and turned. No man talked to her like that. She dried her hands on a rag and said softly, "You pay my wages, *yanqui*, for an honest day's work. But I am no slave, cowed to act on your slightest whims. You did not hire me as a guide, so if I choose not to be one, I will not." Disdainfully, she turned her shoulder to him and picked up the bucket to carry it to the porthole.

He moved so fast she blinked. He, too, had dropped all pretense as he blocked her path. There was naught desultory in body, face or manner when he purred, "Ah, but this will be part of your duties. I want you to accompany me to purchase fresh vegetables. Surely with your skills, you'll make better selections." The movement of his lips was a smooth, taunting mockery of a smile.

Magdalena's grip tightened on the bucket handle. She was tempted to throw the water at that goading face but, as her eyes met his watchful ones, she knew he hoped for such an extreme reaction. He was indeed testing her.

Taking a slow, careful breath, Magdalena set the bucket down and bowed her head. "As you wish." But the glinting gold look she sent up at him promised retribution.

Clint was satisfied. So, whatever her purpose, it was important enough to her to bend that damnable pride. Interesting. Clint stepped out of the galley and swept a hand before him. "After you, Carlotta."

It wasn't easy to stalk with a limp, but somehow Carlotta

managed it. Clint's lips quirked as he followed her down the gangplank after telling Pritikin where they would be. Maid, pshaw! Indian princess, perhaps? But whoever she was, he'd discover the truth about her, he vowed. *And* the woman she resembled.

Carlotta stood haughtily waiting as he hitched the carriage horse to the carreta. He would have helped her climb in, but she hiked her skirts and did the job herself, giving him a glimpse of shapely ankles.

He said nothing until they'd cleared the beach. On a slight rise he paused, looking at the city before him. Santa Barbara was a pretty town, consisting of haphazardly clustered buildings of brown and plastered adobe situated on a low, grassy plain. Mountains surrounded the town on three sides, he judged about fifteen miles distant. While the hills were lush with grass, he saw no large trees.

When he questioned Carlotta about that, she reluctantly broke her brooding silence. "There was a fire some years ago. It burned the trees in the surrounding hills and they have not yet grown back."

"I see. And can you tell me a little of the history of the mission?" He indicated the dazzling white buildings some two miles inland. They watched over Santa Barbara from their hill like benevolent despots. Two towers and an ornate pediment above the portico were each topped with a cross. He couldn't see the mission clearly, but it seemed to be of Roman and Moorish design.

"Spain would not allow the mission to be started until after the presidio was founded. That was done in 1782. The mission site was selected and blessed four years later. It was first made of adobe, but earthquakes damaged it. The padres built with stone then, and it has stood as it is since 1820."

The drab recital said nothing of what he knew must be a colorful history. He was as goaded as she obviously hoped, but he merely clucked to the horse. "Perhaps your memory will improve as we enter Santa Barbara."

Magdalena drew her rebozo over her head as they passed the first building. People thronged the paths, for anything so linear and orderly as a street Santa Barbara could not claim to. The builders of the various houses had situated them where they willed, so that one faced this way, another that, giving Santa Barbara a charming but disorderly look.

Women in skirts and chemises hurried to and fro, baskets over their arms as they bargained for dinner supplies. Two caballeros lounged in a doorway, their long hair queued, their tall figures clad in knee breeches, white stockings and deerskin shoes. Red sashes cinched their narrow waists. Magdalena looked quickly away from their curious stares. Children darted from house to house playing tag, their dark skin and eyes shining with health.

They passed several Indian women laboring in wash tubs while their mistresses sipped morning chocolate on their front verandas. A little Indian man, his broad face showing his Chumash heritage, curried his master's spirited stallion, his hands wizened with toil and age.

Magdalena looked away. The secularization her father had fought for should have bettered the Indians' lot, yet they seemed worse off, if anything. Many had died from disease and the harshness of their toil, yet the administrators Mexico had sent after dissolving the mission system were far worse than the padres had been. They were both greedy and cruel, being more interested in acquiring wealth than assisting the Indians. At least the padres, stern though they were, sincerely hoped to civilize and cultivate the neophytes. Mexico seemed interested only in bilking the vast wealth formerly guarded by the padres. Even now Mexico granted mission lands to those who met the requirements and swore allegiance to the government.

Her brooding thoughts were interrupted when Clint drew the carriage to a halt before a modest adobe with a small vegetable stand set up in front. Clint jumped down and offered Magdalena a hand. She drew the rebozo over her lower face and pretended not to see, easing one leg down to the ground, then the other, as if unsure of her footing. She limped up to the stand and began appraising vegetables, wondering what the devil she was supposed to look for. They all looked alike to her.

102

Clint shadowed her every step, watching her so acutely that she grew nervous. She dropped the ear of corn she'd been fingering and snapped, "If you want my help, then don't hover over me so. I promise not to poison you."

"Not deliberately, perhaps," he teased.

She whirled on him, but paused when she caught sight of the approaching women. She turned hastily away, drawing the rebozo over her face again.

Curious at her reaction, Clint turned. He smiled broadly when a voluptuous señorita, trailed by her duenna, peeped at him before quickly looking away. She was a tasty morsel, from her shining black hair, covered with a white lace mantilla, to her dainty, velvet-shod feet. Her European dress was blue dimity, a fitting accompaniment to her deep blue eyes.

She seemed as curious about him, but every time she looked at him, her duenna tugged on her arm. One tug was so energetic that her silk rebozo fell off her shoulders and fluttered to the ground. Clint bent, picked it up and offered it to her with a smile.

Blushing prettily, she accepted it with a soft, "Gracias," and wrapped it about her shoulders again. When her duenna tried to urge her past them, she jerked her arm away, cocked her head on one side and asked, "Are you the American captain?" The duenna looked disapproving, but she was distracted when Sarita approached and greeted her. Magdalena shrank into the shadows of the stand, turning her back.

"Indeed I am. Captain Clinton Browning at your service." Clint bowed deeply.

"And do you have clothes from Europe on your ship?"

"Yes, I do. But none that would do justice to your loveliness."

Though she seemed uninterested, Magdalena had listened to every word. She prayed Angelina would be too fascinated by the American to look at their carriage horse. Judging from the soft laughter behind her, Angelina probably wouldn't recognize her if she ripped off her disguise and yelled, "Boo!" How adept the American was at charming everyone he met.

Magdalena slammed down the squash she'd been fingering, so angry that even her fear of Sarita seeing her was muted. The man was nothing but an opportunistic scoundrel, flirting with every pretty woman he saw. Angelina was too susceptible to his handsome face. Magdalena made her selections, hardly heeding what she picked. So far Sarita hadn't seen her, but she must hurry away. However, as she filled the sack, she overheard Sarita's low-voiced conversation with Angelina's duenna, Isabelle. Magdalena paused as she listened.

"The *yanqui* stayed overnight, transacting business with the master. He was most curious about señorita Magdalena."

"Was he trading for hides and tallow?"

"I think it was something else. As I served them dinner, I heard Luis whisper to el patron that it was time to ask for the American's aid." Sarita selected some choice squash and put them in the basket she carried.

"Forgive my candor, Sarita, but I've never liked Roberto de Sarria. I can't help wondering what he and the American are involved in," Isabelle said.

From the corner of her eye, Magdalena saw Sarita shrug. "He is el patron, for good or bad. As for the American, who can say? I just thought you'd be curious about him." Sarita paid for her purchases and hurried away, glancing once at the tall, slim woman turned away from her.

Isabelle stalked back to Angelina and took her arm, whispering in her ear.

Feeling too sluggish to care that Sarita had gone without recognizing her, Magdalena selected more produce, she knew not what, then hurried to Clint. She looked at him, at how his hair, his eyes, even his skin, gleamed with health in the sunlight. Odd that his appearance gave no hint of the rot within. Sarita never lied and hadn't even known she was overheard. It was true. Browning was helping Roberto in some way. She longed to scream at him, but she could only watch as he complimented Angelina on Santa Barbara's charms. She couldn't run from him as she longed to, for now, since he *was* Roberto's ally, it was more important than ever that she stay. She could learn much. She could teach him much, as well, she promised herself.

"I am finished," she said in a low monotone, her face turned away from Angelina and Isabelle.

Clint fished in his pocket for some silver, paid the proprietress and turned to watch as the duenna dragged her charge away. He sent a regretful smile after them, well aware that Carlotta was watching.

Angelina called, "I will visit your store soon, captain."

"I'll look forward to it, señorita," Clint responded. Whistling, he climbed back into the carriage to sit beside his sullen maid.

"Now there is the prettiest sight I've seen since coming here," he said happily, glancing sideways at the stiff face next to him.

Silence. So, his maid resented his attentions to another. But why? He'd seen her start of recognition when the girl walked up. It must be she his maid hoped to protect. What reason had he given her to think him so undesirable? And why would an Indian maid even know such a woman, who was obviously of the *aristocracia*?

Questions, always questions, never answers. This little escapade had proved nothing except that his maid was familiar with Santa Barbara and its inhabitants. And that she resented him, for some unfathomable reason. Clint glanced at her again in time to see her eyes widen as she watched an approaching horseman. He turned his head in the same direction, catching sight of Luis, the comandante of the presidio. Good, this encounter would save him a visit to the fortress. Clint waved and called, "Capitan! A word, please."

Luis halted. "*Si?*"

"Have you made progress in locating Black Jack?" Clint asked.

"Not yet," Luis said curtly. He glanced at the silent figure beside Clint, but Magdalena had pulled her rebozo over her face and turned away, so he could see nothing.

"But we will. Even now I have men searching for him. He's been reported thieving in several locations along the highway. He'll not escape me long."

Clint felt and wondered at the start beside him. He was also aware that Carlotta was keeping her face covered, but now was not the time to question her. "If I can be of aid in any way, please let me know. I have a score to settle with Black Jack, too." Clint rubbed his head.

"We'll manage, in our bumbling way." The edge left Luis's voice as he added, "However, let us finish the discussion that we began when you visited El Paraiso. The potential reward is great. Are you interested?" When Clint nodded his head equably, for he was curious to see what Luis was talking about, Luis smiled. "Good. I meet Roberto every few days. Come to see us and we'll talk." Luis tipped his hat, slanting a curious look at Magdalena's covered face, then he proceeded on toward the highway.

Clint clucked to the horse. "Cold, my dear?" he asked solicitously.

Letting her rebozo fall back, Carlotta moved as far away from him on the seat as she could. "No. But the best way to avoid disease is lack of contact." She bit her lip on the words and turned her head away. She jumped down as soon as they reached the wharf.

Now what was he to make of that? Clint wondered irritably as he watched her limp away. Was it him she wished to avoid, or Luis? It was certain she'd feared recognition when Luis approached. Had she perhaps served him and been dismissed? Somehow he thought not. Her reaction had been too strong. Pure hatred had throbbed in her voice when she'd talked of "disease." Why would she hate Luis?

After stabling the horse and carriage, Clint carried the heavy sack to the galley. Carlotta glanced up from scrubbing the grill, and he saw from her closed face that she was composed again. She'd contained the emotion that had led to her outburst, denying him yet again the chance to rile the truth from her. Damn. But there were other ways . . .

He plopped the sack at her feet. "Put it away," he ordered harshly.

He was rewarded by a hostile look, but she took a deep breath and bent to open the sack. He sprawled in the chair before the tiny table and watched her put the produce away. Idly, he began rapping his knuckles against the table. Rap, tap, rap tap.

Magdalena glanced at him in irritation, but his intent blue gaze made her turn back around. Always, he watched her. She knew he'd forced her into Santa Barbara to get a reaction from her. Even now, he tried to upset her. Well, he'd succeeded. She wanted nothing so much as to go to her cabin and indulge in a good cry, and then to flee. She could do neither. She'd wanted proof of his perfidy, hadn't she? Well, she had it, twice over. If he wasn't yet aiding Luis and Roberto in their schemes, he soon would be. He'd admitted his interest. She should be glad to be proved right. But her disappointment made her feel as if she'd been flailed raw, her sins and dreams ruthlessly revealed to all. She was torn between rage and sorrow but could reveal neither.

Gritting her teeth, she tried to pretend she was alone. She'd almost prevailed when she reached into the bag for the last item. She drew out the woven grass basket. She dropped it as if burned. Strawberries rolled over the counter, several plopping to the floor. Two tumbled between Clint's spread feet and spun to a stop.

Carefully keeping her back to him, she picked up the berries on the counter and placed them back in the basket, hoping he couldn't see how her hands trembled at the memories they evoked. How briefly, forbiddenly sweet that time had been. Sweeter than the berries. Until the man who'd made it so had poisoned it . . . That poison burned now in her stomach, making her want to vomit. For a moment, she actually felt faint.

Clint blinked at her sudden clumsiness, his eyes widening when he saw what she dropped. His gaze never leaving that stiff back, he stooped and picked up both plump, ripe berries.

"You missed a couple," he said softly.

He saw her shoulders lift in a deep sigh, then she turned to look. His eyes narrowed on her face, but he could read nothing. When she didn't see the berries, she knelt to look under the table. Clint put one hand on her shoulder and leaned forward. Slowly, reluctantly, she raised her eyes. He plopped one berry into his mouth and chewed and offered the other to her. Their faces were almost on a level as their gazes locked. Something flickered in the fascinating depths of those golden eyes, like a goldfish leaping out of a sun-dappled pond. But then they went still. Dark. Secretive.

She tried to lean away, and his smoldering anger flickered to life again at her illusiveness. Why was she always so secretive if she wasn't plotting something? What did she have against him? He threw the other strawberry to the table and stood, hauling her to her feet. "Damn you, no more lies! I want to know why you came to me. When and where you knew Luis." His voice softened, but was no less grim with purpose when he concluded, "And what you know of another tall, slim girl with gold eyes who loves strawberries."

That odd look flashed at him again. Hurt? Bewilderment? Rage? Something told him it was a combination of all three, but again he glimpsed her iron will as she contained her emotions and looked down.

She shook her head and said coolly, "I don't know what you're talking about."

"Liar!" He shook her, once. "I'll get the truth from you if I have to . . ."

"Yes, señor? Will you beat me to prove what an hombre you are, like the rest of your countrymen?" Her voice was even, but he heard the anger throbbing beneath the softness.

Had some American actually beaten her? Sighing, he tamped down his own ire. His hands gentled on her shoulders. Strangely, whereas she'd been pliant when he shook her, she stiffened under the caress. As if she found his anger easier to deal with than his tenderness. He searched her downcast face. Her lip didn't seem quite so twisted today. He tried to raise her chin to look at her more

closely, but she wrenched away with that surprising lithe-
ness. Her contemptuous look distracted him from her scar.
Once again his hackles rose.

"Dismiss me if you please," she said, "but I'll tell you
nothing." She looked him over, as if he were a worm she'd
found in her shiny apple.

"No, I'm not finished with you yet." The soft words
were both threat and promise.

She shrugged and turned back to the grill, but he stopped
her with a gentle hand on her shoulder. Reluctantly she
turned to find him holding out a strawberry, the stem
gouged out.

"Take this from me, and I may believe you know
nothing." When she held out her hand, he closed his own
over the berry, then opened his fingers under her nose. "Eat
it from my hand," he ordered softly.

He met her outraged glare with a bold smile. "Come, if
you are not the girl I speak of, and know nothing of her,
what have you to fear?"

Magdalena's neck prickled with danger. Reluctantly, she
opened her mouth. She had no choice, but the knowledge
made his challenge no easier to accept. She bent her head
and nipped the strawberry from his hand without touching
him. She straightened, lifting a hand to push the large berry
into her mouth. To her shock, he shoved her hand away,
bent his head and closed his teeth over the portion of the
berry sticking from her mouth. She leaped backward too
late to avoid the brush of his mouth and skin. She gulped the
berry down and met his searching eyes, not moving a
muscle even when he chewed slowly, then licked the berry
stain from each side of his mouth.

"It was very good. Would you like another?" She picked
up a choice berry and held it out. Her control was rewarded
when, after a final searching look into her veiled eyes, he
sighed and shook his head.

Disappointed, Clint left the galley. It had been a crazy
fancy anyway. Despite the eye color and height, there was
little else similar about the two women. That girl in the hills
had been a vibrant, emotional creature. She'd enjoyed their

109

embrace as much as he. She could never accept a berry from him so coolly, for it must surely arouse the same memories. His eyes closed as he allowed himself the luxury of remembering that embrace. When his body responded, he turned to mundane tasks in the shop to distract himself.

When she heard the galley door close, Magdalena's pose slipped. She gripped the counter with white-knuckled hands, trying to deny the sudden heat in her body. So sensually he had chewed, those crystalline blue eyes holding her prisoner, helpless as a fly in glass. *Dios*, why did she still respond to him, despite her knowledge now of his true nature? She hated him, she told herself, for he made her hate herself. She could not afford such weakness.

Taking a deep, steadying breath, Magdalena put the berries in the cupboard. There was one bright spot, at least. She was almost certain she'd hidden her feelings. In this instance, his conceit served her well. He apparently didn't believe the strawberry girl could have reacted so coolly to his challenge. Now, he'd dismiss his notion that she could be the same girl.

She wondered why the consolation was little comfort. No matter how many times she called herself a fool, she could not shake her regrets: that she'd been forced into this role; that he was not the man she'd thought him on their first meeting; that he was her enemy when part of her still longed to call him friend—no, more than friend.

Why was he so uncommonly interested in the girl he'd met only once? Her eyes narrowed. Perhaps she could use that interest to her advantage and hasten her departure from this place she wanted so much to leave. The passion he'd incited, the passion she looked back on with such shame, could be an unexpected boon. To Carlotta he would say nothing of his plans. But could he resist so easily the girl he'd kissed with such ardor?

Her heart beat faster, despite herself, at the memory. Did she risk meeting him again as herself? Did she have a choice? Every day she remained increased the danger to her. She was more inclined to tempt fate than to let it buffet her as it pleased.

As to her vulnerability to Browning, she had only to remind herself that he was Roberto's associate. She would hold the knowledge to herself like a talisman, using it to ward off his treacherous charm. She smiled grimly to herself. She'd never had much faith in such superstitions. She preferred to rely on her own strength and ingenuity . . .

Her employer was brusque with her for the rest of that day, which suited her fine. When she took away the evening tray, she felt his brooding eyes following her. With a sigh of relief, she retired to her tiny cabin.

It was a hot night for early summer, and she was too restless to sleep. She'd warred with her promise to Joaquin and her own impatience since she'd seen Luis ride away. He'd likely stay overnight at El Paraiso. She'd heard no word from Joaquin or Sean, and Friday was still two days away. She wanted something to report. Every day she remained here increased the danger to her. Surely Joaquin would understand . . .

Besides, she was apparently being blamed for robberies she hadn't committed, if Luis was to be believed. Reported in several locales along the highway indeed! Who was spreading such fallacious rumors? If she was to have the name, she might as well play the game.

Before she'd finished the thought, she was out of bed, dressing in her breeches. This time, she drew on deerskin boots instead of her leather ones. Throwing her blouse and skirt loosely over her other clothes, she opened the door and tiptoed down the corridor. She didn't hear the man who eased his own cabin door open and followed her. Once outside, she ducked into the shed, stuffed her outer garments under the carreta seat and went down the beach to fetch Fuego.

Clint ducked behind a stack of crates as a very different figure from the one who'd entered emerged from the shed. Even the fitful moonlight could not hide the shadow of the wide-brimmed hat, flowing cape and sword scabbard. For a moment, Clint was frozen in outrage. He'd followed Carlotta, hoping that she'd somehow lead him to the strawberry girl. This he'd never expected. So, Carlotta was indeed more than she seemed—friend, sister, spy or lover of Black Jack? He cast a grim look at the shed, but he'd have to deal with her later.

To avoid being seen, he gave Jack a couple of minutes head start, then he hurried up the beach. He looked both ways. At first he saw nothing, but then his ears caught a dull thudding. He ran toward the sound in time to see Jack riding up the rise toward the town.

Rushing back to the shed, Clint hurriedly saddled his own rented mount. By the time he traced Jack's path, the bandit was gone. Clint tracked the hoofprints as far as he could, but they disappeared on the hard-packed earthen streets. Clint drew his mount in and debated. If Jack was up to his thieving, he'd likely pick the wealthiest residents of Santa Barbara. Some of the most expensive townhouses were in the area of the presidio. Clint kicked his mount in that direction.

# Chapter 5

"Adversity is the best spur to an adventurous spirit."
Act I, DON JUAN TENORIO

The night itself seemed Magdalena's ally. The silver needle of a moon stitched in and out of threadbare clouds. However, the night that was indulgent of her dark garments and horse was yet a threat. She and Fuego felt their way along the paths, stumbling through holes and over bumps. Her night vision was good, but when the moon was hidden, she could barely see three feet ahead.

Magdalena heaved a relieved sigh when the gleaming white walls came into sight at last. She reined Fuego in and tied him to the crumbling wall. She checked to be sure her sword sheath was securely fastened, then unlooped her reata and tossed it over her shoulder, throwing a pouch over her other arm in case she found something to bring back.

Pausing to pat Fuego's muzzle, she whispered, "Wish me luck, amigo." She turned and vaulted over a low place in the rear wall, giving a mental thank-you to Joaquin for the acrobatics he'd made her learn. She'd have need of every lesson this night.

From her earlier survey, Magdalena knew where to throw her rope. The chapel had a wing on its west side with a roof that sloped down lower than the chapel proper. The tile overhang should be sufficient purchase to pull herself up—*if* she could get the reata looped tightly about it, and *if* the tile was not crumbling with age. Magdalena squinted, waiting for the moon to reappear. When it did, the light was fitful, but she could just make out the eave. With a practiced flip of her wrist, she tossed her reata. It slithered against the roof and fell back down. She repeated the maneuver patiently, sometimes literally throwing blind.

Fifteen minutes later, she'd worked up such a sweat that she decided to take off her cloak. In the dark no one would notice the slight rise of her bosom anyway, even should she be seen. Feeling a little cooler, she went back to work. Ten minutes later, however, she was almost ready to give up and go around to the storehouses, despite the danger of the horses in the corral reacting to her presence.

She wrapped her reata in a neat loop, tapping one foot against the ground. Then suddenly she snapped her fingers. "*Estupida!*" she chided herself. Walking back to the crumbling rear defense wall, she climbed it and wended her way from a low spot on the wall to the highest, sturdiest place opposite the chapel. The next time the moon came out, she muttered a prayer and threw. The reata looped obligingly about the eave on the first try. Magdalena tugged on the rope to tighten the loop, then jerked. It held.

Jubilantly she jumped down, tossed the pouch over her shoulder and gripped the rope tightly in her gloved hands. Bracing her feet against the chapel wall, she walked her legs up it as Joaquin had taught her. Once she reached the roof of the lower extension, she wrapped the reata up and coiled it over her shoulder. From there, it was easy to boost herself up to the chapel and walk across it to the other side. Again using her reata, she lowered herself to the overhang in front of the first lieutenant's quarters, which abutted the chapel, moving one careful inch at a time. She had no idea if Leon

*114*

was inside, but if he'd followed his usual custom, he'd drunk himself to sleep and wouldn't hear her if she danced a flamenco over his head. Blessing the deerskin boots that made her movements almost soundless, she crouched against the side of the chapel and surveyed the inner quadrangle.

The moon came out. She sighed with relief to see the yard empty. The few guards on duty seemed to be in the guardhouse at the entrance. She could see a light across the yard and hear an occasional burst of laughter. Reassured, Magdalena left her rope where it was and jumped the remaining feet to the ground, ducking into the shadows of the overhang and walking next door, to the comandante's quarters.

She tried Luis's door. Locked, as she expected. The windows fronting the building had their shutters closed, probably barred from the inside. So, Luis apparently did not even trust his own men. Not that she blamed him—especially if he had something to hide. More determined than ever, she withdrew her sword and, with its tip, she tried to release the catch. When it remained stubborn, she whittled at the doorjamb where the lock adjoined.

She smiled maliciously when she was able to pry the lock free and shove the door open. Mexico's "finest" would have some explaining to do when Luis returned. She closed the door behind her and felt in her pockets for the candle and flint she'd brought with her. Only then did she remember she'd left them in her cloak. She cursed roundly, then began fumbling in the dark next to the door. Her fingers brushed a lantern on the small table. The flint lay conveniently close. When the lantern was burning, she turned the wick down as far as it would go, but it still cast more light than her candle would have.

All the better to see with, she tried to reassure herself so she wouldn't have to think of the telltale cracks of light between shutters and door. She held the lamp up and scanned the interior. This front room was obviously Luis's office. It held several straight-backed wooden chairs and a massive, scarred rolltop desk in the corner. She set the lantern down on a nearby table and rolled the desktop back. She searched hurriedly, but found nothing out of the ordinary in the various compartments. Requisitions, correspondence with Monterey about various issues, commendations or reprimands for the soldiers, receipts. She closed the desk, picked up the lantern and went to the next room. A spare bedroom, it was empty of all save a simple iron-frame bed and a rickety chest.

When she reached Luis's room, she set the lantern down on the table next to his bed. Methodically she looked through his chest-on-chest. She was disappointed to find nothing but clothes. She went to the tiny bookcase in the corner and took out a tome at a time, flipping through them, looking for she knew not what. It was highly unlikely she'd find her grandfather's last will here. If Roberto had found it, it had been destroyed. But she might find a hint of what Luis and Roberto were allied in. If Luis had sent his men to kill Carlos, he'd done so with hope of reward. Since Roberto would never share the rancho with Luis, then the Mexican hoped for enrichment of another kind.

Besides, since Mexico had ordered secularization of the missions, many of the soldiers had applied for—and received—lands of their own. Luis's parcel was doubtless prime land, as large as the law would grant. So he had no need of land. She looked for something else.

Magdalena stiffened when she heard a door creak open outside. Footsteps shuffled on the hard-packed earth. She blew out the lantern and shrank against the wall. Her bated breath eased when she heard a stream of moisture splatting on the ground. Nose wrinkled in distaste, she waited to resume her search until Leon had relieved himself.

It was not to be. The winds, always capricious in Santa Barbara, had quickened since her arrival. She'd paid little heed to them whistling through the shutters, but when those footsteps paused, then approached the comandante's door, an icy trickle down her spine limned what had happened.

The door, unable to latch because of the lock she'd pried loose, had blown open. Morales was coming to check it.

Magdalena looked frantically about for somewhere to

*116*

hide, but the rooms had no closets and the beds were too low to crawl under. She hurried back to the main room, snatched up the lantern and stood behind the door. If only he didn't call for help, she'd have a chance of disabling him and escaping.

But fate seemed intent on teaching her the consequences of impatience. After appraising the lock, Morales cursed and ran back across the yard, shouting for his men. They answered immediately, more quickly than Magdalena had anticipated. She slammed the lantern down and grabbed up her pouch. The lantern wobbled on the table edge. By the time it had toppled over and shattered on the floor, she was halfway out the door.

Several guards were conferring with Morales in the middle of the compound, but it was the sight of the tall, fair-haired man with them, gesturing vehemently, that gave wings to her feet. As she burst out of the doorway, she heard Browning say, "I found a horse tied to the rear of the presidio . . ." Then she was too busy to hear more.

Leaping up, Magdalena caught the tile roof of the veranda and chinned herself up until she could lever one foot on the roof and boost her weight over. Not a moment too soon, either, for the group turned toward the comandante's rooms, Clint in their midst, the soldiers holding their muskets at the ready. Magdalena flattened against the chapel wall, hoping they would not think to look up.

When they all rushed into Luis's quarters, Magdalena caught the rope and began her spiderwalk up the chapel wall. She'd almost made it to the roof when a shout split the night. She looked down. One of the soldiers had apparently been ordered to search the grounds. His face caught the moonglow. He was looking directly at her.

"*Alto!*" he shouted.

When she ignored the command and pulled herself onto the roof, he put his musket to his shoulder and fired. The shot zinged into the tile near her head, sending clay dust into her eyes. She blinked rapidly, trying to clear them, jerked her reata loose, looped it over her shoulder and stumbled across the chapel roof. She almost stepped over the edge before her blurry eyes saw it. She leaped down to the wing roof, overbalanced because of her impaired vision and skidded on her back. She dragged her feet on the overlapping tiles, grasping with her gloved hands, slowing her momentum enough to stop herself from falling over the edge.

Her heart pounding with fear, she took a deep breath, cleared her eyes as best she could on her sleeve and prepared herself. There was no time to rappel down as she'd planned. More soldiers, alerted by the gunshot, were crowding into the yard. Any moment now they'd search the rear of the presidio for the horse Browning had alerted them to. Not giving herself more time to think, she dangled her legs over the roof, twisted at the waist, grasped the tile edge and lowered herself into nothingness. It seemed she fell a mile before blessed earth whammed into her feet. A sharp twinge darted up her ankle, but she ignored it as she climbed up on the defense wall and leaped into the saddle, jerking Fuego's reins loose and retreating at a full gallop. The winds had chased the clouds away, and now a dim but steady glow lit the paths.

It also illuminated her retreat to the mounted soldiers who rounded the presidio . . .

Magdalena weaved between houses, zig-zagged to the beach. It slowed her progress, but retarded their pursuit. By the time she burst down the incline to the beach, the soldiers were not even in sight. She had the precious time she needed to run Fuego through the waves to disguise his tracks. Only when she'd reached the wooded point did she turn back up the beach—and just in time. Pursuing hoof-beats pounded up the packed sand. Magdalena reined Fuego through the brush to his cavernous stable. She patted his muzzle to keep him quiet as the soldiers neared. Obeying a shouted order, they scattered to search.

Would they see her tracks? Magdalena held her hand over Fuego's nostrils when he lifted his head to answer a horse's whinny. He tossed his head, but subsided when she offered him the carrot she'd filched from Clint's larder.

Magdalena's heart pounded in concert to the trotting

hoofbeats. Up they went, down and around, gradually slowing and becoming confused. Finally, two soldiers paused near enough for her to hear their exchange.

Leon growled, "He came this way, eh? Did he grow gills or wings?" When there was no reply, Leon roared, "Answer me!"

The soldier stammered, "But I s-saw him turn this way. He must be here s-somewhere . . ."

*"Imbecil!* If you hadn't missed your mark, we'd have a prisoner to show Luis when he returns from El Paraiso instead of a broken lock. You'll make a full report to him. You know how strict he is about his privacy . . ." Their voices retreated down the beach.

Magdalena bowed her head against Feugo's hide, dizzy with relief. She had been lucky. A fool's luck, perhaps, but she'd take fortune where she found it. When she deemed it safe, Magdalena lit her lantern, groomed, then fed and watered Fuego from the supplies she kept on a ledge. The throbbing in her ankle grew worse with every step, but she gave it little heed, turning over in her mind the conversation she'd overheard. So, Luis *did* have something to hide. Why else would he be so protective of his rooms? If only she'd had more time to search . . .

Because of her injured ankle, she didn't dare risk going back tomorrow without Sean. Besides, the presidio would be more watchful now that she'd betrayed her interest. Taking off her sword, she wrapped it carefully and set it on the ledge, her ears ringing with the reproaches Joaquin would peal over her head. She didn't even consider not confessing the fiasco. She couldn't deceive Sean and Joaquin when they endangered their very lives to help her.

This time, Magdalena admitted, she deserved every scathing name Joaquin would doubtless call her. Her narrow escape had cleared her head of the impatience that had hazed her judgment. The mistakes she'd made this night seemed obvious now she had time to think.

She should never have undertaken the risk alone. If Sean had been with her, he could have waited near the door and knocked Morales out before he noticed the broken lock.

*119*

She'd made two other stupid mistakes besides: She had forgotten her candle, and she should have propped the door closed to be sure it didn't blow open. But no, she'd let her own headstrong determination blind her, as usual.

For the first time, she seriously considered Joaquin's warnings. Tonight she'd learned the hard way how wise he was. At times, indeed, recklessness was called for. But tonight had not been one of them. The longer Luis and Roberto were unalerted, the better her chance of stealth—and success. Tonight, she and she alone, had destroyed one of their few advantages. The soldiers would be on guard now, even if they concluded she was but a thief. They'd not find it easy to get into Luis's quarters again.

But they had no choice. Something was there. Something incriminating. Why else would Luis be such a fanatic about his "privacy"? If they had to battle each and every soldier to find it, they must go back.

Wearily, Magdalena changed back into her skirt and blouse. She bundled up her disguise, then hesitated. It might be safest to dress here in future. She unwrapped the clothes and folded them neatly on the ledge. Giving Fuego a last pat, she limped out of the cave. At least this was one thing she wouldn't have to pretend to for a few days. However, the sprain was slight and would doubtless heal soon.

She was walking up the *Arabella*'s gangplank when she froze midstep, calling herself every scathing name she could think of. Her mind was no better than mush! Yes, she'd had a close call, but if she let fear distract her, they were all doomed. She tested her weight on the bad ankle. She winced. It would never bear her full weight. If she forced it, it would take weeks to heal. She had no choice but to limp—*on the wrong leg*!

Perhaps, just perhaps, Browning wouldn't notice if she stayed off it as much as possible. But she now knew him to be both ruthless and intelligent. How had he figured out she'd search the presidio tonight? As the logical answer came to her, she paled. If he'd followed Carlotta, then seen Jack emerge from the shed . . . She groaned aloud, thinking furiously. So what if he believed Carlotta had met Jack? He surely had no reason to make the real connection. But what if he reported the meeting to Luis?

Magdalena stayed where she was, seriously considering not boarding the *Arabella*. After a moment, her panicked heartbeat slowed. Browning was too arrogantly determined to catch Jack himself. He'd probably not turn her in. Besides, she sensed that she was close to gaining valuable knowledge. Staying was her only chance of investigating Roberto. She could not leave. Depressed at the added complications, Magdalena limped back to her cabin. She'd opened her door and started untying her blouse before she saw the shape on her bunk. She gave a little gasp of fright and backed away, one hand to her throat.

There came the scrape of flint, then her lantern flickered to life. Her employer, all six and a half feet of him, rose from her bunk, crossed his arms over his torso and asked equably, "Do you make these excursions nightly?"

Her hand dropped to her side and clenched into a fist, but he seemed not to notice. Clint tapped his chin with a forefinger. "Let me see, perhaps you go to market?" He craned his neck to look behind her, one side, then the other. "No. No supplies." He contemplated her darkening face for another long moment. "Ah, I have it. You go to meet a lover. A tall, sinister man with a taste for larceny."

When her head reared back in outrage, he dropped his hands and barked, "You don't like my explanations? Then let me hear yours. What is Black Jack to you? Why do you meet him?"

Magdalena retorted, "I owe you nothing. Even a servant is allowed some time to herself." Her inward relief that he didn't suspect her dual identity gave her strength to stand on her injured ankle and meet his condemning eyes.

"Indeed. Provided whatever schemes she's involved in do not disgrace her master." He stressed the last word, smiling benignly when her breath hissed through her teeth. "I need to earn these people's trust. If it's known my maid is a spy for the man who steals from them, how will I look? I don't know what your purpose was in coming here, but

I'm certain it involved more than a job. Won't you simplify everything by being frank with me? Perhaps I can even help, if you'll let me. Please, prove to me that you're too honest to be a member of his band."

Those blue eyes had softened in the lantern glow from diamond hardness to billowy blue waves. Magdalena could deny their power only by looking at the floor. Once before they'd encouraged her confidence. She'd come close to betraying herself and all she lived for to an enemy, an ally of Roberto's. This man wanted her captured, maybe even dead, and had almost succeeded tonight. She'd forget none of this, no matter how much false charm he oozed.

Breathing deeply, Magdalena answered, "I but walk on the beach when I cannot sleep." When he looked skeptical and strangely disappointed, Magdalena twitched her skirt up to show him her sandal caked with wet sand. "See? Do you believe me now?"

When she realized his eyes were fixed not on her sandal, but on the ankle above it, she lowered her skirts and shifted her weight to her good ankle.

Shrugging, Clint said dryly, "I believe you were on the beach. As to why you were in the shed . . . that remains to be seen." He approached. She stepped out of his path, but when he reached the door, he paused with his hand on the lever, turning to pinion her with a lancing blue stare. "But I'll tell you this, *doncellita*." Leaning forward, he whispered in her face, "I will find out. And you can give your friend a message: I'll find him, too." The door snicked shut behind him.

Magdalena slumped down on the bed as if her bones had been dissected. She was spineless, gutless, witless . . . That man was naught but a *picaro*! Yet, knowing him for an enemy as she did, something pusillanimous in her yearned to lean against the strong shoulder that seemed shaped for a woman's head. Only the will forged in adversity kept her upright when she longed to collapse and have a good cry.

She had cast off a woman's weakness with her woman's dress. If she was to succeed in this charade, she could afford neither indulgence. A man she pretended to be; a man she must act, even if she knew it was a lie. Now, with Browning obviously suspicious of her, such weakness was more perilous than ever. Even if he were not allied with Roberto, she could never share the truth with him. He was still American and not to be trusted. No, her plans were made, her feet set firmly upon the path she herself had chosen. Nothing would distract her. Grimly, Magdalena prepared for bed.

The next morning, she avoided Clint. She left his breakfast tray before he entered the shop and didn't pick it up, knowing either he or Pritikin would bring it to the galley. Indeed, midmorning Pritikin did. He gave her an odd look when she asked him to take the lunch tray in early but did as she requested. She waited until one o'clock to straighten the cabins, then limped into the shop, pausing in the doorway until Pritikin looked up. She drew a little sigh of relief when Clint remained with his back to her, scribbling in his ledger.

To her delight, Pritikin met her with the empty tray, enabling her to leave without Clint even noticing her presence. She was too busy hurrying out to note the frown Pritikin bent upon her limping leg. Magdalena stayed off the ankle as much as possible throughout the day, working at the table in the galley fixing a more elaborate meal than she usually did.

Her luck ran out when she brought the rich beef stew, apples spiced with sugar and cinnamon and boiled carrots into the shop. Clint was leaning against a shelf, ankles crossed, facing the door. The minute she entered, his eyes dropped to her leg. Magdalena faltered in the doorway, looking from Clint's watchful face to Pritikin's sheepish one. She closed her eyes in dismay, knowing she'd been discovered, but she forced them open and blanked all expression as she carried the tray forward. She made no attempt to disguise her limp.

As soon as she set the tray down, she turned to leave. Clint reached out a long arm and grabbed her wrist. "No, my dear. You've fixed us such a lovely meal the least we can do is invite you to share it with us."

"I'm not hungry," Magdalena mumbled.

"Nonsense. All this effort must have worked up an appetite. Come, sit. Your leg seems to be paining you." Gallantly, he pulled out a chair for her at the small circular table. His smile showed too many teeth.

Despite the feeling that she'd be the first course, Magdalena sat down. She could only brazen it out. Perhaps she could make them believe they were mistaken about which leg she had limped on.

Clint and Pritikin sat opposite her. Silently, she served them. Silently, they ate. And silently, they watched her. Magdalena's neck prickled a warning, and she wolfed down her food. When she crossed her fork and knife over her empty plate and would have risen, a gentle but inflexible voice held her. "No."

Pritikin mumbled an inaudible excuse and fled from the cabin.

"The time for evasion is long past. Your game is up, Carlotta, if that's even your name. You are obviously a woman of many talents." When her eyes stayed glued to her empty plate, Clint's voice sharpened on the strop of wrath. "Not least of which is duplicity." He smiled grimly when that got her attention.

Jolted as always by the contrast of those beautiful, compelling eyes in that dark, scarred face, he spoke more harshly than he'd intended. "But even a talent for lying cannot work the miracle of regeneration. What fools do you take us for? Did you really think we wouldn't notice when your left leg healed only to transfer its ailment to the right?"

After a brief flicker of emotion—fear? anger? despair?— her eyes went expressionless again. When she didn't answer his questions, his frustration grew. He slammed his palm down on the table. The pewter dishes rattled and jumped. She didn't bat an eye. Her composure only made him angrier.

"Tell me who you are and why you met Jack. Why did you come to me?"

"I came to be your maid. If I've performed unsatisfactorily, then release me. Hire someone else."

Clint stiffened at the mocking, sideways look she sent him. "You know very well no one else will work for me . . ."

"Yes, and why is that, gringo? Could it be Californios are suspicious of you? You Americanos stole Florida. Now you've taken Texas. Can you blame us for wondering if California will be next? Your government has tried overt bribery. Since Mexico won't sell San Francisco and assist your greedy plans for expansion, will you now resort to force?"

Clint wondered if his face was as red as it felt. Damn Uncle Charles for putting him in this unconscionable position! He wasn't blind to what Carlotta was trying to do. Attack was always one of the best defenses, but her shots were striking far too close to home. Indeed, how could he condemn her for duplicity when his own actions were less than noble? The fact was, he was spying for the very reasons Californios feared: American interest in annexation, peacefully if possible, forcibly if not. At least, forcibly if Charles had his way. And, willingly or not, he was a tool in that cause.

Magdalena's eyes narrowed when Browning shifted his long legs and looked away. She swallowed a bitter tang in her throat. "So, moralize to me when your own heart is pure. At least my motives are honorable . . ." She bit her lip and averted her head.

"Yes?" Clint leaned forward.

She shook her head and rose. She was so upset at his uncanny ability to encourage her confidence, despite her knowledge of his own duplicity, that she unthinkingly put all her weight on her sprained ankle. Gasping, she dropped back in her chair.

The next thing she knew, a large figure was kneeling at her feet. When he tried to raise the hem of her skirt, she flinched, crying, "No! I'm fine. Just let me sit . . ."

But the big, callused hands would not be denied any more than would the man who wielded them. "Come, *muchacha*, let me see. This pain, at least, is genuine." Ignoring her protests, he flipped her skirt back to her calf and set her foot

125

on his thigh. He ran gentle fingers over the puffiness at her ankle. He whistled.

"What have you been doing? Scaling the presidio wall?" His lowered eyes did not catch her shock before lush, curling lashes shielded it.

By the time he glanced up, all he saw was a face flushed from his teasing. "I would suggest packing it in ice, if such a luxury were available. But since it isn't, cold sea water will have to do." He went to the door and yelled an order up to Pritikin.

Returning to Magdalena, he stroked her ankle, his hands all the more soothing for their latent power. "Don't you think you should tell me how you did this?" He frowned up at her. "Jack didn't beat you, did he?"

"I . . . fell when I was walking on the beach."

Clint sighed and put her foot back on the floor. "Very well, I'll ask no more questions for now. You may keep your job despite your refusal to be honest with me for, strangely enough, I believe you when you say your motivations are honorable." His smile was wry, self-mocking and very male. "Besides, I've a fondness for eating. And your skills have much improved. Dinner tonight was delicious."

When Pritikin entered with a bucket of sea water, Clint moved to help her. She waved him away, removed her shoe and stuck her foot in the bucket. She gave a sigh of relief as the cool water lapped against her muscles. She dropped her head against the ladder-back of the chair and closed her eyes. Vaguely she was aware of Clint and Pritikin clearing away the dishes and cleaning up the shop in preparation for tomorrow's business. But mostly she just drifted, giving herself the blessed, unusual relief of not thinking at all. She started when a hand landed on her shoulder.

"You'd better go to bed before you fall out of your chair," Clint suggested. "Tomorrow stay off that foot. You can prepare the meals, but we'll fetch and return the trays."

Magdalena's eyes fluttered open. She straightened abruptly when she saw his gaze wandering from the supple arch of her throat down to where it connected to her chest.

126

She pulled her foot out of the bucket, stuck her sandal back on and rose.

"*Si,* señor." She limped to the door, but her sense of fair play made her turn. She had never suspected him capable of such kindness. He'd no doubt been kinder than he thought she deserved. "Gracias," she said huskily, but sincerely. She turned and exited.

Clint stared at the door after it had closed behind her. What was it about this girl and the other she resembled that made him instinctively want to protect them? Perhaps it was the vulnerability buried so deep beneath the layers of pride. But whatever it was, it was damned effective. He was no longer even angry with her, as he should be. In time, he'd stumble onto the truth. For now, that seemed enough. Shaking his head at his own foolishness, Clint decided to walk to Santa Barbara to drum up some sorely needed business.

Besides, he'd not forgotten his intent when he decided to remain here. It was time to see what he could discover about a certain bandit. He was curious to learn what Santa Barbarans thought of Black Jack, and he was more likely to get an objective answer from a stranger than from Luis or de Sarria. He also wanted to casually bring up Carlotta and see if anyone knew if she had relatives. A sister, for example . . .

He strolled between the adobe houses, looking for someone to talk to, but it was almost dark and few Santa Barbarans were about. Finally he decided to risk a rebuff. He stopped in front of a two-story adobe townhouse with lights flickering in the windows. Entering the swinging picket gate, he walked boldly up the earthen path to the heavy door and knocked.

An Indian maid opened the door. "*Si?*"

"I'd like to speak to the master of the house," he said in his fluent Spanish.

The woman opened her mouth to answer, but a musical voice interrupted. "Who is it, Juana?" Light footsteps sounded on the tile floors.

Through the crack in the door, Clint saw the pretty

*127*

señorita he'd met at the market. He bowed. "Forgive the intrusion, señorita . . ."

Before he could go on, she gurgled a pretty laugh. "No intrusion, señor. *Pase, usted, la casa es suya.*" She opened the door wide and stood back invitingly.

Clint stepped inside, pausing on the woven rug in the small entryway. "That's most gracious of you, but perhaps I should come back when your father is home . . ."

"I am Jose, her brother," said a tall, handsome caballero, entering from a room on the right. He looked Clint up and down, then sent a chiding but resigned glance at his sister.

"How may I help you, Captain Browning?"

Clint caught the cool tone and guarded look, but he had not built his father's business into the thriving concern it now was by timidity. "I'd like to discuss a recent encounter I had on El Camino Real."

Jose's mellow brown eyes narrowed. "What encounter?"

"With a bandit calling himself Black Jack. He's an arrogant devil I'd give much to capture. Luis told me he's been reported in several locales along the highway, and I wondered if you, perhaps, know some of the victims and can share the details of the robberies. The bandit will be easier to capture if some pattern can be assigned to his movements."

Clint blinked when every muscle in Jose's body tensed. What the devil have I done to offend him? he wondered.

"Come into the parlor, señor. We will talk."

Clint eyed that stiff back warily, but followed. Angelina hastened after them, her gold silk skirts rustling over stiff petticoats.

Waving Clint onto a hide sofa opposite the door, Jose took the wine brocade wing chair opposite. Angelina, with a defiant look at her brother, sat down next to Clint, arranging her skirts about her.

Clint glanced with interest about the room. With the exception of the stiff hide sofa, adobe walls and tile floor, he could have been in a drawing room at home. The oil paintings, plush rug and old but elegant Hepplewhite furniture bespoke wealth and culture. As a trader, Clint

128

could estimate the cost of these luxuries. Californios paid, on average, three times as much for their goods as an American from the east coast would. Clint had often wondered why Californians didn't take more advantage of the bounty of their land. Yet even wealthy landowners such as these seemed content to barter their hides at low rates for American and European goods priced at a premium.

Shaking his head mentally at such waste, Clint began, "As for my encounter, I'd just arrived in Santa Barbara when I was invited by the owner of El Paraiso to see his holdings . . ." Clint faltered when Jose's wariness changed to outright hostility. But when he said nothing, Clint continued, "He said he had a business proposal to discuss with me, but before we had opportunity to talk, we were accosted by three bandits, who were led by a man calling himself Black Jack. They took our purses, spooked our horses and left us to walk."

Angelina squeaked, "He did not hurt any of you, did he?"

Why the surprise? Clint wondered. He felt asea, but admitted, "Er, I'm afraid I was rather . . . recalcitrant. One of them knocked me out because I refused to give them my purse."

Jose shot his sister a triumphant glare. "See? All your talk of gallantry is foolish. The man is a ruthless *bandido* who will stop at nothing in his thievery."

Clint looked from one to the other of them. "Do I take it you've had an encounter with him, also?"

"Si. He recently held up our coach and stole my money and a carriage horse . . ."

"Part of your money. He left enough to buy another horse," Angelina corrected.

Jose snorted. "How generous of him to leave me *some* of my own property."

"Nor did he take my jewels." Angelina flashed a hand weighted down with a huge ruby and diamond ring on her forefinger and a sapphire on her ring finger. "He was really most gallant."

Jose threw an impatient look at the ceiling. When he

met Clint's eyes, he spread his hands. Clint grinned in sympathy with his male exasperation. Leaning forward, he said, "I have three sisters, Señor Rivas. I understand your feelings perfectly."

Angelina sniffed and jerked at her skirts.

"Has anyone else been robbed that you know of?" When Jose shrugged, Clint sighed in disappointment. "Well, that's hardly a pattern. Twice on the highway and once on the presidio—"

When Jose made a surprised exclamation, Clint broke off. "Didn't you hear about last night?"

"No," Jose answered. "Was he seen again?"

"Yes. Here in Santa Barbara."

Jose whistled. "When? What happened?"

Clint described last night's events. "The soldiers aren't certain if it's the same man, but I believe it is. I got a good look at him on the beach."

"Yes, señor? Then you saw him disappear into thin air, also?" Angelina folded her hands demurely in her lap when both men looked at her in surprise.

"What do you know of this, Angelina?" Jose demanded.

"Only the 'gossip' you tell me not to heed. Since you only returned shortly before Captain Browning arrived, I didn't get a chance to tell you. When the soldiers trailed *Juan Negro* to the beach, they found no hoofprints, nothing. So now they call him El Halcon. A most suitable name for a man of such cunning and daring, no?"

"No," Jose said flatly. "There's nothing romantic about a man who makes a career of terrorizing others."

Clint nodded his agreement. "Besides, such talk is foolish. He's just a very clever man with a good hiding place. The man who robbed *me* was no falcon."

Jose digested all this in silence before venturing, "Do you suppose he mocks us? Dares us to try to catch him?"

"That's occurred to me, señor. The irony of a bandit breaking *into* the presidio has not escaped me, even if Leon Morales is too dense to think of it."

"Luis will be another matter, when he returns," Jose

130

said. "He'll be furious at the arrogance of the man in daring to break into his own quarters."

"What on earth could he have been after?"

Jose shrugged. "Who knows? Though Luis has been granted lands recently, he has nothing of value in his rooms at the presidio, surely, as the bandit ought to know. That's why I can't help but wonder if he isn't daring us to try to capture him."

Clint smiled grimly. "I don't know about you, señor, but I've always relished a challenge. Won't you help me meet his?"

Brown eyes met blue ones, measuring, testing. When Clint's remained steady, Jose nodded. "I will help if I can. What do you have in mind?"

"Let us both watch and listen. In your trips to and from your hacienda you may encounter him again. Try to find some clue as to his hiding place. I'll do the same here in the town." Clint didn't add that his own servant could provide that clue if he watched her closely enough. Some strange reticence forbade him to implicate Carlotta. However, it wouldn't hurt to ask another question he was burning to learn the answer to . . .

He looked at Angelina. "Tell me, señorita, do you know if my maid, Carlotta, has relations? A brother or sister, perhaps?"

"Carlotta? I do not know her." Angelina looked puzzled when Clint frowned at her reply.

He opened his mouth, then snapped it shut. Carlotta had known Angelina, and Luis as well. But again, until he knew more of her, it was probably best to say little. If she were in trouble, he didn't want to complicate matters for her. Clint smiled at the Rivases' curious faces. "I must have been mistaken." He rose. "*Muchas gracias* for your hospitality. If you hear more of the bandit, please tell me, señor."

The Rivases walked him to the door. Jose put out a hand to stop him when Clint said goodnight and opened the door.

"Señor," he said diffidently, "I don't want to be rude, but can you tell me if you ever discussed your 'business' with Roberto?"

"Ah, you know him, then?"

"Si."

One word, yet so eloquent of distaste. Clint shared the feeling, but his curiosity was stirred as to why this man felt the same. "No, he stayed closeted in his study during my brief stay at El Paraiso. I have not seen him since."

"Good. Good."

Angelina scolded, "Jose, you accuse *me* of being foolish . . . Surely you don't believe Roberto is to blame after all this time. Papa would be furious to hear this. You know what he saw with his own eyes . . ."

"Hush, *niña*," Jose said, noticing Clint's attentive air. "We must not bore Señor Browning with old gossip."

"I'm not bored. I caught snatches of some old tragedy while I was at El Paraiso. I'd be very interested to hear more."

"It's not my story to tell, I'm afraid. But it's a tragic one indeed. A very good friend of mine died under suspicious circumstances."

"So you say," Angelina scoffed. But she subsided when Jose shook his head at her.

He opened the door pointedly, giving Clint no chance to remain. "*Buenas noches*, señor. I will watch, as you suggest. Indeed, I would relish meeting the bandit again when I am better prepared."

Clint had much to think on during the short walk back to his ship. But strangely, it was not the tales of the bandit that stuck in his mind. It was the hints of a mystery so dark and a tragedy so sad that no one felt comfortable speaking of it . . .

When he arrived, he was still deep in thought, and he was reaching out to open the door of his cabin before he realized a slit of light showed under it. He froze with his hand on the handle, then slowly, cautiously, he pushed. The door creaked open; the breath left his lungs; his eyes widened.

There, reclining on her side on the bed, was the girl from the strawberry patch. She had one hand propped under the side of her head, one long, slim leg encased in tight black breeches angled, boot resting on the mattress, over the other. It was a pose both seductive and casual, as if sensuality were as natural to her as the long dark hair flowing down over his pillow. His heart banged against his ribs as he snicked the door shut and approached her, his eyes still devouring every long, luscious inch of the body that had haunted his dreams. A bare foot away, he paused.

"Somehow I knew I'd see you again," he murmured, holding those unfathomable gold eyes with his own. "But it pleases me that you've come to me. I've yearned to see you."

She levered herself to a sitting position, drew one leg up, crossed her arms over it and propped her chin on her wrists. "How flattering, señor. Do you want something of me?" The light in her eyes was both teasing and mordant, as if she mocked him and herself equally.

"And what do *you* think I want of you?" He sat down beside her, twining one hand in that lush fall of hair to tilt her head in his direction. He stroked through the hair with his fingers, holding her eyes all the while. He thought vaguely that the texture was a bit coarser, the color darker, than he remembered, but the lantern was turned low, and he was too pleased at her acceptance of the caress to ponder the change.

"What all men want, señor." As if shy, she looked down, running her tongue over the edges of her upper teeth. If she heard his quick inhalation, she didn't react.

"And what is that, *bonita*?"

"Must I draw you a picture?"

Her flirtatious peep enchanted him as much as her soft laugh, but that mordant light lurked still beneath the gaiety. He was overjoyed that she'd come to him, but he couldn't help wondering why she'd changed her mind after seeming most definite that they not meet again.

"I've always thought action the best way to explain things, myself. Why don't you show me what you mean?" He expected her to scramble away. He was both pleased and disappointed when, after a startled look at him, she slowly lifted her arms and twined them about his neck. He willingly lowered his head at her tug, but that was all. She nibbled at her lip, took a deep breath and closed the remaining gap between them.

All thoughts but one left his brain as her lips met his. Delight, pure but not so simple, tingled through him as those soft, mobile lips both answered his yearning for closeness and incited deeper needs. He let her lead the kiss, but when her lips remained closed, he teased the corner of them with his tongue. At her gasp, he entered her mouth and took command. He searched out every tiny plain and miniature crevice, exploring her with his tongue and lips until he knew every texture. Yet it wasn't enough . . . He crushed her so close that he couldn't distinguish her heartbeat from his. Indeed, in those endless, yet all too brief moments, it seemed they were not two separate, but one, whole. Breathing together, pulsing together, feeling together.

Their intimacy was so deep for relative strangers that it was disturbing, and when she snatched her mouth away and pushed frantically at his shoulders, he let her go. They gulped deep breaths, trembling from the aftermath. When her dazed eyes met his, he wondered if he looked as shaken. Drawing an unsteady hand through the blond hair she'd mussed with her fingers, he decided he must.

"You are a woman of action, indeed," he teased huskily. When her eyes widened and cleared, his own narrowed at the emotions he saw there. Shock, confusion, fear, and, disturbingly, sadness. Sadness, as if she found him lacking, and herself lacking for wanting him. He was reaching out to her when she rose and began to pace up and down as if she couldn't keep still. He thought she stumbled once, but when she boldly turned to face him, he decided he must have imagined it.

She paused in front of him to glare at him. "And you, señor? What kind of man are you? Why have you come here?"

Sensing that his answer was important, he weighed his words. "To trade. And to learn more of your country," he answered as honestly as he could.

"And why do you wish to learn more of us?"

"Because I find you interesting, and because I promised a relative of mine that I would."

"And why do you stay so long in Santa Barbara?" Her ramrod straight back and pitiless gaze had a prosecutory air that angered him.

"Because I like it here."

She looked impatient at the glib answer, but he decided he'd been on the defensive long enough. He rose and bridged the gap between them in two strides. "And why are you so interested in my motivations?"

She shrugged and backed a wary pace, angering him further. "This is why you sought me out? To question me?" When her silence confirmed it, he swallowed his disappointment and advanced another step.

He stalked her across the cabin until she was backed against the door. "Perhaps if you offered . . . incentive enough, I might answer whatever you like." He braced his palms on either side of her waist, not touching her except with thorough, roving eyes. Had he been wrong about her? he wondered. She'd seemed such an innocent that first time, but no innocent could use feminine wiles so masterfully to gain information.

She pressed back against the door. "I don't believe in giving or taking bribes."

"No? Then what was that interesting little display of affection for? Because you couldn't help yourself?"

Finally she looked at him, and he quivered under the impact of that direct stare and even more unequivocal answer. "Yes." She bit her lip and looked away, as if regretting her honesty.

All hostility left him. He lifted his hands to tenderly cradle her face. "Ah, *niña*, we are more alike than you suppose. I, too, find you irresistible. Can we not forget who we are and just get to know one another?" He held his breath.

"Perhaps," she whispered. "But for now, I must leave." When he didn't release her, she looked up at him pleadingly. "Please, señor. It is late, and I have far to go."

"I'll not let you go until you tell me where I can find you

135

again." When she closed her eyes and shook her head, he bent to nibble at her earlobe. "Tell me where," he demanded when she quivered.

No answer. He bent lower to trail a hot series of kisses down her neck, pushing her shirt aside to extend the path across her collarbone. "Tell me," he whispered into her skin. When she shook her head and tried to push him away, he caught her wrists and drew them above her head, lifting his free hand to unbutton her shirt.

When the second button came open, she gasped. "Enough! You win. I live not far from the Gaviota Pass, near the strawberry patch where we first met."

"This is the first time I've regretted winning such a stubborn contest." His heated blue eyes smiled into her uncertain gold ones. When he reluctantly released her, she fastened her shirt and reached behind her for the door handle.

He stopped her with a gentle hand over hers. "Just a moment. Won't you tell me your name?"

"Er, Inez." When his eyes narrowed at her hesitation, she stared guilelessly back.

He sighed. "Very well, Inez. One more question. Have you a half-Indian sister?"

She shifted her feet, as if eager to leave. "No, señor." She turned the handle and slipped into the corridor. "Adios, señor."

His confident chuckle trailed her up the companionway. "No, nina. *Hasta luego*. Soon."

As Magdalena limped back to the cave to dress again as Carlotta, she gnawed savagely at her lip to stifle her incipient tears. Her ankle had felt better after the soaking, but after forcing herself to stand naturally in front of Clint, it pained her again. Still, the throbbing seemed minor compared to her other worries. She'd endangered herself for nothing, for nothing had she learned. She, on the other hand, had aroused his suspicions not only about Carlotta, but about the girl whom he had, previously, deemed an innocent. But, she told herself savagely, he had no right to condemn *her*. Wouldn't a man with nothing to hide be more

136

open? Why did each additional evidence of his betrayal weigh more heavily upon her? Why couldn't she dismiss him as the moral lightweight he was? What was it about this man that made her so reckless, when caution was all that protected her from a violent end?

She rubbed her eyes. She couldn't answer any of her own questions, but one thing she knew: This man was dangerous to her. And not because he was her enemy. He made her weak, and that she could not afford. He'd even pried from her a clue to her hiding place. At that point, it had been more necessary to escape those disturbing caresses than to protect her hideaway. Somehow it had not occurred to her to lie to him.

She was the fool, not he. Even knowing him for what he was, she was drawn to him. She'd not lied when she admitted that she'd kissed him because she couldn't help herself. Expediency hadn't lasted a second in his arms. And what, she wondered grimly as she reapplied the berry stain, did that say about her own character?

Very well, if he was her Achilles' heel, then she must protect herself when she was around him. And she must finish what she came here to do and leave as soon as possible. Resolved if not comforted, she finished dressing and returned to the ship.

# *Chapter 6*

"And knows, God bless her, scarce as much of love as
it is a word that's got four letters."
**Act I, DON JUAN TENORIO**

The following night, Friday, Clint tossed in this bunk, too
restless to sleep. He'd risen early and ridden to the spot on
the Gaviota where he'd first seen Inez. He'd searched
several miles on both sides of the highway, but he'd found
nothing resembling a domicile. His eagerly thrumming
heart had sunk like lead as he drew the obvious conclusions.
She'd lied to him. She had no intention of seeing him again
and didn't want him to find her.

He smiled grimly, now, into the darkness. She didn't
know him well if she thought he'd be put off so easily. The
knowledge that she was so determined he not find her only
firmed his own resolve. Tomorrow he'd search again higher
into the mountains. The decision was not a restful one and
when, an hour later, he still couldn't sleep, he cursed, rose
and dressed. Maybe walking along the beach would calm
him.

The moon cast a romantic glow over the shore. Waves

leaped in to kiss the sands' wrinkles away in their endless attraction, then rushed out again to gather strength for the next embrace. Palms swayed in the salty breeze. Clint leaned against one and breathed deeply. However, when muffled sounds caught his ears, he turned his head and beheld a sight that scattered all thoughts of rest.

There, just ascending the rise into Santa Barbara, was a rider. Clint rushed out onto a clear spot on the beach to get a better view. As if his movement had caught the rider's attention, the horseman paused and turned to look. He wore a cordovan. A full, flowing cape flapped behind him in the breeze.

With a curse and a bound, Clint erupted into action, running to the shed where he stabled his rented horse, watching the rider all the while. With a slap to his black's flank, the horseman galloped toward El Camino Real before Clint lost sight of him. Never had he saddled a horse so fast, but he'd seldom had better motivation. What satisfaction it would give him to capture that rascally thief single-handedly. He was a bold one, indeed, to return to Santa Barbara so soon after raiding the presidio. Clint led the stallion out of the shed, vaulted into the saddle and turned toward the highway.

"Dios, that was close!" Magdalena hissed under her breath. She should have been more careful. What a calamity it would have been if the American had come upon her a minute earlier. She wasn't wearing her hood because she didn't expect to meet anyone so late, and she'd ripped away the wax to savor her own identity. At Clint's insistence, she'd stayed off her ankle all day and had bound a rag around it, so it was much better, and she'd not affected a limp when she reached the point. Still, the memory of that throbbing ankle prodded her to caution like a penitent's conscience.

Reluctantly, she reined Fuego in, put on the hood and tied it down, then replaced her hat. At least Joaquin wouldn't be able to fault her this time for her recklessness.

She continued on, but at a sedate trot. When the sounds of a galloping horse rapidly approaching from the rear reached her, she wasn't alarmed. She reined Fuego to the far side of the highway and averted her head. It was dark, and the horseman would have no reason to give her more than a cursory glance.

By the time she heard the slowing hooves and sensed the rider coming alongside, it was too late. She turned her head to discover yet again that Clinton Browning never fit neatly into her plans. With a curse under her breath, she kneed Fuego, but a large hand caught her reins. A pistol poked her ribs.

"What an unexpected pleasure," purred that deep, familiar voice.

Though her knees shook with nervousness, Magdalena's Black Jack tone was calm. "Indeed, señor. You make your joy at seeing me again most obvious." She sent a wry look down at the pistol jabbing her side.

"And I know our bold comandante will feel the same. Get down." Warily Clint pulled one leg over his saddle, intending to slip to the ground while holding his pistol on the bandit. With his free hand he reached for the reata hanging over El Halcon's saddle.

Violently El Halcon sawed backward on his mount's reins, simultaneously slipping sideways in the saddle. The stallion reared, his powerful body protecting the long figure clinging to the side away from Clint.

By the time Clint had regained his seat and soothed his own jibbing mount, the bandit was several lengths down the highway, bending low over his stallion's neck so as to offer a poor target. Clint aimed anyway, but hesitated a moment too long. He hated to shoot any man in the back, even such a one. He slammed the pistol back into his saddle holster and kicked his own stallion. The nervous animal bolted forward in a ground-covering gallop, but still the gap between the two horses widened.

Clint slapped his bay's rump and also bent low, but it wasn't enough. Then fate smiled upon him. El Halcon turned his head to gauge his adversary's distance and didn't see the tall tree growing beside the highway. One long branch reached out to him like greedy fingers, catching the

*141*

back of his velvet cloak and snagging him from the saddle. His stallion ran a few more lengths, then slowed and stopped. He turned and whickered inquiringly.

El Halcon kicked his legs and threw his weight up and down, but neither branch nor material would give. He tried to untie his cloak, but his weight made the knot impossible to loosen. Every time he kicked, the tie slipped a little higher above his chest toward his neck. With a frustrated groan, he went still. He dangled several feet above the ground, helpless as a fish on a line.

With a gleeful chortle, Clint drew to a stop in front of the bandit. He crossed his arms casually over his saddle. "Shall I leave you to rot?"

Magdalena didn't give him the satisfaction of a reply. She went for her sword, but he slapped her hand away. "Ask me nicely, and I may cut you down," he said.

"To have you deliver me to Luis? Not likely. If I'm to hang, I'd prefer to do so now instead of for the amusement of Luis and his *cholos*."

Clint peered at the tie, for the first time realizing the danger the bandit was in. He leaned forward to examine the knot—and had to dodge a kick from one of those long legs. He cursed. "I've a mind to leave you there." He turned his mount as if to ride away.

The kick had made the knot slip higher still until it was but a couple of inches below Magdalena's throat. Her words sat ill upon her, and they came out more as a demand than a plea. *"Por favor,* help me get down."

Slowly Clint reined his mount back around. He rode right up to her. Mounted as he was, their faces were almost on a level. After staring at her long enough to make her squirm—had she dared—he dropped his reins and raised both hands.

She waited quietly, expecting him to reach for the knot. Her breath hissed through her teeth as, instead, he went for her hood. She kicked out desperately, trying to rear away, but his mount was too close. Just as the knot slipped higher and his fingers touched her hood, another masked rider galloped up, pistol drawn.

"Get back, boyo," Sean ordered curtly. When Clint went for his saddle pistol, Sean cocked his weapon. "Ye'll no' be so handsome with a hole in that bonny face."

Glaring, Clint backed off, then raised his hands. Sean, holding his weapon on Clint, rode up to Magdalena and gave her a knife. She slit through the knot just as her movements made it slip to her throat. Coughing, she fell to the ground. Her knees sagged with relief, but she forced the faintness away and whistled for Fuego. He trotted up.

She mounted, then rode up to Clint, took his pistol and threw it into the brush. By the time he found it, they'd be long gone. "*Adios*, gringo. You'll have to seek another fish to boast about." She turned to ride away, leaving her cloak in the tree. She had another, and she'd never be able to wear that one again without thinking of how close she'd come to hanging herself.

Clint's voice was grim with resolve when he called after her, "The first requirement for the successful angler is something I've an abundance of, El Halcon: patience. We shall meet again." He didn't bother to watch her leave, choosing instead to keep his stony gaze on Sean until that worthy shifted nervously.

Magdalena galloped off, her spine tingling. When she was safely away, Sean holstered his pistol, wheeled his mount and followed her.

Neither of them saw Clint find his pistol, check it over, holster it, than rein his mount into the shelter of the tree that had caught Magdalena. El Halcon had had the air of a man on a mission, but not a lengthy one, for he had no pack on the back of his mount. If he'd passed this way once, he could well do so again. Clint sat down with his back against the trunk and waited. Patiently.

A mile up the highway, Sean drew even with Magdalena. "We worried when ye were late, and 'tis a blessin' we did." He pulled the mask down. The moonlight glinted off his smile. He pretended to wipe sweat off his brow. "In another twinklin' that stubborn man would've had the shock o' his life."

"Once again, amigo, thank you for being there when I

**143**

need you." Magdalena pulled Fuego to a stop and kissed Sean's cheek, smiling when his blush showed even in the moonlight.

"Go on with ye," he said huskily, giving her shoulder a pat and turning his horse about. "I must get back to me traps. Joaquin is waiting." With a cheery wave, he was off. He didn't notice the shadows lurking beneath the tree as he galloped past.

Clint sent a satisfied look after him and settled himself more comfortably.

Before going to the cavern, Magdalena stopped to bathe in the river, using the bar of strawberry-scented soap she'd filched from Clint's shop to wash the stain away from her skin and some of the dye from her hair. Feeling herself again, she dressed, deciding to leave off the breast binding, and rode on to face Joaquin's music.

The moment she entered the cavern, Joaquin stopped his restless pacing and turned to her. "Why are you so late? *Ay Dios mio*, I was crazy to let you go. Disaster will befall us all, I feel it."

When Magdalena dismounted without retorting, Joaquin's dark eyes narrowed. He stepped up to her and pulled off her hood and hat to appraise her features. He shook his head in despair and muttered, "What have you done now, Magdalena? You look just as you did when you were twelve and stole my reata to practice behind the corral."

Magdalena wanted to hang her head as she had then when he'd scolded her. But she was no longer a child seeking acceptance. She was a woman seeking justice; she could hardly mete it out if she couldn't take it. Magdalena straightened, her spine stiffened by the proud generations of Spanish and Irish blood flowing through it.

"I have been foolish, Joaquin, and almost paid dearly for it. I saw Luis ride out of town two days ago and used the opportunity to search his rooms." She ignored Joaquin's hiss of indrawn breath and continued coolly. "I was not cautious enough and was discovered. The *cholos* gave chase, but I had enough of a lead to make it to the cavern

*144*

before they caught up with me. So now Luis is alerted that we're interested in his rooms and will be doubly cautious. I ruined one of our few advantages by my hastiness. I regret it now, but it's done and I can't undo it. And, tonight, the American almost caught me. If Sean hadn't come to look for me when I was late . . ."

Pasty white, Joaquin collapsed on a stone ledge and covered his eyes with one hand. When his hand dropped, Magdalena winced at the sadness in his dark eyes. "Ah, Magdalena, you shame me and make me proud in one breath. But will seeing the truth of your folly keep you from another? I think not."

Magdalena sat next to him and covered his restless hands with one of her own. "Joaquin, what would you have me do? Abandon my lands, my name, my honor, my very life, and cede all to Roberto's treachery?"

Joaquin shook his head. "No, for I know you'd hate yourself if you did. Nor do I want you to leave. I only want you to be cautious . . ."

"Cautious, bah! We are three against an army. Only daring will let us triumph over such odds." Magdalena's tone softened when Joaquin slumped, for once looking his age. "Come, amigo, don't lose heart. Truly, my first rage has cooled. I'll not attempt the presidio again alone. You have my word on my brother's grave."

Joaquin sat straight again and muttered, "Well, that's something, at least."

Looking at him sidelong, Magdalena purred, "But you will agree, will you not, that there is such a thing as calculated daring?"

Joaquin's head snapped around. "Magdalena! You . . ." His scolding sputtered to a stop as he met her laughing eyes. He cuffed her gently on her stubborn chin. "Ah, *gatito montes*, I love you."

Magdalena hugged him, hard. "And I you." She stood. "Now, let us see if we can satisfy each other and come up with a bold but careful plan. I only got to speak briefly with Sean before he returned to his traps. Did he say where he's camped?"

"Si, he's camped near the channel. He returned yesterday and said he's almost got enough furs to bring in to trade."

"Good. Tell him to stay as near the presidio as possible so he can watch the soldiers. When Luis leaves again, we'll strike. I'm convinced he hides something in his rooms that will give us a clue to Roberto's plans, if we can only find it. Meanwhile, it's time to make our first payment to the indios. Give me the silver we took from Luis."

While Joaquin fetched it, Magdalena went to the pitch black rear of the cave and changed into clean clothes. Then she walked up to her falcon, put on her glove, untied its tether and cued it to her wrist. She speared a raw chunk of meat trimming left over from Joaquin's dinner and fed it to the bird. "So, *mi guapa*, are you ready for more adventures?"

"I will bring her with me when I join Sean," Joaquin said.

Magdalena frowned at Joaquin. "What do you mean? I was going to quarter her with Fuego. You can't join Sean. It's too close to Santa Barbara. You might be recognized."

Joaquin propped one booted ankle over the other and crossed his arms over his chest. "So? You are not the only one who can take risks."

Carefully Magdalena tethered the bird. She took off the glove and slapped it into one palm, trying to dampen her temper. "No, Joaquin, it's too dangerous. I won't allow it."

A sleek dark eyebrow rose. "*You* won't allow it? Since when do I need your permission?"

"You agree that I am leader, do you not?"

"Si, but nor am I a hireling to blindly obey your decrees."

Gold eyes met brown ones, but neither wavered. Finally Magdalena flung the glove away and took a step toward Joaquin. "Please, Joaquin, don't do this. I'll worry . . ."

"Good. It's time you did," Joaquin countered inflexibly. "I'll not hide in this cave while you and Sean take all the risks. When I come into Santa Barbara, I'll disguise myself or wear my mask."

Magdalena had visions of Joaquin locked in the presidio

jail, beaten and starved. She shook her head slightly and shouted, "*No!* If I lose you, nothing will matter any more . . ." Her voice trailed off at Joaquin's complacent nod.

"It is not a pleasant feeling, is it?"

Magdalena snatched up her hat, hood and the pouch of coins and stomped out of the cavern. She didn't ride away quickly enough to miss Joaquin's taunt, "But at least you have the comfort of knowing I'll be cautious . . ."

Enraged, Magdalena had reached the Gaviota Pass before she remembered she'd not reapplied her disguise and was not even wearing her hood. She was reining Fuego in to do both when a deep voice startled her.

"So, my dear, we meet again."

A tall figure stepped from behind the tree that had almost been her end this night. Damn him. He must have realized she'd pass this way again. She should have known he'd be lying in wait. Why did her much-vaunted intelligence always seem to desert her around him? She drew a sigh of relief that at least she was wearing plain brown pants and white shirt now instead of her black attire. Magdalena jerked so hard on the reins that Fuego snorted and shook his head. Easily, she controlled him, then answered coolly, "A felicitation I can do without, señor." Magdalena tried to nudge Fuego around Clint, but he caught the stallion's bridle.

When Clint then put his hands about her waist and snagged her from the saddle, Magdalena stifled the urge to struggle and curse him. She had no choice but to brazen it out. He wasn't paying that much attention to Fuego; his eyes were fastened intently on her face. Thank God she'd not reapplied the stain and wax. It was best to meet him thus rather than as Carlotta or Jack, but he was still a menace to more than her safety. Why did her heart thrill, despite herself, at sight of him?

Her face gave no hint of her turmoil when Clint gently shoved her hat back. It hung on her shoulders by its string. Clint tilted her face into the bright moonlight. She met his searching gaze steadily. "What do you want, señor? It's late. I must get home." Ahead of you, she thought.

"I've worried about you. Why did you run away?" He traced one of her high cheekbones.

Their breaths hissed between their teeth even at the slight contact.

His voice went soft and deep. "What we've shared twice now is something to treasure, not something to fear."

Not even possibility of discovery kept Magdalena still then. She backed two safe steps away. "Why do you spy upon me?"

Clint closed the gap between them in one step. "Actually, I was . . . er, hoping to see someone else, but you're much prettier." When her lip curled at his cajoling, he sighed. "You've nothing to fear from me. I want only to help you."

Magdalena responded with a skeptical, unladylike snort. "You want nothing of me, eh, gringo?"

The tall figure stiffened at her mockery. "Perhaps a more telling point is—what do you want from me? Why did you come to me a couple of days ago and use your boundless charms to try to wheedle information out of me?" When she glared at him with dislike, he mourned, "What happened to the girl I met in the strawberry patch? She was as sweet as the moisture I took from her lips. Not bitter as a sour apple."

"Perhaps I've learned much since then. My kind has trusted your kind before—and lived to regret it." Magdalena inched around him as she spoke, but he held out a powerful arm to block her path.

"No, my dear, you'll not leave this little discussion as abruptly as our last one. Come, sit. Tell me what I have done to make you distrust me so." Clint swept a hand before him, indicating a boulder.

After gauging the distance around him, Magdalena begrudgingly sat down. When he sat down beside her, she inched away. She plucked a blade of grass and chewed on it. As her agitation calmed, she realized she'd handled him wrong. Of course he'd be suspicious at the change in her manner. She'd literally thrown herself at him last time. Her attitude now could remind him of his maid if she didn't take care. Distasteful as it was, especially after the way he'd bested her alter ego tonight, it would be expedient to inflate his already swollen opinion of himself. Confrontation would win only his anger and suspicion.

She leaned nearer, confiding, "This is a busy, tiring time for me, señor. Forgive my short temper. Shall we begin again?" His broad grin was so charming she clenched her hands in her lap to deny her response to it.

"I'd be delighted to." Clint slipped two fingers between his shirt buttons and bowed slightly. "Clinton James Browning the Third at your service, señorita. And whom do I have the inestimable pleasure of addressing? You told me your first name, but what is your surname?"

When she didn't answer, Clint turned her averted head around so he could look at her. "Just Inez?"

"Just Inez."

"Ah, a mystery. I do so love mysteries, you know. Now, let me see . . ." Clint nibbled on one fingertip. "Inez . . . Fuentes. No? Ruiz. Montalvo." While Magdalena shook her head, Clint went on, naming every common Spanish surname he could think of, talking faster and faster until her head was flying from side to side. From out of the corner of his mouth he asked, "Dizzy yet?" and held his arms wide hopefully. This time she shook her head demurely, but he saw her mouth quiver.

He was determined to win a smile. "It must be an unusual name indeed. Well, let's see . . . How about Higgin-botham?" The quiver vibrated harder. "Or Pharquar, Fitzhugh-Simmons . . ." Faster he spoke until the strange names ran together. Only when Magdalena giggled did he stop. "Ah, victory at last."

When she looked inquiring, he quoted softly, "'Sing away sorrow, cast away care,' as your much-loved Cervantes would say. See, the world is not such a dreary place with a smile on your lips, is it?"

Her eyes widened. Even in the moonlight he could see the intensity with which she looked at him—as if seeing him for the first time. Before he could comment, she leaped off the boulder. He jumped down to keep her from riding away, but she merely sauntered to a cleft in the rock and plucked a couple of spring flowers. Holding them to her nose, she turned slowly back to look at him.

"Señor, you are kind. But are you also honorable? Will you tell me truly why you have come to California?"

Clint leaned his elbows behind him on the boulder. "Why, to trade, of course."

"Of course. And what else? Already you have been here longer than most traders, and rumor has it in Santa Barbara that your business has not been good. Would it not be more practical for you to sail farther up the coast and try there?"

"Who told you this? Have you relatives there, after all? A certain maid, perhaps?"

She shrugged. "That is not the issue here. If you refuse to answer me, I'll think *you* have something to hide." Her voice was no longer soft. She flung the flowers away and stood straight. "You want my trust and confidences. Give me some reason to share them."

"I have many reasons for staying here and one, at least, concerns you intimately."

"How?"

Clint strode up to her. "I stay partly because of you. You appeal to me, you see. As a thinking man, I wonder about you; as an active man, I admire your grace; as a feeling man . . ." he took her gently into his arms and bent to whisper in her ear, "I want to explore this emotion between us." He kissed his way down from her ear, inhaling the delectable scent of strawberries. When she struggled, he quelled her by holding her wrists behind her back.

"Come, one kiss. If you can deny me the passion I want, I'll leave you be. You have my word."

"Bah, what good is that? You . . ." The insult was smothered by his lips.

This kiss was different to the other two. The warm, masculine mouth rubbed sweetly against her, promising paths of delight if she'd only follow his lead. Slowly he deepened the intensity, showing her his own brand of

150

passion. Magdalena struggled against him and herself, trying to turn away, but he buried his other hand in her hair and tilted her head farther back. He raised his mouth for an instant only to slant it over hers, demanding now rather than asking, but wooing still with flicks of his tongue at her closed mouth. The teasing strokes drained her until all thought of struggling, indeed all thought entirely, ceased. She opened her mouth, greedy as a fledgling hungry for its first bite.

Groaning in mixed passion and triumph, he fed her, letting her sample his lips, tongue and teeth until they were replete and giddy. Only then did he tear his mouth away. Panting, he leaned his forehead into her neck. "Tell me you don't feel this . . . something between us, and I'll leave you alone and never seek you again."

When she was silent, he drew back to look at her. The brilliance of those eyes, golden as the moonlight pouring into them, expressed many things. But joy, alas, was not one of them. He released her and stepped back.

"So, you resent your response to me. While you may be unhappy, my dear, I am not. I've nearly ten years on you, yet I've never met a woman I was more drawn to. Pursue you I will, despite your flighty whims." He stood, knuckles propped on his hipbones, arrogant, unyielding.

Magdalena had been dangerously close to liking him, but this . . . *dictador* reminded her vividly of her grandfather at his worst. Any minute now this brash American would pat her on the head and call her *niña*. Anger stiffened her. She retorted, "Whim, señor? *Mi padre* would not call it a whim for me to be wary of a man who has twice forced himself upon me."

Clint jerked his head back as if she'd slapped him. "That's an unfair accusation. If you'd not enjoyed it as much as I, I'd have let you go. Where are your bruises? Your scars?"

Deep inside where you cannot see them, Magdalena thought, for her emotions did indeed feel bruised. Why was she still so drawn to this man? He had but to touch her for her to forget everything she knew him to be. So wounded he was, looking at her with those fascinating, reproachful blue eyes. Liar, she wanted to scream at him, but she couldn't afford that luxury—yet.

"Well, it matters not. We'll probably not see one another again." She untied Fuego's reins, but he snatched them away.

"Run home, *muchacha*, for now, but know this: I'll find you again if I have to search California's length and breadth. Running from me only makes the chase—and the catch—all the more exciting."

Magdalena jerked the reins back. "Do I look like a fox, gringo?" When he cocked his head to the side as if giving it consideration, she gave a frustrated groan, put one hand flat on his broad chest and shoved him away so she could mount.

He ran to his own horse and mounted, but he was several lengths behind her when he got his cantankerous stallion into a gallop. "Tally-ho," he shouted, laughing as he kicked his horse to a faster pace. Still she drew away, her body moving as one with her mount's, her hair and hat bouncing behind her.

"Dammit, do all California women ride as well as the men?" he called.

She turned her head and saw his jouncing posture for the first time. Fuego slowed as her hands and knees slackened their pressure. Magdalena's mouth fell open. Never had she seen a man ride in such a way. He rode like a . . . she'd not insult her gender so. Like a sack of potatoes. She angled Fuego across the road and folded her hands on her saddle pommel, seeing a golden opportunity to best him. She'd obviously no need to fear his pursuit. It was time he learned women were meant for more than kisses.

"Some of us. Some of us ride better than men." She looked him up and down.

He sighed heavily and slowed his horse to a more comfortable pace. When he was almost even with her, he admitted, "Riding is not one of my talents. Frankly, I despise it."

Magdalena saw the gleam in his eye and knew better than

152

to allow him too close. He might not ride well, but she'd seen how quickly he could move. She backed Fuego, keeping pace with Clint's horse. When she changed the pressure slightly, Fuego obeyed by backing on his powerful hindquarters and flicking his forelegs in the air.

"Show off," Clint grunted. He urged his mount a little faster.

Magdalena took her hat off, covered her heart with it and bowed in her saddle. "If you truly want me to show off, señor, I'll oblige." She jammed the hat on her head, turned Fuego about and urged him into a gallop. Then she kicked off the stirrups, swiveled around and levered her legs under her to face him standing, bending at the knees and swaying to keep her balance.

"You fool girl," Clint yelled, "get down from there. You'll hurt yourself!" He galloped after her.

"Since you are an admirer of Cervantes, señor, cogitate on one of his most practical sayings: 'Let every man mind his own business.'" She touched two fingers to her hat, pivoted and sat in the saddle, all in one unbroken, fluid movement. Her mocking laughter taunted him, and Clint frowned, thinking it sounded familiar. He'd never heard it before, and yet . . . The memory was elusive, as if he looked for it in the wrong place.

Before he could pin it down, disaster struck. Too late, they saw the black bear blocking the highway. With a challenging roar, it stood on its hindlegs, spooking Fuego. He snorted and reared before Magdalena had regained her stirrups. She toppled to the ground—directly in the path of the bear.

Clint saw it all, and by brute strength he held his own stallion's head down when it, too, tried to rear. He pulled his saddle pistol out and sighted just as the bear lumbered toward Magdalena, who was scrambling to her feet. When his terrified mount wouldn't allow him a steady shot, Clint leaped out of the saddle. As Magdalena turned to run, two hairy paws tipped with long, curved claws swiped at her. A loud report rang in the rock-enclosed canyon. The bear toppled over, a hole oozing red mush between its eyes. One paw caught Magdalena's shirt, ripping the back of it. She fell with the bear to the ground.

She screamed and tried to pull away. Clint tossed his smoking weapon aside and ran to her, gently untangling the razor-sharp claws from her white shirt. When he lifted her to her feet into his arms, she clung to him, shivering. He fingered the smooth, supple lines of her spine, sighing with relief when he felt no moisture. He made soothing sounds in his throat and patted her until her quivering ceased.

She looked up at him with wonder in her eyes. He planted a tender kiss on her lips. "Aren't you glad that I shoot better than I ride?"

When he smiled whimsically, her lips trembled into a responding smile that made him catch his breath. Such sweetness it held, such genuine liking. He got the feeling it was the first real smile she'd ever bestowed on him. He bent his head to whisper into her ear. "Would you like me to show you what else I excel at?"

Her smile deepened as she demurely shook her head. She pulled away, then went solemn again as she looked up at him. "You have my deepest thanks, señor."

"The only thanks I ask for is to hear my name upon your lips."

"Clint, thank you." She turned to her mount.

He fetched his pistol and mounted with her. "Don't you think I deserve to at least be told how I can contact you?"

She settled her hat upon her head, then gathered her reins. "If the good *Dios* wills that we meet again . . ." She trailed off and shrugged, then kneed her mount into a trot.

She let him follow her for the first few miles; then, with a look he would have sworn was regretful, she urged her mount into a gallop. His own horse was not as swift as hers, so he could only watch the gap between them widen.

"This won't be the end of it, *querida*," he called. He frowned when soft, mournful words drifted back to him.

"It has to be, Clint." And then she was gone.

He slowed to a trot, then a walk as he contemplated the woman who'd just left him. This third meeting had firmed

154

his sense that there was something between them too valuable to relinquish easily. Whatever her reservations were, or her fears, he would set them to rest. He grinned wryly. If she let him. For this meeting had confirmed something else as well: This woman was unlike any he'd ever known. She had strange talents and a will as inflexible as a man's. Would it bend to his as God had intended? For the first time, he wondered. But only briefly. She was a woman; he was a man. She'd soon savor those differences as much as he did and let him help her in her little difficulties. Women were not meant for the troubles she obviously faced.

He plodded down the highway, confident as Alexander planning his Arabian expedition. From somewhere the thought struck him: Alexander never reached Arabia. He was cut down in his prime and his empire was chopped to pieces. Clint snorted and urged his stallion faster. But the thought remained.

When Carlotta brought the breakfast tray the next morning, Clint was restless. He nodded when she set the tray down, but then bestirred himself. "Carlotta, I've a guest tonight. Please prepare one of your best meals."

Magdalena studied the door's wood grain to give herself time to compose her voice. She'd slept little last night, for once again, Clint had raised hope in her that he was more man than she credited. He was certainly no coward; a coward would have left her to face the bear alone. Had he missed or simply wounded the animal, then he, too, could have been killed. "Very well, señor. Male or female?"

"Female. The pretty señorita we saw at the market stand, Angelina Rivas."

Nodding, Magdalena left. When she reached the galley, she slammed through cupboards to see what she had on hand. She wasn't particularly concerned about seeing Angelina again. That one was so self-absorbed she'd probably not even notice her. But Angelina's duenna was another matter. Even though she and Angelina had never gotten along, their families had often been together. Isabelle,

155

Angelina's duenna, had bandaged many a knee for her. Perhaps Angelina wouldn't bring her. Isabelle would disapprove of this dinner, as would Jose and Tomas.

Magdalena's eyes focused on what she'd set out. Beef liver, onions and squash. Three of the foods Angelina hated most. Magdalena gripped a squash so tightly her nails scarred it. She methodically put the items back and took out the ingredients for the savory beef stew Clint had enjoyed.

But the mundane task of preparation was not distraction enough, and finally Magdalena had to acknowledge the truth. She was jealous. She hadn't really actively disliked Angelina until Clint had become interested in her. She thought of Clint kissing Angelina as he'd kissed her . . . Her stomach roiled in protest. And no matter how much her mind sneered at her for caring, care she did.

Magdalena grunted when she cut the tip of her finger with the sharp knife. She flung the knife away and sat down at the table to suck her finger. So, he was no coward. What did that prove except that he wasn't without some redeeming qualities? He was still aiding Roberto. What other reason would he have to stay so long? He was her enemy, she told herself through clenched teeth; but it did no good. She covered her eyes with the heels of her hands and rubbed wearily. So, *dictador*, *rufian* and *picaro* that he was, she wanted him. Last night had only deepened her forbidden attraction to him. She wanted those kisses that made her forget, however briefly, the harsh realities life had taught her. She wanted those strong arms to shield her, even knowing their protective might was flight from right. In short, he appealed to all her worst instincts: lust, cowardice, weakness, envy.

Rising, Magdalena arched the kinks out of her spine, trying to do the same with her thoughts. She had no rights over Clint, and less reason to want any. Since he weakened her so, her only recourse was to leave. Soon Sean would arrive. He could watch the presidio movements while she tried to recruit a band and did what she could to help the indios. Clint would soon lose interest in Inez and Carlotta. Away from him, she'd be herself again.

Her little talking to herself achieved little. When Angelina arrived that night, breath-taking in her expensive scarlet silk dress with tight, V-indented waist, melon sleeves tapering at the elbow to pearl-buttoned wrists, Magdalena felt herself actually turn green. Even when her parents had been alive, she'd never owned so fine a dress. The fact that she'd never sought one was little consolation when she, the very picture of an india servant, was forced to serve such a vision. Her dismay increased when she saw Isabelle enter behind her charge, a glum look on her face as she nodded coolly to Clint's greeting.

A lace fichu covered Angelina's deep bosom, matching the white lace mantilla over her shining raven hair. She giggled flirtatiously, fluttering her impossibly long eyelashes when Clint bowed over her hand.

"Never has my ship been graced by one so fair," he said, straightening.

"You are too kind, señor. I don't deserve such high praise." She smiled at Clint complacently.

Magdalena snorted, fidgeting where she stood with the tray of wine and glasses. Clint and Angelina looked at her. Mutely she held out the tray, her eyes downcast. Clint took the open bottle and poured three glasses, set the bottle down on the linen-covered table and waved Magdalena away.

"This is the finest Spanish sherry. I think you'll enjoy it," he said, handing a glass to each of his guests.

Warily Magdalena stepped around Isabelle. She felt the woman's eyes on her face as she passed. She sighed in relief when she reached the galley. Her hands shook slightly as she sliced dainty triangles of roast beef and bread. If she kept her face averted, she just might make it through this evening without Isabelle's recognizing her. If only she hadn't planned such an elaborate meal to appease her guilty conscience, she'd not need to enter and exit so often.

Bracing her shoulders, Magdalena picked up the tray and entered the cabin Clint had set up as a dining room. At first she was too busy looking humble to heed the conversation, but then a name caught her attention.

"*Juan Negro*, you may prefer to call him, señor, but I

157

prefer the name more and more are giving him—El Halcon. You may not believe him capable of such a feat, but many others do." As she held the tray out, Magdalena looked from Angelina's teasing expression to Clint's exasperated one. He, Angelina and Isabelle all sat on different sides of the square table.

Clint sighed his impatience. "Who else is spreading the tale?"

Angelina took a triangle and set it daintily on her pewter plate before answering. "Julio Velasquez, Roberto de Sarria's vaquero, has told many how the bandit held a falcon affectionately, almost like a . . . *cómeo se dice?*"

"In English we'd call it a familiar, an animal a witch can change into."

Angelina nodded vigorously. "Si, si, that's it. Since he disappeared so quickly on the beach and harbors a falcon for a pet—who can say that he's not a witch?" Angelina spread her hands wide.

"Aside from the fact that witches don't exist, there's one little matter that needs explaining." Clint's voice was as dry and rustling as autumn leaves.

Swallowing a bite of beef, Angelina queried, "What is that?"

"His horse. If he changed into a falcon, did his horse change into a flea and hitch a ride on *his* back?"

Angelina wiped her mouth on her napkin. "Anything is possible, señor." She shrugged, apparently unimpressed by his logic.

Clint's mild interest in her cooled further. How could anyone be so credulous, even a woman? "Well, whether he's mortal or magical, he'll be in chains or get his wings clipped if your brother and I have anything to say to it." Clint's eyes were drawn by a movement at the door. Carlotta stood there, her face sallow under her dark skin, her eyes going intently from his face to Angelina's. She seemed mightily interested in their conversation. Why?

When he raised an eyebrow at her and chided, "We're ready for the next course," she hurried out. He turned back

to Angelina, but he noticed Isabelle staring after his maid, a frown on her round, unlined face.

"Señora? Is something wrong?"

Still looking at the door, she shook her head slightly, as if to herself, and answered, "No, señor." But she peered at Carlotta's averted face when his maid entered with the dinner tray.

Clint was distracted by Angelina's, "And what do you think of California?"

"It's one of the loveliest, most diverse lands I've ever seen. It's a mystery to me that Mexico has done no more than she has to settle it." When the three women stiffened, he added hastily, "With the help of those of you already here, of course."

"Jose says the life we know is doomed. With every settler, more will want to come until the land is gone. Then greedy eyes will fall on our holdings until the ranchos are no more." Angelina parroted the words between bites of beef stew.

"And you do not agree?"

"If such occurs, it will be long after you and I are gone. Why worry about something I cannot change?" Angelina licked her fingers daintily.

"Indeed. Would you care for more stew?" When Angelina nodded, Clint served her another generous portion, thinking he'd never seen a creature so unabashedly bound by her senses. He both liked her and despised her for it.

Carlotta jerked up the empty serving dish, clattering ladle against rim. He glanced at her in time to see her looking at Angelina with contempt before she lowered her eyes and limped out. There'd been something else in her expression as well. Almost . . . resignation. As if she'd not been surprised to hear Angelina voice such sentiments. As if she'd heard them before. Clint glanced at Isabelle to see her staring thoughtfully after Carlotta. So, he wasn't the only one who considered his maid mysterious.

He listened with half an ear as Angelina continued her train of thought. "Besides, *mi padre* doesn't agree with Jose. What we hold, we keep, he says. Jose is too . . .

159

intense. He sometimes sees trouble where there is none. After all, he is the only one of our people who clings to the foolish notion that Roberto de Sarria was involved in Carlos's death."

"Angelina! I'm sure Captain Browning has no interest in local affairs," Isabelle interrupted with a glare at her charge.

"To the contrary, señora, I'm very interested. Who is this Carlos I keep hearing about?" Clint propped his arms on the table and bent his most charming smile upon Angelina. No one noticed Carlotta's approach or that she hovered in the doorway upon hearing Angelina's reply.

"Carlos was the grandson of Ramon de Sarria, the first owner of El Paraiso. He was killed by Indian renegades shortly after being sent away by Ramon. Carlos's sister blamed Ramon and stabbed him, then fled, leaving Roberto as sole heir to El Paraiso. No one has seen or heard of her in over two years. It's assumed she's dead."

"Was she seen in the act?"

"Not exactly. But my own father saw her come out of Ramon's study holding the bloodied knife, with blood on her gown and hands. What more evidence is needed? If she's not guilty, why did she flee, leaving all to Roberto? She was seen shortly after Carlos's death attacking Ramon with that same knife."

Steepling his fingers under his chin, Clint asked, "And how long after Carlos died was Ramon killed?"

"Several months, I think. Why?"

"That's a long wait for a crime of passion, as this seemed to be. Would she not have killed him right away or covered her crime more stealthily?"

"She tried to kill him . . ."

"Once, you say. Then once again, months later? Something isn't right."

Isabelle leaned forward. "Indeed, señor, I have always thought it odd, too. She was a deeply emotional girl, perhaps capable of such a crime. But not cold-bloodedly. She and Ramon had reconciled by the time he died."

Angelina frowned. "I didn't know you felt this way, Isabelle. You've never agreed with Jose before . . ."

"You never asked my opinion," Isabelle reminded her.

Angelina leaned back in a huff, crossing her arms over her breasts. "You were always lenient with her, but never with me. When she'd come in wearing breeches, covered in dust from head to toe, you'd pat her head. Yet if I got so much as a smudge on my cheek you scolded me."

"I was not her duenna. Besides, you were two different girls. You wanted to be a lady. She didn't."

"*That*, at least," Angelina retorted, "I agree with."

Clint interrupted, "What did you say she was doing when she came out of the study, Angelina?"

"Carrying the knife."

"But what was she doing with it? Wouldn't it have been more sensible to hide it?"

"You didn't know her. When she was angry, she was not sensible."

"But if she'd reconciled with her grandfather, why was she angry? And again, what did she intend with the knife?"

"Now that you mention it, señor, I believe Señor Rivas said at the time that she threatened Roberto with it," Isabelle said slowly. Her large dark eyes met Clint's.

Angelina waved a disdainful hand. "She was merely trying to cover up her crime. What she said meant nothing."

Clint pounced on the words. "What did she say?"

"She called Roberto a . . . murderer . . ." Angelina's voice trailed away, then grew strong again when Isabelle and Clint exchanged a triumphant look. "Now you're both being as . . . unreasonable as Jose. Roberto is no murderer!"

"Forgive me, señorita, but your opinion in this matter is not exactly based upon reason." When Angelina looked affronted, Clint pointed out, "If she was cool-headed enough to divert suspicion to someone else, she was calm enough to get rid of the knife and her bloodied gown. You can't have it both ways."

"But . . . but . . ." Angelina sputtered.

Clint cocked his head. "Yes?"

"But we don't know what happened that night. She was probably angry at Ramon again for some reason. She . . ."

"Exactly. We don't know what happened that night. The evidence you state is damning, I admit, but not conclusive. In my country, at least, even murderers are presumed innocent until it's known otherwise. Is Mexican justice any less fair?"

A snort preceded Carlotta's entrance into the cabin. As she cleared the rest of the table she muttered, "Tell my people about Mexican justice." She paused at the door with the burdened tray to look at Clint. "Will there be anything else, señor?"

His head popped up. So softly and sweetly she'd spoken, in a tone that seemed oddly familiar. He'd never heard it from her before, that he knew. Then where? And she looked at him strangely, too. Searching, measuring. He had the queerest feeing that for once she didn't find him lacking.

His answer was slow. "Only the brandy, Carlotta. Ladies?"

Angelina looked hopefully at Isabelle, but Isabelle shook her head sternly. "Your padre would never allow it, and you know it."

"One glass, then, Carlotta." With a smile and a nod, she exited. She was acting most peculiar tonight. Tense one moment, smiling the next.

A rustling of skirts accompanied the light footsteps that paused beside his chair. Angelina propped one hip on the table and smiled at him. "Captain, are there any new dances in your country you can show me?"

Isabelle's scandalized, "Angelina!" didn't faze her charge.

Angelina leaned down to Clint, seeming not to notice as her arm brushed his. "We've been so grim lately it's an age since we've had a fiesta. Will you not dance with me?"

Clint sent a doubtful look about the cluttered cabin. Crates and rigging were heaped in every corner. But there was a long walkway around the table. Why not? If this pretty, sensual girl wanted to flirt with him, he'd gladly reciprocate. Where was the harm with her duenna present? He sprang to his feet and bowed.

"I'd be honored, señorita." Humming a bouncy tune, he took her in his arms. "As for new dances, there's nothing I enjoy more than a waltz. What about you?"

The brilliance of Angelina's smile was answer enough. Clint had to hold her close in the limited space, so the sight that greeted Magdalena when she returned was a man and woman using a dance—with no music—as an excuse to embrace. Her fingers tightened on the tray until her nails bent, but she said nothing.

She fought to keep her face calm, for she felt Isabelle looking at her, but in that moment she hated Angelina. Always it had been thus. Angelina was a natural coquette. There wasn't a thing in breeches that she didn't try to draw within her fascinating orbit. The ease with which she succeeded infuriated the girl who'd always taken pains to hide her envy. She'd never cared that the boys on neighboring lands had always flocked around Angelina while giving herself a wary berth, for she'd known their reasons. Youths her age were intimidated by a girl who could outride, outfence and outrope them. While she'd never wanted any of Angelina's suitors, there had been times, in the quiet of her heart, when she'd wished for a small measure of that charm or for one handsome boy to look at her with the same longing.

The feelings Clint inspired when he lowered his head to Angelina's level to hum in her ear proved she'd not changed so very much from that adolescent. Envy, pain, confusion, longing all swirled in her mind in a miasma that fogged her brain. But this pain seemed sharper, somehow. She refused to wonder why, for the answer was one she didn't dare pursue. So what if Clint was as susceptible to Angelina as the boys from her childhood? What else could she expect from the gringo? It should be Angelina she was concerned for.

Angry with herself, but more furious with them, Magdalena stalked around their whirling figures to slam the tray down on the table. She was too upset to care that she stepped out of her role yet again.

Clint looked up at the sound. He frowned at the look on

Carlotta's face, wondering what was wrong. He was becoming uncomfortable at the way Angelina was clinging to him, so he used the opportunity to pull her arms from about his neck. He kissed her hand.

"Gracias, señorita. That was most enjoyable. I hope we have the opportunity again. With music." And people. Many people. He'd no mind to marry this pretty armful, and he couldn't help but wonder if she was angling for exactly that. Her behavior was certainly bold for a woman born and cultivated by the *gente de razon*. He squelched the thought that she simply seemed too soft and easy. He wanted a tall, lithe body that had to be coaxed . . .

Turning to Carlotta, he raised a hand when she would have exited. He'd only intended to ask what was wrong, but her resentful glare changed his mind. What the hell was wrong with her tonight? One moment she looked at him with more liking than she'd ever shown, yet now she almost seemed to hate him. "Wait," he ordered imperiously, matching her frown with a scowl.

"You haven't been dismissed. Pour my brandy." He snapped his fingers.

He watched with grim satisfaction as her head reared up. The anger she'd been struggling to hide leaped full-blown into her eyes. She opened her mouth, but then her eyes slipped to Isabelle's curious face. She looked down. He saw her shoulders lift, so deep was the breath she took, then she limped forward and poured him a glass with a steady hand. She set it down on the tray and folded her arms, her pugnacious chin daring him to say more.

He dared. "Well, bring it here." He'd almost forgotten the other two women, so fiercely did he glare at her, trying to goad her into showing her true colors. Let her tell him to go to hell. Fury provoked rashness—and truth. He'd yet have it from her and discover why she'd come here.

Even Angelina seemed shocked at his harshness. "You should not treat your servants so, señor."

"I don't care for that look about her mouth. I'm master here and she'll yet acknowledge it."

Angelina's shaking head seemed to galvanize Carlotta.

Down went her chin, up went her hand to clench about the wine glass. Slowly but steadily she limped toward him and extended the glass. He tried to meet her eyes, but she wouldn't look at him. He'd decided his ploy had not worked, so he was shocked when she released the glass right before he touched it and stepped back. It shattered on the planking, brandy splattering on his fashionable mole-skin pants from ankle to thigh, glass flying, but luckily missing him. Isabelle and Angelina gasped in concert.

The anger he'd pretended to became real. He brushed at his trousers. "What the hell was that for?"

"So clumsy of me. Forgive me, señor. Would you care for another glass?" She poured another glass and advanced on him. Part of her was aware of the way the two women gaped at her unseemly boldness, but the hurt, confused part didn't care.

Prudently he backed a pace, waving her away. "No thank you. I'll get my own. Fetch a broom and clean up this mess." He stepped about her to make his apologies to the ladies, who were still casting appalled looks at Carlotta.

Angelina eyed him doubtfully when he didn't reprimand his rude servant, but she let him take her hand. "I've enjoyed this evening, señor." She looked disapprovingly at the glass on the floor. "Most of it. You must come to our house soon for dinner. Jose will be back from our rancho in a few days. I'll send someone with an invitation."

"I'll be delighted to attend. Forgive this scene, but I had my reasons for acting as I did." When Carlotta marched back in, broom in hand, her back ramrod straight, he added wryly, "I hardly think my maid was cowed."

Angelina threw a hard look at the maid. "Perhaps she should be."

Isabelle's puzzled eyes watched as Carlotta swept up the glass. Clint saw her expression. "What is wrong, señora? You've watched her oddly all evening."

"I don't know, Captain Browning. She . . . reminds me of someone. I don't know who. Her defiance is familiar, wrong though it is."

"Indeed? How interesting." He, too, turned to watch

Carlotta, who was beyond range of their soft-voiced exchange.

Angelina rearranged her mantilla and fichu, fidgeting until they finally turned back to her. "She's only a maid. What is it you both find so interesting about her?" She seemed genuinely mystified as she looked from Clint to Isabelle.

Clint opened his mouth, but Isabelle shook her head slightly. She took her charge's arm. "Nothing, Angelina. You're right. She's but a maid."

But, as Clint escorted them to the door, she looked back over her shoulder at Carlotta until she could see her no longer.

Clint hastened back to the cabin, intent on taking up with Carlotta where they'd left off. Dammit, he'd a gullet full of mystery. First that cursed bandit, then the strawberry girl, now this odd girl who looked so much the maid but acted the princess. Since he had no access to the first two, he'd take advantage of his proximity to the third.

But when he descended to the cabin, he found it empty. Carlotta's cabin was likewise deserted, the bed neatly made. Clint hurried out on deck, but saw no sign of her. He slammed a big fist into his palm. "Damn her! By my eyes, she's delayed the reckoning, but come it will." He stomped down to his own cabin.

Magdalena, dressed as her alter ego beneath her maid's clothes, slipped from a crouch behind the capstan to ease down the gangplank to the beach.

# Chapter 7

"We met here on the level, and each played as his wit
and courage served to beat the other."
**Act I, DON JUAN TENORIO**

Magdalena stuck the minuscule hide pouches in her cloak
pockets. She saddled Fuego, tied down her hood, put on her
hat, strapped on her sword and vaulted lightly into the
saddle. Black Jack had a duty to perform. Besides, only
action would ease this restlessness, this unseemly regret for
things that never were and longing for things that never
could be.

Never had she coveted the man Angelina flirted with, but
neither had she felt so possessive about that man before. No
matter that she had no claim on Clinton Browning. The part
of herself she'd always feared ignored reason; that part
wanted him, right or wrong. Magdalena the bandit scorned
the Yankee, but Magdalena the woman longed to call him
her own. All her lectures to herself about his untrustworthy,
unscrupulous nature were impotent before the longing to
believe in him.

Jerky with frustration, Magdalena reined Fuego out of the

cavern and galloped down the beach. If she'd only herself to consider, perhaps she'd risk trusting him. But she had two others living who would suffer if she were wrong, and four ghosts she'd never lay to rest until she'd confronted Roberto. She *had* to listen to her head instead of . . . Magdalena clamped down on the reins and her thoughts and turned toward the mission.

She paused on the mission road to look at the building that was luminous beneath the moon. Its architecture harmoniously blended Moorish and Roman design, with rounded Moorish towers abutting a pedimented and pilastered front. The living and working quarters jutted out in a long left wing with a series of arches. Glancing at the chapel, Magdalena wondered if Father Franco were within, praying for the fate of his fief and his scattered flock.

For a craven moment, she was tempted to seek him and beg his aid, but she reined Fuego resolutely past the main building west to the Indian pueblo. His hoofbeats rang in the desolate silence as she entered the walled area. The houses were the usual adobes with red tile roofs but were much smaller and simpler than the townhouses in Santa Barbara. They adjoined one another, back to back, along straight, narrow streets. Magdalena saw many doors sagging to one side. She tied Fuego to a post and tentatively knocked on one such door. When she received no answer, she entered and lit the candle in her pocket.

The one room was empty save for a filthy woven mat on the floor. Rats scurried out of the threatening circle of light, one running over her boot. Shivering, Magdalena blew out the candle and stuck it back in her pocket, rushing outside to take deep breaths of the scented night air. The desertion of this hut must have been recent, for the bloodied rags on the mat still smelled of disease.

She walked down the streets until, finally, she saw a glimmer of light under a door. She tossed a sack in the doorway, her throat tight with tears at this ugly end to a noble dream.

How sad Papa would be to see the results of the desecularization he'd fought for, she thought. If he'd known how it would end, he would have heeded the padres' dire warnings of waste, sloth and abuse. If only he'd lived, perhaps he could have helped administer the mission, ensuring that some of its riches reached those they had supposedly been kept in trust for. Instead, the greedy administradores bilked the once rich wealth of the church—with Mexico's tacit consent. How she hated the Mexicans! It was not enough that last November Californios, led by the dashing Juan Bautista Alvardo, had expelled Mexico's latest bumbling gobernador and declared California "a free and sovereign state." Their authority was fragile and could be usurped by either Mexico or the greedy foreigners who coveted their lands.

Mexico sent no troops to enforce her will only because she was too occupied elsewhere. The time would come when she would no longer tolerate even the limited independence Californians had wrested for themselves, or the Americans would switch from diplomacy to war. But whatever the outcome, Magdalena knew the wonderful days of her youth would soon be only a memory. Perhaps it was as well that none of her family, especially Papa and Ramon, had lived to see what had become of the California they'd so loved. This ruination, everywhere she looked, was but the beginning, Magdalena feared.

The vast mission herds were scattered: slaughtered, bartered or pilfered by everyone from the settlers Mexico had granted with mission lands to the Indians who had once cared for them. The bountiful crops were no more, the industries such as shoemaking, carpentry and stone cutting abandoned. And worst of all, the padres' children, the neophytes the friars had been cruel to be kind to, were now worse off than when they'd been forced to labor for the church.

At least then they'd had a measure of dignity. Those who had conformed to the padres' rigid doctrines had known modest happiness and security. They'd obeyed the rules for reward or broken them and been punished, but at least they'd known what to expect. Now they had no one to care for them or fight for their welfare. Weakened by disease, starved as often as not, forced to labor yet sharing nothing of their profits, they had little hope. No wonder so many had deserted and died. What had they to live for?

Magdalena had not expected to have enough sacks to go around, but when she'd walked through the entire village, she had three sacks left, so many huts were deserted. She'd turned to retrace her steps when a sinewed arm caught her about the throat, knocking her hat askew. She gasped for air and clawed at the arm.

It was as inflexible as the harsh voice that spoke in slightly accented Spanish. "What do you here, my fine caballero? No longer will we let you dally with our women without a fight."

The arm loosened to allow her a response. Magdalena coughed, and she didn't have to feign Jack's hoarse tones this time. "Look there, in that doorway, and you'll see why I have come."

She felt surprise tense the muscular man behind her and sensed him peering over her shoulder. She took advantage of his distraction and stamped her boot down on his moccasined foot, simultaneously jamming her elbow into his ribs. He grunted, and his grip slackened. Agilely, she writhed away, unsheathing her sword with one hand, straightening her hat with the other.

The Indian had time for one inhalation before his windpipe constricted away from Magdalena's sword point. "Maybe a fight is what I'm looking for instead, indio," she mocked him.

For a moment they eyed one another, the stocky, swarthy Indian and the tall, lithe figure garbed in black. Then Magdalena sheathed her sword and folded her arms, feet braced apart, ignoring the way he fingered the knife stuck into his tattered pants.

"I see you'd welcome a fight, but you mistake your enemy. Go, look at what I've thrown in that doorway, and if you still want to fight, I'll oblige you."

Warily the Indian inched around her, backing to the doorway so he faced her. He stooped and groped, all without taking his eyes off her.

*170*

Magdalena smiled under her hood. Indeed, she must make a sinister figure for such a man to be so wary. His face was painted, his arms scarred from battle, his features those of a hard and desperate renegade. Magdalena was rather flattered, but quick to foster his impression.

When he picked up the pouch and straightened, she ordered, "Open it."

He complied, dumping the contents into his palm. The silver coins clinked, glinting fitfully in the moonlight. Magdalena relished his change of expression.

The smoldering eyes widened and the hard jaw slackened. "Why do you leave this for my people?"

"Because it is rightfully theirs. It comes from the dons who live on their lands and the soldiers who persecute them. It is little enough recompense for years of slavery, but it is a beginning. Do you see I wish you no ill, that to the contrary, I want to help?"

A reluctant nod, then a simple, "But why?"

Only the wind answered for a moment, then came the enigmatic reply. "Because *mi padre* would want it so, and because your enemies are mine. I want the Mexicans gone as badly as do you. Would it not make more sense for us to ally our efforts?"

"How do you know I fight them?"

"Do you tend the herds painted for war?"

The Indian felt his face. "I tend Don Roberto's herds no longer. Except for my own use." He looked at her boldly, daring her condemnation.

Magdalena chuckled. "Ah, I see we have more in common than I thought. I, too, have 'tended' his herd from time to time." The door behind him creaked open and a timid girl peeped out.

"Miguel, what is happening? Why are you still here?"

Magdalena saw the Indian's face soften as he reassured the girl that all was well. Discreetly Magdalena melted away to give them privacy, but she caught Miguel's plea, "Please, Juana, come with me . . ." before she was out of earshot.

A few minutes later, Miguel walked silently up to her, his

expression glum. "She will not come to my hut in the hills. She has never known the old way of life and says she would not be happy there."

"Perhaps if you had more to offer her, she would come. With money, you can build her a house and buy cattle to begin your own ranch." Magdalena watched his eyes narrow thoughtfully. "A systematic drain on the resources of the dons will be more effective than an occasional rustled steer. Come, join with me and take back some of what is yours."

Miguel leaned back against a crumbling wall and looked at her steadily. "You are El Halcon, are you not?"

Slim shoulders shrugged gracefully. "So some call me. I prefer to be known as Black Jack, but if the other pleases you, use it."

"Already Luis has put a price on your head. Danger will follow you. And those with you."

"As does danger menace those who act alone without support." Magdalena let him digest that fact before adding, "I can promise you nothing. But if I succeed, you succeed. And, amigo, I warn you, I will win, or die trying." She took the last three sacks out of her cloak and tossed them to him. He caught them deftly.

"Distribute this to others in need, and think on my words. If you decide to join us—I work with two others—meet me on San Buenaventura point at midnight two nights hence. If you've friends you trust, who fight well and can keep their mouths shut, they are welcome, too. Whatever your decision, I wish you well." Magdalena touched two fingers to her hat, bowed slightly, then blended into the night to round up Fuego, leaving Miguel staring thoughtfully after her.

When she arrived back at the ship, she was optimistic for the first time in a long while. She wondered how many other disgruntled *vaqueros* had left Roberto. He'd always been a hard taskmaster and had grown worse in recent years, from all accounts, with no one to stifle his ruthlessness. If Miguel joined her, she'd have to question him about the situation at El Paraiso.

Dressed as Carlotta, Fuego stabled and fed, she returned

to the ship, so deep in thought she didn't notice the tall figure planted before her until she'd almost barreled into it. Strong hands caught her shoulders. She looked up into eyes glittering with fury even in the moonlight.

"So, you return from another rendezvous! What lies will you feed me this time?"

Magdalena wrenched away. "I won't bother. Anyone who treats me with the contempt you showed before your guests this night doesn't deserve the hypocrisy of a lie. Even servants have pride!"

Clint snorted his disgust. "And employers deserve respect. If you don't give it, why should I? Especially to a woman who lies and sneaks in and out at all hours of the night?" His hands reached for her again, but she danced away, forgetting to limp.

"I'll soon trouble you no more!" she snapped unthinkingly, her hurt at his actions earlier overriding common sense.

His eyes lifted from her leg to her face, where they latched like leeches. Indeed, her blood drained away when he goaded, "You're no more an Indian than I am. I don't know why you disguise yourself, but Isabelle was not fooled, either. It almost seems she knows you. Odd, is it not?"

"No, I used to work in her household, years ago."

"Ah, I see, that would explain much," he agreed lightly. But his voice hardened when he added, "If I believed you. Which I don't."

With a flick of her hand, Magdalena showed her opinion of that. "Believe what you will. If you wish me to go, I'll gladly oblige. Such a threat I am, I realize."

When her eyes drifted down her own slim figure, then down his muscular frame, he clenched his hands. "Oh, not yet. You'll go when I'm ready to let you, not before."

Magdalena curtsied in mock humility. "Yes, master. Anything else, master? Do you want me to garb myself in sackcloth and ashes, perhaps, to show my penitence for daring to defy you?"

The grinding of strong white teeth was audible even

above the sea sounds before Clint swallowed and answered blandly. "Perhaps I want to see you in less. *Much* less." Clint's mouth quirked in satisfaction when Carlotta stiffened and flounced away. He'd goad her out of that cool control yet and get some truth from her for a change.

Her retort drifted to him on the sea breeze. "Never, for you, gringo."

Clint's satisfaction waned under her taunt. For someone else, then? Jack, perhaps? And why the hell did the possibility bother him?

He still couldn't answer that question the next morning when a tall, red-headed stranger entered the shop just as Carlotta was serving breakfast. She clattered the plate of bread on the table as she caught sight of him, then she looked away and stacked the bread back in a neat pile.

Clint looked curiously from her flushed face to the stranger's watchful gaze. The tall man's bright blue eyes held a mixture of amusement and exasperation as he watched Magdalena limp about the cabin to straighten it. When she flung a minatory glare over her shoulder, his lips quivered, but he turned away to examine a pile of men's garments.

Pretending an interest in the accounts spread before him, Clint absorbed every nuance of their by-play. He'd eat this month's records—and his sorry profit, too—if this pair didn't know each other. The question was, how intimately? And why was he here? He shoved his chair back and rose, pasting his best shopowner's smile upon his face.

"Are you interested in expanding your wardrobe, sir?"

"Aye, eventually, but I've really come for supplies to make me camp up on San Buenaventura point more homelike. I need . . ." Clint automatically collected the staples the stranger listed, but his ears were pricked for more. Subtlety was obviously not the man's strong suit. Now not only Carlotta knew where he camped. As Clint listened to the long list, he became more and more intent, less on the man's words than on the lilting sound of them. Somewhere he'd heard this man speak before. But where? Surely he'd not forget a man of such size, with flaming hair

174

and hyacinth blue eyes . . . My God, that was it! One of Jack's men had been a big Irishman with red hair. This man had held a gun on him last night, allowing Jack to escape when, finally, he'd literally been treed. Clint dropped his eyes to hide his angry recognition. Most troubling of all—this man knew Carlotta.

When the sizable pile was paid for—in otter pelts rather than hides—Clint asked casually, "Have you been in California long?"

"Less than a year. I originally be from County Cork, Ireland. And you?"

"The Chesapeake Bay area. My home is not far from Baltimore."

"And what brings you here?"

"Trading, of course." Clint held out his hand. "Clinton Browning, at your service. And you are . . .?"

The man shook his hand with a firm grip. His generous mouth opened, but then he looked beyond Clint's shoulder. His mouth snapped shut, and Clint's nerves tingled with the knowledge that Carlotta had signaled the man not to reveal his name.

Instead, he said only, "A fellow new to trappin', but mighty fond o' freedom. And justice." Clint's hand was released with this last, which was enunciated with a penetrating look. Clint had the feeling he'd just been warned.

The Irishman hefted the heavy burlap sack over his shoulder without a twitch of a muscle. "Well, I'll be off. The moon's full and bonnie tonight, and I want to be set up to enjoy it." With a casual wave, the stranger was gone.

Clint turned to watch Carlotta dust a shelf she'd already dusted three times. He bit his tongue to keep back a sarcastic comment. Tonight, for once, he'd be ready. Either the Irishman or Carlotta would lead him to the bandit. Hiding a complacent smile, he turned back to his accounts.

Fully dressed, Clint listened tensely. When the footsteps came, incredibly light for a "cripple," he rose and stole out of his cabin. He reached the deck in time to see Carlotta

175

disappearing down the plank. He crouched behind the bulwarks and peeked over them and was rewarded for his caution when she paused at the hut to look over her shoulder. He ducked. When he looked again, she was gone. He sprinted over to the hut, expecting to catch her readying a mount, evidencing no infirmity. He banged the door back on its hinges and stormed inside, only to draw up short and curse. He ran back outside and up the beach. But he was too late, for only moon-washed sands greeted him. Either she'd gone another way or she'd run as soon as she reached the beach. Cursing his stupidity, he walked grimly about, trying to find a trace of her footsteps. If he saw none, he'd go directly to the point, for he was still certain she'd meet the Irishman there. If his suspicions were right, Jack would be there, too.

Inside her cavernous stable, Magdalena saddled Fuego with trembling hands. She paused to rest her cheek against his vital warmth and draw calming breaths. Her nerves had been stretched taut since Sean's visit. Clint had been entirely too quiet all day. She'd caught him watching her, but he'd smiled casually when her eyes met his, as if he'd no reason to start guiltily away. Still, she knew he was suspicious of Sean's sudden appearance. This time, she feared not for herself, but for the tall Irishman she'd come to love like a brother.

After all, Clint had met him twice. Seeing him in the cloak of night, with Joaquin along, would be all it would take to jog his memory. It was vital she elude him if he followed her tonight. As soon as she reached the point, she'd help them move camp. It was too dangerous now that Clint knew where it was. Magdalena reined Fuego out of the cavern, skirting the hill away from the beach, her nerves alert for danger, but she saw no sign of Clint.

After greeting Joaquin and Sean with hugs, Magdalena chided Sean, "Amigo, you not only look angelic, you've the innocence of one. Why did you betray your location to the gringo?"

The two men exchanged glances, and Magdalena knew they'd been discussing her. When Joaquin shrugged, Sean peered into Magdalena's face as he replied, "Ye need to bait the trap to find out if it's a rat or a mouse invadin' yer larder." When Madgalena's eyes widened, Sean added, "Especially when the cat has become fond o' the rat."

Magdalena drew herself up to her full height. "Are you implying I care for this . . . this . . ."

"So 'twould seem," Sean answered. "Else why have ye stayed so long, put yourself in such danger, yet know no more today than ye did when ye began?"

That stung, truth or not. Magdalena blustered, "As usual, you mistake me. Do you think I'd be so wary of our location if I didn't suspect the gringo's intentions?"

Again Sean and Joaquin looked at one another. This time Joaquin answered. "And once you are certain of them, you will leave?"

"In an instant. Now you've questioned my wit, I suggest you consider your own. Hasn't it occurred to you that if Browning does follow us here, he'll recognize us? Is baiting this trap worth such danger?"

When both men looked crestfallen, Madgalena's voice softened. "Come, amigos, let the cats hide and watch for the rat. If he comes, one of us will question him."

And she knew which one, she thought grimly. For come he would, out of curiosity if nothing else. He'd rebuffed both Carlotta and Inez when they questioned him, but he'd not find Jack so easy to refuse. Besides, she had to prove to Joaquin and Sean that Browning meant nothing to her. Most of all, she had to prove it to herself.

It took them only moments to break up the camp, load the mule and move it and the horses into concealment in the thick brush. Still, they'd barely settled behind some short bushes before a gleaming blond head topped the point. Magdalena's throat closed with disappointment. His eagerness to capture Jack only made his alliance with Roberto more certain; here, alas, was more proof. Shamed by her own regret, Magdalena shoved Joaquin back down and stood. Checking to be sure her hood was securely fastened, she strolled out into the open, one gloved hand resting casually on her sword hilt.

"*Buenas noches,* gringo," she said in Jack's hoarse tones. "We meet again."

Clint whirled, his hand reaching reflexively for his sword before he remembered he'd been in too much of a rush to wear one. The derringer he always kept in his jacket, however, was a comforting weight against his side.

He leaned back against a large boulder, propped one foot behind him and drawled, "As I hoped we would. But I fear this meeting may end a bit differently."

"Indeed?" With a mocking glance at Clint's bare waist, Jack tipped his hat back and propped his cheek in his hand, a study in insolent boredom. "You've a legion waiting to come to your aid, then?"

Clint's retort was closer to a snort. "No, but I need none." Straightening abruptly, Clint dashed his hand into his pocket.

The bandit reacted quicker than he had expected, and his sword was fully drawn by the time Clint had the derringer held at the ready. Bright moonlight glinted off pointed and snubby steel, each held by a steady, capable hand.

With a mocking click of his tongue, Clint goaded, "Come, El Halcon, change into your alter ego, for that's all that will save you now. Skillful as you doubtless are with a blade, you can't outfence a bullet."

A star glanced off the rapier's point as it was reluctantly lowered and sheathed. Clint was surprised and relieved at the easy victory, but he pretended disappointment. "How are the mighty fallen. So easily do you go down to defeat. But the reward you'll bring me will go far toward appeasing my disappointment." When the bandit stood with head bent, Clint tired of baiting him.

Briskly he waved the pistol toward the beach. "Come, let's go. Luis is eager to meet you." Clint watched warily as the bandit stumbled over the rough tufts of grass toward him, unaware of the two guns pointed at him a short distance away. When the bandit swayed and fell, Clint frowned.

"What ails you, man? Are you drunk?" When there was no response, Clint bent down, keeping a wary eye on the sword which was still sheathed, the right hand flung wide. Thus he missed the left hand hidden inside the cloak until it whipped to his throat wielding a slim, deadly stiletto. The hood lifted from the ground, wavering before Clint's eyes like a cobra dancing before striking.

El Halcon's whispered warning sent a chill up Clint's spine. "Drop the gun, gringo. I've lost patience with you, and have more reason to dislike you than you know. If you give me sufficient provocation . . ."

Cursing his gullibility, Clint dropped the derringer. Still holding the dagger to his throat, El Halcon rose to a sitting position and picked up the derringer in his other hand. Prodding Clint in the chest with it, he bade him rise and go to the stump near the edge of the point.

Clint looked wildly about for some distraction, but the barrel stabbing into his back was a cold reminder of the bandit's warning, especially when El Halcon enhanced both with a reflective, "Such a crude weapon. No finesse. I've seldom used one. Perhaps you can refresh my memory as to how it works? I've but to pull this little lever, er, it's called a trigger, I believe . . ."

Clint lunged for the stump, breathing easier when the barrel slipped away. He turned and looked at his tormentor.

Derringer in one hand, stiletto in the other, El Halcon ordered, "Remove your belt."

Clint frowned, his momentary discomposure replaced by anger. "I'll do no such thing. Humiliate me if you please, but this will not be the end of it, I swear." He crossed his arms over his chest and stood firm.

The bandit sighed. "You grow tedious, *yanqui,* and my hand tired. I but intend to tie you to that tree so we can have a quiet little chat. If you'd rather I incapacitate you . . ." With a shrug, El Halcon's thumb cocked the tiny pistol, but it was its aim below the waist that made Clint obey.

When the belt was flung at his head, El Halcon ducked. "Anger makes you foolish. Sit before I'm tempted to punish your insolence."

Gritting his teeth, Clint sat and put his hands behind him as ordered. Pocketing the pistol, but pressing the dagger to

Clint's back, El Halcon wrapped the belt around his wrists several times with one hand, dropped the dagger and latched the belt. He didn't notice the frayed belt hole in the dim moonlight. Picking up the dagger, he scooted several feet in front of Clint and sat cross-legged, studying him in brooding silence.

He played with the dagger, balancing it hilt first, then tip first, on his gloved hand. When Clint's angry struggling ceased, El Halcon said in a soothing voice, "You've but to answer my questions truthfully to win your release."

"I'll sit here until the tide stops coming in before I'll tell you the time of day!" Clint glared into the opaque eye slits, leaning forward. An odd look flickered over his face before he carefully leaned back again.

"Then we'll spend eternity together, for I'll not leave until I have some answers." Jack stabbed the dagger into the ground, put his hands on his knees and leaned forward. "First, why were you with Roberto de Sarria that first night we met?"

"Met! You low-born thief, I'll . . ."

El Halcon cut in suavely, "What manner of business do you conduct with him?" When only curses answered him, the bandit's voice grew hard. "One way or another, I'll have my answers. Freely given or taken matters not to me."

Clint snarled, "Then take them, if you can, you coward! Come, torture an unarmed man and show your true colors."

With a supple uncoiling of his long body that reminded Clint more than ever of a snake, the bandit grabbed the dagger and scooted over to Clint on his knees. Turning the blade so it gleamed in the moonlight, he said evenly, "Answer me, gringo, else I may have to prove your estimation of me right."

Stubbornly, Clint turned his head away. Even when the razor-sharp edge of the stiletto was stropped lightly against his jaw, he didn't flinch.

The tormenting voice went on, "Come, don't make me scar your pretty face. It won't be so easy to seduce the ladies, then." The voice took on a sharper edge when he

**180**

still didn't reply. "No? Perhaps there's something you value more . . ."

Clint sucked in a shocked breath when he felt the gentle but unmistakable poke at his groin. He turned his head and met glittering eyes. He'd have given three of his ships to see their color, but it was too dark.

His own tone was as inflexible as the steel still playing lightly over his privates. "I'll tell you nothing. Scar me or unman me, but I warn you it will only make me hate you more. If it takes me the rest of my life, I'll see you dancing at the end of a rope."

When the dagger was abruptly withdrawn, Clint swallowed a relieved sigh but refused to look away from the glittering eye slits. After another thirty seconds, the bandit blew a rueful laugh and returned the stiletto to the sheath strapped high on his thigh. "You win. But, since you won't defend yourself, I can only draw my own conclusions, and it's your own fault if they're unfavorable to you. Whatever allies you with Roberto, it means harm to someone else or harm to California. And this I warn you: I will discover what it is and see you both brought to justice."

Clint's mouth dropped open. He sputtered, "You'll . . . bring us? *You!*—one of the most wanted criminals in California?" He laughed harshly. "I'm allied with that insufferable don in nothing, but you tempt me to try it just to spite you."

Magdalena paused in rising. "I'd like to believe that, gringo, but the evidence says otherwise. You had your chance to tell me the truth. Now I'll discover it for myself." As she pushed her weight upward, she was shocked to find her arm grabbed and forced behind her back.

Leaning forward, Clint shook off the loose belt from his other wrist. He rose, pulling her with him by one arm, then pinning her other arm behind her back as well.

"Come, Jack, change into your winged form and rip my eyes out. No? You've had your fun. Now it's my turn. What is Carlotta to you? Why did you raid the presidio?" When Jack silently stared into the brush, Clint tightened his grip, reaching with his other hand for the stiletto strapped to

Jack's thigh. Before he could touch it, however, a grim and all-too-familiar sound caught his ears. He lifted his head and stared down the bore of the Irishman's cocked pistol.

"Release him, 'an you value yer life, me buck."

Reluctantly, Clint let the bandit go.

Pulling away, Jack threw his comrade an exuberant salute. "Thank you, amigo. I will bind him again. More carefully, this time."

Clint could only fume in silence as, keeping out of the Irishman's range, Jack pushed him down, wrenched his arms behind him and bound him on the last, unused loop of his belt.

Magdalena then slashed partway through the sturdy leather, and sheathed her dagger again. "After you've sawed long enough to make your wrists raw, you should be able to free yourself. See, I am not heartless." She turned, pretending not to hear the soft vow that trailed her into the brush.

"Yes, you are. But have you a soul? If so, it will be mine before we're finished, *bandido*. When we meet again, I'll be ready." When the Irishman holstered his pistol and gave him a cocky wave, Clint gave him a hard look that promised retribution. Then both bandits disappeared into the brush.

Magdalena held her finger to her lips when Joaquin would have spoken. As quietly as they could, they led the animals down the other side of the point.

When they were safely on the beach, Joaquin warned her, "He is no man to be trifled with. You acted foolishly, Magdalena, enraging him with nothing to show for it."

"Nothing? His very presence here proves his guilt. If he weren't allied with Roberto, what had he to lose in telling the truth?"

"Except his pride, lassie," Sean inserted. "Which is no small thing to such a man. We know no more of him than when we started."

"But we will. I've not yet searched his cabin. He has a small chest he keeps locked. If he hides something, it will be there. I only need one more day. Besides, tomorrow we may have at least one new man to join our struggle."

Having successfully diverted them from the debacle on the point and her own confused reactions to it, Magdalena told them briefly of her skirmish with Miguel. "If he brings friends, we should have enough to enter the presidio by the gate. With luck, we can incapacitate the guards before they can sound an alert." They parted after agreeing upon a new campground up the beach in a stand of palms and setting a meeting time shortly after Magdalena's meeting with Miguel.

On arriving at the ship, Magdalena undressed and got into her cot. When, thirty minutes later, heavy steps entered her cabin, she pretended to be asleep. When they stomped out again, she drew a relieved breath. He must have been furious indeed to have frayed the heavy leather so quickly.

Magdalena turned over and buried her head in the pillow, but she knew sleep would elude her until she faced what she'd learned this night of herself and the man she . . . she might as well admit it: Despite the circumstances, she still admired him. Admired his courage, his determination and his wit. But she hated just as much the sly cunning that made him shadow his crippled maid and incited him to do business with a *cerdo* like Roberto. Whatever it took for him to better himself, in status or wealth, he would do. And God help the poor souls who stood in his way.

This night had raised even more doubts about him, and it behooved her to heed them at last. Sean was wrong about him, as fooled by his charm as she had once been. It wasn't pride that had led him to be so cagey to her questions. It was greed, pure and simple. Had he not proved it himself by trying to capture El Halcon for the reward?

When her innate fairness cried out that he had every reason to despise El Halcon, Magdalena buried her head in her pillow again, too depressed to flagellate herself further. But a last admission she must make before she could relax enough for sleep: Sean was right about one thing. She had come dangerously close to allowing her longing to believe in this gringo to divert her from her purpose here. She'd never followed him on any of his outings, nor had she searched the chest that, she'd known from its first dusting, held his most private possessions. Something in her, some flaw she'd been unable to excoriate, longed to trust him still.

But he wasn't worthy of that trust. It was time to proceed with her plans. Tomorrow, she'd search his cabin. And if, as she feared, she found something incriminating, she'd be as ruthless in her pursuit of him as she would be with Roberto. Thus resigned if not comforted, her weary mind and soul finally gave her rest. She slept, only to dream of a tall, golden-haired man who made her happier than she'd ever been in the reality she'd carved for herself . . .

# Chapter 8

"I am a leaf in an unearthly wind; there is a tempest shakes me."

**Act I, DON JUAN TENORIO**

The next morning, Magdalena was not surprised to find Clint in a bearish mood. However, as her own mood rather matched, she had little patience to spare for him.

When she brought his breakfast tray in, he snapped, "I can't stomach that pap this morning. Take it away."

She eyed him narrowly for a long moment, so long that he looked up from the shelf he was sorting. His own eyes slitted. "If you're wondering how I'd look wearing your culinary triumph, I dare you to try it. I'm full to here," he made a chopping motion in the air beneath his chin, "with your deceit, and I'd dearly love a reason to put my hand to your skinny backside."

Pritikin came yawning into the shop, only to back out again when he saw the bristling pair. He mumbled, "I'll be on deck," and retreated with more sense than valor.

Neither of the antagonists even heard him. Magdalena growled back, "And you'd lose it if you tried. I'm full to

185

here," deliberately she imitated his movement, "with your arrogance. You can get your own lunch, since my cooking is so unsatisfactory." She slammed the tray down and flounced out, not even pretending to limp. Let him make of *that* what he pleased.

Clint roared, "Come back here, Carlotta!" Only the sound of her retreating footsteps answered him. His frustration coming to full boil, Clint swiped the tray off the shelf. Porridge glopped over several bolts of his best cloth, and he had to spend a good hour trying to clean them. Instead of calming his rage, the task increased his anger with himself, with Carlotta, with the world in general and with that blasted bandit in particular. Feeling he'd explode if he didn't take some action, he curtly ordered Pritikin to watch the shop and strode off into Santa Barbara.

He was too lost in thought to notice the tall woman, her head wrapped in a coarse rebozo, who followed him. When he entered the presidio gate and spoke to the guards, she slumped against a wall, then pushed herself away and strode firmly back to the beach.

Clint was admitted immediately to Luis. The debonair *capitan*, long of limb and powerfully muscled, rose from his desk and greeted Clint with outstretched hand.

"Captain Browning! To what do I owe the pleasure of this visit?"

Despite the charming smile on his handsome face, Clint rather thought his eyes stayed cool and assessing. As with his friend de Sarria, something about this man bothered Clint, but he was not here to be friendly. Besides, if Luis was as crafty as he sensed, all the better. It took a wily, ruthless animal to trap a fox.

Clint's handshake and smile were both perfunctory. After sitting across from the captain as invited, Clint asked, "Have you had any luck in tracking El Halcon?"

Luis's smile faded. His hands gripped the arms of his chair as he growled, "No. I've men searching the area near where he accosted us, but they've found nothing yet."

"Perhaps you're looking in the wrong place. I myself saw him on San Buenaventura point last night."

186

"Caramba!" Luis half-rose, his expression stunned, but Clint waved him back into his chair.

"He's long gone. The Irishman saved him." Briefly Clint explained what had happened.

When he'd finished, Luis frowned. "Why do you suppose he's so boldly come into Santa Barbara? Is that not an odd thing for a wanted man to do? Isolated robberies on El Camino Real are much safer."

"Indeed, I wondered the same thing myself. And drew the obvious conclusion." Clint paused, arching one golden eyebrow. Luis did not disappoint him.

"There's something here he wants. Badly."

"*Exactamente*, capitan." Clint leaned forward intently. "But what? If we can discover that, we'll have our first advantage against him. And I've a feeling to capture him, we'll need many."

Luis asked archly, "*We* will, Captain Browning? Are you joining my men?"

Clint braced his hands on his chair arms, as if to rise. "I but offer my assistance. Of course, if you don't want it . . ."

This time it was Luis who waved him back into his chair. "No, no, I welcome your aid. I but wonder what you have to gain."

"You know, the bandit asked me something similar. In fact, he seemed devilish interested in what business I had with your friend Roberto de Sarria." Clint wasn't surprised when Luis paled. So, there was some mystery here. Luis and Roberto were obviously allied in something, as the bandit suspected. Clint waited calmly for Luis's next question, but when it came, it was not what he expected.

"Are you sure this was the same man who robbed us? This could not have been . . . someone else? A woman, perhaps disguised?"

Clint blinked. If he hadn't been so astonished, he would have laughed at the absurd notion. When he'd regained his voice, he scoffed, "That bandit is no more a woman than I. And it *was* the same man. He admitted as much. Damned enjoyed reminding me, in fact." Clint scowled, then tapped his fingers against his chair arms. "What reason do you have to suspect anyone asking about de Sarria?"

But Luis had risen to take a bottle from a chest and pour two glasses of Spanish madeira. He replied over his shoulder, "A foolish whimsy on my part. I but teased you, señor." When he turned back around, his face was calm. "Indeed, no woman would be capable of what El Halcon has done. Still, he's but a man, no matter how slippery, and we will catch him."

Clint knew he'd get no more, but he would have sworn Luis seemed relieved. It was intriguing indeed that the Mexican preferred El Halcon's interest over some mysterious woman's. After drinking his wine and agreeing to tell Luis if he found any clue of El Halcon's whereabouts or intent, he left. He played with the riddle Luis had teased him with, but then he dismissed it. Hopefully Jose would have better news tonight when they met for dinner, as scheduled.

When he arrived back at the ship, he growled at Pritikin, "You can take tonight off. I've a dinner engagement in town." He didn't see Carlotta's head pop up from where she sewed at a tear in her skirt.

In fact, he studiously ignored her for the rest of the day, which suited her fine. She spent her time in the galley, straightening it, trying not to think of him at all. Come what may, tonight she was gone from here. If they had a successful raid on the presidio tonight, her presence would no longer be necessary. While she'd not had tangible proof of Clint's involvement with Roberto, she was nevertheless convinced of it.

Time would bear her out. Time would heal the regret that throbbed like a wound in a region dangerously close to her heart. He'd been her enemy from the beginning. Twice she'd let herself be seduced into almost trusting him; she'd not make the same mistake again.

The hours that had once passed slowly flew by in mundane pursuits. Every inexorable minute brought her closer to a parting she couldn't even acknowledge. She watched with bitter-sweet admiration as he left shortly after dark. He was dressed in his finest suit: gray trousers hugging long, powerful legs, wide chest emphasized by a long black broadcloth coat and a pearl gray silk waistcoat with a double row of silver buttons. The ensemble was completed by a gray ascot and black beaver hat.

Never had he been more the *yanqui*, but, ah, such a fine-looking man he was. She hid in the shadows and watched as he started down the gangplank. As if he felt the intensity of her stare, he turned to sweep the deck with his penetrating gaze. She stayed still, knowing her dark clothes would make her inconspicuous. Finally, he shrugged and went on his way.

Clearing a suddenly aching throat, she went below to pack her things and tidy her cabin for the next occupant. She'd seen Pritikin leave earlier, so she should have privacy to perform her last task . . .

Clint shifted in his chair, wishing he'd been able to find a discreet way of getting out of this dinner since Jose had been called back to his rancho. He knew better than to ask Angelina if Jose had made any progress in his investigation. Nor did he share with her his own meeting with El Halcon.

When he could bear her batting eyelashes and languorous glances no longer, he shoved back his hastily emptied plate and rose. He bowed low over her hand. "Forgive my early departure, señorita, but I've much yet to accomplish this eve. The meal was delicious. Please tell your brother to call upon me when he returns."

Oblivious to her soft protest, he slammed his hat on his head and beat a hasty retreat. Outside, he took deep breaths of the night air and removed his coat. So still it was. And quiet. The presentiment that had been nudging him since he left the *Arabella* of some imminent danger pushed harder as he neared the wharf. He'd been bored with Angelina, true, but that couldn't account for the restless urgency drawing him back to the ship. What could be wrong? He'd given Pritikin the night off, and Carlotta was most likely about one of her nocturnal wanderings, so the ship should be deserted.

Yet when his hurrying steps brought him in sight of his vessel, a single light glowed. The location of that light brought him to a dead stop, then made him break into a run. He drew off his shoes when he reached the gangplank and tiptoed the rest of the way to his cabin, pulling the derringer out of his pocket as he went. At his door, he quietly set down his hat and shoes to free his hands, pausing to regain his breath and wipe the sweat from his brow. The still humidity in the air boded a storm. Holding the derringer hidden inside the folds of the coat over his arm, he entered his cabin to face the intruder.

His heart plummeted to his stockinged feet. He'd thought Carlotta capable of many things, but never this. The evidence was damning: her sacked belongings tossed on his bed, his sea chest open, his clothes strewn across the floor, the small chest she even now pried open with a knife. Had he treated her so badly to warrant this thief-in-the-night conduct?

Rage built in him, slowly, steadily, like the storm clouds massing overhead, a rage fed by disappointment—and more dangerous, withal. Her back was to him and she was intent upon her task, so she didn't hear his approach. He hovered over her just as the small lock snapped open and she flung back the lid. Her movement loosened one sleeve of her chemise. It slipped to the side, baring a white shoulder blade that contrasted vividly with the dark skin of her neck and upper shoulders. He'd always suspected she was no Indian, and the proof staring him in the face made him wonder what else she'd hidden.

Just as she reached inside to investigate the chest's contents, he jibed, "Such exemplary thoroughness. I'm gratified to see you keep my most intimate possessions tidy."

She froze. Her head turned to look up at him, her unscarred side in profile to him. Her true identity whammed into him with the force of a sledgehammer. In truth, he blinked, dazed. He could only watch, mouth agape, as she rose to face him. The lantern light shimmered in her eyes, gold eyes that were steadier, clearer, than any he'd ever seen. The wax scar was slipping in the heat of the cabin. That mouth, untwisted now, was one he knew. One he'd tasted. Savored. Longed to taste again.

The bitter gall in the back of his throat burned like acid. Finally, everything made sense. Carlotta and the strawberry girl had reminded him so of one another because they were one person. Carlotta had come to him to spy upon him; Inez had used her feminine wiles upon him for the same reason. Both had lied to him, used him and now robbed him. This woman was as treacherous as she was beautiful. The fact that he responded to her so strongly, growing hard for her even now he knew her for what she was, angered him further. Only one question remained—what was she to Jack?

Her chin tilted. Her posture straightened when she saw his recognition. Thus he met again the proud girl he'd longed for, ached for, worried about. Her courage deepened his sense of betrayal. All along she'd been here within his reach. Here, spying on him; sneaking away without a word; stealing from him.

His confused feelings lurched from shock, to elation, to dismay, to, inevitably, rage. The last tightened in his gut like a fist bunched to strike. He tossed his coat and gun on the bed, trembling with the need to punish this girl who was both more, and so much less, than he had hoped. But first . . . "Why?"

When she stared at him steadily without answering, he reiterated tonelessly, "Why? Why did you come here disguised to spy on me? What have I done to make you despise me so? What is Jack to you? Was it for him that you tried to seduce me the other night, when you came to my cabin?"

Her eyes wavered, then latched onto his again. "You are an associate of Roberto de Sarria's. His friends are my enemies."

He frowned, something in her words twanging a cord of memory. But he was too angry to listen. He stepped closer to her. "We'll pursue that later, but I suspect even Roberto

*191*

de Sarria would not stoop to stealing." His scornful glance went from the knife in her hand to his pried open chest.

Her harsh laughter raised the hairs on the back of his neck. His eyes searched her features, but they didn't match the memory nagging him. "Do you think to visit his—and likely yours as well—sins upon me? He would not stoop to stealing, you say?" This time her laughter had an edge of hysteria.

He took advantage of it to leap across the small gap between them. One instant her head was thrown back in discordant mirth; the next it was firmly upon her shoulders, the knife lifting to ward him off. Her lightning-fast reactions were not quite fast enough. He was able to catch the wrist aiming the knife at his shoulder and twist the weapon away. Only then did he look at it closely.

This time goose pimples swept his body from head to toe in accompaniment to the hairs lifting on his neck. He'd seen this knife before. Only last night it had menaced his throat. And lower. It must be true. She was Jack's lover. Why else would he give her his own weapon? Had Carlotta deliberately led him to Jack, then witnessed his humiliation?

His barely contained rage spewed out like a bursting pustule. He flung the stiletto away and caught her shoulders with brutal hands. "Damn you; damn your lying eyes and strawberry lips. What else are you? How well you play the innocent, when all you are is a thieving whore. What else will you do for your bandit lover?"

The fear and shock that had widened her eyes receded into, incredibly, a flicker of mirth. When she said, "Whatever necessary to help him win," his last vestige of control was lost.

"Good! Then use your body as well as you've lied and stolen, and I may, just may, let you go back to him."

The fear returned to her eyes, but he was too enraged to see it. His mouth swooped down on hers with none of the tenderness he'd shown before. His lips were hard, punishing, those of a conqueror bent on rapine. When she made a muffled sound of protest, he released her mouth to tear the wax away from her skin. He caught a handful of her long hair to arch her throat for the ravaging of his lips. Her struggling only incited him to greater lust. And lust it was, for it was not tempered by the gentle fervor the lost girl in the strawberry patch had inspired in him so effortlessly.

How many ways had she tormented him: the peculiar attraction to the scarred cripple he'd never understood, the growing concern for her welfare; a similar, but stronger attraction and worry for the brave girl who had haunted his dreams; the shattering realization that both were the same girl, no, woman. A deceitful woman who knew how to use her sexual charms to play on a man's heartstrings. Well, no more. The only strings she pulled now were the ones at his groin. Those he'd let her twiddle with gladly.

Thus, he ignored her furious tirade and kicked the bedclothes off his narrow cot, cramming them into a bed of sorts with his foot. Holding her latched to his side, he kicked his cabin door shut, then shoved her down to the floor. When she would have risen, he pushed her back down, holding his hands on her shoulders.

"No, my dear. You used your body to seduce me, and like a fool I let you go. Not this time." He caught her easily when she dove for the knife under the cot. He threw her back down on the makeshift bed, stooped, picked up the knife, went to his porthole and flung it into the bay. Then, striding to block the door, he methodically took off his clothes, adding them carelessly to the pile on the floor. His eyes never left her face all the while. He relished the fear he saw there even as it twisted his gut with regret. Anger warred with tenderness, but stronger still was the sexual hunger both Carlotta and Inez had aroused. All else ceased to matter. Who he was, who she was, who had betrayed whom. There was only this need that at last would be fulfilled. He'd make it pleasurable for her. His conscience almost overrode him when she looked about like a cornered animal seeking a bolthole. Almost.

Finding none, she looked down for a long moment. Then she straightened her shoulders and rose to face him, meeting his eyes, ignoring the hands that were busily baring bronzed, gold-dusted skin. "I ask you not to do this thing. If you do, you'll regret it."

He arched one eyebrow. "Is that a threat? You're hardly in a position to make them. If you think to make me fear your bandit lover's revenge, you waste your breath. He can't hate me any more than I hate him. He could have killed me last night, when you led me to him. You knew I'd follow you, didn't you? One night with me is a small price to pay for such treachery."

When he worked at his breeches' buttons, she turned away, her hands clasping her elbows. He had to strain to hear the words he couldn't, wouldn't, credit. "And if I told you I'd known no man, would you spare me then?"

His laugh was short. "If I believed you—which I don't. Why else would you be so eager to help Jack if you're not his lover? Come, accept me, and you'll not regret it. I promise I can please you more than El Halcon."

When she stayed silent, head bent, he flung his last garments away and stalked up behind her to bump his stiffening length into her supple hips. "Don't make this any harder on yourself than it has to be. I've no wish to hurt you. But I'm determined to exorcise you. Come, it won't be so different to the other men you've known. I promise to be gentle, if you'll let me."

How right she'd been about him, Magdalena thought. If only she'd heeded her brain instead of her foolish heart, she could have been long gone. Her stomach churned with a rage, sorrow and fear she refused to heed. Promise her gentleness, would he, like a sop to his conscience? She'd not allow him the comfort. He was as bad as the swine who'd killed her mother, she sneered to herself, even as a soft corner of her heart knew she lied. This man, at least, had reason to resent her and think her wanton. But that didn't excuse his actions. She'd not make his victory easy . . .

She turned in the circle of his arms to meet the steady blue flames in his eyes. "Rape me like the ruthless American you are, for you'll get me no other way." She raised her hands to claw at his eyes, trying to lift her knee into his groin.

But he was ready for her resistance. He caught her wrists in one hand and wrapped one iron-thewed thigh about her legs to keep her still. For the first time, the laughter in his voice was genuine. "I don't think that will be necessary. I've never known a more passionate woman. And I felt your attraction to me when we kissed."

When she bared her teeth at him and gave a frustrated snarl, he teased huskily, "What a hell-cat you are. Do you know how tigers mate? Such fierceness, nipping and growling. It makes the mating, when it comes, incredibly erotic. Here, let me show you . . ." His head dipped. She flung her neck aside, so he took advantage of the vulnerable cord she'd bared and ran his tongue along it, then took tiny nips, up and down the length of it.

She shivered, she told herself in disgust, but the feel of those strong white teeth teasing her flesh sent strange messages to her brain. When his hand went to the laces holding her chemise closed, she stiffened, ordering, "Release me, gringo!" When the laces tore, her voice rose a notch higher. "I hate you! I'll see you pay for this."

Now her struggles foiled her efforts and aided his, for her loosened chemise followed the path of least resistance and fell, draping low across her arms, barely shielding her bosom. Still he held her wrists, but he took a half-step back to appraise her.

The very air seemed to hold its breath as he studied her. With his free hand, he stroked from one delicate collarbone to another, breathing quicker at the warm silk under his hand. Then he gave one tiny little tug to the ruffle lining her neckline, and the chemise dropped to her waist. Her gasp echoed his as his eyes locked on the high breasts that were fuller than he'd expected. Not large, but perfectly round and firm. A virgin's breasts. He frowned and dismissed the thought, concentrating instead on the tightening eagerness at his groin. He caught a handful of firm white flesh, testing its weight and resiliency, before running a thumb over the deep rose peak.

"Strawberries and cream," he whispered. "Do you taste as good as you look?"

She met his eyes fiercely. "I hope I poison you."

He bent his head so close to hers their foreheads brushed. Still her eyes never left his. As if she were afraid to look elsewhere. "Was hemlock ever so sweet? Come, let us die together."

Her face turned beet red. She struggled again, but went still with a frustrated groan when he teased a bouncing breast with his finger. He cupped the underside of the flawless globe to lift it to his descending lips. She flinched and cried a protest at the touch of his warm lips, but he ignored her and pulled her wrists down to arch her into his mouth.

She stared at the deck above, telling herself she despised him, she'd kill him, but her nipples ignored her will, peaking to meet the wicked slash of his tongue. He feasted for long moments, learning her taste and feel until a trembling took hold of her that had little to do with fear or rage. She tried to whip up her hatred, but the lapping, tugging motion at first one pebbly nipple, then the other, made a liar of her. And that knowledge shamed her as the loss to come could not.

She began to struggle again, crying between curses, "Stop! Rape me and be done with it!"

His chest heaving, he lifted his head at last. "You'd like that, wouldn't you? But rape is not to my taste. I'll have you begging for me before I'm done."

When she shook her head wildly, he caught a handful of her hair and held her head still, forcing her to look into eyes as darkly passionate as the seas beginning to swell about them. "I know you better than you think, Carlotta, Inez, or whatever you call yourself today. It's your stubborn little mind, your wild spirit you cherish more than this delightful casing for them." He released her hair to run his palm from shoulder to hip, and back again. Then he bent so close his breath brushed her face. "It's those I will conquer and make my own!"

He muffled her protests with his mouth, but this time the

kiss was different. It was the aroused kiss of an experienced male, the hungry seeking of a man who would be a lover in truth. When she resisted, he pushed her back against the bulkhead to keep her still with his weight while he quickly stripped her skirt and petticoat down and off. Then, lifting her chin with one hand to take her mouth again, he used the other to caress her from neck to thigh.

The gentle massage sent goosebumps over her body. When he began to rub his powerfully muscled torso against her, she moaned into the relentless heat of his mouth. The smooth hardness covered with golden hairs, rubbing against the breasts he'd brought to such excruciating sensitivity, made her resistance ebb. With a moaning sigh, she gave up and opened her mouth to his probing tongue.

He explored her, flicking his tongue teasingly in and out until she tried to capture it with her own. He avoided her like a skilled duelist, feinting to one side only to lunge to the other, slanting his mouth over hers to thrust deeper. She was so enraptured at the feelings his mouth inspired that she didn't notice when he stripped her last garment away.

But she felt the first gentle touch of that big hand where no one had ever dared to touch before. Her eyes popped open just as he released her and stepped back. For a moment, she was too weak to move.

Leisurely he admired her from smooth shoulders, broad for a woman, tapering into a tiny waist, to the flaring hips and soft bush at the apex of her legs. He shuddered as he gazed at the spot, already feeling the hot clasp as he pushed into her. He forced himself to look away, down to the unusually long, perfectly shaped legs. Never had he seen such flawless skin, or felt such firmness beneath. She was slender yet strong, feminine yet powerful. And he wanted her as he'd never wanted a woman. Finally he looked back at her face, smiling as he watched her perform her own appraisal.

Even as she blushed, she looked. His clothes had not hidden the power of him, but the perfection of his shape had to be seen to be appreciated. Briefly, she forgot how this odyssey of sensual hunger had begun and enjoyed the journey. Such wide shoulders he had, arms bulging with muscles, narrow waist and long, muscular legs. He had the physique of a laborer, yet his hands were proof of his breeding. She longed suddenly to test him in a duel. Would he wield a blade with the promise of his long fencer's legs? Her thoughts led her eyes to the one place she'd avoided. Biting her lip at her own daring, she finally looked at the mysterious muscle she'd felt pushing into her so urgently. She gasped, and the length that was long, hard and thick as a blade, curved in eager readiness, prodded her into awareness. She knew its purpose, and it recalled her vividly to her own.

He saw the change in her expression. He caught her at the waist and lowered her to the makeshift pallet of blankets and clothes. He stifled her protests before she could voice them, but this time the drugging warmth of his mouth had lost its potency. She turned her head from side to side, lifting her hands to claw at his shoulders. He winced, caught her hands with his and pushed her arms slowly, inexorably, over her head.

When she still squirmed, trying to draw up a knee, he sighed. "I thought we'd done with this." When a narrow foot poked him in a spot dangerously close to his groin, he lost patience. It had been too long since he'd had a woman. And it was this woman he'd hungered for, cheat that she was. He'd almost forgotten her deceit in the enjoyment he'd taken from her beautiful body. She'd reminded him just in time. Why should he make this pleasurable for her if she preferred it otherwise?

Pushed beyond his limits, he readied her. He growled like a lusting tiger, "You've made a fool of me long enough. Yield to me, woman." His eyes, hungry, compelling and quintessentially male, delved deep into hers as he levered her legs outward, bit by bit, with his own. When she was open to him, vulnerable, for a reason he could not name, he hesitated, staring into golden eyes that, even now, fearlessly held his own.

Magdalena felt his eagerness hovering at the opening that had moistened to receive him in their previous play. Now she cringed from what she might have welcomed earlier, trying to swing her hips aside, but he was too heavy, too strong, and too aroused. Frustrated but resigned, she accepted unpleasant reality as she always did—with defiance. And unknowingly precipitated what she most wanted to avoid.

Her eyes wild and golden as a tigress's, she snarled back, "Then shaft me well, *perro*, for you'll know my own blade soon enough."

His fierce expression softened, and that hurt her far more than the iron rod pushing the first bit into her, stretching the delicate opening. She couldn't let this be a gentle taking, for that would leave her even more to regret. She turned her scorn for her own weakness upon him in the most explicit of ways: She spat in his face.

His features hardened. Wiping his cheek on her hair, he purred, "Then take it, *zorra*, as you want it!" Arching his back, he lunged forward with all the power in his hips. The flimsy obstruction gave, and he'd buried half his length between her legs before he realized the significance of that tiny curtain of flesh. Appalled, he stayed still to look into her face.

Carlotta's determination not to cry out was apparent in her clenched teeth, but her neck arched so far back with the fierce thrust that each cord stood out. Blood oozed into her mouth from where she'd bitten her lip, but the triumph in those huge golden eyes far overshadowed the pain. She smiled, just a bit—contemptuously, condescendingly.

His blue eyes, softened by regret and shame, grew stormy again at her deliberate challenge. "You little witch, you wanted it this way, didn't you?" When her lip curled in answer, his control shattered. What other woman would meet her own deflowering with such defiance? She was life, she was passion, she was more woman than he'd ever known, and he was aware only of the primitive need to win her. Groaning a mingled protest and acceptance, he took her mouth, withdrawing only to push slowly into her softness again. He lost himself in her and savored the losing. Never had it been so good. He'd make her admit it, too, before he was done.

The heated clasp of her body, slack and open, accepting, burned the last of his regret away. She was his, this strange, thrilling, fiery creature, his and no other's. He pushed again, gently, to stamp himself upon her, within her, tempting her to share this fierce joy. Holding her head between his hands, he probed her mouth with his tongue, tenderly licking the blood away from her self-inflicted wound. Below, in that other, more delicate mouth, he drew out, slid in, a bit deeper each time, allowing the silken sheath to stretch and grow used to him.

"See, *querida*, you were made for me. So well you hold me, as if created just to fit with me." He made other wooing remarks into her mouth, her neck, his blade pushing steadily in and out all the while. He felt her tension drain away as the pain slowly faded, and only then did he allow himself the deep, possessive plunges he yearned for.

Holding her tight buttocks to lift her harder against him, he drew himself out, long, glistening, throbbing with the nectar preparing to spew forth, only to push fiercely back in as if he'd meld his very soul with hers. He felt the quickening of her breath, enjoyed the gliding of her hands over his sweat-gleaming shoulders, and redoubled his efforts to truly make her a woman. His woman.

Magdalena stifled the urge to lift her legs about his waist and meet each long, measured thrust into her body. Why did he not get it over with? He'd had his revenge, and hers had fled with the easing of the pain of his taking. Now the repeated, silken slide to her very depths was not a justification of her hate; it was a purification of it, tempting her to set aside enmity and share this give-take. She turned her head aside from his hungry lips, trying to lock him out. But it was too late. He had opened her mind to the possibilities, her body to the limitless vista of womanhood, and dared her to explore both.

He lifted her hips higher still so that each masterful stroke brushed against some core she struggled to numb, though it ruled supreme. The taking that had begun rough, brutal as the name she'd given it, had become a seeking that plumbed for the womanly urges she'd spent so many years denying. She felt those urges rising, rising to meet him . . .

Clint knew she was becoming aroused, but his elation was all the impetus needed for his starved body to sate its hunger. Throwing his head back, he climaxed with a tortured but triumphant groan, pushing to her womb to sow it with the seeds of a new beginning.

When the potent splashes filled her, Magdalena slumped with relief even as she bit her lip over a protest for him to go on. She'd won, after all. She'd never forgive him for this, but now at least she had nothing to excuse in herself. She didn't try to push him away when he sprawled over her, his great length slowly softening within her.

But when he looked at her, those crystalline blue eyes clear now that passion had found its natural release, she turned her head away. She couldn't avoid his measured warning, however: "Don't celebrate your victory yet, *querida*. We've a long night ahead of us."

At that she tried to push him off. He obligingly fell to her side but wrapped his arms about her waist to anchor her to him.

"No, you must let me go. You've had your revenge, taken by force what I've never given any man . . ."

"To my regret, and your triumph." He bent to her ear to whisper, "I know now what you were doing—inciting me to rage to quiet your own desires. I apologize for hurting you, *chiquita*. Give me another chance to show you what pleasure there is in being a woman. Please."

But she struggled in earnest now, batting with arms, kicking with legs. He simply sprawled on his back, pulled her atop him, hooked both his ankles around hers and held her hands behind her back. When his eyes half-closed in pleasure at the feel of his squirming blanket, she forced herself to stillness, though she trembled with frustration.

For the first time, the hatred in her voice was genuine when she spat, "There will be no other chance. I swear if you don't release me I will hide one cloudy night and plant a knife between your ribs."

He ignored her and lifted his bright golden head, damp now with sweat, to run his tongue along her bottom lip. She flinched and jerked her head back, crying, "Ooh! Are you deaf, gringo? Do you think I'm joking?"

His reply was muffled as he nuzzled her throat. "No, I'm sure you mean it, for now. You're a poor loser." He dropped his head back to smile up at her, his eyes sunny and clear as a noonday sky. "You've given me something precious, and I want to give you something in return. When you see what your loss has gained you, you'll no longer hate me."

Her mouth dropped open at his incredible conceit. He took advantage of its working and silenced it before her fury vented itself in more than a sputter. So sweetly he wooed her, holding her head still with his free hand when she would have pulled back. She resisted, cursing into his mouth, squirming again, but he was far too strong for her. She gave up and let her mouth rest slackly upon his.

But passivity was not what he strove for. Patiently he worked, running his tongue from one luscious corner to the other, flickering just inside only to retreat, teasing her until her mouth tingled with sensitivity. Yet when, with a frustrated moan, she finally opened her lips to take more of him, he drew away to march a line of kisses down her neck. He dipped his tongue into the hollow of her throat, smiling when she inhaled a pleasured breath, only to deny her there as well. His tormenting mouth sucked and nibbled at every inch of skin he could reach—shoulders, arms, upper torso. Then his legs joined the game, rubbing their hairy length up and down hers, but still keeping her spread-eagled, helpless.

Every move she made aided him. If she shifted away from one teasing nip, he merely sampled the new skin she bared. If she squirmed from side to side, he writhed in the opposite direction, rubbing their bodies together with a pleasurable friction that made her glow from head to toe.

Being covered by his brawny length was exciting enough, but lying atop him, feeling the tensing of every muscle, the hair-roughened yet smooth skin, the strength controlled now for her pleasure instead of unleashed upon her, made her head swim. Soon she scarce recalled why she hated him or how this had begun. She only felt the pounding of his heart calling to her own, the flesh that had known her once rising in joy at her eagerness. Lost to herself, she arched her neck back to give him access to her breasts.

At her response, he loosened his tightly reined control. Pulling her higher, he raised his head to sample again the beauteous fruits hanging heavy and ripe for his tasting. He filled his mouth with her, knowing vaguely as he did so that she sustained more than his body. She sated a lonely spirit that had long yearned for just such a woman to partake of. He lavished fervent kisses upon her, moving from one strawberry peak to another until her nipples more resembled rubies, glistening and hard, precious.

Only when she was moaning, her breath coming in little pants, did he free her hands. They dangled limply at her sides, as if she didn't know what to do with them. He lifted them about his neck, cradled her head in his big palms and drew her mouth down to his. His kiss seared away the last of her resistance, fogging her brain with the steam that rose between them.

Neither noticed when the storm heralded its arrival with a clap of thunder, for this tempest of hearts and bodies was more elemental than any turmoil nature could devise. She answered every passioned thrust of his tongue with a lunge of her own, squirming upon him now not in resistance, but in enjoyment of the texture of his skin.

Big, shaky hands drew hers to his torso, showing her how to rub and tease. When she flicked a nail at his own pebbly little nipple, he flinched and groaned, pulling his mouth away to pant in much-needed air. He wrapped her hair around one hand to look deeply into her eyes as slowly, slowly, he inched his other hand down her supple spine, to chart her firm buttocks and lithe thighs. Again he was amazed at the feel of silk over steel. He'd known slimmer women who had more fat. She'd not an ounce upon her. With two exceptions . . . He rubbed his chest against those exceptions, but he said not a word. He'd not chance shattering her pleasurable haze.

Enraptured golden eyes blinked into his, and he knew it was time. Pushing her legs a bit further apart, he finally let himself touch the spot that made her so much a woman. The feel of his seed, still warm upon her, made him clench his teeth over another groan, but he felt a new, slicker moisture as well. Sighing in relief, he caressed the living velvet until she was trembling, her head shaking from side to side as if she didn't understand what was happening to her. He brushed the tiny, tumid button and she cried out, arching her back. He lifted her legs astride him, caught her hips and pushed her back. The feel of that womanly patch, sliding moistly over him, almost sent him over the edge. He dug his fingers into her hips and took a deep breath.

"Lift, *corazonita*." She obeyed blindly, her lips and breasts swollen with the passion he'd aroused. Gently he set her upon the engorged head of him, watching her as he eased into her. "Look, *querida*, at how God made us fit."

She looked down, her eyes widening at the sight of his thickness sliding into her easily, as if this were not the second time, but the sixtieth. The feeling of that maleness probing, then filling her so gently, stretching her inch by inch, accompanied by the sight of him slowly disappearing between her legs, built her arousal to fever pitch. Impatiently she lunged forward, sighing in delight as his throbbing length inhabited every inch of the chamber it had so recently visited. The slight soreness as she stretched about him disturbed her sensual haze not a whit, especially when he teased the top of her slit with his thumb, raising his head to suckle at her breasts.

It was if her body knew this man, as if she had in truth been made to fit with him, and only him, in such a way. The moment was too blissful for doubts, distrust, and gladly she gave herself to whatever he wanted to do with her. Some primitive instinct knew she could trust him, that this moment she'd fought against was meant to be.

Clint sensed her yielding, and it made his heart melt with

tenderness. From his greater experience, he knew how unusual this mating was. For it *was* a mating: a melding of two opposites made to complement one another, rather than a gutter coupling of two lusting human animals. He'd known enough of the latter to feel the difference now. He didn't understand it, especially when there was yet so much he didn't know about this woman. But nor did he question it. It pleased him, body and mind, and he simply settled back to enjoy.

Murmuring English and Spanish endearments, he pulled her down to his mouth. Embedded full length, he let his lips and the gentle flexing of his male muscle, caressing her snug interior, express his feelings.

Attuned to him, she understood, and the tenderness he arrayed about her like a sumptuous cloak brought tears to her eyes. The womanly half she'd denied clamored now with demands. She'd needed this, a man to cherish and depend on, for over two years. Was giving up a part of her independence to enjoy such rapture a loss or a gain? Before she could decide, his demands, and her own, made her sublime thoughts ridiculous. The earth from which they'd come ruled them now.

Her gentle rocking horse became a stallion, chafing at his restraints. When Clint held her pelvis to push her back and forward to match his stride, she gladly moved with her mount. The trot became a lope, the lope a gallop. His back arched as he strove to reach her core; her back arched as she strained to take him deeper. The constant rubbing of his belly, back and forth, on her swollen nubbin, incited first a tickle, then a tingle. Then it became a throb, growing, spreading to encompass every inch of her. When it exploded, sending pleasure so acute it was almost pain from her center to her fingertips and toes, Magdalena gloried in it. For once she gave up a measure of her control and reveled in the loss.

Clint's gaze, dilated with the intensity of his feelings, locked on her face as she threw her head back and stiffened upon him. Shouting his triumph, he took a moment to savor her clenching and release before the flexing drew his hips sharply upward a final time. Suspended in midair, his heels pressing into the makeshift bed, he spent his passion at the very mouth of her womb. The pulsing release was so ecstatic that his head swam, his ears roared. He collapsed, his hands gentling upon her hips, stroking to express his delight.

Magdalena came back to herself slowly. She found her cheek pillowed on his breast, her body sated upon him. She heard the steady drum of rain upon the deck above them, saw the flashes of lightning, felt the softening manhood slipping out of her as he shifted. For a moment, she mourned its passing. But then she lifted her head to look down at him.

He looked back, his expression so contentedly male that reality returned to her with a jolt. His first words shook her further. "Do you see, my dear? You were made to know a man's body, as all women are. But my body, and mine alone." Calmly he stroked her hair out of her eyes, as if the events of this night had given him rights over her.

The truth of what she'd done, what she'd let him do, burst upon her then. Her eyes closed in self-disgust. She turned her head away from his touch and tried to move, but he wouldn't let her.

He lifted her chin and looked concerned at the tears she couldn't hide. "What's wrong? What we've known is something to celebrate. We're attuned to one another. Never have I known a more passionate woman. I will always cherish what you've given me this night." And, when she didn't answer, "Please forgive me for not believing you. I'm sorry I hurt you in the beginning, but I can't regret that this has happened."

Each word hammered into her like a nail, crucifying her upon the cross of her own sins. If only he'd left her be after the first time, she could leave with her head high. Instead, he'd stolen her chastity, and something else she cherished far more: her self-respect. She wanted to crawl off and hide, to never face him again. The pain brought her instincts to the fore. Relaxing at his side, she yawned. "I'm just so tired. So tired." her lashes fluttered shut.

Smiling down at her, he gathered her in one arm and drew a blanket over them. "Sleep, *querida*. We will talk later. You can tell me what is troubling you then, and how I can help." His own words ended on a yawn. In moments, he was fast asleep.

It was easy for her to slip from under his slack arm. She soundlessly scrambled into her clothes, remembering to bind her breasts just in time. When she was dressed except for her sandals, she tiptoed over to the chest and searched it swiftly. She found nothing of interest except a rolled parchment. Her spirits lifted. Was she wrong about him after all? *Dios*, let it be so, she prayed as she unrolled the parchment.

For a moment, she didn't understand the neat drawings. She traced a line from one presidio to another. Notations were made as to how many cannon and men each accommodated . . . Magdalena sank back on her heels and bit down on a cry of pain. She looked from the parchment to the sleeping face of the man she'd just trusted as she'd never trusted any living soul. Searing waves of pain swept away the dregs of his tender passion. That, too, was false. He'd lusted for a woman, any woman. He'd wanted to see her groveling, begging for her own debasement. He'd admitted as much, and how richly had he succeeded. She'd gloried in her own downfall . . .

She looked at him again, so peaceful, so handsome, sated like a god who'd shared himself with a mere mortal. She doubled over to keep from crying out her hatred. For a moment her head swam with it, but then she took a deep breath and forced the blackness away. She lurched to her feet, struck the parchment in her sack and moved to step over him. Her gaze lit upon the swords, crossed in their place on the bulkhead. Her hand reached out to them longingly before she snatched it back. No, that would be too quick. Too easy. He'd know a measure of the torment he'd made her suffer before they were done.

She moved soundlessly around him and went to the door.

There she turned, her eyes casting upon him a brilliant, deadly light. "Dream of your triumph, gringo. You'll know nightmares soon enough." She whirled and was gone, the drumming rain disguising the sounds of her footsteps.

# *Chapter 9*

"Where soldiers gather, there's dice and cards, hot
  tempers, ready blades . . ."

**Act I, DON JUAN TENORIO**

Clint stirred an hour later as the drumming rain diminished.
Even before his eyes had opened, he was reaching out with
a smile on his face, but he touched only crumpled clothing.
He jackknifed up, cursing under his breath. Dammit, he
never should have let himself fall asleep. He started to rise,
but he knew it was useless. She was long gone and would
never willingly come near him again.

Leaning back on his palms, he brooded on the rumpled
mat. There were traces of blood on the blanket. He looked
down. And rusty streaks of it on his own upper thighs. He'd
not needed proof of the girl's innocence, but here it was.
His male triumph had receded under the shock of waking
alone. Now the blood was symbolic not of her loss, but of
his own. He'd found the woman he'd been seeking for all
his adult life, and she'd fled before he had a chance to win
her. She was too innocent to understand how unusual was
the pleasure they'd shared. It probably seemed to her as

though he'd satisfied his lust upon her, though he knew it for a more poignant need.

Why hadn't he believed her? He sighed. She'd played the seductress too well the other night. Her passion to help Jack had seemed too strong to devolve from innocence. Still, evidence notwithstanding, he'd wronged her. Had he desired her less, perhaps he'd have been able to keep his head. But all the regrets in the world wouldn't help him now. He had to find her. Only dire straits could have led an aristrocratic girl, an innocent to boot, to such charades. She obviously needed a strong shoulder to lean on, and he ached to offer it to her.

While trying to decide where to begin his search, he noticed his small chest had its lid thrown back. His depression deepened to despair. "No, please God," he begged out loud, leaping up to scurry to the chest. A moment later, he collapsed on his bed, resting his elbows on his knees to stare glumly at the floor.

He knew as clearly as if she'd told him what she thought of him. He was a lecher, a cheat, a spy. A gringo not to be trusted, much less cared for. A man who'd callously stolen her virginity—and then made her enjoy the loss. He knew enough of her to realize she'd resent him most for that. And he couldn't even honestly apologize, for, though he regretted the roughness with which he'd begun, he knew their joining was meant to be.

As for the other . . . The fact that he'd spied reluctantly and had still not decided to give Uncle Charles the information he'd demanded, would not redeem him. He hung his aching head in his hands, almost overwhelmed. But soon the spirit that made him such a successful trader rebounded. He sat up, swabbed off the blood, and dressed.

She couldn't have gone far. Even if she'd left Santa Barbara by now, he'd find her. Where the bandit was, she was. Somehow he knew it. He puzzled briefly over the relationship between the pair, then he dismissed it. First he had to find her. He picked his pistol up from beneath his discarded coat and put it in his pocket. He debated taking a sword as well; then, deciding he wouldn't need it, he stalked out, his expression grimly determined.

Magdalena stretched her gloved hands out to warm them at the fire. It was already past midnight. Perhaps Miguel would not come. The thought had scarcely formed when she heard a stealthy movement behind her. She whirled, sighing with relief when she recognized the stocky figure.

Arms crossed, legs spread, she said, "*Buenas noches*, amigo. It is good to see you again. Have you decided to join me, then?"

Miguel looked at her steadily. "Yes, but under what conditions? Where do we live, and how? Do I have any say in decisions? What will be my share?"

Magdalena let the suspense build before replying softly, "We live where fortune sends us. In the mountains, on the beach, in a hut we build. Your share will be an equal one with each who joins me. I will receive the same, no more, no less."

"But, as leader, are you not entitled to a greater share?"

"Si, but it is not fortune I seek. Instead, I want my compensation in your complete obedience to my decisions." Magdalena raised her voice. "And the same terms go to any who follow El Halcon."

She smiled beneath her hood at Miguel's surprised look. She nodded at the four packs sitting against a tree. "Do you and your friends accept this?"

Miguel made a beckoning motion with his hand, and three more Indians, dressed in the same tattered mixture of Spanish and Indian clothes, straightened from behind the bushes. They watched her warily, but with grudging respect, their dark faces hard in the flickering firelight.

"Do you agree to my terms?" One by one, she looked at the dark faces. One by one, they nodded.

"Bueno. Now, what skills have you?" After Magdalena satisfied herself that each could wield a knife, two a pistol, and Miguel a sword, she gave a piercing whistle.

Sean and Joaquin climbed up the point. Magdalena introduced them as Mick and Ricardo, letting each man appraise the other, before saying briskly, "Now, we've not a moment to lose. The Americano has let it be known that I am in Santa Barbara. Even now Luis probably has men searching for me. All the better, for it will mean fewer guarding the presidio. My intent is to raid it this very eve."

When the Indians' eyes widened, Magdalena challenged, "Don't you think it time you became the hunter rather than the prey? What better chance than now, on a cloudy night, with many of the soldiers gone? It is the bold who prevail, the weak who fail."

Magdalena flung her cloak back to rest her hands on her hips. "Well? Do you follow me?"

After a hesitation, Miguel stepped forward. "I do. For once it will be the Mexicans who have to defend *their* home." The other three Indians stepped up also.

Magdalena eyed them sternly. "One word of caution: There will be no unnecessary blood-letting. For every soldier we kill, the governor will send ten to take his place. We want to rouse the people to our cause, and only judicious action will win them. They've had enough of ruthlessness. It's time to show that justice and fairness can still triumph." Magdalena looked from face to face. "If any of you join me with blood lust in your hearts, then leave me now. Many wrongs have been done you, but a life for a life is not the way to settle them."

Joaquin peered at her. Magdalena gazed back, conveying her thoughts. Roberto was different. He was no paid soldier. He was a murderer. She would be his executioner, nothing more. She turned again to the men, stifling the conscience that tried to chide her equivocation.

When none argued, she said, "This is what we will do . . ."

The guards at the gate that night were even more bored than usual. The recently passed storm had left a cool sweetness in the air that made a man think of a warm bed and warmer body to comfort him. The five men had not been with the detachment who had searched for El Halcon, and they thought Luis's worries about security were ridiculous. What could one man do against an entire presidio? Their boredom made them quarrelsome, and they were paying more attention to their card game than their post when the first sounds came.

One lifted his head to listen. Was that a horse approaching? A bird cackled, and thinking the wind had distorted the sound, the guard looked down at his cards again. Only one of the men looked up before the night descended upon them. One moment they were huddled over the barrel; the next they were flat on their backs, rags stuffed in their mouths before they could cry out. They glimpsed several Indians and several men in cloaks before they were trussed, dragged to a storeroom and locked inside.

Magdalena jerked her head, and the two Indians who had pistols took up their assigned stations in the middle of the compound, where they could watch every door. Miguel and his other friend joined them after securing the prisoners.

Sean and Joaquin followed Magdalena to Luis's quarters. Apparently the captain still had faith in his men, for he'd left his door unlatched. Magdalena led the way to Luis's room, pulling her rapier as she went. She lit the candle beside his bed. By the time he sat up, blinking at the sudden light, she had one knee propped on his hard bed, her sword nicking him in the throat.

"*Buenas noches*, capitan. Did you have a pleasant rest?" She was amused at the horror with which he looked at her. Shaking her head, she said suavely, "No, I'm not a figment of your worst nightmare. I am real, see?" She patted him on the head.

She nodded when his befuddled expression grew hard. "Ah, that's better. Now, listen well. You are to use your influence with the administrador to guarantee that he quits stealing from those he's been assigned to help. It's no longer worth your while to accept your portion, for you see, for every piece of silver he pays you, I will take twice as much to repay those you have stolen from." She nodded at Sean and Joaquin. One of them began to methodically search Luis's chamber; the other went to the outer office and began opening desk drawers.

When his throat worked in anger, Magdalena eased the pressure of her sword slightly. "Yes, you wish to speak?"

"I don't know if you're insane or just the most arrogant *cretino* ever to walk the earth, but you'll not get away with this. I've a presidio full of men to stop you . . ."

"Come, come, think me crazy if you like, but acquit me of stupidity. Half of your men search for me. You've obliged me so kindly, it almost pains me to, er, force a donation from you to our cause."

Joaquin desisted tapping the walls to look at her sharply. Why was she deliberately riling Luis? As if she wanted him angry enough to act rashly, giving her an excuse to kill him. He'd sensed a recklessness in her since seeing her this evening, and now he was certain of it. Only anger made her so. But anger at what?

Only Magdalena knew the reason for her repressed fury. This man had sent his soldiers to kill her brother. For that alone he deserved to die. But this man was also in business with the man who'd made not only her body submit, but also her mind. Luis's dark face wavered before her eyes and became a paler face topped with gilded hair. They were one and the same, the two of them, and both deserved to be skewered like the pigs they were.

Thus, while Joaquin searched, she continued her taunting. "So brave and worthy a captain you are, such a leader of men—when the odds favor you. But when you're left to face danger alone, what becomes of your boldness then?"

Luis's face purpled with rage. He threw a longing glance at his sheathed sword, which was slung across a chair back. Magdalena closed her mouth on another taunt when Joaquin exclaimed in triumph.

Never taking her eyes from Luis's face, she prompted him, "Yes? Have you found something?"

Joaquin turned from the chest he'd pushed aside to reveal a door cut low in the wall. "In a moment, we will know." He pried open the lock with his knife, opened the door and drew out a small strong box. He searched for the key, but found none, and so indicated to Magdalena.

"The key, if you please, señor," she said politely.

Luis's mouth worked with rage, and she could see by the narrowing of his eyes that he was considering calling out.

"I would not. Your men would only get their heads blown off. I have men of my own stationed in the yard for just such an eventuality. Now, the key. No?" She shrugged, then flicked her sword up to open the nightshirt at his throat. Smiling, she snapped the silver chain off his neck with her free hand and tossed it, tiny key and all, to Joaquin.

He opened the box and gave a long whistle. Magdalena heard the clink of coins, then an odder, heavier thunk as Joaquin dropped something on top of them. The glittering hatred in Luis's eyes told her all she needed to know of its value.

Joaquin's comment merely confirmed it. "I've never seen it in its crude state before, but it's unmistakable. Gold, Jack. Lots of it. Pure nuggets, and some rocks veined with it."

Magdalena tapped one finger against her mouth, her eyes fixed on Luis's rigid features. "Now, where would you get raw gold? And, if you came by it honestly, why have you not claimed your find with the authorities, then boasted of it to all California?"

Luis didn't answer, nor did she expect him to. "Take the box to one of our friends in the yard," she suggested to Joaquin. He looked at her, hesitating, then reluctantly obeyed.

Sean called from the next room, "I found a piddly sum here, Jack. The payroll, maybe?"

"Probably the occasional pittance Mexico so generously grants the defenders of her republic," Magdalena answered. "Leave it. We've better pickings here, and I've no stomach for stealing a man's very livelihood. Unlike some."

His hands flexing, Luis looked again at his sword.

"You want your weapon?" Magdalena asked softly. She stepped back, letting her rapier tip brush the floor. "Take it and strike me down. Punish me as you think I deserve."

Luis leaped out of bed, giving her a flashing glimpse of brown thighs. Magdalena laughed soundlessly, her shoulders shaking with genuine mirth. "Ah, poor capitan, caught with your pants down. How embarrassing." And, as he snatched his rapier from his sheath, "Redeem yourself then. If you can."

Backing into the next room, Magdalena motioned to Sean. He gave her an angry look, but sighed and obeyed, pushing the chairs out of the way until the center of the large room was clear. By the time Joaquin hurried back in, Luis's blade was at the ready, and he was flexing at the knees, preparing for his first lunge.

Joaquin snapped his mouth shut over a reprimand. He'd not disturb Magdalena's concentration, but his look warned of a reckoning.

All Magdalena saw was Luis's face, and superimposed upon it, Clint's and Roberto's. She needed this. Men were such selfish creatures, caring for nothing but their own pleasures. Her blood had spilled this night. The ache between her thighs prodded her on to draw a like amount from one of the men who represented all she despised. Oh, she'd not kill Luis. But it was time he learned just how formidable an enemy El Halcon would be. He'd rush the news to Roberto, and she relished the thought of her cousin's reaction. If only she could be there to see him sweat.

Tossing her cloak to Sean, she ordered, "Stay back. Give us room." Luis gave her no time for the obligatory salute. He closed the slight gap between them with a bound, stretching his lunge so far that his extended left knee brushed the floor. Magdalena saw it coming and turned neatly aside, catching his sword with hers and shoving it outward far enough to overbalance him.

He toppled over, his face flushing with humiliation when, instead of pressing her advantage, she stood waiting, one hand propped on her hip.

"An inauspicious beginning, capitan. Perhaps we should save it for another day when you are more alert." Her mock solicitous tone brought him surging to his feet.

"A lucky strike, merely. We go on. Unless you're afraid . . ."

"As you wish." Magdalena again let him take the

initiative. He was a tall, powerful man, but only a few inches taller than herself. She parried several thrusts, batted aside a lunging stab and countered several awkward feints before she was satisfied. She'd never personally dueled with Luis before, but she'd heard Carlos talk of his strength, but slow reactions. Carlos . . . Having taken Luis's mettle, she threw caution aside and gave her instincts free rein. Her desultory movements quickened.

This time when Luis jabbed at her, she struck his blade aside so hard that his rapier vibrated, ringing in the tense stillness of the room. She didn't give him a chance to recover, following through with a thrust at his belly that was too well-planned for him to counter. If she hadn't gauged exactly how far to extend her arm, she would have gutted him.

Luis found himself suddenly changed from the aggressor trying to pin down a will-o'-the-wisp to the prey defending his life. He was forced to parry thrusts that came from nowhere and feints that slipped under his guard. At first he couldn't believe that El Halcon was so much more skillful. He, as captain, was one of the best swordsmen in the presidio. Surely this scoundrel had the luck of the devil . . . But when El Halcon entangled one of his wiliest moves with insulting ease, whammed his blade aside and stood waiting for him to recover, he could no longer lie to himself. He was facing a swordsman more skilled than any he'd ever known. His life could well be forfeit.

Magdalena saw the fear in his eyes and redoubled her efforts. Good. He was not a God-fearing man, but she'd make him fear the devil before they were done . . . She went through a dazzling series of feints and lunges, stabbing to one side, then the other, forcing him back. Time and again she pulled her arm in. She considered wounding his shoulder, but regretfully decided that she needed him reasonably whole to convey her message to Roberto. Besides, it was time to end it. They'd been lucky so far, but the ringing of their blades and the stomping of their feet were loud enough to awaken even Luis's slug-a-bed *cholos*.

Thus, when Luis made a last, desperate lunge,

Magdalena caught his sword with her own, and, with a lightning revolution of her wrist, wrested it out of his hand. It clattered against the wall and fell to the floor. A few seconds later they all heard running footsteps next door.

Luis's pale face grew confident again, even with Magdalena's rapier tip at his throat. "Now, the tables are turned, *bandido*," he sneered. "You cannot defeat so many."

"Such misplaced confidence in your brave men." She held up one finger. "Listen, capitan."

Indeed, they heard the adjacent door open simultaneous with a shot. Came a loud curse, then the door banged shut. Sean hurried outside, both his pistols primed and ready, to lend his aid. Soon more shots came, but no returning fire sounded—yet.

Luis's reptilian-eyed hatred reflected off the white teeth shining through the hood.

Magdalena allowed him to straighten. She jerked her head at Joaquin. "Find something to tie him with." Then, turning back to the captain, she said pleasantly, "If I thought you'd learned from this encounter, I'd desist your lessons. But I don't think my message has quite gotten through. Perhaps this will help." She lightly drew the tip of her blade down the side of his face, opening a long, shallow scratch that would not be deep enough to scar him. He winced and began a stream of vituperation, wiping at the blood dripping down on his nightshirt. Joaquin forced Luis's arms behind his back and tied him with the rags he'd found, then he stuffed another rag in his mouth. The captain's diatribe became garbled.

Magdalena started to sheathe her sword, then, smiling broader, she approached Luis. She inserted the blade in each shoulder of his nightshirt and flicked upward. The torn garment began to slide down, but before it could unveil him entirely, she pushed him backward. He plopped down in the chair behind him, blood trickling down his chest, his nightshirt falling to his waist. She sheathed her sword, nodding her satisfaction. It would be long indeed ere he recovered from the humiliation of this night. It was little enough punishment for his treachery, but it was a start.

She picked up her cape and swirled it about her shoulders, then strode to the door. She turned. "Adios, capitan. My thanks for a most enjoyable evening." Almost as an after-thought, she added, "And give my regards to your friend de Sarria. Tell him I hope we have similar sport soon. Very soon." Muffled curses answered her.

She and Joaquin no sooner peeked outside than shot slammed into the post near their shoulders. It hadn't taken long for the soldiers to gather their scattered wits. Magdalena saw flashes from doorways all around the compound. Only the cloudy night and the darkness of their clothes had kept her men safe so far.

"Form a circle and get to the gate, quickly, amigos," she called. Joaquin and Magdalena started across the compound in a running crouch, Joaquin firing as they went. A lucky shot knocked Magdalena's hat off, but she didn't pause as she suddenly realized a glaring fault in her plans. The soldiers were fully alert now. They'd pursue them to hell unless they were stopped . . .

When they reached the others, Joaquin closed a gap in the circle, expecting Magdalena to do the same. To his horror, she kept on alone, her flapping cloak making her a prominent target. Then he hadn't time to worry about her, for Miguel screamed and almost fell as he clutched his leg. Grimly, Joaquin supported him, firing with his free hand. The distance to the entrance was narrowing, but it seemed leagues away.

By the time Magdalena made it to the gate, she was panting, but she hadn't time to rest. She swung behind the guardhouse and hurried to the corral. Her hands were on the latch when a shot sounded to the side of her. The ball impacted with a whine into the fence next to her hand. Cursing, she bent down and reached up to unlatch the gate. She flung herself to the ground when another shot boomed, then rolled inside the corral. A powerful hoof narrowly missed her head when a nervous horse shifted out of her way.

Springing up, she slapped the horse on his hindquarters, shouting, "Ayyy!" He loped out of the corral, but into the compound instead of out of the presidio. Were they to be defeated now, when they were so close to success? She was helpless to herd the horses in the other direction, for they milled about, pinning her against the fence. She scrambled up on it and side-stepped the bottom slat to the corral gate. She was safe from being trampled now, but she was also a bold target. This time the shot landed so close she smelled the rancid odor of burning velvet and felt the jerking of her cape. When she reached the gate, she didn't dare jump down because horses were shooting out of it into the narrow corridor between the high, thick presidio inner and outer walls. But nor did she dare stay where she was. She saw another flash simultaneous to the bolt that seared her upper thigh. She closed her eyes as pain weakened her, but she forced the faintness away.

She had only one chance . . . Without giving herself time to think, she took it. She leaped for the back of the next horse that shot out of the gate. She landed with a jarring thump on his hindquarters, wincing as the impact pained her between her legs and jolted her wound. She felt herself slipping to the side and made a desperate lunge for the mane. She caught it just in time to pull herself onto the animal's back. Turning him with his forelock, she angled him across the narrow corridor, forcing the remaining horses to run out of the presidio. The dust they stirred up and the narrowness of the corridor afforded her protection from the marksman who'd aimed at her from the window cut in his quarters. When the right corral was at last empty, she kneed the stallion to the left gate and unlatched it.

These horses were restless to follow, and, whickering, they obligingly cantered out of the corral, into Santa Barbara. By the time her men at last reached the corridor, Magdalena was on the ground, ducked low against the wall, pressing on her thigh to stop the oozing blood.

She scrambled up in concern when she saw them half-carrying Miguel.

"His leg," Joaquin said tersely. Sean positioned himself

at the gate's opening into the compound to keep the soldiers pinned down while the others reached their mounts. Magdalena ignored Joaquin's sharp call and stayed to help Sean. She'd watched him reload enough to understand it, and his percussion-primed pistol was easy to load.

"Are you all right, Sean?" she asked over his fire.

"Aye. And why are ye favorin' that leg, lassie?"

"It's just a graze." Magdalena peered around the corner to see how many horses had made it into the compound. She spied only four hulking shapes before she had to duck back as a shot whined past her head.

When they heard the shout from the street, they exchanged a jubilant grin and ran out the gate. Magdalena bit down on a cry of pain as Sean held Fuego for her, but she was able to get in the saddle by herself.

She frantically waved the others away. "Go, we'll follow."

They galloped off. Magdalena held Sean's skittish horse, unaware that cold blue eyes watched her from the shadows across the street.

Clint had walked Santa Barbara for nearly an hour, looking for Carlotta, when a herd of horses almost stampeded him. He knew of only one place in town that kept so many. Curious, he waited until they passed, then started for the presidio. He arrived in time to see five men gallop off, and two more mounting. Even in the fitful light, he recognized that slim, athletic figure . . . Pulling the pistol from his pocket, he strode boldly into the middle of the street.

"Halt, El Halcon," he warned softly.

Sean froze, one foot in, one foot out of, a stirrup. He fumbled for a pistol before he remembered both were unloaded. His arm dropped back to grip the saddle as he pulled himself into it.

Magdalena lifted her head to stare at her enemy. So cool and in control he looked. So sure of himself. She wished in that moment as she'd never wished for anything that she knew how to shoot and carried an arsenal on each hip. She crossed her wrists over her pommel, mindful of the shouts issuing from the presidio. Soon, very soon, pursuit would come.

"Why do you hesitate, gringo? We are unarmed. Shoot us down." She began walking Fuego slowly toward him.

Clint cocked the pistol and repeated through his teeth, "Halt." Still the bandit came. Clint's hand trembled about the butt with the need to pull the trigger. Only the memory of Carlotta's face stayed him.

"Where is she?" he snarled.

"Who?"

"You know who. Tell me or I'll blow your head off."

"Then do so, for you'll never see her again. She asked me to tell you that."

"Dammit, what is she to you?" Clint cried, his anguish more real than Magdalena believed.

"More than you can ever know." Magdalena was even with him now, looking down upon the head that gleamed dully as the clouds began to clear. She saw his trembling hand, his fixed glare and glittering eyes. "So, you are capable of strong emotion after all, gringo. Carlotta wondered about that. I keep telling her you know nothing but lust and avarice. Soon, I think, she'll believe me."

"You, a thief, dare to preach to me of avarice? I'll find her, I swear it . . ."

Magdalena raised a hand. "Don't seek her. You might not like what you find." When Clint's face paled and his big frame literally shook with fury, Magdalena could bear no more. She leaned forward, croaking in her most menacing voice, "Hate me well, *yanqui*. It will sustain both of us until we meet again." Slapping Fuego on the hindquarters, Magdalena galloped off into the night, somehow certain he'd never shoot her in the back. With a last puzzled look between the pair, Sean followed.

The shot didn't come because the hand holding the pistol hadn't the will to use it. Cursing his own weakness, Clint dropped his arm and watched the pair fade into the night. He told himself that he couldn't shoot any man in the back, even such a one. But a stronger motivation stayed him, one he was only beginning to understand. And one he didn't

222

want to think about at that moment. For he knew, if El Halcon and Carlotta had their way, he would indeed never again see the woman he'd found after so many years of searching. But seek her he would, whether either of them liked it.

Dropping the pistol back in his pocket, he whirled and stomped off toward the docks.

Magdalena took the lead as soon as they caught up with the others. In a roundabout way, she led them to the beach, showing the Indians how to ride in and out of the tide to confuse their tracks. Then she hied Fuego up the beach to her hiding place. The soldiers would comb the area, but it was the safest place she knew. They had need to rest and tend to their wounds. Once inside the cavern, Magdalena leaned from her saddle to light the lantern she kept on a ledge. Eerie shadows flickered on the walls. The Indians looked about uneasily, but emulated her unconcern and tended to their horses.

Joaquin saw how stiffly she dismounted, but when he went toward her, she waved him away. "See to Miguel first." She tried to walk as naturally as she could to where Sean gently laid Miguel on a blanket. She moved to squat, but winced and stood straight instead.

The Indian's swarthy face had a greenish tinge. Gently Joaquin probed for the lead, exclaiming when he found it had almost exited just above and behind Miguel's knee. It had narrowly missed shattering his kneecap. Joaquin smiled sympathetically into Miguel's dilated eyes.

"It will have to come out, amigo. I used to assist a ship's surgeon, and I promise not to hurt you more than I have to. Get me your stiletto, Jack," Joaquin said tersely. When no response came, Joaquin turned his head to look up at her.

Biting her lip to stifle her recollection of just how that stiletto had been lost, she said dully, "It's gone."

Joaquin frowned, for he knew how she'd cherished the weapon, which had been a gift from her father to Carlos. He opened his mouth, but Sean intervened.

"Here, use me huntin' knife. I just sharpened it. I'll wash

223

it good, then run it through the lantern flame." When he had done so, Joaquin went to work. He only had to probe a few times, but Miguel bit so hard into the piece of rawhide they'd put between his teeth that the tough substance tore. When, with an able flick, Joaquin dug the round shot out, Miguel's back arched against the cavern wall. Joaquin swabbed the wound, smeared it with the medicinal paste he'd made from mountain herbs and tied a clean bandage about it.

Magdalena ignored her protesting muscles and knelt to wipe the sweat on Miguel's brow away. "I'm sorry you were hurt, Miguel. But our danger was not without reward." She made to rise and go to the strongbox Sean had taken off Miguel's horse, but Joaquin caught her cloak and pulled her back down. All eyes fixed on the dark, wet patch spreading now to encompass her entire left leg.

The resentment in Miguel's eyes changed first to puzzlement, then to admiration. What manner of man was this who ignored his own wound to comfort one of his men? Bitter experience had led Miguel to expect aggression, cruelty and abuse from white men. Only desperation had led him to throw in his uncertain lot with one he sensed was a member of the *gente de razon*, the exploiters of his people. Desperation, and the tantalizing fact that El Halcon fought those he hated most. But this? This consideration . . . no, it was more than that. This . . . generosity, from a white to an Indian, shamed him. For the first time, he realized it was not only the whites who had prejudice. He looked at his friends and saw from their faces that their thoughts were much the same.

When again the hooded figure tried painfully to rise, Miguel said, "Time enough to see what we've won later. See to his wound, Ricardo. We've need of him if we're to bring justice to my people." And Miguel smiled, the first genuine smile Magdalena had ever seen on his face.

She flopped back down beside him, her throat so closed up that she didn't have to fake her croak. "This will only take a moment. Mick, the box."

When Sean had set the box before her, she took the key

224

from Joaquin and unlocked it. She rested both hands upon the lid, letting the moment build, before she exulted, "See, compadres, what your daring has won!" She flung back the lid.

Everyone, even Joaquin, squatted about her in a circle to cascade the coins and nuggets through their hands. None of them had ever seen so much wealth.

Pablo, a small, plump Indian with a moon-shaped face and a mournful smile to match, asked, "But what are these?" He held a nugget to the light, turning it from side to side to admire its glitter.

Magdalena looked at Miguel's enraptured face. "Tell him, amigo," she urged, smiling.

"*Oro*," he murmured. "Like that the señoras wear on their fingers. It is most valuable."

The Indians grunted their astonishment. When they'd all played with the pretty baubles, Magdalena closed the lid and locked the box. The Indians looked at Joaquin, expecting her to give him the key. Instead, she tossed it up and down in her palm.

"We will count it later. We need someone trustworthy to keep our winnings. You say you assisted the padres with the storehouse ledgers, Miguel?" At his cautious nod, Magdalena offered the key to him. "Will you honor us by doing the same for us? We'll get a ledger book for you."

He blinked his astonishment, looking at his friends for verification, but they, too, stared goggle-eyed at El Halcon. "That is, if Pablo, Benito and Juan don't object?" Dumbly, the trio shook their heads.

When Miguel still seemed stunned, Magdalena gently pried open his hand and dropped the key into it. "Keep it safe, Miguel." She struggled to rise. Joaquin caught her beneath the elbows and heaved her up. "Please excuse me . . ."

Sean turned to unsaddle and rub down the rest of the horses, smiling as the Indians gossiped together about their odd leader. S'truth, her talents were wasted on a female, he thought to himself with typical male arrogance. She should be a general, leading her men against impossible odds to

225

victory, or an admiral, outsailing and outthinking lesser captains to crush a superior fleet. But then, remembering how she looked, the wind blowing her long hair back from her exquisitely molded face, he knew he'd have her no other way. If only she felt the same . . . Sighing philosophically, for he'd accepted at last that she'd never be more than a friend to him, Sean turned and joined the Indians. When they asked him about their leader, Sean told them as much truth as he could without giving away her identity.

As Joaquin supported her to the rear of the cave, Magdalena basked in the feeling that for once she'd done something right. Even Joaquin didn't seem so angry with her any longer.

Indeed, his anger had muted to approval and weary patience. He knew where she'd gotten her leadership abilities, and he couldn't help thinking how proud, but how anguished, Patrick would be at the life his daughter had embraced. He propped her against the rear cave wall while he hung a blanket over two rock outcroppings, then flung their cloaks over them so that even her shadow would not show through the double thickness. She took off the hood with a glad sigh.

"Take off your breeches so I can tend to your leg," he ordered. "We'll get you comfortable before I demand explanations."

Magdalena did so without a second thought, for he'd seen her in less than her long shirt many times in the last two years. She was still too pleased with herself to remember that she bore evidence of another wound she'd received in a far different way . . .

At first, Joaquin noticed nothing. He dipped a clean rag in the bucket of fresh saltwater Sean had fetched, helped her sit down on a padded blanket and gently swabbed the half-inch deep gash that marred the entire outside width of her perfect white thigh. She winced at the sting of the saltwater, but she didn't cry out. It took him several minutes before he'd cleaned all the blood away, for it had dripped from her thigh to her ankle. He flung the rag into the rusty red water, probing along the wound with his fingers.

226

He sat back on his heels, sighing with relief. "The shot grazed you deeply, but cleanly. You'll heal well enough, but you'll have a scar."

"My muscles weren't damaged, were they? I'm so stiff . . ."

"That's natural enough. No, you should have full use of your leg when you're well." He smiled sardonically at her sigh of relief. How like her to worry more about retaining her fencing skills than being marked for life. He doctored her leg, then handed her the clean pair of pants he'd brought with them. She half-rose to step into them, but her stiffness made her awkward. She fell over, her shirt riding up to bare her inner thighs.

His breath drew in sharply. He leaned forward and shoved the shirt higher. Was she wounded somewhere else? How could her blood have flown upward?

Confused at his concern, she followed his glance. She went ashen and jerked the tails down. She tried to rise again, but he caught her arm.

"Where else are you hurt? Surely you weren't shot at . . . er, up . . ."

Magdalena shook her head wildly. "No, no, it's just smeared blood from the wound." But her voice was high, breathless, and he knew she was hiding something.

"Nonsense. Let me see . . ." He tried to shove the shirt back, but she slapped his hand away.

"I'm fine, I tell you." She struggled to her feet and stuck one foot into a pants leg, but there was nothing she could do to shield herself from his frowning appraisal.

The blood was very high on her inner thighs, and it was pale, as if it had been mixed with something else, then half-heartedly wiped away . . . His breath gushed out of his lungs. His gaze leaped to her face.

She met it for only a moment before she looked down and buttoned her breeches with trembling fingers. He leaned weakly back against the wall. She'd been through so much. Now this, too? How had it happened?

He caught her hand and drew her gently down beside him. "Don't lie to me any longer, Magdalena. It's obvious you lost something else this night besides several inches of skin. I don't blame you, but I must know how it happened. It was the American, wasn't it?"

She hid her face in her hands, rocking back and forth. "You don't blame me? *Dios*, if only I could say the same." She drew her hands slowly down her cheeks and looked at him through tear-filled eyes. She'd hoped he'd never learn of this, but now that he had, she owed him the truth. If it hadn't been for her own weakness, she'd have been long gone before the gringo returned. She'd delayed, she knew now, because a part of her was still reluctant to leave him. But that she couldn't admit, even to Joaquin.

She took a deep breath, wrapping her arms about her upraised knees. "He came upon me searching his chest. When he took the stiletto away from me, he recognized it and thought me El Halcon's mistress." A watery laugh shook her chest. "There's irony for you, Joaquin. I was betrayed not by an enemy, but by my own cleverness. He used one of my identities in hatred of the other, not realizing I was both." She buried her face in her knees.

Joaquin stroked her tangled hair and let her cry for several minutes. His eyes were cold and hard as they appraised her, but his thoughts were obviously far away. "And when he discovered you were innocent? What did he do then?"

Flinging her head up, she dashed her tears away. "He reveled in being the first," she spat. "And then . . . then . . ." Her voice broke, as if she couldn't bear to continue.

When his hand tightened with unknowing strength upon her shoulder, she welcomed the pain. "And then he made me enjoy it, the second time. For that, I will kill him." Her voice was flat, and she was too anguished to see the fury in Joaquin's eyes. She lay back on the blanket.

"So, *mi amigo*, you were right. I never should have gone near him. My recklessness has cost me dear. But I did at least gain some knowledge. See there, in my pack."

Joaquin rummaged in the sack she'd brought from the ship and tossed in the rear of the cave. He opened the parchment, bringing it into the light. When he'd looked it over thoroughly, he rolled it back up and flung it against the cave wall in disgust.

"*Americano puerco*! Doubtless he's greedy for our lands."

"Agreed, but I still think he's partnered with Roberto. In what, I don't know, but it probably has something to do with the gold." Magdalena yawned, worn out by her physical and emotional exertions.

"Sleep, *pobrecita*, we will talk more later. I'm sorry I couldn't keep you safe . . ." His voice cracked, then he covered her and stalked to the front of the cave. Magdalena barely heard him as the black waves of exhaustion carried her away.

Joaquin glanced at the snoring Indians and went to Sean, who was sleepily keeping guard. He shook his shoulder. "She's asleep in the back. See that she's not disturbed," Joaquin whispered. "I've a duty to perform. If I'm not back by dawn, go on to the mountains without me." Taking one of Sean's pistols, he loaded it carefully, stuck it in his belt and patted his sword; then he pushed the brush curtain aside to stride into the blackness.

Sean frowned as he watched Joaquin go, but weariness had taken its toll even on his massive frame. It would be hard enough for him to keep awake until Pablo relieved him without worrying about Joaquin. That wily fox could take care of himself . . .

Clint slumped over the table, reaching with an unsteady hand to pour himself the last of the brandy. He was oblivious to the narrow dark eyes watching him from the shadows. The bottle clattered against the glass, but he filled the fine crystal without spilling more than a few drops. He lifted the glass to appraise the amber liquid before taking a deep swallow. He savored the smooth fire burning a path to his gullet. "Ah, there's no brandy like Spanish brandy. No maid like a Spanish maid . . ." His voice shook. He lifted the glass to his lips again, then slammed it down, propped his elbows on the table and rubbed his forehead with both palms.

"Guilty, gringo? You disappoint me," a cool, hard voice mocked from nowhere.

Clint lifted his head to blink at the disembodied sound. When a slight dark man holding a pistol in one steady hand stepped out of the doorway, Clint took a moment to connect the man to the voice. He shook his head a little in an effort to clear it, but the wraith didn't dissolve. "Who are you? What do you want?"

The man came forward into the light, and Clint was certain then, drunk or not, that he'd never seen him before. But, judging from the enmity in those long dark eyes, this man knew him. Or of him. And what he knew, he disliked. Clint's nose twitched as the scent of danger wafted into his nostrils, clearing the haze from his brain. He had to get himself together. Unless he was very, very careful, this man would kill him. The resolve was written plainly in that rigidly controlled face. And his derringer was still in the jacket thrown on the floor clear across the cabin . . .

Clint clasped his hands together on the tabletop, leaning back in his chair. "Very well, since you don't want to tell me that, perhaps you'll share something more pressing: Why do you want to kill me?"

The dark eyes flickered with surprise at his coolness. Joaquin had expected this man, a coward who used his strength on a woman, a drunkard, to whine for his life. Instead, bright blue eyes met his, the drunken glaze clearing rapidly.

"Because you deserve to die. Unless, of course, you'd prefer a more fitting punishment . . ." Joaquin aimed his big pistol at the apex of Clint's sprawled legs.

Clint blanched, but exclaimed, "You're here because of Carlotta! Where is she? Is she well? Is she safe?" He leaned forward eagerly.

Joaquin frowned, again surprised at a reaction he hadn't expected. Surely that was genuine concern in the gringo's voice? "Do you really care if she is?"

"Yes, more than you can know." At his opponent's

skeptical look, Clint added dryly, "Or believe, apparently." He waved a hand to the chair opposite. "Please, sit. The least you can do is set my mind at rest before you spatter my brains all over my cabin."

Joaquin was so puzzled at his unconcern that he obeyed before he realized what he was doing. Indeed, this man was not what he'd expected. Either he was very brave, or very foolish. Which? "I'll give you one chance to defend yourself. It's more than you deserve, but you make me curious, gringo."

Sighing, Clint held up a weary hand. "Please, I tire of being called gringo. Call me Clint, call me Captain Browning, or call me . . ."

"What you really are—rapist!" Joaquin interrupted curtly, the pistol barrel braced on the edge of the table, pointing at Clint's chest. "The woman you took for a maid is a lady with more aristocratic blood in her veins than exists in your whole cursed land. She's no quick toss in the hay for such as you. We kill men for that in this country. I've failed her often enough . . ." Joaquin's voice shook before he steadied it. "But I'll not fail her in this."

Clint stunned him yet again by agreeing, "I don't blame you. If anyone had treated my sister so, I'd do the same." He leaned forward earnestly. "But please believe me—and pass this on to Carlotta—when I tell you that I never would have . . . forced her had I known she was a virgin. By the time I found out, it was too late." Clint looked down. He could make other excuses. She'd incited him, dared him, mocked him. But in the last analysis, he'd used his superior strength to wrest something from her she'd not have willingly given. At least, the first time. But that, too, was something between him and Carlotta.

Lifting his head, he looked squarely at the small dark man. "And I'll not lie to you. Kill me if you think I deserve it, but I cherish every moment I spent with her. If you don't strike me down now, I'll do all in my power to find her and prove that what we knew together was not a lie. It began badly, but ended good. For both of us. And it can lead to better things. She's more woman than any I've ever known, and I long, as I've never longed for anything, to prove to her that I'm all the man she needs."

What was he to do now? Joaquin wondered. He should have shot the man without discussing the issue. But he'd raised some telling points. And what he'd not raised was even more telling. Joaquin knew Magdalena too well. She'd not have accepted her fate tamely. Yet she bore no bruises and had herself admitted that she'd enjoyed what he'd done to her at the end. So, furious as he undoubtedly was, this man had taken her with less brutality than most would have. Yet he made no excuses for himself. As if he in truth held dear—and private—what had passed between them. Indeed, unless he was as skillful a manueverer as Machiavelli, he truly cared for Magdalena. If it were so, he did not deserve to die.

While Joaquin sat quiet, Clint picked up his glass to take a desultory sip. He rolled the brandy around on his tongue, swallowed and swirled the liquid in his glass. Then, taking advantage of Joaquin's hesitation, he flung the alcohol in his face, snatching the pistol out of his hand.

Joaquin cursed, wiping his stinging eyes clear, only to have them filled with the sight of his own gun leveled at him beneath steady blue eyes. For a moment, the adversaries stared at one another; then, to his astonishment, Clint offered the weapon to him, butt first. Joaquin took it in a limp hand.

Clint knew he was taking a huge gamble, but he sensed this man had lived a life based on justice. "I am no threat to you, or to Carlotta," he said quietly. "I want only to assist her in whatever she fights against, get to know her and be given a chance to win her. I'll never again touch her unless she wishes it. I swear it, by the God I sense we both love."

Surely if Browning were truly allied with Roberto, I'd be dead now, Joaquin thought. And the instincts that had clamored at him from their first meeting, making him hesitate, spoke loudly now. *Yanqui* though he was, this was a man of morals. If he joined their cause, he could be a powerful ally. Moreover, he sensed Browning would be good for Magdalena. She was strongly attracted to him.

Perhaps he could even help her accept her femininity and, if he were worthy of her, give her the happiness she deserved.

Joaquin stuck the pistol in his belt, the action speaking for itself. Clint slumped a little in relief. "I will tell her, but it will take more than that to appease her. If you want to aid us, you also aid El Halcon." With the barest smile, he concluded, "She fights closely by his side."

Clint frowned. He'd suspected as much, but he still wasn't pleased to hear it. He'd sworn retribution against that arrogant bandit. They hated one another. How could he aid him in his thievery?

Smiling secretively, Joaquin rose. So, the gringo would be punished, a little, in the choice he'd have to make. He started for the door.

"But where will I find you if I decide to join you?"

Joaquin shrugged. "We'll find you."

"Please, I must know one thing . . . What is Carlotta to El Halcon?"

Joaquin turned. Browning's face was red with his frustration, and something more. Perhaps a little jealousy would do him good. Again, came the ghost of a smile. "She's his refuge; he's her strength..They're each the best and worst of one another." With this peculiar answer, he was gone, his steps so light and swift that the sounds faded before he'd reached topside.

Clint groaned and buried his aching head in his hands. Damn these Latins and their riddles. Would he ever solve the mystery that was Carlotta? Moreover—would he even get the chance?

# Chapter 10

"A greater scoundrel ne'er drew the breath of heaven."
**Act I, DON JUAN TENORIO**

Roberto de Sarria locked the study door behind him. Hands propped on his hips, he glared around the simply but elegantly furnished room. Curse the sly old bastard, where could he have hidden the will? For over two years now he'd searched: Ramon's bedroom, the study, the other bedrooms, the front room, even the kitchen. And he'd found nothing. Perhaps no other will existed, and it had been an empty threat. But instinct told him to keep searching. Only when the will was destroyed—and his cousin was dead—would he be safe.

He was beginning to feel secure in the latter suspicion. Magdalena must be dead. One thing, and one thing only, all the de Sarrias had in common was a will that went beyond stubbornness and became obsession when the challenge was great enough. He himself had so grown to love the land he'd worked that he'd twice committed murder to win it for his own. And, knowing what he had done, Magdalena would

235

not rest until she'd avenged herself upon him. Given the fact that no one had heard anything of her in the past two years, she *must* be dead. With no money, and no skills to survive, how could she have lived?

Even so, he returned to his methodic search. He'd tapped every inch of the walls, searched every cranny of the desk. Now he began on the other side of the room, turning over chairs, feeling behind the seats and frames. He started when a loud knock interrupted him.

"What?" he called irritably, thinking Sarita disturbed him with inconsequential household matters.

"It's Luis. Open the door."

Roberto set the chair upright and surveyed the room to be sure all was normal. Luis didn't know of the other will. Roberto trusted no man, not even his best friend, with something so vital to his future. Luis had sent men to kill Carlos believing that only then would Magdalena marry his friend. When Roberto was sole owner of El Paraiso, he'd agreed to share a portion of his hides with Luis. Fortunately, that had not been necessary, for he'd found something of more intrinsic worth to appease his partner . . .

Satisfied that all was as usual, Roberto unlocked the door, smiling a welcome. "*Buenas dias,* Luis. *Como* . . ." his voice trailed away as Luis came into the study, his face illuminated in the light streaming through the windows.

"*Dios mio*! What happened to you?"

Luis rubbed two fingers along the scratch running from his temple to his jaw, his eyes lightless as a snake's. "El Halcon. He was crazy enough to invade the presidio last night. Now, he'll die long before the governor has a chance to sentence him."

Waving Luis into a chair, Roberto shut the door and sat down opposite him. He frowned at his friend, but before he could voice the question, Luis nodded curtly.

"*Si*, he found the box. All is gone."

Roberto slammed his fist down on the hide-covered chair arm. "How could you have been so careless?" Luis stiffened, but Roberto raged on. "Over two years we've toiled to wrest that bit of gold out of the mountain. How will we ever raise enough to purchase the land from Mexico if we can't retain what we take?"

"*Basta*!" Luis growled back. "What would you have done if you were awakened out of a sound sleep with a sword at your throat?"

That silenced Roberto, but his face was still red with fury when he demanded, "Tell me what happened."

Luis gave a curt sketch of last night's events, ending with a mocking, "The last thing El Halcon said to me before leaving was, 'Give my regards to your friend de Sarria. Tell him I hope we can have similar sport soon.'"

Roberto's nails dug so hard into the tough hide that he scored the leather. "The insolent *desgraciado*!"

Again Luis ran a hand gingerly down his face. "He didn't say so, but I got the impression that this was meant as a message to you as much as to me. Also, Captain Browning came to me several days ago to tell me that he'd been questioned by El Halcon as to his relationship to you. For a man who's met you once, the bandit's hatred of you is strong."

Roberto's fingers relaxed. He bent his head to stare at the floor, then he met Luis's eyes. "Do you suppose *she*'s involved in this in some way?"

The "she" needed no definition for Luis. "The thought occurred to me. But why would a thief take up the cause of a penniless woman at extreme danger to himself? What would he have to gain?" Luis was surprised when Roberto's eyes flickered away from his.

Shrugging his wide shoulders, Roberto answered, "Who can know such a madman's reasons?"

"Perhaps it's 'gallantry,' as the women whisper behind my back," Luis sneered, his opinion of such a useless emotion clear.

Roberto laughed coarsely. "More likely it's something else. She was becoming a striking, sensual woman. She'd not be above using her body to get what she wants. *If* she's still alive. If she isn't what does this bandit want of us?"

Indeed, such was the mystery they had to solve. Both men brooded on it for several long minutes, then Luis leaned back, linking his hands behind his head. "It doesn't really matter. One way or another, we must kill El Halcon. If she's alive, she's probably with his band. We'll find her when we find him."

Roberto rose to pour them each a glass of wine. "As usual, my friend, you are wise. Now, how are we to catch him? You say he has more men with him now?"

"Si. Five or six, at least." Luis took the offered glass, but he caught Roberto's wrist. "El Halcon is more dangerous then we expected. He could have killed me at will last night. Never have I fenced a man with such skill."

Roberto pulled away. "Then you'll have to leave him to me. Now Carlos is dead, not a swordsman in California can defeat me, as you well know." Unconcernedly Roberto sat to take a long, enjoyable draught of his wine. He delicately wiped his mouth with his handkerchief, finishing, "I'll relish seeing him squirm on the tip of my sword. I'll let him beg for mercy before I kill him."

Having faced El Halcon in battle, Luis knew better. Luis hated the bandit too much to admit to admiration, but he knew one thing of El Halcon: he'd face death as boldly as he faced life. That one knew little of the fears that cautioned most mortal men. Perhaps he really was part demon. . . .

Shrugging away the chill, Luis suggested, "Perhaps Captain Browning can be of some use to us. We don't need him to smuggle the gold out with the tallow, yet, but he has travelled the coast widely. He seems to hate El Halcon as much as we do. The tales of El Halcon's gallantry to Angelina Rivas and the indios are spreading. The people seem wary of talking to my men about him. Many seem to genuinely admire his bravery. Those who don't will do anything to spite me as representative of the Mexican government. But Browning, as a trader, can travel among them freely and discover more. I've invited him here to discuss both matters."

Roberto scowled. "The *yanqui* is a fool. He'd be more of a hindrance than a help. Like all his kind, he comes here for advantage. The people are no more likely to be open with him than they are with you. No, I'll have no dealings with that pretty, effete bear. Retract your invitation, and next time ask me first."

The look on Browning's face when he'd offered his aid had been anything but effete, Luis thought, but he didn't argue. That inflexible set of Roberto's jaw meant his mind was made up, and neither heaven nor hell would sway him.

"Very well. I will continue to send my men out in shifts, but I don't know what else to do."

"You should post several guards along El Camino Real. Eventually the bandits will pass, and your men can follow them, then return to you to disclose their location."

Luis rubbed his bent index finger against his mouth, then nodded. "A good idea. I'll see to it at once. Now, when do you go to the cave again? Have the mining supplies arrived?"

Roberto set his glass down with a snap. "No, the shipment must have been lost or stolen. At the rate we're excavating with chisel and hammer, it will be years before we have enough funds to purchase the land from Mexico."

"Perhaps we should bring Julio in to help . . ."

"No, his tongue is too loose. He could never keep such news to himself. If your government learns the value of that infertile, rocky land donated to the church, they'll never sell it."

For the dozenth time, Luis groused, "If only I hadn't received my eleven league maximum farther into the valley, I could have obtained the lands easily."

Flinging one long leg over a chair arm, Roberto nodded glum agreement. "Indeed, your timing was most unfortunate. And I, of course, have far too much land to apply. No, this is the only way. Mexico will leap at the opportunity to get hard currency for her lands for a change. And with Borge making the purchase for us anonymously, no one will wonder where we got the money or question why I want the lands that border my own. How agreeably surprised I'll be to trade for the land, then find a gold deposit."

Luis yearned to put their flawless plan into execution. He was tired of soldiering, tired of doing without the comforts he'd so enjoyed in Mexico. Yet he had no hankering to return. Luis liked California's temperate climate and scenery. He liked even more the easy ways of its people. Here, a man could live as he pleased. Since he couldn't bring these things to Mexico, he'd bring what he missed of Mexico to California. And for that, he needed hard cash.

Currency was scarce in California; even the wealthy traded for goods. But the gold would make all his dreams come true. He could hire a fleet of ships and an army of skilled workers to build the magnificent mansion he dreamed of. While the indios worked his lands, he'd go to Spain and buy the aristocratic Spanish bride he'd always coveted. Then, he'd be content. He'd let someone else run the presidio and risk getting his heart cut out.

Stifling a sigh of longing, he urged, "Send for the supplies again. With the right tools, we should be able to work much faster."

"I'll do so tomorrow, then work the cave in what time I can spare after giving Julio his instructions for the day. Can you join me to help?"

"I'll try to, after sending several of my best men to watch the highway."

Both men rose, Roberto escorting Luis to the door with an arm about his shoulders. "Take care of your face, my friend. This time, I think I will keep our spoils. I'll post more guards, but El Halcon will not dare come here."

Luis wished he had the same confidence, but El Halcon had shaken it out of him. He said only, "I will send for you if we locate him."

"Good." Roberto smiled coldly. "The bandit will learn the hard way that stealing, not once, but twice, from Roberto de Sarria is the worst mistake he ever made."

Magdalena glanced sideways once more at Joaquin. He'd been unusually quiet since they'd risen shortly before dawn to sneak away. She longed to ask him what was wrong, but it must wait until they were alone. She'd seen Sean deep in conversation with him as she was rounding the men up and wondered at Joaquin's satisfied air as he nodded once, as if

240

having a suspicion confirmed. Yet he'd hardly spoken a word since. What was he worried about?

They'd decided to camp in their old hideaway for now. They'd discovered all they could by staying in Santa Barbara. Further delay, now the presidio was alerted, was dangerous. They were safer in the mountains, making calculated raids upon those who persecuted the Indians most. Miguel thought that if they continued to share their wealth, word would reach the renegades high in the hills, and their numbers would swell to impressive size.

Magdalena prayed he was right. She'd need a small army to risk invading El Paraiso. Miguel had told her that Roberto kept almost twenty armed guards near the house at all times. The news was more tantalizing than worrisome to Magdalena, for only a man with something to fear was so nervous. Rage almost overwhelmed her as she thought of Roberto lounging in abuelo's study, but she quieted it as she had of late—by thinking of someone else she hated almost as much.

When would the gringo leave? The measly amount of hides and tallow he'd traded for would have long since sent a genuine trader in pursuit of better commerce. The fact that he'd stayed so long was more proof of his sinister motivations. Now that Magdalena had seen the gold with her own eyes, she knew what those were. Somehow, he was important to Luis and Roberto in their scheme. She must discover how. Perhaps it was too late to prove Luis and Roberto guilty of murder. But if, as she suspected, their gold was stolen from someone else's lands, the governor would not be pleased. And if, on top of that, she found the changed will, then all California would see the fine, respected Roberto de Sarria as he really was. No one would blame her if she challenged him to a duel and killed him.

The glow at the thought was snuffed under the douche of cold reality. Her existence was built on a series of ifs. Sometimes despair almost overcame her. Perhaps she'd spend the rest of her short life on this quest, tilting uselessly at windmills like her lachrymose hero, Don Quixote. But unlike him, her dangers were real. And unlike him, she had no hope of coming to her senses. If she died, it would be as she lived: fighting to her last breath, but facing death squarely if all was lost. She alone had begun this. She, and she alone, would kill Roberto and take the consequences. If death were the cost, then it was a price she was willing to pay.

Feeling somewhat better, she turned to her small party and called, "Come, compadres, we are almost there. We shall rest; then, tomorrow, we take to the road!" Slapping Fuego's hindquarters, she loped him up the steep trail to the cavern, ignoring the twinges in her leg. It was still stiff, but it was better. She hoped by tomorrow she'd be well enough to ride with the others.

She felt almost a sense of homecoming as she dismounted, took several lanterns off one of the packhorses and lit them. There was the barrel they used to wash their dishes. Their closet, the string hung from stalactite to stalactite, still hung secure. Her guitar, swaddled in cloth and then in hide to protect it from the damp, was propped against the wall. El Paraiso this was not, but it was a dwelling she'd selected, and it offered something more vital than comfort—safety.

She waved Sean away after he'd helped Miguel down from his horse. "I'll see to him. You help settle the others."

Magdalena supported Miguel's shoulders as he hopped on his good leg to a jutting rock ledge and sat down with a sigh of relief. When he rubbed at his leg, Magdalena knelt to push his torn pants aside and look at the bandage. She was not surprised to see it soaked with blood. "Ricardo, bring the paste," she called to Joaquin.

She took the clean bandages and medicine from him when he would have done the job himself. "It's my fault he's wounded. Let me see to him." She flashed a smile up at him that gleamed through the slit in her hood. "Besides, amigo, it's best *you* see to dinner. I'll not have our friend here with a bellyache to add to his woes."

Miguel smiled weakly at the joke. He slumped against the wall behind him, watching as she stripped off her gloves and went to work. What white, slender hands El Halcon had. Almost . . . womanish. He realized that this was the first time he'd seen them. He wondered, too, what terrible countenance under his hood made him so afraid for his own men to see it. He was somehow not surprised when, finished tying the clean bandage, El Halcon stood, wiped off his hands and drew his gloves back on.

"There, does that feel better?" When Miguel nodded, El Halcon turned away to help organize the men.

Miguel watched him, observing that only when all had selected a spot for their mats did he select his own, far in the back of the cave, behind a blanket wall. El Halcon was always ready with an encouraging word and he laughed as loud as any at their rough jokes, but there was yet a reserve about him that none, even Ricardo, could fully breach. He slept isolated; even surrounded by his men, he somehow seemed always alone. Miguel thought there was much to be admired, but also much to puzzle over, in their leader.

El Halcon soon came back out to help pass out the stew Joaquin had made. Only when all were served did he take a plate for himself. Miguel ate slowly, more tired and sore than hungry, but he knew he'd need his strength, so he forced the savory beef, carrots and potatoes down.

After they'd sated their hunger, they retired. El Halcon gestured to Joaquin to follow him. When they were seated on opposite sides of her mat, Magdalena drew off her hood and rotated her neck on her shoulders in relief. Then she propped her elbows on her knees, her chin in her hands and looked at Joaquin steadily.

"Well, do you tell me why you've been silent as the grave all day? What do you worry about?"

She knew Joaquin too well to be fooled by his evasive "Nothing. I'm but tired."

Unfolding her legs, she nudged his knee with her boot. "Come, amigo, you badger me until I share all with you. The least you can do is grant me the same courtesy."

Joaquin sighed, but, as usual, she was right. Perhaps it would do her good to talk about the *yanqui*. He knew he'd never change her mind, but if he could plant a few seeds of doubt, then maybe, when Browning came as he inevitably would, she'd let him stay.

Joaquin tilted his head to one side to study her as he said baldly, "I confronted the gringo last night while you slept. I went there to kill him."

She scrambled to her knees with an anguished cry, and he hastily went on, "But I could not." When she slumped back down to the ground, he shook his head at her gently. "*Niña, niña,* if you could see your face. I should have realized that there was much you didn't tell me."

Magdalena lifted her head proudly. Not even to herself would she admit how devastated she'd been to think Browning was dead. "And he told you, I suppose, how he pleasured me, took me away from myself and made me, for once in my life, glad to be a woman? Then he savored my humiliation and showed me how very foolish I had been to trust him, even for those few short moments. . . ."

Joaquin took her hand, twining his fingers gently with hers. "He told me very little, Magdalena. In fact, he admitted that he had wronged you. His actions were not those of a strutting womanizer. His concern was all for you—where you were, if you were all right, how you were feeling . . ."

Magdalena jerked her hand away. "Bah! He's fooled even you. You disappoint me, Joaquin."

"And you, *niña,* will disappoint me if you don't try to understand what happened between you with your mind instead of your emotions. Isn't it time you admitted that you care for this *yanqui*?"

Magdalena shook her head wildly. "No, no, it isn't true! He made me lust for him, that's all. Never could I care for such as he."

"And what if you're wrong? What if he is an honorable man? Will you let him help us then?"

"Never! Twice now I've trusted him, only to find out he's an ally of Roberto's and a spy on my people. What wizardry did he work upon you to fool you so?" She looked at him with combined horror and incredulity.

"No wizardry, Magdalena. I've lived my life by trusting

244

my instincts. I can't stop now. And that instinct tells me Browning cares for you and would make a powerful ally. We don't know why he drew the map. Perhaps it's for his own trading purposes . . ." At her scoffing sound, Joaquin leaned forward to pierce her with keen dark eyes. "He took my gun away, Magdalena, then gave it back to me, asking me to tell you that he is no threat to us. If he were truly allied with Roberto, don't you think he would have killed me then?"

For the first time, a flicker of doubt shadowed Magdalena's pale features, but she shook her head adamantly. "Another trick. He *wants* us to believe him so he can spy on us." When Joaquin would have spoken again, she put her fingers over his lips. "No more, Joaquin. You'll not convince me. I don't dare trust him."

With those revealing words, she turned away from him on her side and pillowed her head on her hands. "Now please leave me. We've much planning to do tomorrow."

Sighing, Joaquin rose, but he couldn't resist a parting shot. "Sleep well, little coward. Run away to your dreams. Maybe there, truth will find you." He departed to his own pallet.

Truth was indeed her bedfellow that night, but it took a most unusual form. It had soft golden hair that billowed through her fingers, big, rough hands that caressed her sweetly and a hard, driving body that possessed her utterly. Heart, soul and mind were lost to her, but she celebrated the loss. For again, after so long, she belonged. She was wanted. And she wanted in return.

Magdalena awoke with a start around dawn, her heart pumping, her body trembling with arousal. Slowly, slowly, the vivid images faded. She shut her eyes to stem the tears. It was her body that betrayed her. Joaquin was wrong. Her heart was not involved at all. And if Browning came near her again, she'd kill him. Then, she'd be free of this peculiar fever. Rising, she dressed and went to rouse her men.

Clint shifted wearily in his saddle. He was getting better at this damned uncomfortable way of transport, but he still

245

didn't like it. However, a horse was vital to this task. Somewhere here, in the mountains north of Santa Barbara where El Halcon had first accosted them, he'd find her.

Two days ago, he'd left Pritikin in charge of the shop and begun the search he knew could well be fruitless. But he had to do something! The encounter with the slim Latin hadn't reassured him in the least; indeed, it had made him more anxious than ever to find Carlotta. If there were a mysterious bond between her and El Halcon, then he had to find her before it cemented him out. Things had not progressed between the pair to an intimate point—at least, not yet. Unless . . . unless she'd taken him as a lover since he'd initiated her into the joys of the flesh. Rage consumed him at the thought, rage so strong that he trembled with it.

She was his. By God, she'd given herself to him. Not the first time, but the second. For a woman such as she, who held herself in high regard, that was no small commitment. But he had to find her and make her admit it before the bandit had a chance to press his suit. That would be revenge enough on El Halcon. A man of such arrogance would not enjoy the part of jilted suitor. Clint's anticipatory smile screwed up into a grimace as his stallion stumbled over a rock, almost launching him onto the ground. He pulled the bay's head up just in time, then sat motionless, breathing heavily. It was definitely time for a rest.

Dismounting, he led the bay into the shade of a large tree off the highway and tied the animal up. Then he pulled some tortillas and jerky out of his pack, uncorked the bottle of wine he'd brought and slumped tiredly back against the tree to eat his lunch. He was just wiping off the mouth of the bottle to recork it when he heard someone approaching. His fingers froze around the bottle; then he tossed it aside, uncaring that the remainder of the wine soaked into the ground, and rose to hide as best he could behind the bole of the tree.

A few seconds later, a lone rider rounded the bend. Clint strained to see his face under the shady, wide-brimmed hat, but it wasn't until he'd passed that he glimpsed the familiar features. Clint eased from behind the tree to watch the man's brisk progress down the highway. Now what was Luis doing out here? They were past the Gaviota and shortly beyond the turn-off to El Paraiso. Perhaps he was heading to Monterey or San Francisco? Without pausing to wonder why he felt an urgent need to follow him, Clint tossed aside his half-eaten tortilla, untied his horse and vaulted into the saddle.

Ignoring his protesting muscles, he urged the animal into a trot. When, after several minutes, he still couldn't spy Luis, he kicked his stallion into a lope, sighing with relief as the jouncing of his sore rear eased. Still, he saw nothing ahead of him. He should have caught up with Luis by now, for the man hadn't been traveling above a brisk walk. Confused, Clint drew the panting stallion up and turned him about, scanning the sides of the highway as he retraced their steps. At first he saw nothing, then a movement caught the corner of his eye.

There! High up on that scrub-covered hill, Luis was letting his animal pick his way up the treacherous slope. Even as Clint watched, the horse slipped and regained his footing. A moment later, they rounded the side of the hill and were lost to sight.

Clint sighed. The last thing he wanted to do was follow him, but Luis was behaving oddly and Clint sensed tracking him would gain him valuable information. Whatever Luis and de Sarria were involved in, for example. And an enticement—or a club, whichever seemed handiest—for El Halcon. Clint reined his stallion off the highway and began his ascent.

Several times, when his stallion slipped and snorted in fear, Clint grabbed the saddle pommel and cursed himself for a fool. Only the memory of Carlotta and the urgent need to prove to her that he could aid her cause—as well as pure stubbornness—kept him going. When he at last turned the corner where Luis had disappeared, he held his breath, expecting to see Luis looking at him over a pistol bore. But the only challenge came from a mocking oriole. Clint craned his head, looking up, down and around. He had a clear view here of the valley below and the slopes above, but Luis was not in sight.

At another time, he would have enjoyed the lush green blanket, embroidered with cattle, spread below. Absently he reflected that this must be the northern boundary of de Sarria's rancho. He sat and peered about for a good five minutes, frowning, then he shrugged and urged his mount carefully higher. The man was here somewhere.

If it hadn't been for the sounds echoing in the noon stillness, he would have missed the narrow cleft. He had in fact passed it before the clink of hammer on stone reached his ears. He drew the stallion up and dismounted, leading the animal behind him. There was a narrow trail here, almost level, so the footing was safe. He tracked the sounds to an outcropping. Clint scrutinized the rock face, but he saw no opening. He felt along the gray stone before he noticed that the obliquely angled slab had an entrance behind it, half-covered with overgrown scrub and curly manzanita trees, just large enough for a horse to squeeze through. Clint tied his animal to one of the trees and entered.

When his eyes had adjusted to the dimness, he went toward the weak light in the back of the cavern. Soon he heard the murmur of voices. He slowed and peeked around the corner, glimpsing Luis and de Sarria, stripped to the waist, arguing about something. The cleft widened here, and their two horses waited patiently, as if this were a common outing for them.

Clint moved in to listen, but now he was close enough to the light to see the cleft walls. He blinked, wondering for a second if somehow the sun was shining through cracks, for narrow, jagged streaks shone like rivulets of molten heat. He blinked again, then had to cover his gasp with his hand as he realized what he was looking at. This narrow cave was interlaced with ribbons of the substance man has coveted since time immemorial: gold.

Clint was no more proof against the fascination than most. He looked around in pure delight for several minutes before the argument grew heated enough to impinge on his bedazzlement.

Luis sucked on a swollen thumb, then drew it out of his mouth to snarl, "I say we put some of your indios to work. They've not intelligence enough to know what they're doing. We'll just tell them you want the pretty rock for decorating the hacienda . . ."

"They might believe that, but they know full well the boundary of my lands ends short of this mountain. All it takes is for one of them, just one, to mention what they're doing. I'll not have all California consider me a thief." Roberto did not mention that his Indian *vaqueros* had become restless of late. The harder he tried to suppress rebellion, the more it stirred. Many of them would delight in making him look bad.

Whatever his faults, Luis was no hypocrite. "That's exactly what we are, amigo," he pointed out dryly.

Roberto flung down his hammer and chisel to glare at his friend. "We are no such thing. We'll legally purchase this land . . ."

"For a pittance of its real value . . ."

"And can do much good for California . . ."

"And ourselves . . ."

"And for me, too," Clint said, stepping boldly into the middle of the chamber, silencing the argument.

They stared at him with mingled shock and dismay, then Roberto snatched a pistol out of the coiled holster he'd set nearby. "You've made your last mistake, gringo. Really, you are a fool . . ."

"Am I, de Sarria? Or are you? If you were as wily as you think yourself, you'd realize what an asset I can be." Clint leaned casually back against the cave wall, propping one foot behind him. "I have contacts all over this continent. Some may question where I get the gold to broker to buyers back east, but no one will doubt my right to keep my supplier anonymous."

The pistol didn't waver. "We already have a broker. We've but to get the gold to him and he'll convert it for us into pesos."

"At the best price?"

Luis nudged Roberto's stiff arm. "The least we can do is hear him out."

Roberto hesitated, then he sighed elaborately. "So talk, gringo. Every man should be granted a few last words." When Clint didn't bat an eye at the taunt, for the first time some of the contempt in Roberto's eyes faded.

"My cousin owns an assaying company, actually. He'll give me, as his cousin, the best possible price. And I, as a trader, can see that you get the best quality goods at a discount for your capital, after you purchase the land."

"And what do you gain?" Luis asked.

"I ask for half the share you'd give your Mexican broker, the contract to ship all you buy to California, and that you recommend my company to your friends. Many of the rancheros hereabout have been reluctant to trade with me, but if the respected Roberto de Sarria sets an example . . ."

As usual, Roberto was susceptible to flattery. His relaxed arm dropped a notch lower as he considered Clint's offer. In truth, he had much more to offer than Borge. Emotion, even strong dislike, never clouded Roberto's judgment where profit was concerned. He looked at Luis, hesitating.

Clint saw him wavering, then he played his ace. "Besides, I have one more thing to offer that may be of little material value but of great interest to you nevertheless."

"*Qué?*" Roberto asked warily.

"I know a way to get into El Halcon's band. I have reason to think he'll accept me."

Luis and Roberto both started, then approached Clint, eagerness in every step. "How? Why?"

"That I'll keep to myself, I'm afraid. Rather in the nature of insurance." Clint looked at the gun, still half-pointed at him.

Luis poked Roberto in the ribs. "Put that down. He's one against two."

Disgruntled but convinced, Roberto holstered the pistol and crossed his arms over his chest. "Very well, gringo, talk. If what you say is true, I may indeed overlook our . . . differences."

"How very generous you are, de Sarria," Clint said dryly, making no effort to disguise the dislike he reciprocated in full. "And I meant what I said. My methods are my own. You should be interested only in results. If I am able to infiltrate El Halcon's band and earn his trust, I promise to share all I learn of his plans. If you know in advance where he will strike, an ambush should be easy to arrange."

Casually, Clint stuck his hand in his pocket and pulled out his derringer. "Do you believe in my interest now? I could have shot you both while you were arguing." Clint stuck the pistol back in his pocket.

Roberto bridled at the insouciant insult, but Luis slanted an I-told-you-so look at his friend and asked Clint, "What happened to your aversion to riding, Browning? This was no easy climb to make, even with a trained horse."

"There's little I'll not dare when the incentive is great enough," Clint responded, admiring the gold veins. Roberto looked resigned, but somewhat reassured, as the *yanqui* acted true to his kind. He jerked his head at Luis and turned about to walk to the rear of the cave.

While Luis and Roberto deliberated, Clint walked this way and that to appraise the kaleidoscope of light and dark glittering in dancing patterns, as if turned by a giant, invisible hand. He was rather proud of his acting ability. It had not been easy to swallow his distaste and offer his aid, but joining them offered the best chance of proving their larceny. It also gave him something to offer El Halcon.

A few minutes later, Roberto and Luis came back. "Very well, we accept your offer." Roberto stabbed a warning finger into Clint's chest. "But if you betray us, I'll take great pleasure in killing you with my own hands."

Clint looked coldly at the gouging finger, then up at the dark eyes of the man a head shorter than himself. Roberto drew his hand away and turned to put on his shirt. "And if you have mining supplies, most especially a good pick, we'll gladly take them off your hands."

"It's not something I commonly stock, I'm afraid." Clint appraised the small chunks they'd wrested from the stubborn rock. Actually, the *Arabella* did number a pick among

251

its tools, but he had no motivation to assist their excavation.

When Clint turned to leave, Roberto called after him, "Come to my rancho if you discover anything. I'll get word to Luis." Clint nodded without turning and disappeared outside.

As he carefully rode back down the mountain, he wondered if he'd done the right thing. True, when they turned the gold over to him, he'd have tangible proof of their activities, but he'd also implicate himself if he were not very, very careful. And if El Halcon discovered the uneasy alliance, he'd probably not take time to listen to explanations, much less believe them. Subterfuge had never been Clint's forte, yet in the space of a few short months he'd acted as "scout" for his uncle, agreed to aid two ruthless men in their larceny and was now hopeful of joining a robber band. Given a choice, he'd participate in none of these activities.

He sighed wistfully, remembering the snap of billowed canvas coursing him along the limitless blue Pacific. He was tempted to continue his journey up the California coast. But the scope of that vision narrowed to two eyes, changing from sad, dusky gold to tiny blazing suns, and he knew he couldn't leave. Ever after he'd be haunted by what had become of her, what he could have had with her if he'd not taken the easy course of retreat. Risking his life by staying was perhaps foolish, but risking his integrity by leaving was unthinkable. He turned his horse back up El Camino Real to resume his search.

Magdalena pulled her second-best hat down low over her hood and cooed to her restless falcon. "Soon, my beauty, you can hunt," she soothed. "I, too, am eager." She looked at her men, stationed half on each side of the highway, with herself, Joaquin and Sean closing the vee. Even two days later, Miguel was too ill to join them, and she missed his calming presence. She hoped the others would not be too nervous. Despite the gathering dusk, she could see their anxiety.

Beside her, Joaquin spoke softly. "How do you know

Ramirez's habits are still the same? Two years is a long time. Perhaps he decides to stay at his rancho for a change."

"And miss his weekly fornication with his mistress?" At Joaquin's hissing sound, Magdalena added impatiently, "I've neither time nor patience to dress my words up. It's too late for the niceties to matter to me now. No, Ramirez is too old to change. He'll come soon, sneaking away from his devoted wife and daughters, as if they don't know what he's doing, and has been doing, for years. Then, two days later, sure of his manhood, he'll go back to his rancho to prove himself yet again on his Indian maids."

Joaquin couldn't quarrel with her scorn, for he'd always considered Ramirez a poor imitation of a man, but there was a fervency in her voice that troubled him. Since that night with the American, she'd been different. Despite the blows fate had dealt her, she'd never dodged them; she'd taken them on the chin, picked herself up and gone on without bitterness. Now, she seemed bitter toward all men. She'd even desisted her friendly pats on Sean's shoulder.

Before he could speak, the sounds of carriage wheels came. When the old, springless vehicle was upon them, Sean fired one of his pistols in the air. "*Alto!* Stand and deliver!" he roared.

When Magdalena looked at him curiously at the odd term, he sheepishly shrugged his wide shoulders. "Sorry, Jack, got carried away. For a twinklin', I thought meself on the London turnpike."

If the term was unfamiliar to the Californios, the meaning was not, especially when the vee quickly formed into a circle about the vehicle. The coachman whined and pulled his horses in, dropping the reins to reach for the glorious sunset. Magdalena weaved Fuego through her men to the carriage.

"*Por favor,* señor, step d . . ." Her request was cut off by the blast of a pistol. The shot missed her head by a hairbreadth only because she leaned down to open the door. She unhooded her falcon and launched it in the air, threw herself from the saddle and stooped, using the door as cover, to wrench it open. She waved her angry men away from the line of fire and raised her voice.

"You may have one shot left, but I suggest you aim well. If you take it, it will be your last," she hissed in El Halcon's most menacing voice. When there was silence, she softened her tone. "Come, Ramirez, be reasonable. We have no designs on your life. Is what you carry so valuable?"

A plump, trembling hand grasped the edge of the carriage to support the squat, shaking body that descended. Ramirez drew his plush cloak, lined with silk and frogged with gold, about himself and looked up at the robber who had stood and was stark against the crimson backdrop of the sunset.

"I carry nothing but a few silver pieces," he quavered, offering his slim purse. He was shaking so badly Magdalena almost pitied him, but she accepted the purse and tossed it to Pablo, who caught it in one hand and kept his pistol raised with the other.

"Forgive my skepticism, but if I may search your coach . . ." Magdalena moved to round the door.

With a nervous glance at the hulking riders surrounding him, Ramirez blurted, "*No*! Er, that is, I've nothing else of value."

Magdalena looked from his sweating face, to the black interior of the coach. His boldness had been surprising. His nervousness now was more what she'd expect of him. The conclusion was obvious. She debated briefly. They could storm inside from the door and the opposite window, but not without serious injury or even death to herself or one of her men. There had to be a better way . . .

Leaning back against the coach, Magdalena glanced at the deepening sky. "It should be dark soon. I've never liked the night, you know. If only we had some kindling, we could build a fire . . ." She tapped her gloved fingers against the side of the coach, affecting surprise when a dry piece of wood flaked away. Making sure her voice was loud enough for the coach occupant to hear, she said, "We'll use this poor excuse for a coach. It's past its serviceable days, anyway."

To Sean, she called, "Bundle some twigs and grass and bring me a torch, Mick."

An appalled Ramirez pleaded weakly, "No, it will take months to get another coach from Mexico."

"You have my sympathies, señor, but I think your coach needs fumigating. You've varmints aboard." When Sean brought her the lighted torch, Magdalena blew on it to get it burning briskly, holding it so the smoke wafted into the coach.

A hoarse cough rewarded her. She broke off a twig at the bottom, turned it to catch the air until it was half-engulfed in flames, then tossed it in the coach. When a curse came, accompanied by a slapping sound, Magdalena flung the torch on the ground, leaped up into the carriage and caught two handfuls of velvet to pull the man out. She lost her balance under the strain of his weight on her sore leg and fell backward, allowing him time to recover his own equilibrium. He whipped his second pistol up, a pretty, silver-tooled thing that seemed more art than armament, and pointed it at her chest.

Magdalena heard the clicks of the cocking pistols all about her at the same time that she recognized the man's face. "No!" she screamed, closing her eyes as she awaited the explosion.

But all that came was an angry screech and swooshing wings. With a cry of pain, the man dropped his pistol. For a moment Magdalena was so relieved that she slumped back against the ground.

"Bless you, Linda," she whispered, as if her falcon could not only hear, but understand. Then, trembling slightly in the aftermath, she rose and dusted herself off. She didn't reprimand Pablo and Benito when they cuffed the man's face and drew him out into the middle of the road. However, when Pablo lifted his pistol to bring the butt down on the shining dark head, she said sharply, "No! Just hold him, for now."

She looked at Sean and flung her head at the coach. Silently, he obeyed and pulled out everything it contained, not even bothering to open the small trunks. Whatever they held would not go to waste. If none of them could use the clothing, there were poor Indian families aplenty who could.

When Ramirez squawked more protests, Magdalena drew her sword and pressed the tip of it to the paunch overhanging his stylish breeches. He stopped as if she'd cut out his tongue. "That's better. Whatever trinket you took your mistress will doubtless not be missed. You deserve worse punishment for your treachery and infidelity."

She pricked him in the belly. When he cried out and wrapped his arms about himself as if she'd gutted him, she turned away with a disgusted sneer. She walked boldly up to the man standing tall and unafraid between the Indians. "So, Jose, you hate El Halcon enough to kill him."

Jose's eyes flickered in surprise, and this time Magdalena could have cut her own tongue out. He'd never told her his name during that last meeting . . . She hurried on, though she knew it was too late to cover up the mistake. "I let you go, this time. I don't know how you knew I'd rob Ramirez, but I compliment your wit. Just see it isn't your undoing in future. And remember, I stopped my men from killing you. If you again threaten any of us so, I can't promise we won't retaliate." To Pablo and Benito she said, "Take his purse and let him go."

Jose shook the Indians off after they'd pulled his pouch from his cloak. Caressing his sword hilt, he challenged, "Why wait?" When Magdalena turned away, he taunted, "Afraid, El Halcon? This will tarnish your false glory a little."

Whirling back around, Magdalena retorted, "Good, for I want no glory, false or otherwise. I seek only justice for myself and the oppressed."

Jose snorted his disbelief. "You have little the look of a judge, unless you preside in hell."

"Think of me what you like. But before I'm done, all California will know the truth." Magdalena stomped away to open the pouch of fresh meat she kept for Linda. Giving a choked cry, the falcon swooped down to alight on her beckoning wrist. Magdalena carried her to a boulder and set her down to let her feast. Then she turned back to Jose and Ramirez.

"Go, amigos. I'll be generous and leave you your horses—as long as you don't try to follow us." When Jose cast a glance toward his pistols, winking in the sun's last rays from their snug position in Sean's belt, she added, "Those we'll keep. To arm any who join us." She gave him an airy wave, which earned a sputter of fury from him.

Ramirez, however, caught his arm and jerked him into the coach. The coachman, a chubby Mexican, watched as El Halcon mounted; then he perched on his seat and whipped his horses back north toward his employer's rancho.

Magdalena mounted and fetched Linda. After strapping the small trunks on their horses, Benito and Pablo also mounted. The little party started off, south on the highway toward the cut-off to their mountain aerie.

It could have been tiredness, or the night, or carelessness, but whatever the reason, none of them noticed the soldier who slipped from the shade of the tree to follow them. And all were too far away to see the weary rider who passed the retreating coach.

Jose, who looked out the window as he heard the horse approach, exclaimed, "Captain Browning! What a fortuitous encounter." And to the coachman, "Stop the coach."

Jose jumped down before the coach had halted and strode up to Clint. "Quickly, let me mount behind you. El Halcon just attacked us. If we hurry we can catch him."

Clint gave Jose an arm up, his tiredness dissipated. "Tell me what happened. But first, why didn't you meet me for dinner last week?"

"I thought if I nightly rode the highway I'd have a better chance of encountering the bandit again. For almost a week, I've been either riding my own horse, or traveling with someone else along El Camino Real. Tonight, my diligence was rewarded."

But he sounded less than jubilant, Clint decided. "I don't see any prisoners, so I take it you didn't capture him?"

"No, nor kill him either, as I tried to."

For a reason Clint couldn't understand, he stiffened with alarm. "Did you hurt him?"

"No, the crafty fox outwitted me again." Jose explained how El Halcon had "persuaded" him out of the coach. "And he has more men with him now."

"I know. The reason you didn't see him until tonight is that he's been in Santa Barbara." Clint filled Jose in on what had happened there in his absence.

After that, they silently peered into the gloom up ahead until Jose reflected absently, "I got the oddest feeling El Halcon knew me. He called me by name and knew of Ramirez's er . . . propensities. But my mind shies away from the hint that this thief could be a member of my class." Jose frowned, remembering something else that troubled him even more. He'd been ready to kill El Halcon and the bandit must have known it, yet he'd ordered his own men not to fire. Could it be he was more than a bandit? Before Jose had an opportunity to ask Clint's opinion, they spied a rider up ahead.

Immediately Clint drew his own horse in before the man could hear them. Judging from his low position in the saddle, the rider did not want to be seen.

"Dismount," Jose suggested. "We'll muffle your stallion's hooves."

Clint was puzzled, but he obeyed. Using a knife to slash his sash into four strips, Jose quickly lifted the bay's hooves and tied the strips under and around each one. When Clint offered an arm up again, Jose shook his head.

"You'll go faster without me. If you'll give me a gun in case I come across a bear, I'll be fine until morning. I've camped in these mountains before. Someone will come along tomorrow to give me aid."

Clint gave Jose his saddle pistol, along with extra shot. Then, impulsively, he held out his hand. Jose shook it firmly. "If I do indeed find El Halcon, when I can, I'll let you know where he camps." Waving, Clint clicked his bay into a trot.

Soon, due to his quicker pace, he sighted the man they'd

seen before. Because of his bay's muffled hooves, Clint was able to come in close to the man without alerting him.

Though he stood up in his stirrups, it was too dark for him to see whom the rider tailed, but he had a very good idea. When the soldier turned off the highway, clearing the trees and brush lining the edge, Clint glimpsed a shadow far above him on a mountain trail blocking the stars and moonlight. Whether wraith or man, the shadow moved with an uncommon grace that was familiar to Clint. Naggingly so.

His heart beating faster, Clint brought up the rear of the odd cavalcade, weaving a path high up into the mountains.

# *Chapter 11*

"We're square then, on the round. The game's a draw."
**Act I, DON JUAN TENORIO**

Clint drew his winded animal in, panting himself at the exertion of riding up these mountains twice in one day. Still, his effort had been rewarded. Ahead, the light glimmering from a cavity in the mountain told him he'd found El Halcon's hiding place. His heart pounded even faster. Was Carlotta within? While he sat, debating the best way to make himself known, the man in front of him turned his stallion about and stealthily descended the way he'd come. Clint's few doubts about his identity dissolved.

Quickly, Clint reined his horse around the trail bend and dismounted, pulling himself into the rocks above. He hung there precariously until the rider drew even. Springing away from the rocks like a crouched cougar, he tackled the rider from his saddle. After a brief tussle, Clint subdued the man with a crack to the jaw. Clint then snatched off the soldier's belt and used it to tie his arms behind his back. He hauled

261

him to his feet, picked up the Mexican's fallen sword and prodded him in the back with it.

"You wanted to find El Halcon. And so you shall. Face to face." Leading both horses with his free hand, he pricked the man in the back again. "Move."

So did Clinton James Browning III join the band of El Halcon, Alta California's most notorious outlaw. Not with finesse, nor even with guile; but with a bribe and a challenge. He strutted into the cavern, certain now that he had tangible proof of his loyalty El Halcon would let him stay. This was much better bail than dangling de Sarria in front of him, for it involved no personal implication in wrong-doing. At last he'd find Carlotta and teach El Halcon the fallacy of arrogance. Had he known the lessons El Halcon would also teach him, he might not have swaggered so. The first two he would learn that very night: how El Halcon reacted to challenge and bribery.

At the sounds of the horses, Magdalena looked up from bandaging Miguel's leg. Each man who had a pistol drew and cocked it. They peered at the dark cave opening, then scrambled to their feet when Clint entered, pushing the soldier ahead of him. No one noted in the tense moment that Joaquin stayed seated with remarkable complacence.

"*Buenas noches*, El Halcon," Clint said suavely, ignoring the guns and hostile faces. "I've a gift for you to show my goodwill." Clint shoved the Mexican forward so hard that the man stumbled and fell to his knees. He turned his head to spew curses up at Clint, then fell silent as a shadow moved over him to block the lantern light. Swallowing, he looked up.

Magdalena still wore her cloak and hat. Tall, garbed in black, she was all the more menacing for her stillness. She stood over him as if trying to decide which part of his body she'd like to cut off first. The Mexican inched backward on his knees. Still, she didn't move. Her hands hanging loosely at her sides, she stared at him for minutes on end until even Clint's nerves began to wear.

All thought she was assessing the value of—and purpose behind—the gift. All except Joaquin. He knew it was not the Mexican who disturbed her. He felt the tension, the anger, the confusion evanescing from her like a black mist. He remained seated, wrapping his arms about his legs to still his need to plead with her. She had to let Browning stay of her own accord. *Dios* give him the words, he prayed . . .

"Well, El Halcon? Does my gift please you? I found him sneaking away outside. By tomorrow, had he escaped, you'd have had the entire presidio's company breathing down your necks." Clint quit searching the shadows for Carlotta and focused all his attention on the man standing motionless before him.

Still, no answer came. Clint waited a moment longer, then went on loudly in an effort to disguise his own growing nervousness, "I want to join your fight. We've had our differences, but someone, er, close to me has convinced me you're more than a bandit. If you are, I'll be as loyal a follower as you could hope for."

El Halcon started as if coming out of a trance. Even his voice was hoarser than usual. "Tie him up," he ordered Benito, jerking his chin at the Mexican. While Benito obeyed, he turned his head to look at the American.

His stance became aggressive. One foot pointed outward, as if settling itself for a lunge, and a caressing hand alit on his sword hilt. "Him, I haven't decided what to do with. You, I have no doubts about. Leave, while you still can. I'd not trust you to scratch my back—much less defend it."

Clint sighed in relief. Good, a fight was better than that odd, sullen silence. Clint somehow knew El Halcon would respect a man who could best him. Clint linked the reins of the horses casually about a sharp outcrop and folded his arms. "I'm not leaving. We both know this has little to do with my trustworthiness. You dislike me for the same reason I dislike you. Well, only one of us can have her. Can you not be a sporting man and offer me the same advantage you have? Allow me to press my suit, and if she chooses you, I'll step aside. You have my word, on my father's grave, that I will not betray you."

The Indians looked from the tall, handsome gringo to El

Halcon. Their conversation was incomprehensible, but a blind man could have sensed their hostility. They moved back a bit from the wide, clear space in the center of the cavern. Blood would spill this night . . .

El Halcon's scornful, choking laugh sent shivers up Clint's spine. "Once, Carlotta believed you, but she knows better now. She showed me the map you drew . . ."

"I drew it under duress," Clint said moodily. "And I didn't want to deliver it to the man who blackmailed me. A moot point now, anyway, since Carlotta took it. It would take me weeks to draw it again."

A long hand sliced through the air before Clint had drawn breath. "A convenient excuse for treachery."

Clint stiffened. "And what excuse do you use for thievery?"

"None. I am a thief. I freely admit it. But if you have such scorn for me, why do you wish to join me? And you must think me as big a fool as I think you if you hope to convince me your only motivation is a woman who despises you."

The devious bastard hoped to make him lose his temper, Clint realized. Aware at last of the strong emotions emanating from beneath that hood, Clint worried at the reasons for them. He squinted around the cavern again, but unless she hid in the back, Carlotta was not present. Had something happened to her?

His teeth ground together over his even reply. "I think you too clever for your own good. Those who see treachery everywhere make more enemies than friends." It took all the determination in his towering frame, but Clint managed to set aside his own hostility and extend his hand. "Please, let us call a truce. All I ask is that you give me a chance to prove my friendship . . ." El Halcon advanced with a fluid grace that struck Clint as familiar, but he had little time to consider it.

The long, slim hand raised as if to take Clint's—then struck his aside with a slap that echoed in the cavern. "That for your spurious friendship!" El Halcon hissed into the fading echoes.

Silence, tense with words spoken and more unexpressed, reigned for a good sixty seconds. Joaquin levered himself to his feet, his face drawn with worry. Ah, that stance was so familiar. So tall and stiff she stood, outraged pride in every line. Not reason, not laughter, not fear could reach her now. Only blood would satisfy her. Browning had lost his chance to retreat. He'd not leave this cavern now—at least not as he'd entered it.

Joaquin looked at the American's rigid features, and some of his worry receded. He, too, was spoiling for a fight. Perhaps only physical violence would relieve the emotional pressure that seemed to press on the cavern walls. Magdalena must face the American. More important, she must face the things he made her feel. When his life was balanced on the tip of her sword, she'd see at last how unfairly she'd tilted the scales of justice. For Joaquin knew she could never kill Browning. It was time she knew it too. And, even in the unlikely event that the American prevailed, Joaquin knew that he'd not kill El Halcon, for on the bandit rested the goodwill of the woman Browning wanted. Joaquin smiled. It was a piquant situation he hoped they all could laugh at, in years to come.

Slowly, Clint raised the Mexican's sword, a fine rapier, and pointed it at the base of El Halcon's throat. The Indians, who had let their pistols drop, raised them again, but Browning's only threat as a verbal one.

"Very well, *bandido*, since you've no use for the hand of friendship, I'll make my point in another way. I want to see Carlotta. *Now!*"

Instead of flinching away from the sword as most would have done, El Halcon actually leaned in closer, forcing Clint to relax his arm. "You shall not. Carlotta is mine, as she has always been, as she will always be. No man will ever have her again."

When Clint's arm trembled and his face flushed with fury, El Halcon's voice grew mocking. "But me, me you can have. Do you want me, gringo?" El Halcon cocked his head on one side, still ignoring the blade at his throat, to study the red face a half foot above him. "I see that you do. How happy I shall be to oblige you."

At last El Halcon stepped back. The slither of sound as he drew his sword acted like a thunderclap on his audience. The Indians muttered among themselves, shaking their heads. The American was taller and stronger, and their leader had not fully recovered from his flesh wound. But they knew enough of El Halcon not to interfere. Nor had they seen him fence . . .

Sean had, but he, too, was worried about Magdalena's leg. He took a step forward, but a hand grabbed his arm. Joaquin shook his head. Nibbling at his lip, Sean turned back to watch.

Clint drew off his coat, but left on his boots for protection from the rough cavern floor. While El Halcon removed his cloak and hat, Clint surveyed his dueling grounds. Only in the middle was the cave floor relatively level. Near the back, moisture would make footing treacherous; to the sides, the floor sloped upward as stalagmites pointed warning fingers toward the cave ceiling. Two more lanterns were lit, but still the lighting was ghostly, transmuting shadows where there were none and brightness where darkness lurked.

Despite the disadvantages, Clint's heart pumped with eagerness. At last he'd demonstrate to this fiend that arrogance was not a Californio monopoly. Oh, he had no intention of killing El Halcon. A minor flesh wound would show that he was not to be taken lightly. Only when he'd proved himself would El Halcon begin to respect him.

He'd have to be careful. He sensed El Halcon truly hated him, and doubtless the bandit was good with a blade. But Clint had fenced since he was eight and had met few indeed who could defeat him in a fair fight. As El Halcon turned to face him, his form a tall, lithe silhouette against the light, Clint pushed all thought of Carlotta aside and concentrated on the challenge before him.

El Halcon flexed his knees, then assumed the en garde position. Clint did likewise. Their blades rasped together in the briefest of salutes before Clint beat El Halcon's sword away and attacked with a long, athletic lunge. El Halcon turned aside and simultaneously caught Clint's blade, pushing it outward with his own. Still extended in his lunge, Clint revolved his wrist to disengage and jab again.

But where El Halcon had been, he found only air. He blinked and straightened, amazed at the speed with which El Halcon had leaped backward. Clint was a bit off-balance when El Halcon engaged with a rapid, two-step lunge. He barely deflected the steel reaching for his side, and the close call shook a little of his confidence away. Warily, Clint backed a step. He parried several side to side stabs, preparing a series of feints and counterthrusts in his mind. His greater height and strength should give him a definite edge.

When he whammed El Halcon's blade aside far enough to give himself an opening, he launched into the series, feinting to the left, jabbing to the right and following up with a lunge. El Halcon read his moves with insulting ease, countering his crafty jab with an upthrust parry that jarred Clint's wrist, so strongly was it executed.

Bewildered, for he'd just used—and failed with—one of his best maneuvers, Clint decided to allow El Halcon the advantage while he studied his technique. But again, El Halcon foiled him. He teased Clint with tantalizing taps and slides down the length of Clint's blade, daring Clint to attack. Yet, whenever Clint was tempted into slicing into the apparent opening, he found it closed and his blade slapped away. El Halcon matched his physical taunts with a verbal one.

"Come, prove your manhood yet again, this time on one who is not helpless to fight back." El Halcon entangled Clint's straight-armed lunge, pulling Clint's blade outward with such strength that the hilt slipped in his hand. Only by whirling sideways, letting his body rather than his arm take the force, did Clint retain his weapon.

El Halcon waited for him to recover, one hand propped lightly on his hip, his blade sagging toward the ground. Clint refused to take the bait. Eyes steadfast on the glittering eye slits, Clint waited for El Halcon to engage. He'd played into El Halcon's hands long enough. Already he was slightly winded. The aggression that normally served him well was counterproductive against this man. He used strategy like a chess player, fencing several moves ahead and reading his opponent with a skill that Clint had never faced. But he was not the only one who could make defense a guileful attack . . .

For several minutes, they circled one another, their experimental raps and jabs, rapier against rapier, echoing in the waiting stillness. The Indians watched with mouths agape. Even those who didn't fence knew uncommon skill when they saw it. Sean still worried at his lip, but Joaquin was calm, as if he already knew the outcome of a battle that seemed uncertain to the others.

Finally, when Clint's nerves were stretched to the limit, and he was contemplating taking some of the tempting openings El Halcon offered, the bandit tired of the game. His leisured, sliding steps became a primitive dance. Forward and backward he weaved, his rapier a slithering snake that writhed over and under Clint's increasingly frustrated parries. The hissing sound of their coupling blades, the weaving black hood, made Clint feel he engaged a changeling, a man who moved so lithely and struck so quickly that he was more reptile than mortal. Sweat ran into Clint's eyes, blurring his vision until the reaching swordtip became a forked tongue with fangs of steel behind it.

Clint grew angry at himself for letting the bandit unnerve him so. Perhaps he lacked the man's agility, but he was considerably stronger, as El Halcon would discover to his cost. Swiping sweat away with his free hand, Clint whammed a straight-armed thrust aside and, while El Halcon's blade was wide to the right, riposted with a quick jab so powerful that El Halcon was not able to block it in time.

To Clint's frustration, the man seemed to realize that. Instead of trying an abortive parry, El Halcon twisted his body sideways, then he stumbled, as if one leg gave out. There came a ripping sound, then a half-inch of white skin appeared at El Halcon's side, decorated with dots of bright blood. Clint had little time to celebrate the graze, however.

Instead of slowing El Halcon, the injury seemed to energize him. Bringing his blade up in a shining arc, the bandit rammed Clint's extended rapier toward the cave ceiling. Clint's recovery time allowed El Halcon to leap around to face him again. He rubbed one of his legs with a free hand. His body was uncannily still for a split second, then he erupted into motion.

El Halcon engaged with the savagery Clint had sensed all along. No testing or holding back now; El Halcon yearned for blood. He went into a series of furious thrusts and parries that beat against Clint's sword until he thought either his blade or his wrist would crack. He was able to block each in the nick of time, but the wall of steel pressing in upon him forced him to retreat. He knew El Halcon was setting up for a final lunge, but he was too busy parrying the attacks on his side, his belly, then his heart, to prepare a countermove in his mind. Helplessly swept along on the tide of his opponent's fury, Clint knew that he'd be lucky to escape this encounter alive. Again, he'd underestimated the man. But this time, he had more to lose than pride . . .

Clint felt the cave sloping up beneath his feet and realized he was approaching the side wall. Soon, he'd be trapped between stalagmites unless he was able to slit an opening in the deadly steel net slowly closing about him. Clint tried to move aside, but a blade sliced so close to his side that he felt the swoosh of air. He leaped three steps backward, hoping to give himself room for a last, desperate lunge. He realized too late that El Halcon anticipated the move and was ready to meet it. Like a juggernaut he came, barreling forward in a running lunge on the balls of his feet, his blade wide to the right as he reached for Clint's left shoulder.

Clint knew he was obeying El Halcon's dictates, but there was little he could do to deny him. His only opening was to the right, and he took it, thrusting with all his might. His own strength was his undoing. El Halcon's blade darted to trap the thrust he was obviously expecting. His body braced for the clanging embrace and met it with the full force of his lunge. Clint's sweaty hand slipped on the hilt as his entangled blade was jerked away. The rapier fell to the stone floor with a deafening clatter.

The tinny echoes died under the duelists' pants. Clint didn't try to back off. He stood tall, his chest heaving with his exertions, and waited for El Halcon's pressing swordtip to pierce his throat.

Magdalena's wrist ached, so hard did she clench her hand about her hilt. She panted, a thousand thoughts going through her head as she met Clint's steady blue gaze. If he had cowered or pleaded, she could have run him through as he deserved.

But he stood erect, like a man with a clean conscience, his face as implacable as the pain in her heart. Do your worst, he dared her silently. I don't fear death.

The tension built in her head until she thought she'd explode. "Beg for mercy, gringo, as Carlotta begged, and perhaps I'll show it," she goaded.

He leaned forward until the blade pierced the base of his throat. He rubbed the spot with his fingers, then extended them, smeared with the carmine life-paint, to hold them near her side.

"See? It's the same color. We both bleed good red blood. We both care for Carlotta. We both admire strength. We have more in common than you'll admit, bandit. I accepted your challenge gladly, and you won fairly. You are more skillful than I and deserve your victory. Take my life if that's what you want, but I'll give you nothing of my self-respect. Beg I will never do."

Magdalena closed her eyes to block the sight of his stern features. *Dios,* why did he always do this to her? Just when she was certain he was beneath contempt, he displayed this strength of character that reminded her so vividly of the three men she'd loved and lost, and labored now to avenge. Her arm trembled with the strain of holding the weapon while her heart and mind battled.

Joaquin's eyes felt gritty as he watched her struggle with herself. He didn't fear for Browning; he feared for Magdalena. Even before life had pushed her into this dangerous charade, she'd been a woman at war with herself. Now, when she'd buried every feminine instinct she'd ever possessed, she was challenged by a man who made her long to dig them all up and dust them off one by one. And for it to be this man, whom she had every reason to suspect, was perhaps more than she was able to face at this point in her life. Had he been wrong not to intervene? Perhaps it would have been best for the American to leave, after all . . .

Finally, Magdalena's emotions calmed enough for her to see the situation logically. Very well, Browning was not to be trusted. Perhaps she'd pay with her life for her foolishness, but she could not kill him. She knew that now. And somewhere, deep in the heart she seldom acknowledged, hope glowed like a bright, unquenchable flame. Could a man of such courage really be the rogue she'd named him? She must know for certain, one way or another.

Besides, she'd be mad to let him go. She'd keep him close, where she could watch him on *her* terms for a change. If he proved himself loyal, then perhaps, just perhaps, she'd let him join them. But first, he must learn the folly of challenging El Halcon's authority, for she didn't dare appear weak before her men. She glanced over at them, seeing the confusion on their faces at her hesitation, and the worry on Sean's and Joaquin's.

Magdalena eased the pressure, smiling as Clint relaxed infinitesimally. Despite his brave front, he'd been concerned. Well he should be . . . She inched the weapon down from his throat, only to pop the buttons off his shirt as she went. When it gapped open, she pushed it off his shoulders with the blade.

His chest seemed gilded, the beautiful curvature of his hair-dusted torso accented by the sweat glistening in the lantern light. Magdalena strove to ignore the tempting expanse and equally seductive memories, and nodded her agreement.

"You're right, gringo. I do yearn for blood." With her swordtip, she traced the sworling hair from one nipple to another. When his breath had quickened again with alarm, she flashed the rapier down to his side and carved something into his flesh with all the delicacy of a surgeon. She stepped back.

Clint's eyes followed everyone else's to his side. He'd welcomed the quick-hot darts compared to the deep thrust he'd been expecting, but when he saw what she'd written into his flesh, in the same spot where he'd grazed her, his face paled. By contorting his waist partly sideways and partly back, he was able to see why her men first snickered, then roared, as blood oozed into the shallow scratches. As neatly as if she'd penciled it, EH stood out against his side. She'd branded him as if she owned him.

A feral growl shook his chest as he took a step toward El Halcon. "You arrogant bastard . . ."

El Halcon sheathed his sword and folded his arms across his own shaking chest. The strangled sounds of his laughter infuriated Clint more. If his sword had been within reach, he'd have seized it, but an Indian had long since claimed it. Clint could only clench his hands and cringe inside at the laughter resounding in the cavern.

Finally, El Halcon cleared his throat and jerked his head at Clint. "Tie him up and take him to the back of the cave. We'll be his hosts while he contemplates the wisdom of lying to El Halcon."

Clint bit off curses beneath his breath as two Indians hustled him off, but El Halcon had already turned away. He walked up to the Mexican prisoner who had watched the entire exchange with frowning intensity.

"So, what do you think of El Halcon now?" he asked lazily.

The man, of medium height and build with a long, thin mustache quivering above a long, thin mouth, answered, "I think you the most skilled swordsman I have ever seen." His reflective tone hardened, matching his sneer. "But a fool for letting him live. If you really think him an enemy, then why don't you kill him?"

Rocking backward and forward on the balls of his feet, El Halcon retorted, "Luis has taught you well, I see." He became still. "I take no lives carelessly, *cholo*. I value my own too much to waste others." As skepticism crossed the

Mexican's face, El Halcon shook his head ruefully. "What a young man you are to be so cynical. Ah well, perhaps your stay with us will be the making of you."

El Halcon caressed his sword hilt again, his voice icing over. "Or the breaking of you. Don't mistake my compassion for weakness. When I deem it safe, I'll let you go. If you try to escape, you'll see how much I can have in common with Luis, when forced to."

Magdalena whirled away, ordering Pablo to carry rations back to each of their prisoners. She dropped down beside Miguel to finish his bandage. She knew he and his friends watched her curiously, but she waited for them to speak.

"Who taught you to fence?" Miguel asked diffidently, speaking for the others, as usual.

Magdalena hesitated, then answered truthfully enough, "A man who was once a great fencing master of Spain." She patted Miguel's knee below the healing wound and rose. "When we have time and a more suitable camp, I will fence with you, Miguel, if you like."

It was an honor for a caballero to offer to fence with an Indian, as they both knew, but neither referred to it. Miguel nodded his eagerness, but he frowned as he watched her turn away and pick up a plate of rabbit stew. While she ate, Ricardo cleaned her graze through the hole in her shirt. They were a devoted pair. Miguel wondered what the relationship was between them.

Benito, who sat beside him, shared all their thoughts when he said, "Never have I known a stranger man. On the road earlier he risked his own life when he could have ordered us to take the coach. Tonight, he spared a man he seems not to trust. Yet I sense a hatred in him that awaits only the right moment to release itself. If it's not the money he's after, then why does he fight?"

A shrug was the only answer Miguel could come up with. "We shall doubtless know soon enough. But tonight, for the first time, I feel certain that I've done the right thing in joining him. He is truly not like the others. Honor is not just a word to him." Miguel smiled at his friends. "Fortune is smiling on us at last."

Magdalena ignored Joaquin's inquiring gaze and set aside the last of her stew. She was tired of the curious glances. Had she really acted so strangely this night? Perhaps it was time for a distraction. Oddly, she felt a lightness of heart she'd not known in a long time. The energy she'd expended in her duel with Browning had wearied her, but rejuvenated her, too. He was there, tied up, at her mercy. She could see him, even touch him, any time she wanted to . . .

Ignoring her aching leg, she rose and went to the trunks they'd stolen from Ramirez. Sean joined her. "Lassie," he whispered in her ear as he assisted her in prying open a lock, "Ye've a bear in chains back there. By me way o' thinkin', ye'd best kill or befriend the man, but holdin' him prisoner will make him dangerous."

"Bah! He's more girth than grit. As long as we keep him tied, what can he do?" She flung the lid back and beamed the bright, confident smile upon him that glowed even under her hood. "Besides, don't you know that bear baiting is one of our favorite sports?" She turned away to the trunk, and only Joaquin knew her well enough to raise an eyebrow at her bravado.

Sean desisted, but as he watched her shuffle through the men's clothes, he mentally shook his head. He'd known too many men from too many walks of life to be so complacent. As Joaquin obviously believed, the American would make a powerful ally or a dangerous enemy. Did Magdalena really know which she wanted? There was something between the pair, something he both envied and worried about. For almost two years he'd hoped she'd turn to him, but her eyes when she looked at the American had finally convinced him that the longing was futile.

Still, despite the twinge of resentment, he wanted only the best for Magdalena. She not only deserved, but desperately needed, the love of a good man. Since she didn't seek his, he'd do all he could to see that she accepted another's. It remained to be seen if the American was that person.

Magdalena shuffled through the clothes, tossing fine velvet garments to the Indians hovering over them. They passed the breeches and jackets around, but only Pablo was

274

short enough and pudgy enough to wear them. He drew the maroon velvet jacket, richly braided, on over his tatty shirt and strutted up and down, affecting Ramirez's bandy walk. Miguel, his face alight with glee, snatched up a fringed shawl, drew it over his wide shoulders, and placed his hand on Pablo's arm.

"Come, *mi caballerote*, escort me to the patio," he simpered, batting his short eyelashes.

Pablo gave him a languishing look and patted the capable hand on his arm. "Señorita, it will be an honor." They minced across the cavern.

Miguel still stumbled a bit, but his gait was dainty enough to remind Magdalena of one of her most detested duennas. When he turned his head and winked at her, she smiled, then joined in the laughter. She turned back to the trunk and delved deeper, throwing a lovely pair of deep red boots to Benito.

He turned them over in his hands, looking awed at their texture and gloss. He ripped off his moccasins and heaved and tugged until he finally got them on his feet. He rose unsteadily and stomped to get the tight-fitting shoes to conform to his broad feet. He took a bold step—and fell face forward, saving his craggy features from the even craggier floor by catching his weight with his hands.

He scowled in mock anger at his snickering comrades, then oofed and grunted as he pulled the boots off. "A man can't wear these and ride a horse—or a woman—and concentrate on any part of his body but his poor, aching feet." He flung them aside with a disgusted look, but Juan snatched them up.

"Perhaps that depends on the man. I've always had a liking for a tight fit." Juan smiled wickedly and drew the boots over his own narrower feet.

Miguel came back to scoff, "And you're just the man to ride a woman with your boots on. In and out, the quicker, the better."

Since Magdalena's hood shielded her deep blush, only Sean and Joaquin knew how embarrassed she was. They exchanged a wry look, but Magdalena forestalled Juan's raunchy retort by opening the other trunk. She drew out a fine linen nightgown, trimmed in lace, and held it up to Sean. From the rear of the cave, Clint glumly watched their play.

She rose, twitched at Sean's arm until he also rose, then held the garment up to his brawny frame. "A perfect fit," she teased, despite the fact that the material barely covered his chest. She pulled his head down and stuck the garment over his head, wriggling it down his big body over his protests. Then she stood back to appraise him. Shortly before, she'd rejected death; now, she wanted to embrace life.

And Sean needed to hear again the laughter she so rarely expressed. Intuitive to her needs, he played along. He planted his big fists on his narrow hips and glared. The sleeves barely reached past his elbows, and the buttoned-down front gapped at the strain. The flounced hem trailed past his knees. And that cherubic face topped all, completing the picture of a little boy disgruntled at the dress-up his sisters forced him to play.

The Indians whooped, slapping their thighs. Miguel poked Juan. "There's your señorita, adorned and ready for bed. What a face she has." He pushed Juan toward Sean.

Sean turned such a withering look on the snickering pair that they swallowed their laughter. " 'Tis an insult I'll let pass this time, but I've used me fists to teach proper respect for this benighted face before, and I won't quibble about doin' so again." Angrily he jerked the nightgown over his head.

Magdalena swallowed her own laughter. He didn't mind being made the butt of their jokes until he was teased about his face. Tactfully, she changed the subject by turning toward the trunk again. She stiffened at the crackle of paper and held up a small ledger. "Look, amigos, fate has smiled upon us again!" She found a small bottle of ink and a quill tucked in a leather case and tossed all to Miguel.

"Inventory everything in here. Pick what you like, but see that each has an equal amount. What you don't want,

276

we'll give to the renegades. Do you still think you can find them, Miguel?"

At his nod, she pulled out the last garment and drew the shrouding paper away. She gasped and raised the dress slowly, reverently, to the light. It was a topaz silk gown trimmed in cream lace at the low V-neck and the off-the-shoulder puffed sleeves. The tiny waist tapered to a point below the stomach, accenting the bell-shaped skirt. Yards and yards of shining silk were in turn embellished with tiny lace flounces that started at knee level and grew wider until they reached the hem, where they were swept up and to the sides, like an opening curtain. The lace at bodice and hem was sewn with tiny gold beads that glittered as Magdalena turned the dress this way and that.

Magdalena dropped the dress back into the trunk as if she'd been burned. She made a harsh sound of disgust. "He values his mistress highly, it seems. I've never seen Señora Ramirez so finely gowned." She almost bit her tongue through when she realized what she'd said, but the Indians seemed more curious about her odd reaction than the fact that she'd seen Señora Ramirez.

Still caught up in the rare revelry, Miguel drew the dress out as she rose, holding it up to his leader's stiff figure. "Why, it would almost fit," he said in surprise.

Magdalena moved back so quickly she stumbled. "Give it to your lady, throw it to the birds or burn it. But I never want to see it again." She whirled away. "I'm going to bed." And she stalked off to her pallet at the rear of the cave. Joaquin clicked his tongue, then, wearily, he retired to his own pallet. Sean soon did likewise.

Frowning, Miguel wrapped the dress carefully and placed it back in the trunk. It was too fine for any of their sweethearts or mothers to wear without drawing suspicion down upon themselves. Perhaps they could sell it or barter it. But why had El Halcon reacted to the garment so strongly? After they'd parceled out what they wanted, and Miguel had carefully listed each item in the blank pages in the back of the ledger, they closed the trunks and pushed them to the side of the cave.

Then they retreated to their mats, as solemn now as they'd been ebullient earlier. They didn't even bother to express their feelings this time, but each knew the other's thoughts. Would they ever understand the man who was slowly winning their loyalty? And could they ever completely trust such an enigma?

On her pallet, Magdalena tossed and turned, but sleep would not come even after all was silent. She felt stifled in the hood, but was afraid to take it off for fear she'd oversleep in the morning. From where Browning sat in the far curve of the cave, he could see behind the blankets that shielded her from other eyes. She made a mental note to see that he was moved in the morning, but for now, she didn't want to even think about him. The sensual touch of silk had revived too many memories and longings she had to constantly suppress. And somehow, in a way she didn't understand—and didn't want to understand—Browning's presence made those feelings more acute. More troublesome. And more to be avoided.

As she'd avoided Browning's stare when she'd drawn even with him. Still, she'd felt his glower all the way to her toes. She couldn't really blame him for his anger. The scratches she'd inflicted on him had been bandaged, his new shirt buttoned and a blanket thrown over him to protect him from the night chill. Even so, seated as he was, his waist tied to a stalagmite, his hands bound in front of him, he could hardly be comfortable.

"He deserves the minor discomfort," she grumbled to herself, turning once again.

As if he heard her, a deep, taunting voice called out of the darkness, "A guilty conscience doesn't make a restful bedfellow, does it, *bandido*?"

Magdalena gritted her teeth and screwed her eyes shut even tighter, but the voice went on, "You wounded me when I was defenseless, then laughed about it with your men. I saw you all cavorting in your stolen finery. And you dare to tell me Carlotta prefers you to me? Prove it. Quit hiding her and let me see her."

"The only thing I wounded, gringo, was your pride. If I

let you go unscathed, how can my men respect me? A leader keeps his authority only if he exercises it. Besides, your own cut is not as deep as mine. Some think I was foolish to spare you. I may see their reasoning if you don't shut up and let me sleep."

"I'll never rest until I find Carlotta. Why do you hide her from me?"

The worry in his voice flailed at her raw nerves, and her retort was harsh. "Because she doesn't wish to see you. Could it be you speak so eloquently of guilt because your own troubles you so?"

A long pause came, then the voice, smooth as the silk she'd fondled, said, "You seem to know much of my relationship with her. If you are the suitor you claim to be, then why would she share our . . . intimacy with you?"

She could think of no reply to that, so she blustered, "It's none of your affair, gringo. Now shut up or I'll gag you."

Blessed silence descended, but it was soon broken by a distempered grunt and a curse. "Dammit, man, if you want me to sleep, you'll have to loosen these bonds. My back feels like it has a poker thrust up it."

Deciding she'd never get any sleep unless she complied, Magdalena scrambled up and hurried over to him, feeling her way along the cave wall in the darkness. When her boot touched him, she bent down and felt for the knot behind his back.

A kick sent her sprawling over him, and the next thing she knew, her arms were latched to her sides as he looped his bound wrists over her head and crushed her to his chest. She struggled to get away, but succeeded only in straddling his lap. The memory of the last time she'd been positioned over him so was all the more vivid for the many times she'd suppressed it. She went rigid.

Clint's triumphant glow faded as other, more tactile feelings, grew. For a moment, he was appalled at himself. Had he leanings he'd never suspected? He flexed his arms, crushing El Halcon tighter to his chest. No, he'd not imagined it. The proximity of this body aroused many emotions in him, but hatred was not uppermost. He listened to the soft breaths, felt the rapid thudding of the heart against his, before the evidence was so damning that he could no loner deny it. Astonishment replaced his dismay. What he contemplated was so unlikely that he doubted his own sanity.

Perhaps the darkness was the cause; perhaps he was asleep and dreaming. But whatever the reason, the body pressing so tightly to his had none of the iron-hard muscles he'd expected. Firm it was, from buttocks—he felt the twin spheres pressing into this thighs—to the calves mashing his sides. But if this wasn't the body of a woman, he was crazy as well as blind. There was only one way to know for certain . . . He began inching his hands back over El Halcon's head so he could feel the apex of the legs straddling him.

Magdalena took advantage of his loosening grip and vaulted off his lap. "*Bellaco*! Deceitful rat! I hope your back cracks in two!" She stalked back to her pallet. She flung aside the blanket that she'd huddled under earlier, her skin burning from hairline to toes. Damn him, and damn these things he made her feel. Why, oh why, of all the men in the world did her stupid, contrary body lust for his? And that's all it was, she told herself fiercely. Anything else was impossible. Ever.

Twenty feet away, Clint struggled with an idea that seemed even more impossible, his discomfort forgotten. He actually pinched himself to be sure he wasn't dreaming. Had the real El Halcon sneaked out under cover of darkness and sent Carlotta in? For only once before had he felt a woman of such firmness. Only one night had he had with her, but it would be forever emblazoned upon his memory. He could probably sketch every inch of the body he'd known so briefly, but so thoroughly. His own had signaled the truth to him before his mind had even suspected. Even now, he ached with reaction to that other . . . someone squirming upon him.

Yet . . . It was impossible. Carlotta and El Halcon simply could not be the same. No woman could fence so well, be so brave, lead such a motley group of men. If she did, then she'd be unnatural, too strong to need anyone. Too strong to need him. Yes, somehow Carlotta had switched places with El Halcon. That was it. Perhaps she even wanted to see him as much as he wanted to see her. That heady possibility chased his astonished dismay away. No, the world wasn't completely topsy-turvy yet. In the morning, he'd unmask Carlotta and make her admit why she participated in such a wild charade.

But still the worry nibbled at the edges of his complacency. He was able to relax only by promising himself that one way or another, he'd get to the truth. If Carlotta played El Halcon, she'd never admit it to him, but there was one way to find out for certain. The man he'd fenced with bore a graze on his side . . .

Pushing his tiredness away, Clint twisted sideways and began sawing his wrist bonds, back and forth, the sharp ridge protruding from the stalagmite he was tied to.

# Chapter 12

"Had I not seen it, I'd not think it true."
**Act I, DON JUAN TENORIO**

Joaquin and the other men stirred when the sun rose. Joaquin checked on Magdalena. Finding her deeply asleep, he decided she needed her rest after the eventful night. He checked on the two prisoners, who were also oblivious to the world. He turned away, unaware of the blue eyes that slitted open to watch his retreat.

After a quick breakfast, the men went about their assigned tasks. Sean and Joaquin took several sacks with them to gather grass for the horses. Miguel tied Ramirez's wrapped garments to his saddle. Pablo pocketed the pouches they'd filled last night with a few silver coins each and mounted his horse to follow Miguel, Benito and Juan out of the cavern. The clip clops of the hooves died away.

Clint waited a few minutes to be sure they were really gone, then he snapped his frayed bonds, rocked back and forth to loosen the rope about his waist, and pulled it around and unknotted it. He spared a last glance for the sleeping

Mexican, who was tied up in the farthest cave recess, but the man didn't move. He was isolated from the rest of the cave by a curving wall and a huge rock tower, and Clint was satisfied that the coming heated exchange would have no witnesses. Rising, Clint stretched to get his circulation going, then he snuck the short distance to the adjacent mat.

He appraised the long, still figure. In the clear light of day, he wondered at his sanity. True, the loose shirt hid much, as did the hood still tied down at the neck, but he'd seen El Halcon too many times to doubt his eyes now. Those long, powerful fencer's legs were too athletic to belong to a female. He must have been drunk with tiredness last night. Just to ease his mind, however, he'd prove to himself that he'd imagined the womanly curves against him. He crept to the front of the cave, grabbed up a short length of frayed rope and a knife, and snuck back to El Halcon.

The man was sleeping on his back, his hands lax at his sides. Gently, slowly, Clint caught one hand, brought it to the other, then wrapped the rope about the wrists. The figure stirred, stretched . . .

Magdalena's eyes snapped open. She looked at the man bending over her, his bright hair mussed, his jaw stubbled, and for a moment she was disoriented. Once before had she seen him so, when he'd almost touched her heart as deeply as he'd touched her body. That residual longing, swollen now with the vivid dreams he'd awakened her from made her reach out to him. Only then did she realize her hands were tied, that Browning held a knife to her throat—and that the look in his eyes befitted a nightmare more than an erotic dream.

Her fluttering heart stilled. Her hands dropped. She closed her eyes to block his face, hating him for her weakness, herself for her steadfast belief in his honor despite the evidence. Perhaps she'd pay now for that gullibility with her life: This man had reason to hate the bandit he thought she was. Very well, let it end now, as it had begun between them. With lies. She'd not beg for mercy. And she'd rather die than admit El Halcon was the woman who'd writhed above him in pleasure.

She opened her eyes and looked at him steadily, using El Halcon's gravel tones, "So, gringo, you win. Slit my throat and prove your superior strength on an unarmed man."

Stony blue eyes lowered from a steady perusal of her masked face to a more leisured one of her body. "Maybe what I have in mind is far more devastating to one of your bent." His expression an amalgam of curiosity and wariness, Clint slipped the knife beneath the hood and began to inch it up.

El Halcon stiffened and swiped at him like an outraged panther. "Leave me be! Kill me, but at least grant me dignity in death."

The knife paused. "Dignity? Like the dignity you granted me? Not once, not twice, but thrice now you've made mock of me. Above all, El Halcon, you fear exposing your face. Why, I've asked myself. Well, I'm about to discover the reason. And pray to God it's one I can live with."

With that obscure comment, he again tried to lift the hood. Again El Halcon squirmed away, lashing out with his bound hands, striking Clint's cheek hard enough to snap his head to one side. "Leave me be. Who I am and why I hide my face are none of your concern . . ."

"No? Perhaps you're right." El Halcon relaxed, then stiffened again when the smooth, deep voice added, "But then there's another way to find out what I need to know."

So saying, Clint moved the knife down to flick at the top button, the second, the third, of the black silk shirt. Magdalena was too stunned to react swiftly. By the time she swung her hands upward, he was ready. He snatched them with his free hand and held them above her head. Furiously, she squirmed, but when she felt the last button give way, she went still. Fearfully, she raised her eyes to his. He looked like he'd been kicked below the belt . . .

Clint's heart pounded so hard in his throat that he felt sick. He'd been so sure he was wrong, so certain this . . . person could be none other than the bandit—the *male* bandit—he'd expected. But his hopes and prayers were dross, for those delicate collarbones were too dainty for a man's. He'd run his tongue along them too many times to not recognize them now.

The binding above the ribcage was too high for a bandage. Already knowing what he'd see, he sawed through the cotton strip. Beautiful breasts, high, round and pink-tipped, tumbled free, taunting him with their nipples stiffening in the early coolness of the cavern. Breasts he'd suckled and savored like a rare, exotic candy. Breasts he'd longed to taste again. The anamoly of this bounty, the very essence of femininity, beneath the sinister hood, above the long, strong legs, would have thrilled many men. What a coup it was to have known such a woman, to have initiated her into the ways of women, some would have boasted— those who would have savored the encounter like a fine meal, then forgotten it until the next tasty morsel.

But Clint? Clint felt only creeping dread. For he wanted more of her than a moment . . .

Slowly, knowing he must, he dropped the knife and tugged the hood off. There she was again; the woman he'd dreamed of. High cheekbones, broad forehead, triangular face of a rare and haunting beauty. And those eyes. Eyes the like he'd never seen before and would never see again. Deep gold, melancholy, fearless. Their very steadiness pained Clint until he had to look away from her challenge. One chance only was left. Though he knew it for a futile one, Clint pushed the shirt away and worked at the bandage on her side. When it came loose, he grunted as if she'd punched him in the gut. There, low on her side, were the marks he himself had inflicted in their duel. No shadow of a doubt remained. This . . . walking paradox was El Halcon.

Clint let her go and fell back on his hands to drop his head on his chest. Dear God, in his worst nightmare he'd never dreamed he'd solve the riddle of Carlotta and El Halcon with one devastating answer. Now that he could deny it no longer, he realized the evidence had been damning. He'd just been too stubborn—and too afraid—to heed it.

The haunting gold eyes that no amount of wax and stain

could hide. The fluidity with which she moved when she thought no one watched. Her fascination with the rapiers in his cabin. The firmness of her body, the power of her legs. Carlotta's nightly forays hadn't been inexplicable after all: She disappeared, and El Halcon appeared. Still, he hadn't seen it. Hadn't seen it because he hadn't wanted to.

The wistful girl in the strawberry patch, the sad but proud maid and the arrogant fiend of a bandit were one amazing female. Hence the Latin's obscure comment: "He is her strength; Carlotta is his refuge." How apt, and how revealing, if he hadn't been so willfully blind.

Why did she do it? And why did he care? The latter, at least, he could answer. The strawberry girl was the ideal mate he'd always sought. Proud, passionate, but vulnerable, needing his strength. The Carlotta-Inez he'd deflowered had only strengthened his fascination. She'd been so much the woman when he'd loved her resentment away. That woman, he had something to offer. That woman had need of him.

But El Halcon? This . . . woman needed no man. She was a law unto herself, a spirit nothing could conquer. She'd give not an inch of herself; every smile, every favor would have to be fought for. Won by guile, force or might of arms, but never bestowed. How could he hope to win such a woman? Did he even want to try?

Clint finally lifted his head to look at her. Her fingers trembled as she tied the binding about her breasts, knotting it awkwardly with her bound hands. She drew the shirt closed and buttoned it, then pulled her hood over her head again. Even though he knew what lay under it, her disguise seemed as impenetrable as ever. For a moment, he was almost repelled. It wasn't right for a woman to pursue such a course. She should have a wedding ring about her finger and several toddlers tugging at her skirts. He'd wanted to give Carlotta-Inez all that and more. But El Halcon would find those things a burden, the man who wanted to give them to her a threat.

He knew he should flee this attraction rather than pursue such a doomed relationship, but he still stared at her, fascinated, unable to twitch a muscle. The knowledge that he'd coupled with this creature boggled his mind. He simply could not coalesce the three discrete pictures into one image. Was it horror or wonder he felt? He honestly didn't know. But whether she was a snake or a siren, he was caught in her allure . . .

Magdalena took his white-faced silence for disgust. She swallowed her tears and lifted her head proudly when she finished dressing. She felt obscene in her nakedness, even now, fully clothed. She could have borne his lust better than this. How much easier if he'd fondled her, even raped her, than bared her to prove a point, then shrunk away as if contact with her would befoul him. She wanted to slink out and hide like a mortally wounded animal, but she could not. She had come too far, had too much at stake for the luxury of regret. Magdalena Inez Flanagan de Sarria had willfully disobeyed a lifetime's dictates to become El Halcon. She gave up all rights to her grand name, all pretensions to womanhood in the process. Only by redeeming the honor of both could she rightfully reclaim them.

Nothing could sway her from those ends. Not the disappointment in the blue gaze staring at her; not her desperate need to be what he wanted her to be; not even her own self-disgust. She said emotionlessly in her own voice, "So, you know El Halcon's secret. What do you intend to do with it?"

Rubbing a hand over his face, Clint answered honestly, "I don't know. I'm still trying to reconcile the woman who caught fire in my arms with the man who outfenced me last night."

Magdalena was glad her blush couldn't be seen under her hood. She lifted her bound wrists. "Release me, and you need never do so. Despite my reservations, I'll risk letting you go, if you swear, on all you hold dear, that you'll tell no one where we hide or who I really am."

"That's easily enough promised," he said, sawing through her bonds. "One, I don't intend to leave. And two, I have no idea who you really are. I know you by three names, none of which, I suspect, are correct."

Magdalena drew a soundless sigh of relief. So, no one had told him her story. Something good had come of this debacle after all. Even if he told others that El Halcon was a woman, *If* they believed him, then they'd still not know it was she. Only when her relief subsided did the first part of his statement penetrate her dazed mind.

She rubbed her wrists, repeating slowly, "What do you mean, you don't intend to leave?"

"Just what I say. I've found Carlotta. Not as I expected to, perhaps, but your dual—I should say triple—personas don't change my reasons."

Magdalena rose and strapped on her sword. Feeling somewhat better at its familiar comfort, she planted her legs and crossed her arms over her chest. "The Carlotta you seek doesn't exist. Even if she did, you could never have again what you want of her."

"And what is that?" Clint rose lazily to face her.

Magdalena blushed at her boldness even as El Halcon said bluntly, "To lie with her. Why else do you seek her?"

"Such a pretty opinion you have of me. What have I ever done to justify it?"

"Your sins may seem minor to you, but rape, collusion and spying are not virtues I would encourage in my men."

"Nor would I expect you to." Clint took three steps forward until she had to tilt her head back to look at him. "But heartfelt desire, alliance for a greater good and self-preservation are surely human qualities even one of your—staunch morals can respect." Clint sent a mocking look to Ramirez's smaller trunk, which now contained only the wrapped dress.

Magdalena said through her teeth, "You know nothing of my motives. Don't condemn what you don't understand."

"*Exactamente, niña,*" Clint purred, his eyes bright even in the dimness.

Biting down a frustrated groan, Magdalena whirled away from him. Why did he always change black into white, evil into good and lies into truth? It must be his physical hold over her that made his words seem so powerful. Any other man she could rebut and send handily on his way; Clint

289

Browning tied her tongue into knots and turned her brains into mush. For that reason alone, even if he did speak truth, she had to send him away.

Taking a deep breath, she turned back to face him. He stood casually, one massive shoulder propped against the cave wall, one ankle crossed over the other. As if she didn't frighten him, or sway him.

On her mettle now, Magdalena snapped, "On that I will agree. I don't understand you, gringo, and you don't understand me. Two such different characters would be foolish to form an alliance, no?"

"No. That very difference makes me valuable, for I see the world in a different way to you and your men. I can also move freely about. You cannot."

Again, Magdalena told herself his words were more seductive in their guile than in their logic, for her need to get away from him was growing desperate. "No. My mind is made up. You cannot stay. Take your mount and leave." She stalked away to the front of the cave.

Clint stayed where he was, watching her. Every word he'd spoken had been true, but he'd still not admitted why he really wanted to stay. Now the shock of her identity had worn off, he could admit that reason, if only to himself. For good or ill, he was fascinated by this woman. The astounding fact that she, a lady of the aristocracy, had the nerve, determination and, most amazing, the ability to lead her rough band successfully against an entire presidio only increased her power over him. Disconcerted he might be, but he was not, alas, disgusted. As he should be, he told himself.

She changed personalities with her clothing, but there was something of her in all her guises. Only by gaining her trust could he form a whole picture—one, instinct told him, he would cherish. If she'd let him . . . But he could only knock down one obstacle at a time.

He scowled into space, searching his tired brain for something, anything, that would convince her. His wandering gaze landed on the mats near the front of the cave. His face relaxed. Pushing himself away from the wall, he strode across the cavern to where she was half-heartedly eating an apple. She had to take tiny bites and chew carefully to keep her hood from getting in the way.

A deep, amused voice made her jump. "Don't your skirts and petticoats seem appealing about now?" He winked at the peel she'd shorn from the apple and tossed away.

She was too upset to see humor in his pun. Swallowing, she retorted, "No. Nor were they ever. I'll take my hood and breeches any day over the constrictions women are bound by."

When he looked both surprised and intrigued, she hastily changed the subject. He already knew too much about her. "Where is your horse?"

"With the others. Where he'll stay." Clint folded his long length to sit down beside her. He held up a hand at the protest forming on her lips. "You'll not change my mind with threats, curses or pleas. I stay. I'll waste no more breath trying to convince you my reasons are honorable. Time will prove that to you. Then, we'll see if Carlotta-Inez was truly a figment of my imagination."

Because Magdalena knew she was not, she leaped to her feet and roared, "My sword is solid enough. Get out or feel how real it is!" She clenched one hand about her rapier's hilt.

Clint lounged back on an elbow, propping his other arm over his upraised knee. For a man who'd just been threatened, he looked remarkably calm. "You do get riled up, don't you? Here's the first lesson you can learn from me: Threats made too often and not followed through on lose their effect." He smiled up at her as if he couldn't hear her teeth grinding together. "If you were going to kill me, you would have done so last night. Fairly. Now I'm not even armed."

For a moment it seemed El Halcon would strangle with rage, then she blew a bitter laugh and sat down to eye this strange character with genuine interest. "Why do you want so much to stay?"

Clint almost took pity on her bewilderment, but she wasn't any readier to hear his reasons than he was ready to admit them. "Because I want to help you, El Halcon-Carlotta-Inez." He wrinkled his nose so lugubriously at the string of misnomers that she had to chuckle. "Won't you tell me your first name, at least?" When she shook her head, he sighed, but went on. "So, are we decided, then?"

Looking at him, Magdalena almost wavered. So earnest he seemed. So honestly eager to help her. Those blue eyes that had mesmerized her from the beginning glowed at her like twin camp fires, promising warmth and safety if she'd only believe in him. Making a little sound of distress, she turned away—and shook her head.

Clint's heart sank with disappointment, and his reply was harsh. "Very well. If it's bare knuckles you want, then you'll find I've a taste for brawling and little patience for prize ring rules."

She didn't understand the strange reference, but his tone was warning enough. Warily, she turned her head to look at him.

Holding the eyes he could barely see within the hood, Clint stated, "You let me stay, or when they return I tell your gallant band who really leads them. I wonder how they'll like being told the man they think so fearless is really a female too cowardly to face her own womanhood?"

She flinched as if he'd slapped her, but he went remorselessly on. "Your hopes of recruiting more men will be as forlorn as mine are of winning your trust. What man will allow a woman to dictate to him so?"

As if he'd conjured them up, they heard horses coming up the trail. "Well, what's it to be?"

"Damn your black soul to hell, you can stay," Magdalena spat. "But you're on your own. Don't expect any quarter from me." She pushed herself to her feet and stomped to the cave entrance.

"I don't, my dear lady bandit. An optimist I may be, but a fool I'm not. You've challenged me often. Now, I've one for you: Test me as you will. I'm the man you need. As you'll admit before too many days have passed."

Magdalena snorted, flinging over her shoulder, "If I live to see them and don't forfeit my life to your treachery."

292

Joaquin and Sean looked surprised to see Clint standing up to greet them. They glanced at Magdalena, sensing her anger, but she said only, "Have you seen the others? Shouldn't they return soon?"

"It's early yet. The renegades never stay in one place long. It may take them the day to find them." Joaquin nodded at Clint. "Have you decided to let him go?"

"No, I've decided to let him stay. And may God have mercy on all fools." Magdalena scurried out of the cavern.

Joaquin jerked his head at Clint. "Come, help me carry the grass to the horses." With a last moody glance outside, Clint obeyed.

They dumped a large pile for each animal, then Joaquin tended Rojo and Sean's mount. All the while, he assessingly eyed the American. When Browning ignored him and flopped down to nibble a blade of grass, Joaquin broached the obviously touchy subject.

"What did you say to get El Halcon to let you stay?"

Clint's head veered around in a glare. His mouth opened, then he sighed. "I was going to tell you to mind your own business, but that . . . girl obviously means much to you."

When Joaquin looked startled, Clint admitted, "I blackmailed her. I told her I'd tell her men she's a woman."

"How did you discover that?" Joaquin threw down the currycomb and sat down beside Clint.

A rueful smile played about Clint's lips. "I'm not as slow as I sometimes seem. I should have realized it weeks ago. I would have, if I hadn't been so reluctant to see it." He twitched the grass out of his mouth and flung it away, then sat up. "There's obviously a bond between you. How could you let her behave so foolishly? What does she hope to gain by this . . . this . . . quest?"

It was Joaquin's turn to smile sadly. "A reason for living. I admit, I first tried to dissuade her, but I see now that neither of us really had a choice. Magdalena could never live with herself if she didn't try to . . . " Joaquin's voice trailed off as he realized what he'd said. By the look on the

American's face, he knew if was too late to cover the mistake.

Clint leaned forward eagerly. "Magdalena? That's her real name?" He tested the name several times on his tongue, as if it were a flavor he'd long sought and been denied. "It suits her. A tower. A woman above other women."

Joaquin held his breath as he awaited more, but Clint seemed to connect her name to nothing. Joaquin's breath escaped slowly through his teeth. "We may have little chance of winning, but slim is better than none." Joaquin extended his hand. Clint shook it. "Keep it to yourself, but my real name is Joaquin. I welcome you to our little group. If you want to throw in your lot with us, you have my gratitude. Give Magdalena a chance to know you. If you truly cared for Carlotta as you claim, then you will love Magdalena with all your heart."

"Don't you think I have a right to know what I'm involving myself in? She is obviously more than a bandit. What does she seek so diligently?"

"That, I can't yet reveal." Joaquin glanced toward the entrance and saw that Magdalena had returned and was glaring at them. "Perhaps another time. When we know you better."

Clint watched him stride off, then he lay back, crossed his arms behind his head and stared at the cave ceiling. "Magdalena, Magdalena," he whispered. It was a lovely name, for a rare and lovely creature, but something more teased the back of his mind. As if he'd heard the name before, since arriving in California. Unable to corral the vague memory, he finally let it go. Rising, he went to join the others.

He found the trio seated in a half-circle, planning their next raid. Magdalena was saying over Joaquin's objections, "But we must. I don't care how many armed guards he has posted, we've delayed too long already. If the will is destroyed, I'll have little chance of proving my claim . . ." She caught sight of Clint and broke off.

He met that angry glare calmly. "Don't let me interrupt."

He sat down beside her and offered his hand to the large, red-headed Irishman. "Clinton Browning."

Sean gave him a sly wink. "Sean O'Malley, though this group knows me as Mick. No hard feelins', boyo? If I promise not to hold a gun on ye again?"

"Not any longer, though, at the times, I could have wrung your neck." Clint looked at Magdalena reflectively. "I would have done the same in similar circumstances."

The answer brought a broad smile to Sean's face. "Then 'tis glad I be to have ye join us."

"It's nice to know that *someone* welcomes me."

Magdalena turned away from that needling look and went to polish her sword. She said over her shoulder, "It's settled, then. Tomorrow, we ride." She ignored the three men for the rest of the day, seeing to her own equipment.

It was almost dark when the Indians at last returned. They were not alone, however. Magdalena set aside the guitar she'd been strumming and rose, her heartbeat quickening.

She stood silently and let the four newcomers, each short but powerfully built, look about the cavern warily, then eye her with even more foreboding. Finally, when Miguel nudged one, he stepped forward.

"It's a legend among my people that these caverns are haunted by spirits. You've the look of one, but are you evil or good?"

Magdalena slowly walked up to him and held out her hand. Reluctantly, he shook it.

She stepped back. "You can see for yourself that I'm flesh and blood just like you are. But we've more in common than you think, . . . er . . ."

"Pico," he grudgingly supplied.

"Pico. We both fight injustice to find our place in this land we love. I can promise you nothing except that I will do all within my power to see that your people are rewarded for their years of patience." She flicked a casual hand at the bulge in his shirtpocket. "Does that not prove that I'm sincere?"

"We've been promised reward before. Land. Cattle. Until the drink steals first our wits, then our holdings."

"You'll find no drink here. Our dangers require a clear head. My only rule is that you and your friends obey my orders without question. We all share the profits equally." She watched as he turned to his friends.

After a heated debate, Pico nodded and looked at her again. "We stay, for now. But if you lie to us . . ." The Indian's face hardened, and his hand dropped to the knife sheathed to his thigh.

"That's fair enough. Now, sit with us and eat, then I want you each to show me how you fight . . ."

Clint watched as Magdalena gained the Indians' respect by the sheer force of her personality. At one point she took Sean's knife and faced off with Fernando, a battle-scarred brave. Clint almost bit his tongue off over the protest he knew would be useless, but his every muscle tensed to go to her aid if the Indian got too aggressive.

He should have known better. Magdalena was not an expert with a knife as she was with a sword, but her dancing movements were so agile that she kept ever out of range. The Indian paused, frustrated, and she hooked her foot behind his ankle and neatly downed him.

When he glared at her, she offered him a hand. He ignored it and rose himself, his face crimson even in the dim lantern glow.

"Come, amigo, don't be angry. I but wanted to show you a trick I learned long ago." Her voice softened. "From one very dear to me. Another ploy he taught me is to use my cloak. So." She caught a fistful of velvet and whipped the garment up and around, showing how it could entangle a blade. "You can do something similar with your serape."

Awkwardly, he duplicated the movement, but he looked so clumsy that his comrades laughed. He glared at them, then shrugged.

Her voice quivering, Magdalena encouraged, "That's not bad. It takes practice. We'll do more in the morning. Soon, we ride on El Paraiso."

The name cut into the buzz of conversation as cleanly as a knife. Clint's eyes narrowed; the Indians stopped in midsentence and swiveled to look at her.

Miguel, as usual, expressed all their concerns. "But Don Roberto's land is not like the others'. He has many guarding his hacienda . . ."

"Precisely. So he must have much to lose, no?" When no one disputed that point, El Halcon's voice grew even hoarser than usual. "Few have been unkinder to your people than Roberto de Sarria. He makes you live in hovels and whips those *vaqueros* so foolish as to flout his authority."

Pico stepped forward. "My sister was a maid at his hacienda. He got her with child, then cast her out. Yet when I dared ask him to send her food and clothing, he threw me off his land and said I would never work for a don again." Pico smiled, his teeth gleaming predator-white in his dark face. "I have not. It's more fun stealing their cattle than tending them. Me, I go gladly with you."

His friends stepped forward even with him, then Miguel and the last three followed suit. El Halcon nodded. "Thank you for your trust in me, my friends. I'll not abuse it, if it means my life."

After the Indians had dispersed to bed down, Clint stayed where he was, troubled by his thoughts. The feeling nagged at him that Magdalena's hatred of de Sarria was a clue to her identity, but even that mystery didn't tantalize him at the moment. Somehow, he *must* make her desist this insane masquerade. Her words, so foolhardy, so brave, so devastatingly sincere, reverberated in his head: "If it means my life . . . if it means my life . . ."

What was he to think of such a woman? She had no right to be so brave, he thought in frustration. It was a crime against nature, not to mention herself, to flout her very gender in pursuit of some silly goal even a man would stand no chance of winning. Well, whether she sought it or not, or accepted it or not, he'd protect her. Despite herself, if necessary. Somehow, in the short time he'd known her, she'd become important to him. He could not leave her now no matter how infuriating she was; he would not stand idly by and let ambition or quixotism endanger her.

He found the resolution easier to make than to act on in the days that followed. Magdalena asked nothing of her men she wasn't willing to do, usually first. She always took the lead during their robberies, until Clint grew to dread them. Few resisted them, but she had some close calls that made Clint sweat in contrast to her amazing coolness. The next night, they lucked upon none other than the administrator of the Santa Barbara mission.

At first, he was arrogant. He even threatened Magdalena with a knife, but she caught the blade in her cloak and slapped the flat of her sword down on his wrist. She gave the knife, a fine, gold-inlaid dagger, to Pico.

At her order, the Indians stripped the man to underdrawers and boots. He wasn't physically abused, but by the time they'd taken his purse, horse and garments, he was thankful to be alive. When the Indians got a little too enthusiastic in taunting him, she reprimanded them until they reluctantly backed away. Then, pressing her sword to his throat, she warned that they'd meet again if he didn't quit cheating those he'd been chosen to help. She assisted him on his way with a kick in the rear, and he lit off like a terrified rabbit. Clint wondered if she found the encounter consolation for the one she really wanted.

At Joaquin's urging, she'd reluctantly agreed to wait to raid El Paraiso until the new men were better trained. They were fierce fighters but lacked discipline. Many of the men guarding Roberto's house were soldiers from the presidio, and they would not be as easy to cow as their robbery victims.

Thus, Clint had ample opportunity to observe her during the days when they trained and the nights when they haunted the highway. But always from afar, for she suffered not his company. If he approached her, she turned away to chat with one of her men. Her wariness heightened his frustration to torment.

Several weeks later, he was no closer to understanding her than he'd been when he joined them. It was as if she'd stared down the grim reaper himself; as if she had more to fear of living than dying. She wasn't reckless, exactly. She always planned their forays in advance, and he had to admit that she had ambush skills a general would have envied.

Sometimes they boldly blocked the road just around a bend. Sometimes they came whooping out of tree or rock cover. But they never raided in one place long, for they knew soldiers had been sent to search for them. Their raids went south of Santa Barbara and north to San Luis Obispo. And their cache grew steadily despite the fact that they always shared a portion of their goods and coins with the Indians in the area.

As their skills improved, their legend spread. Travelers carried tales of them north to Monterey and south to Baja California. El Halcon took on mythic proportions. On the rare occasions when he went into Santa Barbara, Clint heard El Halcon's name bandied about by servant and aristo alike. His gallantry to women, it was said, proved he was really a caballero who'd fallen on hard times. It was apparent to Clint that every woman secretly hoped to meet him and every young buck longed to duel him.

Clint would have found the situation amusing if it hadn't been so perilous. On one of his trips to his vessel to see how Pritikin was doing, Clint was waylaid by Luis as he tried to sneak away.

"Captain? A word, por favor."

Warily, Clint turned to face Luis. "Yes?"

"How does your search go?"

"Better than yours, perhaps. I've come across the bandit a time or two, but so far I've found no way to infiltrate his band."

"Do you know anything of my man?" Luis described the soldier Clint had captured.

"No, but if I hear anything, I'll send word." Clint looked around the beach. It was deserted, but he lowered his voice anyway. "How progresses the mining?"

Luis also looked around before whispering, "Much better. The supplies finally arrived several days ago. We hope to have enough to send with you within a few weeks."

"Good. Then I'll be in touch." And before Luis could protest, Clint mounted his horse and galloped toward the highway. He didn't see Luis frown after him, rubbing his bent index finger against his mouth as he always did when cogitating, then whirl and stride briskly away.

A lone horseman rode from behind the shelter of palms, pausing to look from Luis's back to where Clint had disappeared. A troubled look on his face, Miguel rode on toward the mission to see his sweetheart. He couldn't stay the night now as he'd planned. He had to get back and warn El Halcon . . .

When Clint returned in early afternoon, he found the others at their interminable practicing. He watched Magdalena duel with Fernando. Tirelessly she led him through each classic fencing position, showing him how to angle his blade for best advantage, when to thrust, when to retreat.

They'd moved their camp to a secluded canyon with a large, grassy clearing, so the breeze caressed them. Even now, at the end of June, during the day's height, the heat was not extreme. This area, it seemed, seldom knew the fluctuations in temperature that Clint was used to.

Wildflowers bloomed in profusion not only across the field, but in the crannies of the surrounding hills. The sky above arched over their heads like a gigantic cobalt bowl, fired by the Master's hand. The largest bird Clint had ever seen floated effortlessly in the midst of that bright blue, calling raucously. Its bright orange head stood out against its black body and the surrounding heavens. Clint followed its graceful flight in awe, remembering that Joaquin had told him the bird was called a condor.

Sighing, he looked back at Magdalena. She seemed oblivious to all but her fencing. Was she truly so numb to all joy and life that only her quest had meaning for her? Suddenly, he couldn't bear it. The woman he'd held in his arms had generated a joyous fire for life that had warmed him as nothing else had before or since. He'd find her again if he had to strip El Halcon's disguise away piece by piece . . .

Striding boldly forward, Clint clapped his hands and called, "It's time for a rest! What say you all to a bath?" As he grew nearer to two sweating Indians panting from their exertions, he wrinkled his nose. "It's past time." Clint lifted his arm to smell himself. "Phew! It's a wonder my horse doesn't run when he sees me coming."

Ignoring Magdalena's glare, Clint went to his saddlebags and took out the bars of soap he'd fetched from his ship, throwing one to each of the Indians. They turned the creamy oatmeal bars over in their hands, sniffed suspiciously, then looked back at Clint.

"You'll feel rested when you're clean. I promise." When no one made a move toward the clear-running stream nearby, Clint sighed and unbuttoned his shirt. "Stink like pigs if you like. But pretty soon we won't need to announce our presence when we halt a rider. He'll smell us coming a mile away!" Clint rinsed his shirt out and draped it over a branch to dry, then pulled off his boots and socks.

The Indians looked from El Halcon's still figure, to Clint, who was peeling off his pants. They sniffed the soap again; then, led by Pico, they walked toward the water and began fumbling with their own clothes.

Joaquin and Sean looked worriedly at Magdalena. She still held her sword, and her back was rigid. Joaquin didn't have to see her eyes to know what she looked at.

Clint shucked off his tight-fitting underdrawers and stretched lazily. Every proud inch of him gleamed in the bright sunlight, from his glittering head to his long, bronzed feet. His fine body hairs caught the lazy rays, burnishing him from top to toe with forbidden luster. His hands on his hips, he cocked his head to one side. "Come join us, El Halcon. Don't be shy. We're all the same, no?"

The Indians paused in their splashing to look expectantly toward the bank. To a man, they were dying with curiosity to see what El Halcon looked like. They waited.

Still he stood frozen, facing the American. Joaquin finally intervened, for he sensed Magdalena's growing rage. "El Halcon values his privacy. I'll take him to the end of the canyon and keep watch . . ."

"An excellent idea," Clint said, jerking on his pants again. Bare-footed, he fetched his thin towel, tossed it over one shoulder, took a long, wrapped bundle off his horse and caught it under one arm. He looked at El Halcon. "I'm ready. I'll be glad to keep watch for you." He took a step toward the head of the stream, but paused and looked over his shoulder when El Halcon didn't follow.

"Come, come. You've nothing to fear from me." Clint paused. "Or do you?"

Again, the Indians looked at them curiously. Why was El Halcon behaving so strangely?

Joaquin moved forward, but this time it was Sean who held him back. "No, 'tis past time they had an accountin' t'ween them. She'll hold him off 'til judgment day unless he forces her to face him . . ."

Joaquin couldn't disagree with that, so he stayed still as Magdalena looked from Clint, to the watching Indians, back to Clint. She snapped her sword into her sheath so decisively that the clanging echoed through the canyon. "Very well, gringo. Prove indeed that you are to be trusted. Mick, see that we are not disturbed." She whirled and stalked up the stream, leaving the Indians whispering.

When the water curved under the shelter of several willows, she stopped. Clint had followed her silently and he halted to face her. For a long, tense moment, they stared at one another, the lithe, black-garbed figure and the handsome, bare-chested man.

He dropped the bundle and towel and held out his hand. "Come, sport with me," he pleaded huskily.

When she stiffened and backed a step, he shook his head wryly. "Not in that way. Haven't you ever played in the water with only the sun to cover you?"

For a moment it seemed she wouldn't answer, then she muttered, "Long ago, when laughter came easily to me."

He closed the gap between them and lifted her chin to look deep into the steady eyes, gleaming at him through the hood. "Then let it come again. Let us call a truce. Fine, I'm not to be trusted, and you are the most exasperating woman alive. But can't we for once forget that and live for the moment? Who knows when we'll have this chance again?"

Her eyes flickered down, and he held his breath as he awaited her response. Only the murmuring of the swaying trees and the sleepy chirp of crickets could be heard over the pounding of hearts too long denied.

But only that denial kept Magdalena sane, and she didn't dare give an inch lest she lose the breadth of the world as she knew it. For weeks now he'd watched her, daring her to talk with him, even spar with him. But she could do neither without threatening the walls she'd built around her embattled heart. She should have realized he'd not accept her rejection. He thought she was susceptible to him, and *Dios* help her, but she was. This was but a ploy to get her to lower her barriers. Only by seeming to accede, and by resisting the seduction she knew would come, could she rout him for once and all.

She flung her head back to draw the hood over her head. She unpinned her hair and ran her fingers through it, holding his hungry eyes all the while. "Very well, captain. I confess I would love a bath. But you must give me your word you will not . . . press your attentions."

"You have it," Clint said huskily, his eyes on her fingers as she began unbuttoning her shirt.

He heard what sounded suspiciously like a snort, but when he glanced at her, she was looking down at her task. She made no show of her unveiling. She undressed as if she were alone, briskly, efficiently. When she was stripped to underdrawers and breast binding, he expected her to stop. He prayed she would stop, for already he was straining against his breeches. Instead, she stripped the tight-fitting cotton down her long legs and untied the binding to stand proudly before him.

Garbed only in wind and sunshine, she was even lovelier than the picture he carried always in his head. He felt as if he could absorb every curve and hollow through his thirsty pores, and he'd taken a step toward her before he realized she was holding out her hand. Dumbly, he pulled a bar of soap from his pocket and dropped it in her palm. She glided toward the water, her long hair blowing in the breeze, baring, then shielding her strong, graceful back and the upper curve of her buttocks. She walked into the water until it was waist-deep, then turned toward him and scooped up handfuls to wet her breasts and neck. Rubbing the soap in her hands, she lathered every inch of wet, gleaming white skin.

When he still stood as if rooted to the bank, she tilted her head to one side and called, "Come, this was your idea. Won't you join me?"

Gritting his teeth, he hesitated. If he went in with his breeches on, she'd know how she aroused him. If he took them off, she'd certainly know. "What the hell," he muttered under his breath, and peeled his pants off.

He was amazed to feel himself blushing, but she, the witch, had her head bent to wash her neck, and didn't even see the state he was in. He splashed into the water grumpily, and when she still ignored him, he snapped, "That *is* my soap. Unless you've appropriated it as you do everything else."

She quirked an eyebrow, worked up some more lather, and flipped the soap at him. It thunked against his chest, where he caught it. He glared at her, but she merely proceeded to wash her breasts.

Compulsively, he watched her, his hands still crossed to hold the soap to his chest, as still as if he'd been laid in his crypt. But every part of him was achingly alive as he watched her hands suds those taut, high globes. She worked quickly, then rinsed as matter of factly, and he winced at the waste.

She held out her hand again. He looked at her stupidly. "The soap, please," she prompted. After he'd handed it over, she remarked idly, "For a man who wanted to have fun, you look more as if you're being tortured. Me, I'm enjoying this. You should have suggested it sooner."

A low, rumbling growl was her only warning before a wet, angry Goliath accepted her foolhardy challenge. She found herself jerked against a massive, heaving chest. As she looked up into glittering cobalt blue eyes, she thought vaguely, "And me without a slingshot . . ." Oddly, his thoughts seemed to be on a similar bent. It wasn't the first time they'd been so attuned . . .

"You must have been Salome in an earlier life, such

pleasure do you get from tormenting me. But this time, you'll dance with a partner . . ." He lowered his lips over hers.

The kiss was hard, hungry and without reserve. She resisted as best she could, but she, too, had been affected by his nakedness. Her senses, already aroused by the sight of him, rioted beyond her control at the feel of him. Their torsos, slick with water, rubbed together as he bent her backward over his arm and consumed her mouth. Only when she moaned and opened her lips to his questing tongue did he lift his head.

Panting, he growled, "So, it's a bath you want? I'll be glad to oblige." He dove for the dropped soap, came up and tossed his head free of the water.

Her haze was cleared by the stinging droplets, and she tried to turn for the shore. Big, rough hands caught her at the waist and pulled her back.

"Oh no, you don't. You're not clean yet . . ." He turned her to face him, moved her to shallower water where a boulder split the stream's course, then lathered her shoulders and set the soap on top of the boulder. Using his palms more than his fingers, he rubbed her shoulders, her arms, lifted them to clean her armpits, then turned her, shoved her hair aside and massaged her back. The firm, circular motions relaxed her despite herself, especially when he didn't threaten her more intimate areas.

When her muscles were lax under his hands, he pushed her back against the boulder and lifted her left leg to his chest. His hands froze in their languorous course up her thigh. It had been flawless the last time he'd seen her so, but now a long, ugly gash marred the outside of it. On which raid had she sustained the wound? he wondered vaguely. And how many more could she survive before she was too late convinced of her own mortality? He closed his eyes, but the horrific vision he saw made him open them again. Moaning harshly, he lowered his mouth to the scar and soothed the length of it with his tongue.

Her drowsy eyes opened and dilated when she felt the caress. She tried to pull away, but he held her firm to lather

**305**

her long leg and massage the tensile muscles with both hands, anchoring her foot against his chest. In a few minutes, her eyes drifted shut again.

She didn't protest when his hands drifted higher, for they circled her thigh with smooth, nonthreatening motions. She was thus unprepared when he lathered his hands and gently cupped her mound. She gasped. Her eyes popped open as she tried to pull her leg away, but he locked it under one arm and stepped closer, imprisoning her between sun-warmed, smooth rock and passion-heated, smooth flesh.

She protested, "No, you promised . . ." but he seemed not to hear.

His big hands were gentle as he lathered her buttocks, hips and in between. Taking advantage of the slick friction, he rubbed the tell-tale little bud raising its glistening, eager head for his attentions. Using alternately one finger and his palm, but sustaining constant pressure, he caressed her to limpness, then he pushed her atop the boulder and lowered his mouth to her breasts.

Their sighs of pleasure mingled, drifting away on the breeze. He suckled her as if she sustained him, as she did; she squirmed against that gentle hand as if it exalted her, for it did. The weeks of conflict might never have been as they celebrated how closely they could commune. She arched her breasts into his mouth, his prisoner more than he'd ever been hers.

When she stiffened and cried out, he rested his cheek against her heaving breasts and savored the pumping rush of life he'd created. Then, like the honorable man he was, he let her slip back into the water, turned away and briskly soaped himself, hoping the action would relieve some of his tortured aching. Many times had he paid for the pleasure he'd stolen from her that night . . . And how many more times would he have to pay?

Magdalena drew a shaky breath and straightened. Her body still sang, and she felt as if light glowed from every pore, rescuing her from the darkness she'd known for so long. Could a man of such generosity be the scoundrel she'd named him? She watched him, her eyes puzzled, for she

306

knew enough of men to realize the satisfaction had been hers alone. Had this been an atonement for his roughness the first time, or another trick to leave her vulnerable? For she did feel vulnerable, open to him as never before. While she was still trying to figure him out, he finished, rinsed himself and stalked out of the water.

She no longer tried to lie to herself as she watched each long, strong muscle flex as he dried off. More than ever he reminded her of a golden idol, for he was surely too perfect to be real. Could it be that the beauty of his mind matched that of his form? She longed to believe it so, as she admired the harmonious play of arms, back and buttocks as he briskly wielded the towel. Somehow, despite her efforts to guard against it, this man had weaseled his way into her heart. He was important to her, *yanqui* or no, spy or no. For once, she would allow herself to listen to the heart that bade her trust him instead of to the mind that warned her off. She rinsed herself and waded out of the water to his side.

She took the towel from his hands and dried off his broad shoulders. He stiffened, refusing to face her, and she had a suspicion as to why. A gurgle of laughter filling her chest, making her giddy, she teased, "Salome had a head as her prize. What I want is much lower." She dropped the towel and draped her arms about his hips, reaching for him.

A growl reverberated in the strong back, one so primitive that she froze. He caught her hands and whirled to face her, pushing his long, aching length into her abdomen. "Is this what you wanted to know, witch? Your powers are intact." He forced her fingers about the throbbing shaft. "I'm on fire for you and will gladly douse it in your body if you'll tell me you come to me in trust, if not in love. Do you believe I wish no harm to you, that I'll give my very life to protect you?"

Magdalena was both shocked and aroused anew at the pulsing life in her hand, and it took a moment for his words to sink in. When they did, her unfocused gold gaze snapped up, sharpening on his. Her hand dropped away. She stepped back.

She forced her brain to function again over the protests of

307

her body. Had this seeming tenderness been another of his tricks? What better way to earn her trust than to bring her pleasure, then deny himself? He'd not quibbled about her "trust" the first time. Why did he do so now?

Clint saw from the look on her face that he'd failed. That beautiful body believed in him. Perhaps even a corner of her heart did. But her mind was as closed to him as ever. His sacrifice had been for naught. He clenched his hands and took a step toward her, but when she backed away at the look on his face, he stopped. Shaking himself like an enraged dog, he turned away and drew on his breeches. He had to get away from her or do something he'd regret . . .

He bent, picked up the long bundle and threw it at her feet. "I had hoped you'd accept this gift in the spirit in which it was given, but knowing you, you'll probably view it as a bribe." He stalked off with the bitter comment still ringing in her ears.

She paused in drawing on her own clothes to pick it up and unwrap it. She blinked as the sun glanced off the long, polished blade and the precious inlay of one of his prized rapiers. Why had he given it to her? Now, when she'd hurt him? For, unless he truly was an actor beyond compare, there had been as much hurt as anger in those storm-clouded eyes as he'd left her.

Reverently Magdalena rubbed the sword up and down her breeches leg, testing its supple length. He must have known how touched she'd be at the gift, yet he'd not given her a chance to thank him. Perhaps she was being unfair to him. She could at least give him a better chance to prove himself. Pulling on the rest of her disguise, Magdalena drew out her old, reliable rapier and replaced it with the new one. It fit neatly in her sheath. Carrying the other weapon, she strode quickly back to camp, determined to apologize to Clint and give him a fair hearing.

However, before she reached the others, Miguel, who had just arrived, drew her aside. When he was finished talking with her, her bright eyes dimmed. They became hard as brown agates as they found the tall, golden-haired man who was sitting off to himself, brooding on the trees in the distance.

Magdalena strode up to Clint and drew out the rapier he'd given her. "It's not as tempting as you think, gringo, nor are you." She flung it at his feet. "Keep out of my way. And if we're ambushed, I'll know whom to blame." She stalked off to talk to Joaquin,

Clint's chin almost met his chest, so deep was his sigh. What was the use? Why the hell didn't he pack up his gear? He tenderly wiped off the blade and went to his supplies to wrap it up again. But when he was done, he came back to the others and silently accepted his plate of food. His eyes sought hers across the fire, but when she met them, he almost groaned. Something had happened to cause that sullen distrust. She'd softened enough to him at the stream to at least want his touch. Now, she skewered him with her eyes.

His wandering gaze landed on Joaquin. That one, too, looked at him askance. Clint raised an eyebrow. When darkness had fallen and the men had paired up in their usual groups, Clint rose, lazily stretched and went over to Joaquin, taking advantage of the fact that Magdalena was talking to Pico.

# Chapter 13

"There is a magic in your every
word, that like a philtre turns
my will to wax, ready to
take whatever print you give it."
**Act I, DON JUAN TENORIO**

Joaquin moved aside on the fallen log he was sitting on to make room for him. Clint returned Joaquin's glare measure for measure. "What have I done now?" He spoke softly so he wouldn't be overheard.

Joaquin shrugged. "Talk to El Halcon."

"Why? She hears only what she wants to hear."

"Perhaps because what you say is not to be believed."

Swiveling on the log, Clint straddled it and crossed his arms over his chest. "Surely I've the right to know what I'm charged with?"

Joaquin hesitated, looking over to where Magdalena was again showing Fernando how to use his serape during a knife fight. She'd been almost happy when she returned from the stream, until Miguel's news had taken the glow from her eyes, the lilt from her voice. Now, she seemed to hate Browning as much as ever. Joaquin looked back at the handsome face screwed at the moment into a scowl. If he

couldn't fully trust this man, how could Magdalena? When
indecision came to him, Joaquin acted now as he always
did—on instinct. Perhaps the American had a reason for
talking to Luis. But *Dios* help them all if he lied.

"Miguel saw you talking in a secretive manner to Luis
when you went into Santa Barbara. What could you
possibly have to say to him?"

A grim look settled about Clint's mouth, but he answered
easily enough, "Very little. He approached me as I left my
ship, I didn't go to see him."

"But Miguel said you both looked around warily, as if
you feared being overheard."

"I'm afraid I . . . prevaricated a bit with him. When I
was trying to learn where Carlotta and El Halcon were, I
told him I'd help by infiltrating the band if I found them
first. He wanted to know if I'd made any progress."

Browning met his eyes steadily, and Joaquin was inclined
to believe him. Yet there was a . . . reserve in his voice
that troubled him. "That's all that passed between you?"

Clint's hesitation was infinitesimal. "That's all."

Joaquin sighed. The American was hiding something, but
they had to take a chance on him. If they cast him out now,
Magdalena would never again trust any man. That is, *if* she
survived the coming confrontation with Roberto, *if* he
couldn't hold her off long enough for Father Franco to act.
Joaquin smiled wryly. He couldn't really fault the American
for keeping his own counsel. Magdalena will be furious
when she finds out what I've done, Joaquin thought.

Joaquin would have risen, but Clint caught his arm.
"Since it's confession time, I've a demand of my own to
make: Tell me who she really is, and why she pursues
this . . . folly." When Joaquin sat back down and eyed
him broodingly, Clint warned, "If I have to, I'll go to her
and make a scene. As angry as she obviously is with me, it
wouldn't take much to make her lose control. And I've
already observed that when El Halcon loses his temper,
subterfuge does not come easily to him."

Perhaps it's time, Joaquin thought. If Magdalena's behavior was straining Browning's patience and fragile loy-

alty, then maybe he should understand why she acted as she did. Joaquin rose.

"Come. Into the shelter of the trees." After they seated themselves on the ground, Joaquin began.

And so it was that Clint at last heard the true story of Magdalena Inez Flanagan de Sarria, alias El Halcon. The darkness and Joaquin's Latin propensity for drama conjured vivid images for Clint. So many times had Magdalena obliquely referred to her brother. He'd sensed her deep love and stifled grief. To know that she'd so tragically lost first her parents, then her brother, and lastly her grandfather, the latter two to Roberto's treachery, made her behavior much easier to understand. No wonder she was obsessed with hatred of de Sarria. Nor could Clint fault her wariness of Americans, considering how her mother had died.

When Joaquin drew to a weary close, Clint sat quietly, his throat aching with compassion. That's why her name had been familiar. He'd heard Roberto's maids whisper it when he'd visited El Paraiso that time, though Angelina had never said it when she'd related the bare details of the tragedy. What a torment it must be to have a man of Magdalena's own blood murder her last two relatives, then pin the blame on her. She'd lost everything to Roberto: her brother, her grandfather, her lands, the honor of her name. Indeed, what else had she to live for but vengeance?

His eyes sought her out. There she stood, her long, slim body outlined by the firelight as she draped the Indian's serape. What had she been like three years ago, before she'd cast off her woman's ways along with her skirts? Now she seemed so invincible, so self-sufficient. But he'd seen the vulnerability, the pain in her, when her guard slipped. He'd held her in his arms and felt the womanly needs that no clever disguise could hide. He'd sensed her jealousy of Angelina, felt her ambiguous reaction to the lovely gold gown. Yes, she was very much a woman, though she was not free to admit it yet. How he longed to go to her and pull her to his breast. Only that, no more. To comfort and sustain her, to show his admiration for her indomitable

313

spirit. But she'd fight him if he couldn't find a way to prove how deeply he cared for her.

"So, captain, do you still think her unfair?"

Clint had to clear his voice to steady it. "No. I think she's the most amazing female I've ever met, and I will do anything necessary to get her to reciprocate my admiration."

Satisfied, Joaquin patted Clint's shoulder and rose. "If it's any comfort, she already does, in some measure. You are the only man who's ever grazed her in any of her duels, and she's secretly pleased that she can't manipulate you. But winning Magdalena's admiration and trust are two different things. You'll never have her love without both."

Even after Joaquin had returned to the fire, Clint sat in gloomy contemplation. Trust him she never would if she discovered he'd promised to broker for Roberto. Thank God he'd obeyed his instincts and not told Joaquin the whole truth. They'd never believe he'd hoped to gain evidence against Roberto and Luis. With a tired sigh, Clint heaved himself to his feet. She'd led him a wild chase, one which seemed likely to quicken, but he'd shadow her until they both dropped, if necessary. For, no matter how his mind mocked his choice, Magdalena Inez Flanagan de Sarria was the woman his heart had settled on. Even if he fled, she'd remain as much a part of him as flesh and bone. She was the only woman he'd ever loved, and whether he bled to death on this wild coast or was forced to watch her die, he could not leave her. Feeling somewhat comforted, Clint sought his bedroll. At least it seemed they were to rest for a few days, so he could relax his guard for her safety.

At dawn, hoarse, familiar tones proved the supposition false. "Come compadres, a coach is on the way. A coach with many outriders, so the take should be rich." Ignoring their grumbles, Magdalena prodded them into dressing. "You've become lazy, riding only at night. Be sure you all wear your masks. I want no deaths, mind. We outnumber them, so they shouldn't resist long."

Clint cast her a jaundiced look, but he, too, rose. He wondered if she'd slept at all, for she'd still been practicing with one of the men when he drifted off. From the sweat gleaming on Fuego's shiny hide, it appeared she'd at least risen very early. After a quick breakfast of tortillas and honey, she led them out of the canyon onto the highway. She was too intent on the road to notice when Clint kneed Pico's mount aside and took his place at her side, where, despite everything, he knew he belonged.

When they reached a sharp bend in the highway, she ordered several of the best marksmen up into the rocks, then told the other men to push large boulders into the middle of the road. They'd barely finished when the sound of whirring carriage wheels came. They dashed into the cover offered by the crannies and scrub lining the sides of the highway.

The carriage rounded the bend, and the driver cursed and sawed desperately on his reins. The leading outrider tumbled head first off his horse when the animal went from a trot to a dead halt in an instant rather than jump over the boulders. The second outrider was more fortunate: He slipped sideways when his animal reared but was able to keep his seat. When the three outriders in back rode forward to help calm the frightened coach horses, Magdalena made her move. She waved to the men in the rocks. As they fired, she reined Fuego onto the road.

Amid the confusion of dust, smoke, cursing men and whinnying horses, Clint was able to ease his mount in front of hers. Pulling his pistol, he shouted, "*Termino!* Drop your weapons!"

The soldiers, already frightened at having their hats shot off, obeyed with alacrity. Benito galloped after the man who'd been thrown and was trying to run away, and herded him back to the others.

With a fulminating look at Clint, Magdalena rode wide of him, kicked his mount in the hindquarter when again he tried to block her and neatly fit Fuego in the gap as Clint's mount jibbed in protest. She crossed both hands on her saddle pommel and appraised the scene.

All the outriders already had their hands tied behind their backs and were being efficiently searched, but the coach door remained ominously closed, the curtain down over the window. Magdalena eyed the group of soldiers, then urged Fuego a few steps closer to both the sergeant and the carriage. She cast an irritated look at Clint when he stayed glued to her, then looked back at the sergeant.

"Who warrants such a fine escort?"

He glared at her without answering until Sean shoved a pistol into his belly. "No one. We but take this fine new coach to the comandante in Santa Barbara."

"And you need five outriders to do it? Bah!"

"What does El Halcon know of military ways? You're but a thief, sneaking like a rat in the night."

Casting a pointed look at the early morning sun, Magdalena said suavely, "How gratifying that you know my name. Let us see if your passenger is as knowledgeable. Open the door."

The sergeant leaned back against the rear carriage wheel, crossed his arms and spat at Fuego's hooves in answer. Shaking her head, Magdalena urged Fuego forward to do the job herself.

Clint had paid more attention to that still, dark curtain than to the exchange, so he was alert when it fluttered. It might have been the breeze, but then the bright sun winked off shiny steel as Magdalena drew closer. Clint kicked his foot free of his stirrup and shoved it desperately into her side. She fell sideways just as the retort of a pocket pistol echoed up and down the highway. The shot zinged into the stubby tree that had formerly been blocked by her head.

She landed with a thump on her posterior and glared up at Clint. He, however, had already vaulted from his saddle to jerk open the carriage door and pull the would-be murderer from the carriage.

An irascible, decidedly familiar voice complained, "Not so rough, bandit. If you pull my arm from its socket, how am I to give you my purse?" Clint groaned and snatched his hands away as if scalded. This was a complication he decidedly did not need. He shoved the passenger forward before the man could get a good look at him and shrank back into the coach shadows.

Standing, Magdalena dusted herself off, then swaggered

316

forward to appraise the gringo. For gringo he obviously was, from his beaver top hat, to his starched shirt and neat cravat, down to his sober but rich brown silk vest, to his expensive broadcloth beige breeches and fancy high-topped leather shoes.

She picked up the small pistol Clint had snatched and flung to the ground, turned it over in her hands to admire the fine silver inlay, then pocketed it. "Though you wanted only to acquaint me with it, I'd rather know it intimately," she said.

He was a tall, well-built man with reddish brown hair, long sidewhiskers and piercing gray eyes. His naturally florid complexion grew redder at her insolence. "Alvarado feared you might try to stop me, but his men are as ineffectual as I suspected." He sent them disdainful looks that were returned in full measure.

El Halcon smiled at their mutual hostility. "So, you know the governor, do you? How interesting. Now why are you such a favored guest?"

Clint prayed the man would realize his peril and hold his tongue, but the American was a strong believer in the power of not only his own position, but the might of the government that backed it. "Because I've been sent to California by the U.S. state department to offer our assistance in your recent troubles with Mexico. Charles Garthwaite is my name, of late American ambassador to Mexico, though my role is more . . . tactful now."

Magdalena stiffened. Her men grunted in anger, even some of the Indians—for they, too, were Californios. "We don't need your assistance. Our *diputacion* has declared us a free and sovereign state until Mexico restores the constitution. Have you seen any military movement against us? Mexico has accepted our right to self-govern."

Charles clicked his tongue at this naivete. "Mexico has left you alone because she's too busy to commit troops to subdue you. That will not always be the case. Wouldn't you like another neighbor as an ally?"

The hoarse tones grew dry. "Neighbors with ill intentions are enemies of the worst sort."

317

When he would have argued, she sharply waved him to silence. "*Basta*! Your purse, señor." He flipped it toward her. She opened it and whistled, clattering the weighty collection of good Yankee gold. Closing the purse, she tossed it to Miguel, then walked around the American, appraising him from all angles. "Now, what to do with you?"

The arrogance of Charles's stance, shoulders thrown back, head high, didn't wilt as she played with her sword hilt. "Why, let me go on my way, of course. You have what you wanted, and I've more important things to worry about."

Magdalena looked toward the soldiers, who were avidly following the exchange. She had a feeling Alvarado had sent them more as guards than escorts. Alvarado was California's first native-born governor, and if he could quell the sectional resentments between north and south Californios, then he stood a good chance of being the leader they'd long needed. Perhaps she could rid him of one of his worries . . .

"Tie his hands before him and give him your horse, Pico," she ordered softly. "You can ride double with Benito."

"No!" Charles tried to strike Pico's hands away, but when Benito poked him in the back with the business end of his pistol, he subsided. His glare at the slim, black-clad back that had already turned on him, however, indicated what kind of prisoner he'd be.

Magdalena took the carriage leads and knotted them several times, then she mounted and looked at the soldiers, one of whom they'd untied so he could release the others. "We've need of your horses, but you can keep the carriage animals. You should all fit in the coach." She looked at her men. "Ready, amigos?" At their enthusiastic nods, she turned Fuego about, flinging over her shoulder, "Give Alvarado my regards and tell him I'll keep his . . . guest occupied for a time. I will not harm him. Adios!"

They moved off. She looked around for Clint, and he knew she'd a few choice words to share with him, but he had more to worry about at the moment. When they reached camp, he strode up to Benito and Pico and said he'd keep an eye on the prisoner. After they'd gone he took off his mask to say glumly, "Hello, Uncle Charles."

He didn't notice when Joaquin gave them a piercing look and eased closer.

Charles goggled at his favorite nephew. "Clint? What the hell are you doing with these bandits?" Then, imperiously, "Turn me loose!"

"I can't. And I suggest you keep quiet about our relationship. For both our sakes." Clint just shook his head when Charles barraged him with questions. One, however, he chose to answer. "Yes, I drew your cursed map. But it was stolen from me, and I've lost my taste for spying. Call in your note if you will, but you'll blackmail me no more. Now, your life is not in danger, but the dignity you value so highly is. El Halcon is a California patriot and is already suspicious of you. Don't give him further reason to distrust you or you'll never be released."

"This is ridiculous! When the state department hears of this . . ."

"Yes, Uncle, what then? I suspect they'd be astonished to hear of your presence here."

When Charles stared him impassively in the eye, Clint knew he was right and irritably demanded, "Dammit, why must you always persist in thinking that you know more than beast, man or God Himself?"

Charles favored his nephew's exasperated criticism with a sniff. "They're considering my idea. I merely thought if I had first-hand knowledge of the unrest here I could prove my point to them. It was obvious you were in no rush to get back with the report I requested."

A smile edging his lips, Joaquin tiptoed away and pulled Magdalena aside. She listened, and her shoulders straightened, as if a weight had been lifted. Then she strode over to the still arguing pair. "I would have a word with you, Browning."

With a last minatory look at his uncle, Clint followed her to the distant stand of oaks. She leaned back against a broad

319

trunk and propped one foot behind her. "I don't know whether to thank you or curse you, gringo. You were damned interfering, but you saved my life, and for that I'm grateful. But don't do it again."

"What?" Clint blinked at her innocently.

"Put your broad back between me and the danger you imagine I'm in." She waved her hand at him impatiently when he would have retorted. "No, I agree that's not accurate. The danger is real, but so is my need to face it."

Clint sighed, but he knew it would do no good to argue with her when her chin was set at that angle. Still, he'd keep her safe, no matter the cost to her pride. "Is that all, El Halcon?" He emphasized the title he despised.

Her foot dragged down as she shoved herself erect. "Yes, that's all, unless you have something to tell me. About our prisoner, perhaps?"

Clint shrugged. "No, nothing, except that he bears watching, but he also merits careful handling. If he is who he says he is, he has influence." He turned and strode away, unable to bear that acute, searching stare any longer.

Slumping back against the tree again, Magdalena clicked her tongue at her own stupidity. She had hoped Browning would admit to his relationship with the *yanqui*. He, too, it seemed, had been forced into a distasteful charade, if his words were to be believed. Joaquin had been so certain that neither of them had seen him hiding behind that dense bush, but perhaps he was wrong. Why else wouldn't Browning leap at the chance to clear himself? Every time she dared open to him even a bit, he slammed another obstacle up between them. Almost as if he did it deliberately . . . Magdalena stretched wearily, then walked back to camp, sure of only one thing. She'd have to watch Browning and his uncle carefully if she wanted a clue to the character of each.

In the weeks that followed, Magdalena knew Garthwaite watched her at least as closely. After the first couple of days, he quit arguing with them about his release and took an interest in their camp. The Indians were equally curious about him, but wary, withal. One and all they gave him a wide berth. Garthwaite, in turn, seemed genuinely fascinated by their different dress, habits and their skills with horse and reata. Magdalena took advantage of that fact and began a series of casual discussions with him about the differences between their countries.

"Is America truly as vast as I've heard?" she asked him during a lunch break one day.

"Yes, it's a grand land. Our countryside is as varied as your own. We have everything from forests, to praries, to deserts and swamps. Now, if Texas joins our union, we'll grow even more."

Magdalena's easy tone took on an edge. "With lands stolen from Mexico. It seems your government cares little how you achieve this 'growth.'"

Setting his plate aside, Charles lounged back on his elbows. This was just the type of argument he enjoyed. He arched an eyebrow at his nephew, who was sitting nearby, but Clint shook his head and swept a hand in his uncle's direction. Charles eagerly accepted the challenge, for he sensed El Halcon was a man of some intellect. It was this type of man, brave, resourceful and practical, whom they must win to their side if they were ever to fulfill America's destiny of stretching from sea to sea . . .

"On the contrary. We were very careful not to officially involve ourselves in the Texas Revolution. It was planned, organized and executed by settlers invited at Mexico's request . . ."

"*American* settlers who were encouraged in their efforts by the government they still considered themselves part of. Do you expect the same to happen here?"

"Tell me, if Santa Ana had declared himself dictator here as he did there, how would Californios react?" When El Halcon's only reply was grim silence, Charles smiled his satisfaction.

"So the Texans stole nothing, except liberty, as doubtless you Californios would do if you were invaded by Mexico. Besides, if we're to argue about who stole what, then we'd have to agree we're all thieves, in the end. Spain took these lands by force from the peaceful Indians who lived here, did

*321*

she not? And virtually enslaved them for her own purposes? Just as our British and Dutch ancestors stole what lands they couldn't buy. Unfortunately, the world is not the utopia idealists would have it. It's a raw, mean, vibrant beast that can be tamed only by the strong."

"And you fancy yourself with a whip and chair, eh, señor?" El Halcon needled with a sideways look. When Charles would have retorted, El Halcon held up a silencing hand. "Intellectually, I see your logic, but nations are moved by much more. Tell me, señor, would you agree to become part of *our* union and call yourself a Californio instead of an American, taking on our ways and our laws?"

When Charles recoiled, an appalled look on his face, El Halcon's teeth gleamed behind his hood. "So you see, you may be right that we are all thieves in the end—I can hardly call myself otherwise—but we are also all human, with the fires of freedom burning in our breasts. What man, of any nationality, will willingly give up his right to self-govern?" With a courtly bow, El Halcon tipped his hat and strode off to three Indians, who were practicing with a reata and arguing among themselves.

Clint smiled at Charles's disconcerted look and sauntered over to watch as Magdalena took the rope from Benito and showed him how to hold it properly. "With skilled subtlety, a reata can be used for much more than subduing cattle . . ."

"Like subduing a woman, perhaps?" Clint interrupted, twirling his own rope.

The Indians laughed, even though Magdalena stopped whirling her reata and glared over her shoulder at the American. "What do you know of it, gringo?" she scoffed.

"More than you think, *bandido*," Clint answered, and in the next second, his looped rope landed neatly about her shoulders. He began reeling her in like a landed fish. "For you see, I've been practicing."

Magdalena dropped her own reata, wrapped Clint's rope about her gloved hand and jerked it sharply. Clint was not expecting it and he stumbled forward, allowing enough slack for her to slip the loop over her head.

"Show me just how much, gringo." She picked up her

rope and pointed with it to several stumps with enough dead limbs still attached to make them a tricky target. Positioning her reata, she twirled it so skillfully that the movement looked idle rather than practiced. A second later, the loop neatly hooked the bottom of one stump, where Magdalena pulled it taut. "Your turn."

Clint eyed the stumps doubtfully, for they were some distance away, but he gamely whirled his rope above his head. To his relief, his loop landed almost as precisely as hers had. He flung her a triumphant look, which she returned with a condescending smile.

"A lucky throw. Show me more." She sat down on the fallen log next to Charles.

Determined now, Clint turned to the two other stumps and flung his rope about them one after the other. He bowed to the band's applause, his smile growing broader when he saw Magdalena also clapping, if reluctantly. Wildcat, he thought, fight me to the end even over something so inconsequential. His eyes narrowed on Charles and Magdalena, who were exchanging an adult look, as if indulgent of his boyish enthusiasm. Clint slapped the rope against his boot. If they only knew how much alike they were, despite their different backgrounds. Perhaps it was time he gave their understanding a little clarity . . .

Smiling wickedly, Clint twirled his reata again, high above his head. "And there's one more use a good reata can be put to, wouldn't you agree, El Halcon? You first demonstrated it to me." When she threw him a puzzled look, he added, "The unseating of lofty pretension . . ." So saying, he looped his rope about the angled branch sticking out of the log they sat on and tugged sharply. The log rolled forward. With a grunt and a thump apiece, Charles and Magdalena toppled off, landing on their backsides. The canyon resounded with the laughter issuing from the men, Clint's loudest of all.

When they'd regained their breath, the pair sat up and threw similar glares at Clint, but his mirth, brilliant blue eyes watering, broad shoulders shaking, was so infectious that they smiled. Charles stood and offered a hand down to Magdalena. She took it and let him pull her up.

"Gracias, señor. It seems your countryman, at least, thinks we have something in common."

Charles eyed his still laughing nephew with mingled affection and exasperation. "That he does. I've never been able to convince him he possesses the same quality in good measure."

"Perhaps I can help you with that . . ."

Looking from Clint to her and back again, Charles agreed dryly, "Perhaps you can at that."

Thus Charles and Magdalena grew to a mutual respect for the perspicacity of the other, and even a qualified liking. However, Magdalena was careful that he and the Mexican prisoner were bound when they left camp. They always assigned a guard, not only to watch over the prisoners, but to protect their increasing wealth.

The newest recruit, Reno, kept much to himself. She'd taken him in over the band's objections, for he'd deserted from the presidio and was of Mexican descent. He seemed to trust them even less, so Magdalena had assigned him the important task of camp guard in an effort to build his own esteem and his respect for her. This time, she'd badly miscalculated . . .

They'd rested for several days, so the men were spoiling for a fight. Magdalena was also, if for a different reason. Despite Joaquin's pleas otherwise, she knew that soon they must attempt El Paraiso. For too long had she waited. It was time to face her enemy. Roberto was a wily swordsman, but she had right on her side and she was confident she could defeat him.

Thus, when they heard the welcome sound of carriage wheels, Magdalena rode with more exuberance than usual to block the road. Only when she faced the carriage squarely did she recognize it. She groaned to herself, but it was too late to draw back. Her men had already surrounded it. Magdalena glanced at Clint who, as usual, was riding next to her. His mask was securely fastened, but that magnificent head of hair and those sculpted, sensual lips

324

were a dead giveaway. She leaned over to whisper, "Stay back, out of sight," and urged Fuego forward.

Clint frowned, hesitating, then he followed her to the side of the carriage. Whether she knew it or not, she needed him. This time, however, when a pistol nosed out of the window and leveled at her head, Magdalena jerked on Fuego's reins. Obediently, he minced sideways until they were out of the line of fire.

Magdalena drew the black to a halt behind the carriage. Did all of California want to kill her? Muttering under her breath, she smashed her hat down, tightened the cord under her neck, stood in the saddle and leaped lightly atop the carriage. "Give me a pistol, Sean," she ordered curtly. "Your saber, please, Miguel." Both men eyed her doubtfully, for she was skilled with neither weapon, but they obeyed.

She stuck the pistol in her belt, took the saber in both hands and plunged it into the tough tanned leather roof of the carriage. A scream and a curse sounded from inside. Magdalena coolly ducked behind the carriage seat. When two reports sounded simultaneously to two singed holes appearing in the roof, she went back to sawing the saber back and forth. It would be easier just to pull Jose out of the carriage now, before he reloaded, but a little drama might teach him how dangerous it was to strain El Halcon's patience.

In a few seconds she'd sawed a hole big enough to look through. Lying prone, she peered into the dim interior. She was surprised to see Angelina looking up eagerly, when she'd expected her to be cowering in a corner. Jose was almost finished loading one weapon. Quickly, Magdalena stuck the barrel of Sean's big pistol in the small hole.

"Drop your weapons. Really, I'm supposed to be the *despreciable bandido*, but I've never known a more bloodthirsty lot than you pampered dons. Now drop your weapons and get out of the carriage, or I shall take great pleasure in parting your hair into a new style you will not like!"

Jose gritted his teeth in fury, but he flung his pistols down and leaped out of the carriage, offering a hand to his sister.

He watched the detested, hooded head swing around, but his contempt was as ineffectual as using buckshot against a grizzly. Oh, what he wouldn't give for ten minutes alone with the bastard. And what had happened to Clint?

He was turning to look when that hard, hoarse voice ordered, "Search him, Pico. He could be carrying another weapon." When Pico's search yielded nothing but an empty purse, Jose smiled nastily.

"'A fool and his money are soon parted,'" he quoted softly. "And, despite appearances, I'm no fool."

"So you've a liking for proverbs, eh, señor? As our dear departed Fernando de Rojas would say, 'The use of riches is better than their possession.' And my men and I can put them to far better use." Magdalena tossed the weapons back to their owners, grasped the rim of the carriage seat and vaulted lightly down. She strode up to Jose, appraised him from head to toe, sniffed, then stepped so close to Angelina that her cloak brushed against pink silk skirts.

"*Buenas dias*, little pigeon." When soft color flooded Angelina's plump cheeks, Magdalena chuckled and traced the pretty portrait with a gloved finger. "Come, don't you think your lovely dress should be accented by jewelry such as that you wore on our last meeting?"

Angelina stuck her bare fingers behind her back. Her blush deepened, though her fascinated blue gaze never left the eyes behind the ugly hood.

Jose blustered, "My sister has nothing to hide! Keep away from her!"

Magdalena didn't even look at him. "If she has nothing to hide, then she won't mind a polite search, will she, señor?"

"*No*! You insolent knave, I'll . . ." A large, ungentle hand clamped over his mouth, pulling his head to one side. Jose's muffled protests subsided as he met precautionary blue eyes.

Clint shook his head slightly and mouthed, "He'll not harm her."

Perhaps because Clint and Jose watched so tensely, or perhaps because she'd always delighted in teasing Angelina, Magdalena's mischievous urges got the best of her.

326

Putting both hands lightly under Angelina's arms, Magdalena traced the hourglass figure in a leisurely path that resembled a caress more than a search. When she reached the knees, she patted each and slowly retraced her path upwards. Guffaws sounded from her men, not a few of them envious.

Angelina's face was pinker than her dress now, and she shifted restlessly as the gentle hands skimmed her back to her hips. Jose was struggling against Clint's grip, and it required two more men to hold him still when Magdalena, with a discreet cough, brought her hands up to lightly run them over Angelina's deep bosom. She froze, then smiled.

Angelina seemed mesmerized by the white flash of teeth, and she didn't move when the searching fingers dipped into her bodice to remove a wadded man's kerchief. Magdalena stepped back, her smile deepening. "Gracias, señorita. What better place to hide valuables than with treasures?" She eyed Angelina's chest suggestively. Her men laughed louder; Jose struggled harder. Clint cast his eyes skyward.

Unknotting the white linen, Magdalena fingered through the small cache. She clicked her tongue, honing her sharp stare upon Jose's furious face. "It was most ungallant of you to endanger your sister for such a paltry sum." Magdalena picked out the few silver coins and handed them to Miguel, then she tied the two rings and the pearl droplet necklace back into the cloth and offered it to Angelina.

"You should not think so ill of me, señorita," she reprimanded gently. "Did I not let you keep your jewelry last time?"

"Jose made me do it," Angelina blurted. She cast a triumphant look at her brother. "See, I told you he'd not take my things."

"Mine are expendable, I suppose," Jose retorted.

Magdalena met Angelina's exasperated eyes and smiled. "Men are such obdurate creatures. He's lost a few coins yet equates it with a kingdom." Magdalena reached into her own pocket and palmed a like number of coins. She offered them to Jose. "Here, señor. Smooth your ruffled feathers."

Jose jerked free of one of the grips on his arm to knock

the coins away. They rattled against a carriage wheel, then dropped to the ground.

"It's not the money, you insolent rake! It's your arrogance that eats at me!"

The slim, gloved hand clenched, then dropped to Magdalena's side. *Dios*, she was weary of this. She looked at her men, who watched, tense, expectant, and suddenly, her masquerade became a curse instead of a blessing. How was she to always be what they expected? Did she even want to, any longer?

The words she spoke then were passionately sincere, if not wise. "And what of your own, señor? Were you thinking of your sister or your own pride when you made her hide your valuables? What if I had been the desperado you think me? I might have decided I wanted more than jewels and money." When Jose paled, Magdalena's voice grew even more inflexible. "Perhaps it's time you realize that w . . . women have dignity, too. Honor is important to them, also. Why do you and your kind find that so difficult to understand?"

When she saw how strangely her men looked at her, Magdalena bit her tongue to stifle it. Jose, too, frowned, as if he'd suddenly been forced to see her in a new light. Magdalena glanced at Clint, and those sympathetic blue eyes impacted on her like a blow to the gut. She had to turn away to hide the moisture pooling in her own eyes.

Mounting Fuego, she called over her shoulder, "Let them go." She started loping away, then she drew Fuego in so sharply that he reared. Her inimical glare encompassed Jose. "And I warn you, Jose Rivas. If you once again try to kill me, I will return your hatred in full measure. *Comprendes*?" When he nodded reluctantly, she urged Fuego back on his hindlegs, giving him the cue to dance backward and paw the air with his forelegs.

"*Hasta luego*, señorita!" She tipped her hat, then was gone in a cloud of dust. Her men followed silently, still wondering at her odd manner. No one noticed when Clint lagged in mounting his own horse, exchanging a few words with Jose before he, too, followed.

By the time they reached camp, Magdalena had regained control of herself. It was too late to repine the life she'd chosen. Too many depended on her now. If she, the leader of the band, did not prevail, then she condemned the others to fugitive lives. Only the will, and proving Roberto's treachery, would excuse what she had done. They'd acquired enough wealth to rescue her men from the poverty that had made them join her. It was time now to win something as important: vindication.

Nevertheless, as they all dismounted and tended to their horses, it was hard for Magdalena to forget the contempt in Jose's eyes and the hatred in his voice for what she had become. Carlos had loved Jose like a brother, and they'd been much alike. Would Carlos also revile her for refusing to accept an unkind fate? For many months she'd appeased her own conscience by telling herself it was for him, for him and the rest of her family, that she did this. But was that really true? Was it justice she wanted? Or vengeance?

For the first time, she didn't know . . .

If only she'd been able to rip off her hood and reveal herself, she could have demanded of Jose if he'd have acted differently in the same circumstances. But of course, that was impossible. Notorious as he was, El Halcon was still safer than Magdalena de Sarria would be. But she was tired, so tired, of this life . . .

She'd barcly completed the thought when Miguel touched her shoulder, making her jump. "What is it, Migucl?"

The answer came from an unexpectcd source. Charles, laced securely to a tree trunk, answered, "You must have a lot on your mind, El Halcon. Can't you see that your guard has disappeared?"

Magdalena glanced about. Reno, indeed, was not to be seen. She looked at Miguel again, but his grim expression was answer enough. "The money . . ." she whispered.

"Gone," both men answered simultaneously. The band, most of them finished grooming their mounts, came closer to listen.

Charles added, "But he went north on the highway not

more than thirty minutes ago. If you hurry, you may catch him."

Magdalena fumbled at her saddle, but Clint, who'd heard the exchange, was already in his own, as were Sean and Pico. Clint said, "Don't worry, El Halcon, we'll get it back." With a slap to his mount's hindquarters, he led the way out of the canyon. Magdalena noted vaguely that his riding skills had much improved. Though he still sat in his saddle awkwardly, as if he disliked it, he didn't bounce around like he used to.

Magdalena let her saddle drop and plopped down on it. She didn't hear the angry mutters of her men; she didn't see Joaquin's worried look. Her gaze was focused inward. For two nights now she'd barely slept, but she knew her weariness was as much of the spirit as of the body. For once, she didn't mind staying behind. She was in no condition to lead anyone at the moment. Besides, though the admission was difficult for her, somehow she knew Clint would bring Reno back. Her belief in him had grown gradually, fostered by his refusal to defend himself. He'd let his actions speak for themselves. And if those actions had raised eyebrows among her men, she no longer cared.

When she was tired, he always offered a hand to help her down from her horse. When she was quiet, he directed the band's conversation away from her. When she was in danger, he saved her. What she'd heard had been wrong. He was no ally of Roberto's, surely. If he'd had treachery in his heart when he spoke to Luis, then soldiers would have come for them before now. Perhaps, just perhaps, he was the man she'd first thought him.

When the three men rode back in the late afternoon with a sullen Reno between them, Magdalena was relieved, but not surprised, at Clint's success. She rose to face them when they shoved Reno down from his horse. Pico returned the chest to Miguel, who immediately opened it and began counting. When Reno saw Magdalena standing over him, he scrambled to his feet and glared at her.

Magdalena shook her head sorrowfully. "Ah, Reno, you disappoint me. Why did you steal from us?"

"Because you will be captured soon, when the governor sends more men. The soldiers we robbed will insist upon it. Even El Halcon will not prevail against such odds. What use is your treasure to you when you are dead?"

Magdalena raised a hand in the air when the angry mutterings grew louder. They subsided to a murmur. "Our newest member does not believe in our cause, *compadres*. What do you suggest we do with him?"

After a tense pause, the answer came without words, but with a volume of meaning. Miguel's knife was flipped, point-first, into the dirt at Reno's feet. Pico's followed, then Benito's, then Juan's, and so on, until Reno was virtually encircled. With his hands bound behind him, his face drawn, his throat working in fear, he was not an imposing figure.

Charles, untied now, watched from the fallen log. Clint sat next to him. He glanced at his uncle and smiled slightly at the fascinated look on his face. Despite its ill beginning, he realized this . . . visit had been good for his uncle. Charles had been forced to see that Californios of every stamp, from the elite the governor came from, to these less-than biddable Indians, were not the bucolic simpletons he'd taken them for. They neither needed, nor sought, American protection. They were as fiercely determined to rule themselves as Charles's own Revolutionary ancestors had been. Clint knew these few weeks had illuminated far more to Charles than all their heated arguments over the years. And Magdalena would teach him even more. Clint focused again on Reno's trial, but he did not fidget like Charles did, for he already suspected the outcome.

Magdalena looked from the resentful faces of her men, to Reno, to the knives at his feet. She strode forward to pick one up and play with it, then she turned to the band, holding the knife high so the sun reflected off of it. "Does this mean justice to you?"

Several nods came, though Miguel and Pico didn't respond.

"I see. For stealing all we've worked for over these months, you'd take a man's life. A fair exchange indeed."

331

Magdalena lowered the knife along with her voice. "I'll not say you nay, *compadres*, but I suggest you think on this: If stealing warrants death as punishment, then each of us deserves to die."

"But El Halcon," Juan protested, "we did not steal from one another."

"Ah, I see. Stealing from others is all right, but not from a friend."

"No, that's not what I mean," Juan said, exasperated.

"Then what do you mean?"

While he groped for words, Magdalena stuck the knife in her sash and crossed her arms over her chest. "Never mind, Juan. I agree he deserves punishment, but not the ultimate one. If mercy abounded more in this world, then most of you would not be here. Can you truly resent the cruelty your people have suffered if you mete the same?" They looked down at that, and some actually shifted their feet like censured little boys when she added, "I can't help wondering if you'd have voted so if it had been Pico, or Benito, who'd committed the deed."

And, softly, "Can your sentence have something to do with the fact that he is Mexican? Worse than that, he's a former soldier?" Not even a bird dared disturb the silence then. Charles was literally on the edge of his seat as he glanced from the tall, still, black figure to the restless circle of Indians. Their eyes went from El Halcon, to Reno, and back.

One by one, then, they slowly walked forward to retrieve their knives. Magdalena applauded them softly. "Ah, you are to be congratulated, *compadres*. There is hope for our country yet." She pivoted and walked up to Reno, her voice growing hard again. "Don't look so relieved until you hear your punishment." His half-smile was wiped clean.

"Were you truly Luis's secretary?"

When he nodded, she said, "Bueno. Then your penance is three-fold. One, you will be responsible for keeping the camp clean and the dishes washed. We will not rotate that task as we have in the past. Two, your share of the earnings will be confiscated and distributed to the others. And three, you are responsible for recording the stories of each of the men. Find out why they joined me, what injustices they suffered. Then, if I'm captured, at least the men will have a written defense. And it will be a lesson, too, to explain to you why the Chumash hate you and your kind so."

Reno nodded in silent agreement. He deserved harsher punishment, and he knew it. It would have been swiftly forthcoming if Luis had been in command. However, his relief came a bit too soon.

After a few steps away, Magdalena whirled on him again. "One other thing, Reno." When she spoke in that tone, every man attended. "If you betray us again, I won't wait for the men to pass judgment. I'll punish you myself. Now, amigos, to work." They scattered to their assigned tasks.

Magdalena approached Joaquin and drew him aside. Clint watched them argue with a sinking heart. He feared he knew the subject. Charles's wondering voice was a welcome distraction.

"What manner of man is this bandit, Clint? I confess I thought you mad when I first found you with him, but now . . ."

A smile that was a fine blend of melancholy and pride stretched Clint's full mouth. "You see he's much more than he seems?"

"If I spent a year with this group, I don't think I'd understand him. He's such a peculiar mixture of nobility and larceny, fairness and ruthlessness, wisdom and hot temper."

If you only knew, Clint thought wryly. He watched her move about camp, organizing things as she always did, but he sensed the tiredness in her. She didn't bustle like usual. While dinner preparations were under way, he fetched several items from his supplies and went up to her.

"Come, El Halcon, it's time you rested." When she looked up at him wearily, he took her arm and drew her away from her discussion with Miguel about the state of their winnings. She followed unusually obediently as Clint led her up the stream, out of sight.

Miguel frowned after them. For weeks now something in

the American's attitude toward their leader had bothered him. The word that came to mind seemed ridiculous, but he could only call it protective. As if El Halcon needed protection, Miguel snorted to himself. No, it must be something else.

Charles, too, stared after the pair even after they'd disappeared. It wasn't only the dashing bandit who acted oddly; so did his nephew. Charles shrugged. Patience would serve him in the end, as it always did. If anything was peculiar, it would come to light eventually. For now, there was much to be learned from the others. Charles rose and approached Pico.

When Clint and Magdalena reached the lovely, sun-dappled spot in the stream where they'd bathed before, they stopped by unspoken agreement. Magdalena turned to look up at Clint.

"Thank you for bringing Reno back," she murmured, cupping his sculpted cheekbone in her hand.

He quivered at her touch, for she offered it so rarely. "Haven't you realized yet that I'd go to the ends of the earth for you? And give my very life to protect you?"

Stepping back a pace, Magdalena pulled her hat and hood off. The smile she bestowed on him then constricted his chest. It was a lovely, womanly smile, but it was triste, too. As if his words both pleased and saddened her.

"Ah, even you, who know me better than anyone save Joaquin, don't understand. Can't you see that I don't *want* your protection? I appreciate the gallantry that makes you offer it, but you still insult me." When his brow crinkled, she sighed and put both hands on his shoulders. "Never have I known a man such as you, Clinton James Browning. How is it you both delight and depress me, make me weak and strong, all at once?" She shook her head in mystification.

Pulling her hands about his neck, he favored her with a smile of his own. It was all man, that smile, and her eyes widened at the hunger in it. She tried to pull away, but he only drew her closer. "I knew you'd come 'round eventually. It was just a matter of time." His smile deepened when her eyes, which had been huge with uncertainty, narrowed and stabbed into him. She relaxed against him, but he wasn't fooled.

"So, I've fallen into your hands as you planned all along, Browning?"

He nibbled at the side of her neck. "Like a ripe peach. And you taste just as luscious." He hid his smile against her neck.

"Have a care you don't break a tooth on my pit," she warned sweetly.

"Ah, but your pit isn't hard. It's soft as butter."

She blushed when he bumped his hardening lower body into hers. She knew he was teasing her, but his arrogance was still infuriating. She forced a flirtatious smile to her lips. "Is it? Would you like to try it again?" It was her turn to smile when he raised his head to look at her suspiciously.

"Are you offering?"

"What does it sound like?"

"Like a baited trap."

"Clint, you wound me," she said with a pout.

"Better you than me," he responded dryly, but he was inwardly delighted with her abrupt transformation from Amazon to girl testing her wiles.

"I knew your gallantry couldn't be sincere."

"Sincerity given is oft-returned . . ." He let his meaning trail off as he fixated on that lush mouth.

"You want me to prove I'm willing to couple with you?"

He winced at her plain-speaking. "That would be nice, but you need a few lessons in the art of coquetry. For example, you should fling the back of your hand to your forehead and sigh, 'La, sir, your boldness fair makes me faint.' "

Magdalena's nose wrinkled, but she gamely obeyed. When he released her, she stepped back and flung her hand to her forehead so dramatically that he thought she'd tip backward. "La, sir, your boldness fair makes me faint," she said in a swooning tone not one of her men would have recognized. Then she spoiled the effect with a disdainful grimace.

Grinning, Clint fell to one knee before her. Peeling her glove away, he kissed each finger from tip to knuckle, then stuck her forefinger in his mouth and sucked until she did indeed seem a bit unsteady. He drew his mouth away. "And I would say, 'My boldness owes all to your beauty. Take pity on my eager heart, milady.' " He stuck her hand to his breast so she could feel the pounding there. He opened his mouth to prompt her, but to his delight she needed no more guidance.

She lifted his hand to her own breast, where he could feel a like throbbing. "And so I shall, sir, for my own heart gladly answers."

Ah, there she was again. The woman he'd occasionally glimpsed and longed so to see in all her glory. Did his ears and eyes deceive him because he wanted her so badly? Or had he at last won her trust—and perhaps even more? He inched upward to his feet, afraid if he moved too quickly, she'd vanish. But she stood docile as he gingerly caught her waist and drew her against his chest.

"Ah, Magdalena, Magdalena, how I . . ." His declaration both ended—and began—with a kiss. He had to coax naught from her, for she returned his ardor in full measure. Their lips met, clung, then melded. Dark head and blond tipped sideways so the joining could be more intimate. Tongues twined together like vines seeking earthy sustenance. And each found it in the joyous passion of the other. For moments snatched from the jaws of an unkind destiny, they gave and took in that communion that only man and woman know. It both fortified them for the temptations still to come and made them weak with need to consecrate this moment.

Gasping for breath, Clint snatched his mouth away. Another minute, and he'd not be able to control his urge to meld with her in an even more intimate way. He looked regretfully at the lowering sun. Alas, there was no time for that. He lifted her chin to meet her luminous eyes, then kissed her tears away.

"*Querida*, if you only knew your power over me," he muttered between kisses. "You both humble me and make me proud. You are woman as I've always dreamed of her, and you bring out all my manhood, at its best and worst."

When he looked at her and smiled gently, she blinked away the last of her tears. "Why does this have the feel of a warning?"

"Intuitive, as always. You know, I've often suspected it's your instincts that make you such a formidable leader, and now I'm certain of it." But he shook his head when she would have questioned him further. "Put your hood on, and all will be clear in a moment. What I do, I'm doing to help you. Please remember that when you're angry with me." He looked at the sunset, myriad hues splashed on the heavenly canvas by a Master's hand, then glanced at the slope above them. Tiny pebbles cascaded down.

He pulled Magdalena into his arms to distract her from the distinct sound of a man's stealthy descent. "You've beaten the odds magnificently so far, my love, but it's past time they were tipped in your favor . . ." He lowered his head to kiss her protest away through her hood.

Thus did Jose Rivas find his new friend and the fierce El Halcon. He froze in drawing his sword and stared in horror at the scene. He'd thought Browning odd at times, but never this odd. Bile rose to the back of his throat.

His eyes were bleak when Browning lifted his head, looked straight at him, then gently turned the figure leaning against him about. El Halcon gasped, then grabbed for his sword. Jose did likewise, and the sound of drawn swords was sibilant in the silence.

Browning held El Halcon at the waist when he would have gone forward to meet Jose. Ignoring the furious glare sent up at him, he focused his attention on the appalled don. His smile was wry. "I don't wear chemises under my shirts, Jose, as you're obviously thinking. You've always suspected El Halcon was a member of your class. Well, you were right."

Magdalena gasped and tried to break away, but Clint's

337

grip was inflexible. He held her pinioned to him with one arm and raised his free hand to her hood.

"*No!* Damn you, how could you betray me like this?"

Jose's head reared upward, for Magdalena had forgotten to disguise her voice. He shook his head, as if his ears had deceived him. But they hadn't, nor did his eyes lie when Clint gently but inexorably drew off El Halcon's hood . . .

# *Chapter 14*

"Conquered by love, who is love's conqueror . . ."
**Act I, DON JUAN TENORIO**

The rushing of the nearby stream, the hoot of an owl
rousing early, sounded alien to Jose's ears. This was a play
he watched, not reality. That white face, staring at him
defiantly, didn't really belong to Magdalena. She *could not*
be El Halcon. It was intolerable to think that a gently reared
girl could have been forced to such dangerous subterfuge.
And yet, somehow it fit, too. For the girl just flowering into
womanhood had been brave enough, bold enough and
foolish enough to defy the powers she blamed for her
brother's death. Jose's weak legs collapsed. He sprawled on
the bank, laying his sword beside him on the grass.

Only Magdalena's trembling conveyed the depth of her
distress. With a furious look up at Clint, she shoved him
away and stood tall. "Come, Jose, share your joy with me.
I can see how pleased you are to see me alive," she sneered.

Shaking his head slightly from side to side, Jose murmured,
"Ah, *niña*, forgive me, I am glad to see you. So many times

339

have I wondered what happened to you. I had hoped you'd gone to Monterey and made a good marriage . . ."

"Which is a woman's only alternative, si?" Magdalena split a disgusted look between a silent Clint and a sad Jose. "I need no champion for my cause, my two fine caballeros. I, and I alone, decided to become El Halcon. I have accomplished much, and may yet win all. Yes, what I do is dangerous, but can either of you say I have not done it well?"

When neither Clint nor Jose argued with that, Magdalena tossed her head. "Yet instead of being proud of me, you would both be happier if I had bowed my spine and traded a tawdry gold band for honor, justice and my heritage." Her raised voice lowered to a weary timbre. "Never, gentlemen. While I yet breathe, I'll not sell my body to sully my name." She picked up her hood to pull it back on, but Jose sprang to his feet and caught her arm.

"Who will be left to be proud of the name de Sarria after you die? Tell me that, Magdalena! Do you think Carlos would be happy to see what you've become?" When she paled and averted her eyes, he sighed. "Forgive me, that was unfair. Had he lived, you'd not be here."

"Had he lived, he'd have done the same. Don't you know that, Jose?" She lifted her head to look at him.

He looked back into those indomitable gold eyes and said succinctly, "Yes, Magdalena. But he was a man. You are very much a woman." He stumbled, so hard did she shove him away.

"Bah! You're hopeless, the pair of you. Never will you credit me with wit enough to fill a thimble. Think what you like, do as you like. But I go on." Jerking the hood back on, picking up her sword to sheathe it, she stalked off.

When a distressed Jose would have followed her, Clint caught his arm. "No, man, leave her be for now. I'll talk to her later."

Jose slumped back down on the ground, shaking his head. "Never would I have believed it, if I hadn't seen it with my own eyes. How long have you known?"

"Weeks, months, years. It seems an eternity, yet just

yesterday, too. For what it's worth, I reacted with a similar dismay." Clint's smile was reflective. "But it didn't last long. I fear for her, yes, but I must admit I've seldom seen men better qualified as leaders. Most of her men would lay down their lives for her."

With a comprehensive look over Clint's face, Jose said, "As would you."

"Without hesitation. As you can probably tell, I love her."

"And does she return your love?"

Clint sighed. "I think so, but she's fighting it. I'm afraid until this thing with Roberto is settled, she'll have room for no man in her life." Clint sat down next to Jose. "You can help, if you will. Carlos died as you suspected, Jose—by Roberto's and Luis's order. And Roberto killed Ramon by his own hand when the old man changed his will. So Magdalena has right on her side. What has El Halcon done that is so terrible?"

"It's not her thievery that my people so much resent. It's her support of the Indians, even the renegades who rustle our cattle. The administrator of the mission lives in fear that El Halcon will swoop down upon him like a bird of prey if he so much as gives a seed away."

"It's high time someone stopped the wholesale barter of goods that were supposed to be held in trust. This is a bad thing?" Clint shook his head and entreated, "You are eloquent. Make your people see the good she's done. Stir up support for El Halcon among them. When she confronts Roberto, maybe she'll have the townspeople on her side. The Indians for miles around already adore her for the horses, clothing and money she's shared with them."

Jose rose and stretched wearily. "It will seem odd if I go from reviling El Halcon to praising him, but I'll do all I can." He began to turn away, but then, as if compelled, he looked pleadingly at Clint, who rose to face him. "Keep her safe, Clint. Please . . ."

"I've been doing my best, Jose. I can only tell you that no one will harm her while I live." Jose nodded, then climbed back up the slope and disappeared.

Clint watched him go. So, Jose had a tendre for Magdalena. He wondered if she knew. Somehow he doubted it. But when this was all over, he might still have an epic battle on his hands. Why should she select him, an outsider, over a wealthy man of her own kind who obviously adored her? Clint shook his head at his own fears and returned to camp. One problem at a time. First he had to deal with a wonderful, stubborn, gallant, very angry woman . . .

The moon was full that night when Clint snuck over to Magdalena's pallet. It was set apart from the others behind a stand of brush. She was sleeping restlessly, and he was able to stuff his kerchief in her mouth and tie her hands before she awoke fully. Heaving her over his shoulder, he snatched up her blanket and staggered up the stream. She was no lightweight, especially kicking and squirming.

When he reached the secluded stand of willows, he tossed the blanket down and carefully set her on her feet. When she tried to kick him, he caught her foot and overbalanced her. She landed with a plop on her posterior, and then had no more room for resistance, for she was covered by a very large, very heavy and very determined man.

Finally, when her struggles weakened and then ceased, he took the kerchief out of her mouth, but he kept her hands tied. She shifted to the weapon of her voice, and she might have slashed a less resolute male's self-esteem to shreds. Clint, however, merely cocked his head and listened to her tirade.

"You cowardly *bellaco*, I hate you! You've interfered in my affairs for the last time. You can't subdue me with your words, so you use your strength upon me. After promising not to . . ."

Clint grunted when she jabbed him in the ribs with a sharp elbow. He sat astride her kicking legs and moved her arms above her head to smile down at her. He flicked at her loose bonds. "If this is what it takes to keep you with me, then needs must." He met her glare with a charming smile. "Besides, I'm the one dodging blows, and I warrant I'll be the one sporting bruises tomorrow." He rubbed his cheekbone, where she'd landed a lucky punch. "You've a mean right, my love."

The whimsical remark ending in an endearment only seemed to infuriate her more. "Don't call me that! I haven't given you leave . . ."

Clint snorted. "If I'd based our relationship on what you've freely given me, I'd be a pauper begging for alms." He settled more comfortably on her hips and added mildly, "Now, if you've a mind to change that, I'll not turn down your generosity." His free hand went to her shirt and played with the buttons.

Abruptly, she switched tactics. "You want me generous, eh, gringo? Release me and you'll see how generous I can be."

Clint made a fist and brushed it against her jaw, returning her sultry smile with a challenging one of his own. "You'll show me the full length of your nails and the strength of your teeth, eh, *bandida*?" When she looked disgusted at his easy reading of her, he leaned so close his lips brushed her ear. "I know you better than you think, my love, and would know you better still. But first we have to talk. You've less reason to be angry with me than you suppose."

Moving off of her, he waited until she scrambled to her feet, then caught her at the waist and plopped her into his lap. When she still struggled, he turned her about, forced her legs about his waist and lifted her bound hands about his neck, hooking his wrists behind her back to crush her against him. He smiled genially into her glittering eyes.

"Now, my love, hit me and you're like to poke yourself as well." He flinched and looked at her reproachfully when she pinched his neck. "In a moment, I'll let you kiss it and make it better." When she still squirmed upon him, his teasing tone sharpened. "Enough! Hear me out, and then if you still want to use me for a punching bag, I'll let you."

When finally she subsided, he sighed, slashed through her bonds, replaced her arms about his neck and lifted his hands to cup her exquisitely molded face. "Jose Rivas is an honorable man, and he told me once that he suspects

343

Roberto is to blame for your brother's death, despite the evidence. Instead of making an enemy of him, Magdalena, you should have enlisted his aid." He studied her still face and thought he saw a flash of pain in her eyes before she veiled the moonstruck gold with long lashes.

Determinedly he went on, "I suspected once he knew your true identity he'd not only cease hounding you, he'd strive to see you cleared. I was right. He left me tonight with the intent of rallying Santa Barbarans behind you." When still she didn't look at him or answer, he dropped his hands to her shoulders and shook her slightly. "You can't survive this masquerade, much less prevail against a man like Roberto, without support. Why can't you see that? Why won't you let us help?"

When she looked at him at last, he almost wished she hadn't. The pain was replaced by a cold determination that chilled him. "Because it is I who was betrayed, and it is I who must clear my name. If I begin to let you and Jose make my decisions, next you'll be offering to duel Roberto for me. Is that not so?"

Clint met her eyes without remorse. "I would gladly do so, even though I suspect you have the better chance of winning."

Her expression softened a bit. "For that, at least, I thank you. I can even forgive you for your cursed interference, for I realize your intent was kind. But you weren't thinking of Jose at all when you told him where we camped, were you?"

"What did I do to harm him?"

"You tarnished an image he's held bright for two years. He was more sad than glad to see me." Her voice shook as she added softly, "He despises what I've become."

"That's not true, Magdalena. The man was shocked down to his fancy leather boots. When he's had a chance to recover, he'll understand."

She shook her head. "No, he'll never approve. And he's right about one thing—Carlos would be appalled if he knew how I'd lived these two years. But what else was I to do?"

It was a cry for reassurance he'd never heard from her

before. He was both touched and troubled by it. But he didn't hesitate to take advantage of her confusion. Had he a chance to convince her to leave, after all? The desolation in those huge eyes moved him more than he could bear. He drew her head into his chest. "You had few options, Magdalena, and you have, as you said, accomplished much. Most of your men were already renegades surviving by thievery, so you haven't led them astray. Indeed, you've given them a pride in themselves that they've never had before. And for the first time in their lives, they've hard cash to assist them in their dreams. You've shared generously with the Indians, and you've put the fear of God into Luis's soldiers. The men say their friends report less abuse hereabouts than in the past. Even the administrator of Santa Barbara is rumored to be honestly trying to assist the Indians . . ."

"And what have I accomplished with Roberto? Pico says he is meaner than ever," she interrupted bitterly.

"You can't save everyone, Magdalena. Don't you think it's time you basked in your accomplishments and hung up your sword? Lady Luck has smiled upon you thus far, but she's a fickle dame. And if the governor really comes . . ."

She lifted her head. He couldn't fathom the odd look in her eyes when she responded, "What are you suggesting?"

"That you've done enough. That you return home with me as my wife. That you put away the darkness of death and vengeance and embrace the light. Love, happiness, children." He searched her eyes, but she veiled them again. His heart pounded like a death march in his throat as he awaited her answer. When she didn't betray by so much as a twitch how she felt, he rushed on. "I love you, Magdalena. You must know that by now. I only want to keep you safe. And, if you'll give the feelings a chance, I think you have a . . . regard for me." When still she didn't answer, he gently raised her chin and insisted, "Is that not so?"

Again, when her eyes met his, he flinched as if struck. A maelstrom of feelings churned in those huge golden pools, sucking him into her swirling anger, frustration and despair. He didn't know why, but somehow, he'd betrayed her. *This*

345

was the way she accepted his declaration? When she carefully drew her arms from about his neck and stood, he didn't try to stop her.

She backed a few paces. "How can you still understand so little? Flattering as you doubtless think your offer, I find it the lowest insult." When he frowned up at her in bewilderment, she sighed and walked back toward him. Squatting, she said through her teeth, "One last time will I say this. I would betray my family, my ideals, and, in the end, you if I did as you suggest. You say you love me. Tell me why."

"Because you've the courage and intelligence of a man, yet are very much a woman," Clint said without hesitation, lifting his hands to bring her to him.

She struck them away and rose again to glare down at him. "Interesting qualities. Do you truly think I would still possess them if I deserted my men and my goals so easily?"

He opened his mouth, but she didn't give him a chance to respond. Striding up and down, she said passionately, "You see no paradox, but I see a vast one. I am a woman, true. Only now am I realizing how much. For that, I am grateful to you." She whirled and pinned him against the tree trunk with eyes as straight and true as golden spears. "But I resent you for pandering to your own ego and my weaknesses. I swore a solemn vow over two years ago to bring Roberto to justice or die trying. Do you think because I'm a woman honor means any less to me?"

Clint rose to face her. "Women were not meant to duel and defend their honor. You've succeeded admirably so far, but what happens if you don't find the will or if you make even one mistake when you face Roberto? He's one of the best fencers in California, I've heard."

"Then I die," she said with chilling equanimity. "But I'd rather be dead than to betray all I hold dear."

He shook his head in violent rejection. "*No*! I won't allow it!"

"You've no right to stop it. I *must* fight my own battles. Until you understand that, there's no hope for us. If you

346

truly love me, you'll accept me as I am, as I have at last accepted you."

"What do you mean?" He took an eager step forward.

"You are an American, the nephew of a man who has all but admitted he wants to annex my country, by force if necessary." When he started, she smiled grimly. "Joaquin overheard you both arguing. I have good reason to hate you and your kind and to wonder if you are as loyal as you seem, but I have no choice." She pressed one hand over her heart. "This cries out for me to trust you, and I can deny it no longer." She shook her head when he surged toward her. Reluctantly, he stopped. "But that fact doesn't change reality. I may, indeed, die. Or, before this is over, you may no longer want me. It is not only my heart you must understand. It is your own. Do you truly want to ally yourself with a woman who will be your equal, or nothing? Decide that, and then we will talk." She turned around and strode back into the night.

Clint leaned against a sturdy tree, but still his world reeled about him. Part of him wanted to shout with joy, another with frustration. She loved him, she'd admitted as much, his optimistic half exulted. His practical half growled that she was the most infuriating woman he'd ever had the misfortune to meet. What other woman but Magdalena could so easily bless him and curse him in one breath? Her way or not at all. But could he blame her? Wouldn't he react the same if she expected *him* to change to suit *her*? Would he really want her so if she agreed to let him fight her battles or to flee before her work was done?

The questions had answers somewhere in his muddled brain, but they were beyond him at the moment. Every instinct he possessed cried out for him to protect her. He'd become responsible for his three sisters and his mother at the tender age of eighteen, and he was accustomed to thinking of women as needing protection. Strong as she was, Magdalena was still a woman. *His* woman. And it was natural for him to want to be her champion.

His sigh blended into the wind. He looked up. The Almighty was decked in all His majesty tonight. The moon shone like a solid gold orb resting atop a diamond-scattered, vast velvet cloak. Such beauty God blessed them with. Love was the greatest gift of all. Had he and Magdalena found it, only to fritter it away because neither would compromise? His sigh was deeper this time, but it gave him no solace as he pushed away from the tree and glumly walked back to camp.

Magdalena heard his return. She switched sides yet again, but she could not get comfortable. Defeated, she gave up trying to sleep and sat up. She rested her chin on her knees and looked at the heavens. Somewhere up there Carlos, her parents and her grandfather watched her struggle. Were they proud or sad? She'd been so certain when she began that she was doing the right thing, but she was certain no longer. Did she insist on confronting Roberto to redeem her name or to satisfy her blood lust? Magdalena searched the stars, glittering like a host of lost souls above her, but she knew the answer could be found only in her own heart. Those jalousied gates, however, stayed closed to the light. Only action would illuminate them. Whether it was satisfaction or justice she sought, only facing Roberto, sword in hand, would free her to seek a new destiny.

She lay back down, still staring upward at the scintillating points of light. When they began to blur before her eyes, she arched her arm over her forehead. Her thoughts, however, were not so easily denied. She had Clint to thank—or to blame—for these new doubts. His sunny smiles highlighted the gloom that had darkened her spirit for over two years. In his cheerful presence, good vengeance and hate became a crutch rather than a boon. He made her long to cast away her sorrows and laugh with him. He made her yearn to embrace the womanly garb and ways she had long scorned. He made her want to bed with him and know again the temporal but cathartic ecstasy he'd once shared with her.

In truth, he was so much *hombre*, and she longed to be his *mujer*.

Magdalena no longer distrusted the feelings he stirred in her. She no longer doubted his honor. He'd had too many chances to betray them and had not. He was, indeed, very like Carlos, as she had thought that spring day so long ago when he'd awakened her in the strawberry patch. She should have trusted her heart instead of her brain. She'd have saved them both a lot of grief. Yet, because she did . . . love him, she didn't dare accede to his pleas. He made her weak, when she must be strong. And even if she did flee with him, they'd be unhappy, for she'd resent them both.

No, their only chance at being together lay in defeating their enemies. Then, he'd accept her as she was. She repeated the words to herself: "*their* enemies." For her enemies were his. If she stayed, he would fight at her side. Some of the sadness lifted from her heart. Newly resolved, she pulled her blanket tightly to her chin and settled down for sleep.

It seemed but minutes later before the stirring of the camp woke her. She stood, yawning, and peeked around the bush to see the men rounding up the horses from the rough corral they'd fashioned. Joaquin walked over to her with the morning cup of chocolate he always brought her, part of the few luxuries Clint fetched from his stores. This quiet time, sheltered from the others, was one they both treasured. Their arguments about the day's plans had only strengthened the bond between them.

While she sipped, he searched her tired features. "Did you not sleep well, *niña*?" Shrugging, she peeked around the bush again for Clint, who was helping to round up the horses. Twice monthly they divided into groups of two and took the horses they'd stolen to the Indians who lived along the highway. The branded horses they gifted to the renegades high in the hills.

Smiling at her wistful sigh as she looked at Clint, Joaquin took her empty cup and said gently, "Why don't you stay here today? You need a rest. I'll assign a guard to camp." And he turned away before she could protest. He glanced over his shoulder. Amazingly, she pulled on her hood and sauntered from her bower, seeming content to obey.

A huge shadow blocked the early morning sun. She

looked way up into Sean's merry blue eyes. "Top o' the mornin' to ye, lassie," he whispered in her ear.

"And to ye, me handsome divil," she whispered back.

His grin broadened at her good humor. "I go into Santa Barbara today. Is there anythin' ye need?" He put a finger against her lips to stifle her protest. "I'll be safe enough. I'm deliverin' the funds to the mission, with a mite o' me own to the padre for the church. Tomorrow is me birthday, and I swore years ago to make a donation to the church every time the Lord saw fit to grant me another year."

He took his finger away and beamed down at her so sweetly she'd not the heart to argue. This was obviously important to him, but still, she worried. Of all the band, he was the most distinctive, with the exception of Clint.

"I need nothing but your safe return, amigo. Please be careful."

Sean squeezed her shoulder and promised, "That I shall be." He went off to collect the pouches from Miguel and to saddle his horse.

Magdalena was not surprised when Clint was the guard Joaquin selected. She shook her head at Joaquin as he rode off with Miguel, each of them leading a horse, but he only grinned back at her.

Clint crossed his arms over his broad chest and stepped in front of her. "And what shall we do with our day, El Halcon? Practice our fencing? Have another reata contest?" He leaned close and lowered his voice so his uncle and the Mexican couldn't hear, "Or continue our conversation from last night? In a more . . . meaningful way."

One look at his teasing expression told Magdalena all she needed to know about his state of mind. He didn't take her any more seriously now than he had when she was his poor, crippled maid. To him, El Halcon the bandit and Magdalena the woman were two separate entities. She'd never make him understand that if he would have the one, he'd have to accept the other.

Depressed, she just shook her head, walked around him and sat down next to Charles, who was yawning and nibbling at his usual tiresome breakfast of tortillas and honey. They no longer bound Charles when there was someone around camp to watch him, for he seemed content to remain. The Mexican, however, was another matter.

Though he said little and seemed to make a model prisoner, Magdalena knew he hated them and would track them like a bloodhound if she let him go. For that reason, she hadn't dared to. And, as a precaution, she'd moved their camp from the cave to here. Though he sometimes made her uneasy, she was confident that he could not harm them as long as they watched him. Consequently, he wasn't isolated from the group. What her men knew, he knew.

Magdalena glanced at him as she passed. "Have you had breakfast?"

A show of teeth was his only answer, but Charles replied, "Yes, I took him something."

Favoring Charles with a smile, she fetched her own breakfast and sat down next to him, still ignoring Clint, who sprawled next to Charles. She ate only half a tortilla before she sighed and crumbled the remainder for the birds.

"Why do you do it?"

She looked at Charles.

His expression was an odd blend of censure and admiration as he went on, "You're deceiving no one, you know. Even your men are no longer fooled by your disguise."

Magdalena carefully wiped her fingers on a rag, then she drew her gloves on, smoothing each finger. "What do you mean?"

"You can play the mean hombre as well as any actor I've seen, but your hood, hat and cloak can't hide what you really are." Charles's eyes narrowed when El Halcon stiffened slightly and looked away. "A gentleman used to a soft bed and food more refined than this." Charles kicked a piece of tortilla into the distance. A bright-eyed robin was not so disdainful of the morsel. Bolder than his fellows, he swooped out of a tree and pecked up the bit of corn in one bite. Chortling his triumph, he flew back to safety.

El Halcon straddled the log to face Charles, the glimmer of teeth relaying his slight smile. "One does not always suit the life one is born to. Perhaps I enjoy stealing and terrorizing so much that I don't mind the discomforts."

"Humph! The man who lectured his men about mercy and justice was not inspired by larceny. Truly, why do you persist in this calamitous course? Any day now Alvarado will probably send men to capture you."

"Why do you seem content to stay? Every night here extends your mission by a day," El Halcon countered.

Charles drawled, "Ah, but I'm a prisoner, remember?"

With a pointed glance at his free hands, El Halcon retorted, "By choice, I think. Of late, at least."

Charles shrugged. "I'll learn much of what I need to know here. Why Californios act as they do. Their values, morals and history. What could be a more fertile ground for knowledge than this struggle between the landed gentry and the Indians?" When El Halcon snorted, as if he didn't much like being part of an experiment, Charles added slyly, "Besides, I want to be present when you're captured. You're a silver-tongued devil, but it will take a fancy speech indeed for you to talk your way out of this."

El Halcon bowed from the waist. "I thank you for your confidence in my abilities."

"You've abilities aplenty, but unless you've a wand up your sleeve or wings attached to your back, your time of accounting is nigh." Charles seemed torn between satisfaction and sorrow at the fate he envisioned for his captor.

"Perhaps sooner than you think, *yanqui*," El Halcon said, rising. "I shall endeavor to be entertaining sport for you." With a sardonic tip of his hat, he sauntered off to fetch his reata.

Clint, who had listened silently to their exchange, frowned after him. At the worry in his expression, Charles asked, "What is the . . . man to you, Clint? Why are you so protective of him?"

The battle between Clint's conscience and fears was brief, the outcome never in doubt. Charles would be more likely to throw his support to them if he knew Magdalena's story, but he'd already betrayed her confidence with Jose. If he did so again, she might not forgive him.

352

So he said into Charles's expectant silence, "Because his cause is just, and he has few enough friends who truly understand him to worry what happens to him."

"And you're one of them."

"Yes."

A simple affirmative, that, Charles thought, but with a world of meaning behind it. Where did that leave him? How could he hope to see El Halcon captured when his nephew would probably fight to the death to avoid that end? Charles sighed. This mission was growing more complicated all the time. Despite their often antagonistic relationship, Charles was very fond of Clint. He viewed him as the son he'd never had since he'd refused to have his single-minded ambitions swayed by a wife.

He looked at El Halcon, who was poetry in motion as he twirled the reata about his body. The fibers seemed alive, obedient to his slightest whim. Up, down and around his head, waist and feet they played, then back again. Grudgingly, Charles admitted to his admiration for this strange man. If he were honest, he'd have to admit he didn't want to see El Halcon captured, either. Despite his arrogance, the bandit deserved a better end than the quick drop down a rope or the fusillade of a firing squad. And, being the type of man he was, Charles's thoughts turned to what he could do to help.

Little, it seemed. His reception in Monterey had been chilly. His association with the government seemed to be more of a liability here than an asset. Still, there must be something . . .

El Halcon seemed restless that morning. He gave Clint a wide berth and fidgeted about camp, patting the horses, polishing his sword, twanging at his guitar. But Charles noticed that his eyes often went to the lean-to where they kept their goods. Then he'd snap his head back around, as if resisting temptation. Finally, after lunch, when their few dishes had been washed and put away, he entered the lean-to, exiting carrying a small trunk.

With a curt, "Please don't follow. I'll be back soon," he strode up the stream.

353

Both Clint and Charles watched until he was out of sight. "What the devil . . ." Clint muttered to himself. He rapped his knuckles against the log for a good thirty minutes, then, with a pithy curse, he sprang to his feet. After checking the Mexican's bonds, Clint offered his pistol, butt first, to his uncle.

"I need your help, Uncle," he said gravely. "Will you guard the camp while I'm gone? Something's troubling h . . . him, and I must find out what."

Charles took the weapon and nodded. "I'm honored at your trust in me, Clint. You have my word as a gentleman that I'll take my responsibility seriously."

"I never doubted it, Uncle Charles," Clint flung over his shoulder, already loping off up the stream. Charles settled the pistol on his knees and met the Mexican's sneer with a cool smile.

Sheltered in the willow bower, Magdalena kicked her black garments away and drew the lacy ruff over her shoulders. *Dios,* she was sick of black. If she lived through this, never again would she willingly wear the color. She attached the tiny hooks down the bodice that were cleverly concealed behind a lace band. She smoothed the rain-soft silk over her hips and twitched at the lace-ruched hem. But no matter how she pulled, the last ruffle still stopped a good six inches above her ankles. Other than that, the dress was a perfect fit, with its long-waisted style.

For days now she'd struggled against the urge to try it on, to see for herself if she could still look like a woman. Today, she'd used the dress as an excuse to escape Clint's hungry stare. Now she had it on she was almost afraid to look in the water.

Would she be a hag? Or worse, a mannish-looking woman aping a lady? For so long she'd dressed like a man, talked like a man, lived like a man. Since she no longer wore chemises, the silk felt good against her bare skin. But would it look good on her or merely embellish her failure to be the woman everyone seemed to think she should be?

She inched toward the water, lecturing herself as she

went. "*Estupida*! You'd rather face a troop of soldiers than confront your own image in a dress. You pride yourself on your courage, but you're a coward when you fear to fail. You might as well resign yourself to this life, for you'll never be Clint's woman, or anyone else's, if you can't accept your own womanhood." She walked up the stream to a small side pool that was the closest thing to a mirror she had. A sapling grew there, drooping fragile arms into the water. She held on to a slim but strong branch, took a deep breath and leaned out.

The wind ruffled the smooth blue surface, and at first she saw nothing but a blurred outline. Then the ripples calmed, spreading outward in widening circles, leaving a glassy circle in the middle that reflected back a mysterious image. Long hair, lush and shimmery as sable, decorated each side of the gold wraith. And wraith she seemed, a ghost from a time long ago, yet also a portent of the future. The creature looking back at her was no longer the girl who'd danced so gayly at that last disastrous fandango; she was a woman grown. There was a stability, a resolve in that face that had not been there two years ago. Adversity had forged it, but a greater power had pounded it, smoothed it and polished it to tensile strength.

Clint. And the love she bore him. She'd not sought it, had in fact struggled against it, but it was as much a part of her now as the curves that made her female. For female she was, had always been and ever would be. Living like a man had made her see what she missed of being a woman. If she survived this, never again would she resent her skirts or what they covered. Finally, instead of struggling against that knowledge, she embraced it. The woman who savored swordplay was the same woman who longed for children. The female who rode and roped like a man was the same female who now luxuriated in the feel of silk against her skin and longed for her lover's gentle touch.

Clint had not endowed her with any special qualities, but he'd clarified them for her. Seeing herself in this dress proved that she still not only looked like a woman, she felt

355

like a woman. And for the first time ever, she *enjoyed* being a woman.

Society's lessons were cruel. For many years she'd embraced the notion that a lady could not enjoy fencing and fighting. She'd thought herself flawed, a boy erroneously born in a girl's body. But it was not herself who was flawed; it was the culture that had stultified her.

It was as if dawn suddenly seized a land where darkness had ruled. Her heart was bright for the first time in two years, its shadows banished by revelation's sublime light. Hearing a gasp behind her, Magdalena straightened and turned, knowing what she'd see. It was natural, it was good that Clint had followed her. He stood in a shaft of sunlight. Dressed in a white shirt, his breeches beige, his hair winking back every precious ray, he seemed light personified. Everything about him, his looks, his heart, his mind, was good and bright. She walked toward him, her arms outstretched, compelled to share his luminescence.

Clint stood rooted, afraid to believe his eyes. There she was, the woman he'd occasionally glimpsed. She was stunning in the dress, with her white shoulders gleaming above the low bodice, her tiny waist accented, the fluid gold silk caressing her limbs as she glided toward him. The sunlight caught every bead on the dress and made her glitter like something too precious to be real.

But he was moved more by the inner Magdalena than by the outer casing. Never had he seen her look at him so. As if she'd come to terms with herself and what he made her feel, and reveled in her conclusion. As if she loved him beyond self, beyond life. As if he represented all that was good in her life. All these things, she meant to him. She was two steps away when his paralysis erupted into a giddy rush of motion. He scooped her up into his arms and twirled them about, spinning harder when she laughed.

"Laugh, my lady, my own. You have such a rare, beautiful laugh," he shouted. His ebullience was contagious, it seemed, for she truly did laugh harder. Her husky chuckles were music to his heart.

"You'll be hearing it more frequently, now, *querido*."

He stopped, shifted her higher into his arms and looked deep into gold eyes that were rainwater clear. No shadows or reserve there for the first time ever. "Say it again," he whispered, his big body trembling.

"*Querido*. My love, my darling . . ." The last word was muffled by his lips.

His kiss was tentative at first, for he feared to believe the messages her body and heart were sending him. But the passionate devotion her lips communicated was of grand design, as if at last she felt architect of her destiny—a destiny she wanted to share with him. He was so moved that his legs collapsed. He plunked down on the bank, cradled her on his lap and lavished kisses upon her cheeks, nose, forehead and throat.

"*Mi vida*, how I love you," he whispered between kisses. "I'll make you happy, I swear I will . . ."

But talk was not what she wanted, it seemed. She splayed her fingers through his hair and hauled his head back to latch her mouth to his. For the first time ever, *she* kissed him. Aggressively. Hungrily. Arousingly. With a flood of energy that both depended on him as conduit and fed on its own source. Her lips were unskilled but eager, slanting across his with urgent suction. When he opened his mouth and challenged her tongue into battle with his own, they each quivered in arousal.

Clint was hard for her in an instant. Ah, what she did to him, heart, soul and body. The decay of death and revenge no longer ate at her heart; instead, she fairly vibrated with rejuvenated life. He would celebrate with her . . .

Easing her down on the bank, he spread her thick, lustrous hair about her head in a fan. Then he drew back to look at her. She met his darkened eyes serenely, her lips stretched in a winsome, womanly smile.

"Do I please you, *querido*?" she asked huskily.

Clint's answer was wordless but nevertheless explicit. Taking her hand, he pressed it to the straining front of his breeches. Her breath caught. For an instant, it seemed she'd pull away, then she cupped him gently.

Over his own gasp, he croaked, "As you feel, my love.

357

But Magdalena, be very sure this is what you want. For if I bond with you in this way, I'll never let you go."

Her hand moved in a circular massage upon him. With her other hand, she worked at the buttons on his shirt. Her smile, her eyes, her voice became sultry with the passion he evoked. "Perhaps it is I who will keep you prisoner . . ."

With a groan, he swooped on her mouth. He filled her with his tongue, flicking in and out to entice her with a sample of the greater intimacy to come. Never freeing her lips, he felt blindly for the dress hooks. His hands shook so he was barely dexterous, but finally the gold silk began to open. He snatched his mouth away, panting. Her eyes fluttered open beneath him. They were the exact shade of the dress, sparkling like crushed topazes in the speckled sunlight beneath the tree.

He held them with his own heated ones as, inch by inch, he widened the gaping bodice. He could feel that her skin was bare beneath it, but he didn't look down, even when he pushed each sleeve past her shoulders and bared her to the waist. Still he stared deeply into her eyes, savoring their startled widening when both his large, tough hands cupped the fragile globes. He had to bite his lip on the need to look down, but he wanted more to see her reactions, to know that she enjoyed this as much as he did. For, starved as his body was, his heart was hungrier.

Both were fed as, gently, he kneaded her, cupping, pressing and caressing, watching her reactions all the while. Her eyes began to darken, the pupils to dilate, yet still she stared into his own as if mesmerized. But when he circled each puckered nipple with his fingers, then plucked them gently, her back arched like a bow. A low moan vibrated from her throat. Her eyes closed.

His heart thundering so loud his blood sang in his ears, he looked down. His big, dark hands were in intimate contact with the secrets this woman had kept from all but him. His hard and ready staff surged eagerly in his breeches until he groaned in actual pain.

The sound reached Magdalena through the haze of love and passion. She opened her eyes to see his white teeth clenched, his eyes fixed on what his hands did to her body. Instincts eons old guided her then. She pushed the loose shirt off his shoulders, unlatched his belt and unbuttoned his bulging pants. His pulsing flesh leaped out at her, hard and majestic as a scepter, kingly in size. But he no longer frightened her, for she knew the realms of joy this monarch offered. And she wanted to share them with him, now, in the fullness of her love, as she'd never wanted anything, not even vengeance. She worked her hands up and down upon him until his eyes, too, closed.

With an earthy curse, he finally caught her hands and panted, "No more, my love. Give me a moment. I want you too much." He caught her hands and pushed them over her head, then he lowered his mouth to her exposed flesh.

Her breath quickened until her chest was moving up and down like a bellows, feeding the licking flames at her breast. His cheeks hollowed with suction as his mouth pulled gently upward every time her breath expelled. Soon she was squirming beneath him, trying to free her hands, but he persisted at the sensual torment for long, long moments. She became a pillar of flame in his arms; he could do naught but warm himself in her.

He snatched the dress over her head and laid her white perfection against it. The rich material made a fitting backdrop, for every inch of her was precious. From her sablelike hair, to the topaz eyes, down her ivory chest to the ruby nipples, and further still to the mink muff at the apex of her thighs, she was untold riches. If he kept her for a lifetime, he could never assay her full value to all that made him man.

Her hands clutched at his shoulders, his waist, his hips. "Come to me," she moaned, her head tossing from side to side.

He kicked his breeches down and off, then pressed his long, bronzed body to her side. His groan drowned out hers when his starved manhood pressed with a will of its own into her supple hip. Almost, he climbed atop her, but this second time was more than a redemption for the first time;

it was a confirmation of the love he'd labored long for. He had to make it perfect.

So he restrained himself, though his brow beaded with sweat, and ran his hands over every warm, satin inch. He marveled again at her feminine power and reveled in his joy: This woman of immutable fire had selected *him* as her mate. He ran his hands lightly over the moist juncture of her legs as if to verify that his lonely dreams had really come true.

But the slick fluid, the hard, eager button, were real enough. And finally, when his caresses were more torment than pleasure, it was El Halcon the woman who plundered *him*.

She squirmed under his knees and latched onto the power pressing urgently into her hip. "Enough, Clint. Come to me and let me show how much I love you." She pulled at him.

Unable to wait another heartbeat, he gladly obeyed. Shoving her legs apart with his knees, he lowered his hips into the warm cradle of her thighs. Cupping her cheeks in his hands, he watched her face as he pushed slowly into her. Her mouth opened in an O of amazement as man filled woman, and woman surrounded man. The first time had been too fraught with anger for them to savor to the full. But this, this was heaven on earth, warmth where there had been cold, sustenance where hunger had growled.

They savored the intimacy as he stayed still for a full minute, keeping her legs splayed apart with his own so she could feel each throbbing inch. Still, the surcease of his heart's hunger soon made his body's more insistent. With a sigh of pure joy, he gradually withdrew, then as quickly pressed deep again. He was careful to linger at the top of his stroke. Her hip motions quickened, urging him on.

She, too, watched his face as he reached farther, delving for her very womb as if his manhood must find her womanly essence to claim it for his own. And she wanted to give it to him, so she met each plunging stroke with an upthrust of her hips. The friction of their rubbing loins built her needs to equal his. Soon they were flying together, earthbound only in body.

His thrusts grew more urgent, pressing her into the earth with their power. Her teeth bit into her lip to stifle her pleasured moans, but he whispered harshly in her ear, "Let me hear it, love. Show me how I make you feel."

And with the next long, sliding stroke, she did. Her body arched beneath his as the spasms took her. She cried out, clutching him close as her only anchor when the earth fell away from her.

His manhood swelled in response to her clench-release upon him. Her cries were proof of her joy, so he restrained himself no longer. He withdrew one last time, poised above her, glistening with her moisture and his own, then plunged deep, reaching, reaching. With a groan and a gush, he let go, filling her with the joy she'd brought to fruition. His cries mingled with hers as his starved passions were sated as never before. He collapsed upon her, a welcome weight.

When their sobbing breaths slowed, he moved to her side, still remaining within her, and cradled her to his chest. "Ah, my love, you've saved a dying man. Another day, another minute without you, and I'd have withered away."

Impishly she tightened her feminine muscles upon him, savoring his little grunt of pleasure as she teased, "Withered? As a tree branch, perhaps."

"And I would root myself within you and never come out," he whispered into her ear, nuzzling it.

"We should make an interesting spectacle when I face Roberto, then."

His kisses stopped; he raised his head. Carefully he asked, "What do you mean? I thought since you came to me . . ." Her expression closed so quickly that his words drifted away.

"You thought because I love you that I would betray my honor?" Her voice was dangerously calm. She twitched her hips away from his.

The loss of intimacy saddened him. The emotion that quickened his heart this time had no relation to joy. "No, but I thought you would want to be with me, as I want to be with you."

"I do." His relieved expression tightened again when she

added, "But not with lies between us. This love of yours, is it dependent upon my submission to your will?"

They rolled to their feet. Their joy had fled as if it had never been; they were antagonists again. The sight of that beautiful body, stiff with resentment, only made his own anger greater. "No, but it's dependent upon your survival!" he shouted.

Her eyes closed. A weary groan escaped her. Without another word, she rinsed in the stream, then pulled her black attire on. As quickly as that did he lose his love. It was El Halcon who faced him now.

Implacable as ever, she said, "Then keep it. I've no need of a love that is conditional. Upon *anything*." Briefly he had his Magdalena back again when she sighed, "For you see, dead or alive, my heart will always be with you . . ." But she turned away from his pleading, outstretched hand.

Flinging the dress back in the trunk, she closed the lid. She carried the trunk with her as she walked back up the stream. The tears blurring her eyes belied her steady steps, and she paused around the curve to wipe them away. Her heart felt as if it had collapsed in her chest, but she breathed steadily under the crushing weight.

She'd done all she could. Proved her love to him in the most intimate way. Still, he wouldn't accept her. She could do naught else, but endure and go on. Her most important task yet remained, and she must concentrate on that and not let Clint or anything else distract her. Grimly, she hefted the trunk to her hip and walked away from her only hope of happiness.

# *Chapter 15*

Magdalena was both refreshed and weary as she walked back. Would it be ever thus? She found brief happiness, only to have it snatched away by forces beyond her control. And they *were* beyond her control, for at this late date she had more to think of than herself, or even the honor she'd sworn to avenge. What of her men—Joaquin and Sean if she abandoned them to go to America with Clint, and the indios who'd come to think of her as their champion? How could Clint expect her to desert them all for the admittedly wonderful clasp of his arms? She loved him, true, but love should enrich the spirit, not weaken it. She could only go on and hope that, eventually, Clint would come to understand that and accept her as she was, as she'd accepted him.

However, the fates had given her little reason to be optimistic in the last few years, and she had to pause again to wipe her tears on her hood. One thing, at least, was certain: She could delay her raid on El Paraiso no longer.

One way or another, she must complete the journey begun the day she fled the birthright that Roberto stole. Clearing her mind of all but determination, she walked into camp.

Magdalena was relieved to see Sean just riding in. She returned the trunk to the lean-to, avoiding Joaquin's inquiring glance, and went to meet the Irishman. She patted his lathered stallion. "Did something happen, Sean? Why did you return so quickly?"

He dismounted, answering cheerfully, " 'T went right as rain. Father Franco took the pouches and agreed to give them to the most needy o' the Indians in the village."

"Was that wise? You know he must suspect the source."

A shrug of his massive shoulders indicated Sean's lack of concern. "He's one o' yer staunchest supporters. He'll not gossip to the soldiers." After he'd unsaddled and rubbed down his stallion, Sean led the animal toward the distant grove. "If ye'll excuse me, I must cool him down."

Magdalena frowned after him. His manner was odd, but when Joaquin joined him, she turned away. Maybe Sean would tell Joaquin what troubled him. Magdalena went to Miguel to see how their mission had gone.

Safely out of earshot, Joaquin asked tensely, "Well?"

"The good padre says he told the governor all, but Alvarado is skeptical of such an incredible story. A woman, the notorious El Halcon? Moreover, an aristocratic woman who claims to have had her honor and lands stolen by her own cousin, one of California's largest landholders?" Sean's voice was harsh as he repeated Father Franco's account of his conversation with the governor.

Joaquin kept pace while Sean walked his stallion up and down to cool him. After a grim silence, he said, "It seems we've no choice, then, but to raid El Paraiso and look for the will. I had so hoped . . ."

Sean inserted roughly, "Aye. But ye can hardly blame the man. I'd doubt the tale meself if I hadn't lived it." Sean pulled the stallion to a stop.

Slowly, Joaquin turned his head, for he sensed he'd not like what Sean had to say next. He was right.

"Alvarado is comin' here himself to investigate. He's

bringin' twenty volunteers with him to help capture us."
Sean smiled grimly as Joaquin, who rarely cursed, reached
new heights of profane eloquence.

Finally Joaquin ended with a simple, "When?"

"Father Franco didn't know. He just said soon."

After a longer pause, Joaquin sighed. "Perhaps it's for
the best. When Alvarado discovers for himself that El
Halcon is a woman, he'll be lenient, if his gallantry to
women is true. He may even listen. I'd rather see
Magdalena captured than killed, as will happen if Roberto
discovers who she is. If he can't kill her in a fair fight, he'll
send assassins, just as he did with Carlos."

After they exchanged a grim, agreeing look, they turned
back toward camp. They wondered at Magdalena's animation as she talked to Charles, and Clint's grimness as he
watched. Sean jerked his head toward the trio. "What's
eatin' at the American now, do ye suppose?"

"The same as ever." Joaquin chuckled.

Sean smiled wistfully. "Ye mean, 'A perfect woman,
nobly planned, to warn, to comfort, and command.'"

"That's a saying *apropriado*. Who said it?"

"A British poet named Wordsworth."

Joaquin's eyes twinkled as he looked at Clint. "Perhaps
you should acquaint the American with it."

"I've a feelin' he's heard it," Sean rejoined dryly.

Actually, Clint's thoughts at that moment dwelt less on
Magdalena's virtues and more on her faults. Vixen, she
shows me the door to heaven, then slams it shut in my face,
he fumed to himself as he watched her spar with Charles.
She admits she loves me, gets me whetted for more, then
turns her back to go on with what she really cares about.
She has a damn peculiar idea of love. Women are supposed
to follow their men. What does she expect me to do? Give
up my business and move here with her?

And why not? countered a voice that had been disturbing
his peace frequently of late. If she wins this battle, do you
really think she'll desert what she's fought so hard for? Is it
fair for you to expect her to?

But I've a business to run, he protested. And she's a

365

rancho to run, the voice pointed out. She can hire someone to do that for her. So can you, the voice said, continuing, and you've been wanting to establish a new office in the west. What better place than California? When this land is settled on a grand scale, as will inevitably happen, you'll be entrenched.

Clint shifted restlessly. Damn the woman, she was altering his very way of thinking. Even the truths he'd long held inviolable were crumbling. How could he continue to think men were naturally superior to women when he now loved to distraction a woman who seemed his equal? No, it was time to admit it. She *was* his equal, in strength of character, if not in physical strength. And his greater brawn had been of immense help in their duel, he admitted wryly. Besides, she'd fascinated him so precisely *because* of her unusual qualities. Would he really want her to be less than she was?

He turned to look at her. Even disguised, her movements were so graceful as she gestured with her hands that he wondered why none of her men suspected her gender. He glanced around, and found Sean and Joaquin watching her indulgently, Miguel frowningly. Clint examined the Indian. His eyes were puzzled, his head cocked to one side as he studied his leader's unusual animation. It was just a matter of time, Clint thought, before he discerns the truth.

Before Clint could consider the consequences of that, the rest of the Indians returned to camp. When the California sunset was splashing its pyrotechnics across the sky and they had just concluded dinner, Magdalena rose and stood in the circle formed by her lounging band. Clint, whose overworked emotions had worn him out, straightened from his slump against the log. Carefully he set his plate down. He sensed the decision in her by the way she pivoted, looking at each man in turn. His heart began sledging against his ribs, and he bit his lip to stifle a protest as she began to speak.

"*Compadres*, for many months we've faced danger together. Some of you have suffered wounds in our cause. I would have spared you those if I could, and I'll not have you hurt more on my account. Because I so appreciate your loyalty and because I am fond of each and every one of you, I must be honest with you now."

Clint looked about. Each man hung on her every word, as if aware that part of the mystery of El Halcon was about to be solved. Charles leaned forward, intent on the tall, still figure made even more imposing by the sunset's spectacular backdrop. Joaquin's face was calm, but Clint sensed his worry by the way his fingers worried at his shirt cuffs. Clint looked back at Magdalena.

"Many of you suspect that I became a bandit for more than greed." Miguel fidgeted under her pointed stare. Humor was audible as her gravelly voice continued. "Congratulate your own acuity, for those of you who suspected such were right. I can't supply full details, but over two years ago, Roberto de Sarria killed my brother, then, several months later, my grandfather." She let their whisperings crescendo and subside before she went on. "I swore then to avenge their deaths. I have a way to prove his perfidy. A certain document remains hidden at El Paraiso, and I must find it."

"But El Halcon," Miguel inserted hesitantly, "how do you know it still exists?"

"I don't. If Roberto found it, it was long ago destroyed. But I suspect he has not. If he felt secure, he'd not have so many armed guards." Magdalena stared at Pico and Miguel, then she looked at the others. "Some of you have reason to hate de Sarria almost as much as I. To you I say, I would appreciate your support tomorrow at dawn, for I go then to El Paraiso, even if I go alone."

Clint's ears buzzed so with his alarm that he barely heard the concerted sigh, the pregnant pause, then the hushed exchanges as her men debated. Dear God, she was going to do this thing. His love, his pleas, made not a particle of difference to her.

After a couple of minutes, Magdalena interrupted. "But know this. I ask. I do not order. Facing experienced soldiers on their mettle will be far more dangerous than any task we've faced. But we may have much riches to gain, as well.

367

I have reason to think de Sarria has more gold at his rancho. Enough to divide among you and let you live comfortably for many years to come. If so, we'll need to steal no more."

After a few more minutes, Miguel stepped forward first, followed by his three friends. Then came Pico and the men he had brought with him. More hesitantly the latest recruits stepped forward. Lastly came Reno. He looked at Magdalena a trifle defiantly.

"Do you trust me to join you?"

She held out her hand in answer. He'd come far in the past weeks. His task of writing down each man's story had given him a perspective on the whole group that none of the others had. She'd watched his sullen distrust gradually disappear as he grew to respect not only her, but the rest of the band. She'd recently had him reinstated in Miguel's ledger.

"I will welcome you at my side, amigo," she said, shaking his hand.

Then she drew away and concluded softly, "You honor me yet again, *compadres*. No matter how tomorrow ends, my heart is at peace. May justice prevail. Now, let us sleep. We must rise before dawn to make our plans."

While the men dispersed, Clint stayed frozen in place, his heart in turmoil. When Magdalena finally turned to him, he opened his mouth to barrage his protests, but a smooth voice cut him off.

"And me, El Halcon? What am I supposed to do?"

Magdalena rested one elbow in her palm, tapping her fingers against her cheek, while she contemplated Charles. "This is not your fight, señor. Besides, I would have thought you'd relish our danger."

"Perhaps I want to be there to see your end," Charles countered dryly.

"Somehow I think not. Come, admit you now see that we are fair men fighting for justice, not the outlaws we seem."

When Charles didn't reply, Magdalena shook her head at him. "Stubbornness must be a *yanqui* trait." Her eyes slipped slyly to Clint, then she looked at Charles again. Her voice grew serious. "You can help, if you truly want to, by guarding camp. That one," she jerked her head at the watchful Mexican soldier, "would be glad to sound the alarm against us."

Charles nodded gravely. "I will be honored, El Halcon." When Magdalena began to turn away, he stopped her with an outstretched hand. "I wish you luck tomorrow. You're going to need it."

"For once we're in agreement, señor." Magdalena shook his hand, then turned away to talk to Sean and Joaquin.

Charles looked down at his rigid nephew. "It will do you no good to spout your objections, you know."

Clint sighed. "I know, but I've got to try. I feel in my gut this will end in disaster." Clint rose and went toward the trio who were in a quiet tactical discussion.

"Yes?" Magdalena broke off her agreement with Sean's suggestion and turned to him politely.

"I'd have a word with you, *El Halcon*," Clint growled.

"In a moment." And she turned her back on him.

Clint was so enraged that he was tempted to jerk her off willy-nilly, but he restrained himself and stalked to his supplies instead. Had he known how sadly Magdalena watched him go, he might have obeyed his instincts.

Joaquin and Sean exchanged a look. Sean squeezed her arm. "Don't ye think ye should be kinder, lassie? He's but worried about ye."

"Kindness is a soft emotion, Sean. I must be hard now. Harder than I've ever been in my life. I won't underestimate Roberto. Now, if we disperse and come at the hacienda from all sides, we'll have the best chance. Two of us must go to the men's quarters, block the door and stand guard. With surprise on our side, hopefully we'll have an hour, at least, to look. We must make every effort to disarm the lookouts quietly. We should use pistols only as a last resort."

Sean and Joaquin nodded. Joaquin asked, "Where do you think we should search first?"

"The study is the most likely place, since abuelo transacted all his business there. But that's also the first place Roberto would have looked. Any ideas, Joaquin?"

"Not a one, *niña*."

"Then the study it will be."

Magdalena searched the faces of her two dearest friends. She looked away so the flickering firelight wouldn't catch her glimmering tears. She reached up and hugged Sean. "I love you, amigo, like the brother I lost. Never will I forget what you've done for me."

Only Joaquin saw and understood Sean's grimace of pain as he fiercely hugged her back. "And never will I forget ye, either, lassie." He pushed her away and beamed his broad, cherubic smile upon her. "But what prattle. 'Tween the two o' us, didn't we hold off an entire presidio?"

Magdalena nodded. "Si. And we are fifteen strong now, all of us more skilled." She hugged Joaquin also. "Be careful tomorrow. I couldn't bear it if anything happened to you."

"It's not myself I worry about, *niña*." Joaquin cupped her face in his hands, wishing he could rip her hood off and look at her lovely face. "It will be good to see El Paraiso again, no? Even under such circumstances." When she nodded, he patted her cheeks and urged, "You will be careful? Remember what I've always taught you. It is the duelist with the coolest head and the quickest feet who lives to fight another day."

Magdalena flashed him her boldest smile. "How could I forget?" She pulled away, blew them each a kiss, then strode off to her pallet.

Sean and Joaquin exchanged a wry look and retired.

Dropping down beside a glum Clint, Magdalena chided, "You look like someone has walked over your grave."

"It's not *my* grave I'm concerned with."

"Oh? Do you stay at camp?"

Clint bridled. "You know I go, and live or die with you."

"Then fear for your own life and let me look to mine. Would you put this load of guilt upon a man you went into battle with?"

When he was silent, Magdalena drew off her hood and shook her head wearily. "Don't ask me not to go, Clint.

370

Please don't insult me so. I cannot bear it when I . . ." She bit her lip.

"Yes?" Clint rose on his knees to clasp her shoulders. "Say it!"

She flung back her head and stared him in the eye. "I love you. I would spend the rest of my life with you, whether it be a few hours or fifty years." When he tried to draw her into his arms, she pushed him away. "But I'll not cling to you. Vines are parasites, slowly draining strength from their hosts and ultimately bringing about their own demise. Is that what you want of me?"

"Don't be melodramatic. A woman is supposed to depend on her man . . ."

"Does that not depend on the woman? Some may be happy in such a relationship. Not I. If that is love, I want no part of it." She caught his hands. "Please, try to understand. If the positions were reversed, and you were trying to regain the name and lands stolen from you, would you like it if I begged you to flee with me?" When he frowned, she went on, "I thought not. But I," she released one of his hands to stab her thumb into her chest, "would not ask you to do so. It would be an insult to your honor and to the love I bear you. For I would rather see you die fighting for what you believe in than to see you live a coward."

Clint snatched his hands away and enclosed her so fiercely in his arms that she could scarcely breathe. "What good is your honor to you in the grave? These lips," he brushed her sensual mouth with his own, "eaten by worms, these proud bones," he squeezed her arms, "mouldering to dust. I would keep you with me, Magdalena, at whatever cost to your pride." He lifted his head to look at her pleadingly.

She buried her face in his chest for a moment, then she gently pushed him away. "Then *you* are the parasite."

Clint's bright head bowed. He drew a deep, shuddering breath. "Very well, my love." He tipped her chin up. "It may be the last time I call you that, but if such is your will, I'll no longer try to dissuade you." He lurched to his feet and pointed down at the wrapped bundle on the ground behind him.

"But please, take this. It will give me some comfort knowing you're armed with the best. We'll talk more tomorrow, after the raid." And he went off, his eyes blurring, his ears ringing with the words that hung between them. "If we've breath left to speak . . ."

Magdalena's hands trembled as she rubbed the sword to lustrous glory. This time, she would wear his gift with pride. And perhaps, just perhaps, it would give her the edge she needed—that timorous balance between life and death. But more important, it was a symbol of their love: shining, pure and strong. The love that, *quiera Dios*, would bend, but not break. Wrapping it back in its rags, Magdalena set the blade aside and drifted off to sleep, her mind rested for the first time in many weeks.

The men were quieter than usual when they roused for preparations several hours before dawn. They listened intently to Magdalena's plan, nodded and saw to their weapons. Pistols were loaded more carefully than ever before, knives and swords inspected for weaknesses, reatas checked for fraying. Even Charles seemed subdued. He watched silently, asking no questions nor making any of his usual caustic observations.

As they mounted, Magdalena explained the lay of the land about El Paraiso. "It's surrounded on three sides by rises. If they've lookouts posted, we'll have a difficult time sneaking in with this full moon. The rear, however, is a level, brushy stretch that offers good cover. We'll have to make our way around, and this will slow us, but it offers the best chance of surprise. Now remember, not a pistol fired if we can help it. Again, try to incapacitate rather than kill."

She looked at Miguel, who usually led them in prayer before their raids. "Will you do the honors, Miguel?" His prayer was more frevent this time, and even those men who were not devout bowed their heads.

After they'd mounted, Magdalena tipped her hat to them. "I salute you, amigos. You make me proud." And off she galloped, leading the way up El Camino Real.

Charles waved them out of sight, his back to camp. Therefore, he was unprepared for the blow that felled him like a marked tree. He didn't see or hear the man who took the best remaining horse and galloped out of camp, going only a short way up the highway before cutting through a rugged mountain trail.

Two hours later, after tying their horses in a copse distant from the house, Magdalena and her men crouched and darted from bush to tree until they reached the hedge at the rear of the hacienda. Magdalena cocked her head and listened, then peeked above the trimmed bushes. Two guards only, one at each end of the house. From their casual posture, hats pushed back on foreheads, backs against the hacienda's adobe wall, it was clear they were not expecting trouble.

Some distance to the left behind them, she could just make out the hand house, its white-washed walls shining under the moonlight. Magdalena jerked her head at Reno and Pico, who had volunteered to lock in and guard the sleeping hands. They followed her pointing finger and slithered off in a belly crawl.

Sean and Joaquin swung about in a wide circle to come at the hacienda from the sides; Magdalena, Clint and the others ducked around the hedge and crawled, inch by inch, toward the back. Still, the guards made no threatening moves, though they were in the open now. Magdalena glanced about. It was almost as bright as day. Only a glance would betray them, yet they were but twenty meters away, ten, seven . . .

Reno's hoarse shout came too late. "*Aqui hay trampa*! Run . . ." He ended with a gurgle.

They each scrambled to their feet—in time to meet the men swarming out of windows and around the sides like rabid rats. Realizing the hacienda was alerted, those who had weapons wasted no time in firing them, throwing themselves to the ground to dodge the returning fire. Clint picked off one of the guards approaching from the back; Miguel took the other. Several more encroaching soldiers fell, groaning, grabbing shoulders and legs. Acrid black smoke wreathed about them, creating chaos but a welcome screen as well. Several of the band members cried out, rubbing arms and legs, but they lurched grimly to their feet to meet the challenge of their lives.

Then it was hand to hand combat with fists, knives and swords. Magdalena shoved Clint's barricading body aside and engaged the first man she came to. Joaquin took on two swordsmen at once, using his cloak as he had taught Carlos. Clint faced a tall, brawny man with a reach as long as his own. Sean battled a smaller man who was as deadly and agile as an asp. With several of the soldiers badly wounded from their fire, they were not outmanned by much. But these were not frightened civilians eager to barter their goods for safety; these were trained soldiers, some of them former convicts, with little respect for life.

Magdalena herself discovered the difference soon enough. The sergeant she was dueling kicked a pile of dead, trimmed clippings in her face. Blinded, only her instinctive, protective action with her cape saved her life. She felt his blade rip into the heavy velvet, and she wrenched to the side, wiping her eyes with the back of the gloved hand gripping her sword. By the time his blade was free, she was facing him again.

It took only a few engages for him to realize he was outclassed, but he pressed savagely on. "El capitan wants you taken alive, El Halcon, but he didn't say in what condition." And he kicked at her knee after barely batting away her lunging stab.

Magdalena saw the move coming and rolled aside, bounding to her feet to engage him again. Her hat came off in the process, but she didn't notice. She'd seen this *cholo* before. He was one of Luis's most depraved soldiers. Carlos had suspected him of raping one of their maids. And he was wearing a sergeant's uniform now. When had he been promoted? And why?

"Your masters won't take me in any condition, Raul. I have no wish to kill you, but if you force me . . ." She stepped back from a savage jab, shoving his blade outward with her own.

A harsh laugh greeted this warning, and he stabbed

374

again, only to be blocked again. Magdalena sensed he was
pressing her backward, but she didn't understand why until
she glanced over her shoulder. The pear tree she herself had
planted was ringed with stones, and he hoped to trip her up
on them. She whammed his blade wide to make room and
hopped around the ring, but she forgot how much the tree
had grown since she'd been in hiding. The tallest branches
were even with her head, and her hood caught on one in her
leaping move. She felt the protective covering tearing away,
but she was too busy defending herself from Raul's frustrated jabs to save it. In seconds, she was exposed, her hair
still pinned up but her face bare to the moonlight—and to
Raul's shocked gaze.

His blade sagged. "Señorita Magdalena?" he squeaked.

It was her turn to sneer. "*Si*, Raul. Don't tell me you're
too squeamish to kill a woman . . ."

His blade came back up in a thrust that slammed her
rapier skyward. "No, for you remind me of another who
boasted just so before he crowed no more . . ."

Magdalena untangled her blade from his and backed a
pace. "What do you mean?"

"Your brother, when I killed him. He died well. Will
you?"

His ugly, leering face swam before her eyes as she
realized at last what he was saying. This man . . . no, this
*animal* had killed Carlos. He actually bragged about it now.
Had he been promoted for the deed? Rage misted her
vision, slowing her reactions, and she felt his blade slip
under her awkward parry, stab again and rip into her shirt
sleeve. Automatically she jerked away and knocked his
blade aside, preparing her attack in her mind. She'd butcher
him like the swine he was and see his blood feed the ground
to repay what he had spilled . . . The haze cleared away
from her eyes, leaving the gold depths crystal clear, steady
on Raul's face.

He drew in a shocked breath at that look and braced
himself. Her thrusts were so vicious and so well-plotted
that, despite his greater strength, he had to back away. His

375

parries became more and more feeble as he read his doom in that calm, lovely face.

"*No!* Spare me, please, I . . ." His plea was severed by six inches of steel. He dropped his sword and clutched his neck, his carotid artery cascading its contents over the uniform he'd been so proud of.

Her expression pitiless, Magdalena watched him fall to his knees, then drop face forward on the ground. She nudged him with her boot, wishing he'd rise up so she could kill him again. But he was still, and she knew he'd play assassin never again. She stared at the stain oozing into the ground and remembered how Carlos had looked that night. She wanted to bend down and wash her hands in the viscous carmine pool, but she forced the urge back. Without a particle of remorse, she wiped her sword on Raul's immaculate coat back.

"Are you mad?" A familiar voice pierced her macabre joy. She blinked in confusion at Clint, until he jerked her hood over her head. "I don't think anyone else saw, but leave now. We'll finish . . ." He shoved her aside and came at the man who would have speared her in the back.

Magdalena was soon engaged again, but now savage energy released the dark urges that had lain dormant in her for so long. The smell of sweat, blood and fear in her nostrils became an exotic perfume instead of a stench. Just as she prepared her offense to spear her opponent in the heart, his hat fell off and she glimpsed his face. He was just a boy, a boy bug-eyed with fear. With an effort, she capped her welling rage and instead gashed him in the thigh. He fell with a groan. She kicked his blade and spent pistol out of his reach and looked around again.

Vaguely she realized that the battle appeared to have gone in their favor. All her men except Fernando were still fighting. She bent and felt his pulse. Nothing. Her brilliant hatred dimmed under the shadow of remorse. She bowed her head.

She pried his fingers loose from his serape and folded both his hands upon his chest, above the saber gash. She'd not trained him enough. But she had little time for grief.

Another soldier swooped down on her—and this one, too, she recognized.

She bounded up. "You treacherous dog, you set this trap, but you'll end caught with us . . ."

Their former prisoner fought bravely, but he was no match for her. Her feet slipped in a slimy red spot, but she merely wiped her boots on clean grass and lunged at her adversary. She felt invincible, energized. Nothing could defeat her. A few more to dispatch and she could go to Roberto . . . Magdalena whammed a powerful thrust aside and lunged with the counter prepared in her mind. His parry was too little, too late. She yearned to skewer him end to end, but some remnant of sanity made her alter her aim. In the last fraction of an instant, she turned her wrist. Her swordpoint pierced his shoulder rather than his chest. He dropped his rapier and stumbled backward.

Mechanically she veered from him toward her goal. The locked door. Roberto. No doubt he and Luis hid inside like the cowards they were. She was but several steps away when Sean and Clint both turned from their wounded opponents and saw where she was going.

"No, lassie, they'll kill ye . . ." Sean cried.

And from Clint as he ran toward her, "Look out, Magdalena!" She caught a movement in the corner of her eye and whirled just as a wounded soldier steadied his aim against the corner of the house.

Everything happened at once then. A second before the soldier fired, a powerful hand shoved her sideways to the ground. Sean, who'd been running in from the rear, was caught in the line of fire.

As she fell behind a bush, pushed by that unseen hand, Magdalena glimpsed the sticky red flower blossoming over Sean's chest. He lurched to the ground. Clint tore his tiny pistol from his boot and fired at the soldier. The man slumped sideways, a neat hole in his forehead. Magdalena scrambled up to go to Sean, but a kick from another felled soldier made her lose her balance before she'd taken two steps. She landed heavily behind the bush, the back of her head striking a large rock. Lush, starry blackness enveloped her as she tumbled end over end into nothingness.

Clint rose from stuffing his kerchief over Sean's wound to look for Magdalena. Just then, Joaquin left his last adversary, who was moaning and clutching his shoulder, and caught Clint's arm.

"Look!" He pointed.

More soldiers were galloping down the slope in front of the house. There looked to be twenty, at least. Tired as they all were, they'd never hold them off.

"Retreat!" Clint shouted. The band obeyed gladly. Miguel carried Fernando off over his shoulders, while Pico dragged Reno's body. Clint and Joaquin searched frantically for Magdalena even as the soldiers neared the front gate. The few clouds in the sky chose that moment to hide the moon's watchful glow.

Clint groaned and tore at his own hood in frustration. She'd insisted he wear it, saying he was too easy to recognize. "And I, too, would keep you safe," she'd said huskily.

Pain seared through him like wildfire as he was forced to accept the fact that he had to flee, leaving her wounded or worse, or be captured with her. One last time he looked, fumbling along the ground. But his blind search was interrupted by Joaquin.

Torment and weary resignation combined in his voice. "We'll not help her if we're captured ourselves. Come, help me get Sean away and we'll return for her." Clint hesitated, but the first of the soldiers were dismounting now, and a bullet zinging by his head made him face reality.

Cursing bitterly, he hefted Sean over his shoulders and ran toward the horses. The others were loping away. Even burdened with Sean, fear for Magdalena made Clint swift of foot. *I must get back to her, I must get back to her,* beat his thoughts in cadence with his running steps.

Joaquin used Sean's reloaded weapons and his own to hold the first of the soldiers at bay while Clint laid Sean as gently as he could over his saddle. Clint felt for and found a faint pulse. If Sean died, Magdalena would probably never forgive him, for the bullet had been meant for her. He'd gladly take that chance just to hold her in his arms again. Please God, don't take her from me, he prayed as they galloped away.

By the time the soldiers ran back and fetched their own horses, the bandits had blended with the night. However, as they conducted a search of their wounded, they had a most pleasant surprise awaiting them . . .

Magdalena groaned as a prodding foot shook her aching head. When the prod became a kick, she shoved the boot away and sat up. She swayed from side to side, but had no time for misery as she was hauled roughly to her feet.

"Come on, El Halcon, we're all eager to meet you," sneered Luis. He nodded at the two soldiers who had brutal clasps on her arms, and they pushed her toward the back door.

Magdalena blinked against the light they shoved her into. The vicious excitement that had sustained her in the battle had deserted her, leaving her groggy and afraid. Had she imagined that last nightmarish scene? Surely God wouldn't take Sean from her, too. And if it were true, who had pushed her down? Clint had been too far away.

Had the others escaped? They must have, she decided, for the soldiers meandering about herded no prisoners. A measure of strength returned to her, making her pounding headache bearable. As she was manhandled past the *sala* from whence a wide-eyed Sarita stared, down the hall to Roberto's study, Magdalena knew she'd need all the vigor she could muster. The confrontation she'd both longed for and feared was nigh, but it had not come as planned. She was well aware that she'd be lucky to escape it with her life. Once Roberto found out who she was . . .

She sat gladly when she was pushed into a chair before the desk. Ah, how familiar this room was. She ignored the triumphant man lounging against the desk and absorbed the ambience that brought back so many memories. Abuelo, bent over his records. Carlos, offering her a glass of sherry. Her parents, sitting cozily side by side on the short settee before the fire built more for decoration than for heat. She felt their warmth, their love, as powerfully as she felt the evil reaching out to her.

This room that had held such joy, was it also to be her crypt? Taking a deep breath, she lifted her head. There, his hair curling above his ears into two horns, stood *El Diablo* himself. He looked her up and down, savoring her humiliation, for the soldiers had tied her hands behind the chair back before being dismissed. Only Roberto and Luis would witness her unveiling. She took what little comfort she could from that.

When both men still stared at her silently, she knew they hoped to unnerve her, to see her beg for mercy. Closing her eyes, she concentrated on another image called up by this room: how abuelo had looked with Roberto's knife stuck in his chest. Her sluggish heart began to pound again.

If she was to die, it would be on *her* terms. She rested her head against the chair back and crossed her legs, bouncing one idle foot. She knew an infallible way of wiping that detestable smile off Roberto's face. "It's good to see your slimy presence has little befouled El Paraiso, Roberto. Perhaps even you have wit enough not to tamper with something so above your touch." Her voice was her own.

Roberto's smile did indeed freeze on his face. Luis started and paled to a sickly hue. They exchanged a disbelieving look, then Roberto leaned forward and snatched off Magdalena's hood.

"*Madre de Dios!*" whispered Luis, his eyes saucer-wide.

But Roberto said not a word. Somehow, despite all his arguments, he'd known she lived and that she was involved with El Halcon in some way. But this . . . He never would have expected even Magdalena to be so bold. A chill ran up his spine as she stared at him calmly, with a slight smile. He had her trapped, yet she didn't seem afraid. Somehow, this meeting he'd longed for was not turning out as he'd planned. Where was the fear, the pleading he'd wanted to revel in? He searched her features and saw the changes in her. She had a few lines in her face now, but they only added to the power of her personality. She'd been a girl when she left; now she was a woman. A woman who would die trying to defeat him. He wiped a hand over his face, as if to block the power of that gaze, and he actually moved back a step before he caught himself.

Magdalena's smile widened at the betraying movement. "It is good to see you again, too, cousin," she said softly. "For years I have dreamed of this meeting." When he didn't reply, she affected surprise. "Aren't you glad to see me?"

Her mockery stiffened him. He resumed his lounging posture and smiled cordially back at her. "Indeed. You'll never know how I, too, have longed to see you again. How fortunate for me that you are the infamous El Halcon."

"That's ridiculous, Roberto," Luis scoffed, throwing himself into a chair next to Magdalena. "At first I wondered . . . but think, man. It's just the kind of crafty thing El Halcon would do—send a woman to deceive us. Those renegades would never follow a woman, nor could a woman fence like that fiend . . ." His voice trailed off when those enigmatic gold eyes turned upon him.

"Your assassin would not agree with your assessment of my skills, Luis—*If* Raul still lived to form an opinion on anything. It was with the greatest joy that I severed his neck. He deserved a slower end for killing Carlos, but," she shrugged elegantly despite her bonds, "it was some satisfaction to see his face as he died."

It was that shrug that did it—the casual contempt in it was decidedly familiar. So, it was true. That a *woman* could have made such fools of them . . . Luis rubbed his face. The wound El Halcon had inflicted on him had long since healed, but he felt it throbbing now as if it were fresh. His hand lashed out before he'd put thought to action.

Magdalena's head knocked back against the chair from the force of the blow, but her smile didn't waver, despite the trickle of blood now decorating it. "Do you feel better now, most brave and bold capitan?"

"Five of my men dead," Luis snarled, reaching out to strike again, but Roberto caught his arm.

"Save your passions, amigo. There is a more pleasurable way to expend them, is there not?"

381

Both men turned to look at her in a new way, a way that made her skin crawl. The fear she'd so far held at bay sprang free. She felt her face changing, but she was powerless to control it. Death she could face; not this.

Roberto's self-confidence seemed to have returned. He strutted toward her and unpinned her hair. When the silky mass tumbled about her shoulders, he brought a handful to his face and sniffed. "Clean enough, I suppose. I expected you to bear the stench of your Indian lovers. Did you rotate from man to man nightly?" When she didn't answer, he flicked her own hair at her nose and dropped the heavy tresses. "I suppose our pleasure needn't be delayed to give you a bath." And his hands lowered to the buttons on her shirt.

He undid them casually, his dark face showing both his hatred and his lust. "You could have been my wife and saved your brother and grandfather, but you spurned me like the *cerdo* you named me. If anyone is to blame for their deaths, it is you."

His reasoning was so monstrous that Magdalena's sick horror at what they were going to do to her dimmed under pure, shining hatred. She strained at her bonds, but when she couldn't break them, she lashed up with her knee.

Roberto staggered back with a groan, his hands clutching his deflating erection. He landed on the settee and slumped there, panting.

"I wouldn't sully my feet with you, much less allow you such intimacy," Magdalena spat, still struggling. "Release me, you cowards, and give me a sword. What victory will you have proving yourselves upon a defenseless woman? Gladly will I duel you both at once."

Shaking his head at her, Luis went to check on his friend. When Roberto's eyes opened, the look he sent at Magdalena made her swallow. "Release her and tie her face down over the chair back. We'll fuck her like the bitch she is. She's never been reminded that she's only a woman, but she'll know it before she dies. We couldn't let the notorious El Halcon escape, of course." He smiled across at Magdalena.

She shivered, but when Luis approached her, her eyes

narrowed upon him. He prudently veered around and came at her from the side, pulling a dagger from his belt. He easily avoided Magdalena's sideways kicks and held the knife to her throat.

When her struggles ceased, he loosened the knot holding her hands tied and ordered harshly, "Turn around."

Her every muscle strained to strike out at him, but the knife was so tight to her throat that her breathing was constricted. She knew he'd relish the chance to kill her, but even so, she had to try. When she began to turn, her arms were free for a blessed moment. She slammed both her fists up, reaching for his chin, but he blocked her punch and backhanded her across the face, once, twice, until her ears rang. Quickly he pushed her over the chair back, looped the rope about her wrists and tied them to the legs of the chair. For once strength defeated agility, and Magdalena soon found herself in the most humiliating position of her life, her knees barely in the chair, her waist draped over the back. Their laughter as they watched her squirm brought tears to her eyes despite herself.

"Not such a wildcat now, is she?" Luis sneered. He stepped in front of her and casually untied her breast binding. He gave a surprised grunt when her breasts tumbled free. He hefted one appraisingly, squeezing the globe with rough relish.

"Come over here, Roberto. She's full of surprises yet."

Roberto walked carefully over to them. A wickedly slashed eyebrow rose as he, too, reached out. When Magdalena couldn't control a shudder at the feel of his hands, he bent until his eyes were level with hers. "Ah, how good to see you're as weak as all your kind," he said, flicking at a tear on her cheek. "Had you accepted it earlier, you'd have enjoyed a different fate."

But Magdalena's position had offered her an unexpected boon. Resolve flowed back into her sapped limbs as she saw the fine stitches on the back of the chair. Stitches that had not been there when she left El Paraiso. Stitches that looked new . . . Roberto was still looking for the will! If only she could get free, she might yet win.

She lifted her head and met Roberto's murky black gaze with eyes as golden as the sunlight peeking through the window, eyes that beamed into his and knew him for what he was. "But fate seldom acts as we wish. For either of us, cousin. You're still not safe. Your stolen lands will always be in danger as long as you can't find abuelo's last will."

When Roberto's rude hands dropped away, her voice grew stronger. She looked at Luis's frowning face and clicked her tongue. "So the saying is true. There is no honor among thieves. He's never told you, has he, that my grandfather changed his will and left all to me? And he hid it, like the clever man he was, before telling his nephew. Not that he ever believed Roberto would kill him . . ."

"Is this true?" Luis demanded, looking at Roberto.

"She'll say anything to save herself. Besides, what difference does it make? We've more riches to win from the gold . . ."

"If you don't have legal claim to El Paraiso, our whole plan is at risk."

"It doesn't matter now that I've never found the will," Roberto pointed out, his voice as hard as his face. He looked back at Magdalena and smiled. "For when she dies, I will be the last remaining heir."

Luis seemed to take comfort from that. But his relieved sigh was interrupted by Magdalena.

"Oh yes? How do you know I haven't married and given birth?"

That silenced both men briefly, but then Roberto waved a dismissing hand. "That's hardly likely with the life you've been leading. Besides, it doesn't matter. Your bastard would have no proof. Now, my dear cousin, you've cleverly delayed us long enough, and I thank you. I'm feeling my . . . regard for you returning." His eyes on her breasts, on display for them because of her position, he massaged the growing lump in his breeches, cupping one breast with his other hand.

With a coarse laugh, Luis stepped back and bowed. "She's all yours, amigo. It is right that you have first taste. Just leave enough to go around."

Magdalena began struggling again, but Roberto seemed to enjoy that. He squeezed her breasts as they bounced, and she couldn't help but see that his vigor was indeed rapidly returning. If only he'd lean a little closer . . . Her teeth ground together.

Instead, Roberto strutted around to her side. She lashed out with her feet, but the high chair arm kept her from connecting. Then she felt his fingers on her breeches' buttons.

"Now, cousin, I show you all you're really good for . . ." Roberto purred.

As he tightened his fingers in the waist of her pants to pull them down, a peremptory knock sounded at the door. Roberto cursed. "What the hell do you want?" he shouted.

"It's Clint Browning. Open up, de Sarria. I've news for you."

Roberto looked at Luis. "Why not?" Luis said. "Browning should be happy to see the notorious El Halcon as she really is. Perhaps we'll even let him share . . ."

"That depends upon his news," Roberto said, crossing the room.

Both Luis and Roberto were watching the door, so they didn't see the relieved tremors Magdalena tried to subdue. Nothing on earth, however, could have kept her gaze averted when Clint walked through the door. Her eyes shone like beacons in her bruised face, but they dimmed somewhat when he scowled at her and slammed the door behind him.

"What's going on here? Who's this woman?" He seemed to look her over with an appraising eye.

Luis said with relish, "Meet El Halcon, capitan."

Clint started. "Surely you jest. I've just come from the bandits' camp. Their leader is indeed missing and they've obviously been in some kind of skirmish, for many of them are wounded. Now would be a great time to attack. I came as quickly as I could to let you know where they hide."

"Excellent, excellent. I'll alert the men," Roberto said, turning toward the door.

But Clint held up a hand to halt him. "A moment, please.

385

What's this nonsense about this woman being El Halcón?" His eyes darkened as they made a thorough examination of her face, lingering on the bruises, but he seemed calm enough as he looked at Roberto. Only Magdalena noticed how his hand drifted to the pistol at his waist.

Roberto crossed his arms smugly. "No nonsense. This woman has played us all for a fool, but as you can see," he flung his chin toward her, "it is we who will have the last laugh."

"Do you care to join us?" Luis asked casually, as he would offer a cheap glass of wine.

Clint's eyes dropped to the floor as he shrugged his broad shoulders. "Why not? But first, we've business to discuss. I must sail soon. Have you enough gold ready?"

"Sí, I was going to come to Santa Barbara tomorrow and leave a message," Roberto answered.

"Well, I can save you the trip. Where is it?"

Roberto's eyes went to his desk, but then he looked back at Clint. "I will give it to you when I'm ready, gringo. Now, do you join us in teaching this bitch how foolish she was to ape a man, or not?"

Magdalena had long since buried her cheek against the smooth leather of the chair back. Oh God, had she been wrong about him after all? How could he ally himself with these two and still claim to love her? Had he come even now to crow over her instead of to save her, as her heart yearned to believe? The blow was too much, on top of the others she'd sustained. Her body wilted as, for the first time in her life, she waited for men to decide her fate.

Thus, when the sounds came, she flinched, expecting blows to land on her exposed body. Instead, there came a dull thud as a heavy weight crashed to the floor, then a muffled cry and a crack, followed by another thud. Her heart pounded with dread and hope combined as footsteps approached her side. Her bonds were slashed through, and she was hauled into a pair of strong arms and crushed against a wide chest. In another first, she shrank against that chest, bathing it in her tears. Weakly as the vine she'd scorned, she clung to him.

Clint lifted her chin. He shook his head grimly at her expression. "You little fool, even now, you didn't trust me, did you?"

"Forgive me for my moment of doubt. But how could you agree to help them?" Her question was more a cry of pain.

He shook her gently. "To help you, of course. The gold is proof of their larceny." Briefly he explained how he'd come upon them and their plan. He ended whimsically, "But the fat's in the fire now. They can no longer doubt where my loyalties lie."

When she didn't smile, he turned her head from side to side and scowled at her bruises. He cast a mean look at the two limp figures on the floor, but his hand was gentle as he covered her left breast as if to support her weary heart. "Did they hurt you, Magdalena?" He fumbled with her binding and shirt, his hands trembling slightly.

"Only my pride, and they scared the wrath of God into me." She pinned her hair up with shaky fingers, then buttoned her pants. When he urged her toward the window, she balked.

"No, I must search for the will. Roberto admitted he never found it."

"There's no time."

In confirmation of his words, there came a knock at the door and a worried, "Capitan, is everything all right?"

Clint opened the window and stepped over the sill, offering his hand to her. She hesitated, looking back at the two unconscious men. The score she had to settle with them had lengthened this day. Free from that demeaning position, hatred invigorated her anew. Her hands flexed as she stared at Roberto.

"Give me your pistol, Clint," she droned.

He looked at her askance and reached out to lift her upon the sill. "Are you mad? You'd bring every soldier down upon us. No, Magdalena. I know they both deserve to die, but it will have to wait for another day. Besides, it's not right to kill even two such men in cold blood."

"No? That's what they've twice done to people I loved.

And would have done to me, after degrading me in every way possible." She tried to pull away, but he flung his chin at the door where the soldier had begun kicking at the lock.

"You're coming, now, woman, willing or not," he grumbled, pulling her by the waist over the sill. Magdalena struggled against him until he whispered in her ear, "What of Sean? Miguel promised to take him back to camp and look after him, but he was seriously hurt."

She slumped against him. Fear for Sean was a cleansing antidote to hatred's poison. "Take me to him." They'd barely cleared the sill when a shadow blocked the early sun. Magdalena gasped when she saw the soldier's uniform, but Clint looked amused as he glanced at the three guards who seemed to be enjoying a nap.

"Efficient as ever, Joaquin."

Only then did Magdalena see the face under the broad-brimmed hat. Joaquin's eyes sparkled with unashamed tears as he gingerly traced her bruises. "We came as quickly as we could, *niña*, but we had to catch up with the others. We couldn't leave Sean alone."

Her throat working, she rasped, "Take me to him."

Clint led the way to the horses concealed in the brush behind the house. They'd mounted and were on their way before either of them noticed that Joaquin hadn't followed. Magdalena cast worried looks over her shoulder, and finally pulled up.

"Joaquin!" she called. Silence.

She looked at Clint, and he answered her unspoken plea with action. "I'll find him, Magdalena. You go on to camp. I'm not sure . . ." He wheeled his stallion and galloped back through the brush without finishing the sentence.

But the rest of it rang in Magdalena's weary head: ". . . how long Sean will live." Magdalena was beyond weariness by the time, hooded, she reached camp. She didn't even notice the lack of welcome from the men as she hurried toward the long, still form lying on a pallet near the fire.

The bright red head seemed dulled, as if the life that kindled it was all but extinguished. Two big hands rested limply upon his chest. The bandage Miguel had wrapped about him was saturated with the blood that had drained all color from his once ruddy face. Magdalena froze at his side, looking from Sean to Miguel, who hovered over him.

Miguel looked away from her anguished eyes. That was answer enough, even without the slight shake of his head, but Magdalena still couldn't accept it. She fell to her knees beside Sean and took his hands, tightening her grip as if she would embue him with her own life.

"Sean," she quavered, "please, wake up. Speak to me."

For a moment there was no response, then the pale eyelids flickered and the barest pressure of his hands returned her clasp. "Is that ye, lassie?"

Magdalena gave no thought to subterfuge, even though she knew every man in camp listened. "Yes, Sean. I'm back safe, thanks to you and Clint."

"I'm glad . . . ye deserve happiness, lassie. Don't be afraid to reach for it."

"But you'll be there to share it with me, me handsome boyo."

A harsh, grating cough disturbed Sean's wavering smile. Drops of blood appeared beside his mouth. He weakly licked them away. "I don't think so, darlin'. But I've no regrets. What better way to end than in the defense o' . . . friends? Dear one . . ." He coughed again.

Magdalena threw herself over his chest, trying to support his racked body. "Sean, please, please, don't die on my account. I'm not worth it . . ."

"But ye are, lassie," Sean gasped as his cough subsided. This time he didn't bother licking the brighter, heavier drips of blood away from his mouth. "I love ye, ye know," he whispered, his voice so weak Magdalena could barely hear him. "Yer the finest lass I've e'er known, and it's proud I am . . ." He struggled for breath.

His gasped words were hard to understand, but every one was a spike in Magdalena's heart. ". . . to spend . . . me last . . . birthday with ye . . ." His whisper died away. He sighed, his chest rising with the movement, tried to smile at her once more, then his eyes closed peacefully. His slack hands dropped from about hers.

Magdalena shook his shoulders, her voice thick with tears. "No, damn you, you can't die! Not again, I can't bear it!" But once again, the heavens had taken their own. She knew it, and there was nothing to do but bear it, after all. Burying her head against him, Magdalena wept.

When strong hands clasped her to a familiar chest, she hiccuped and tried to stop her tears, but her head was forced against that steady, dependable heart. "Cry, *querida*. Honor him with your tears." And the floodgates were unleashed anew. Some thirty minutes later, she felt sane again, if not better. She lifted her head and looked around.

Clint shook his head grimly. "I couldn't find a trace of him. No horse, nothing. Had he reason to go to Santa Barbara?"

She opened her mouth to answer, but a hard voice interrupted. "Well, *El Halcon*, don't you think it's time you were truthful with us? Three are dead today because of you."

Magdalena followed Miguel's pointing, accusing finger to where two more blanket-covered bodies lay.

Clint stiffened and rose, pulling Magdalena with him. Deliberately, he tightened his arm about her. "That's not her fault. You all know it was the Mexican who betrayed us."

"But it was a woman who sent us on such a foolhardy mission," Miguel returned harshly.

Silence enfolded the camp. The day had turned bad. The sun hid behind massive gray clouds as impenetrable as battlements; the wind sighed like a weary sentinel. Magdalena's spirits sank to a nadir she'd never known, but she reached deep within herself for a strength untapped. She gently pushed Clint away and stood tall.

One by one, she met the accusing stares of her men. Miguel had suspected, she knew, but the others looked torn between shock and horror. It was true. Three men had died today because of her. Good men. One of them more than a friend to her. She looked at the blood on her hands. She'd killed Sean as surely as if she'd pulled the trigger herself . . .

With a steady hand, Magdalena worked her hood over her head and turned to face her accusers.

# Chapter 16

"The balance of your destiny hangs on the knife-edge between good and evil."

**Act I, DON JUAN TENORIO**

Thunder rumbled in the background like a starving beast. But this was a beast she had roused. She'd fed its hunger on her own blood-lust, and she must confront it or be consumed. Lightning crackled, starkly illuminating the condemnation that had replaced respect: Each and every one of the Indians looked at her with varying degrees of resentment.

"*Mujer!*" she heard them whisper, as if her gender had caused their downfall. The muted scorn was as painful to her as a kick in the gut, but she drew a deep breath and met their eyes as she always had. Directly.

"You've much to blame me for, *compadres,* it is true. I should have left more than one guard in camp."

From where he sat slumped on his blanket, Charles grimaced and rubbed the knot on the back of his head.

"We should have trained longer and waited until our numbers had grown before attempting El Paraiso." Her voice wobbled as she stared at the three blanket-covered bodies. "We lost much and gained nothing." She looked down at the blood on her hands. Sean's blood. She wiped her palms absently on her pants, but she knew she'd never be clean again.

Still no one spoke. The hardness in the faces of men she'd come to care for both pained her and stiffened her. She quit fidgeting with her hands and lifted her head. "I take full responsibility for what happened. The weight of it I will carry to my grave. But I remind you that I warned you all of the dangers, and you volunteered to go with me. What can I do to make amends? I can't bring back those who have died, though . . ."—she had to steady her voice before going on— ". . . I would give my own life if I could."

Magdalena's gaze lingered on Miguel. He looked away and crossed his arms over his chest, closing himself in. Suddenly she was angry. She strode toward him. "What should I have done differently? If you had such reservations, why did you not speak them earlier?" Magdalena shook his arm.

His onyx-hard eyes glittered when he retorted, "You should never have deceived us. Had we known . . ."

"Yes, Miguel? Had you known I was a woman, what then?" She flung his arm away in disgust and stepped back. "You'd not have followed me down the street, much less down the highway. Is that not so? Well?"

"Si!" He shouted, goaded. "A woman thinks with her emotions and makes a dangerous leader . . ."

"True, it was *my* emotions that would have condemned Reno to death without trial. It was my *emotions* that made me train you all until I ached, and see that you were fed before taking my own plate." Her lip curled when her men had the grace to look away.

She whirled, stalked to the lean-to and fetched the small but heavy chest. She walked back and threw it at Miguel's feet. "So, take the spoils my emotional leadership led you to. I'd not lead you any longer even if you wanted to follow, which you obviously don't." She picked up a saddlebag and flung it at Miguel. He caught it. "Count out my share,

394

Sean's and Joaquin's and divide the rest among you. Then get out of my sight."

"But what of . . ." Miguel gestured toward the bodies.

"*If* it's not too much to ask, the others can dig while you count out the money." Her sneering tone grew bitter. "I'm such a weak woman, you see . . ."

Miguel bit his lip, but he nodded at his friends, who silently went to work. Magdalena fetched water from the stream and bent to the final task she could do for Sean.

Clint watched her. Her eyes were dry, her hands steady, but her very composure worried him. He glared at the muttering Indians, but they would have to wait. He didn't go to Magdalena as he longed to, for sensitivity to her feelings held him back. He had comforted her all he could; she must say good-bye to Sean alone.

"I can't fault your taste, nephew, but I don't envy you your wooing."

Slowly Clint turned to meet Charles's shrewd gray eyes. "You don't seem surprised, Uncle. How long have you known?"

"I've suspected it for weeks, but her behavior—and yours—yesterday after you both returned from the stream convinced me."

"But how?"

A wry smile stretched Charles's long, thin mouth. "Whatever your faults, Clint, you've no . . . odd propensities." When Clint frowned in confusion, Charles pointedly eyed his nephew's crotch. "I've never seen you hard with excitement over a man."

Color flooded Clint's face, making it ruddy even in the gloom.

Charles looked at Magdalena. "She's an amazing woman, and she'll not make a comfortable wife. You do have marriage in mind, don't you?"

"*If* she'll have me. And *if* . . ."

Charles sighed. "Yes, indeed. She's not one to welcome protection, and I fear the dangers she's yet to face are all too real."

"But she'll not face them alone, if I have anything to say about it." Clint rose and went to help move the bodies.

When each were put in their final resting places, Miguel led a brief liturgy over them. Magdalena bent and arranged Sean's rosary over the clean white shirt she'd dressed him in. She bowed her head, crossed herself, then turned away as the first clump of dirt was dropped on that peaceful, cherubic face.

"Would that you were here to help me carve a cross, abuelo," she whispered.

Clint's eyes narrowed. "You mean your grandfather carved your brother's cross?" he asked Magdalena.

"Si. But Sean's will have to wait." She helped put rocks over the graves, then walked blindly past Clint.

"Forgive me," Clint heard her mutter.

Again, he longed to go to her as she sat isolated on Sean's blanket, running her hands over and over it, but something in her posture stopped him. His heart pounded with alarm as her eyes settled on him, then moved away as if she hadn't seen him. Did she suspect?

It seemed so, for when the men had divided the supplies and money and packed their horses, she rose one last time to face them. "One question before you go—who pushed me out of the way of the shot that killed Sean?"

No one replied, but several telltale glances went to Clint. He released his pent-up breath and strode forward to face her. "I did. I had no idea Sean was behind you, but even had I known, I would have acted the same." He didn't look away even when her eyes dilated and darkened.

"So, it's true," she whispered. She bent her head, as if this additional burden was more than she could bear. He took a great stride toward her, but she waved him off and backed two paces.

"No. Anything we could have had died with Sean. You had no right to take his life to spare mine. You have no more respect for me than—" She jerked her thumb at the silent group of Indians. "I'm but a woman, all along you've claimed. So be it. Then I've the right to reject you as my suitor."

"Magdalena, I . . ." Clint pleaded.

"No, Clint. It's too late." There was a weary world of sadness in her voice. That toneless despair was something none of them had ever heard from her before. Miguel's hard features softened, but she didn't notice as she went on. "Many times have I tried to explain to you how I felt. No longer. We come from different worlds, I guess, and we can't bridge our differences. I've not the strength to try any longer. I must save all my energies to help Joaquin. Roberto must have him, either at El Paraiso or at the presidio."

"But what can you do alone?" Miguel spoke the fear for Clint.

She didn't even glance at him. "Roberto will gladly exchange Joaquin for me." She whirled away, then stopped. Slowly, she turned back around. "I regret we have ended so, amigos. You go with my prayers. *Vaya con Dios.*" And she stumbled to her pallet, her feet dragging on the ground.

The Indians looked at one another, hesitating, then they mounted their horses. "*Vayan con Dios,*" they echoed. The sounds of their horses loping away dissipated on the canyon's humid air.

Magdalena buried her face in her arms and told herself she wouldn't cry, but tears seeped out. When she heard footsteps approach, she was too weary to turn over to look. Friend or enemy, it no longer mattered. The last friend she had was locked away now. Because of her.

Her heart if not her mind recognized that touch, however, when gentle hands smoothed her hair and a warm blanket was dropped over her.

"I'll be back, Magdalena. Depend upon it. Sleep now. You must rest if you're to win this last battle." Clint's footsteps retreated.

She heard a murmur, then the creak of saddle leather and fading hoofbeats. Then she was alone. Alone as she had claimed she wished to be, but her solace was melancholy at best. The weather complemented her mood. The restive elements would neither relieve themselves in a stormy burst nor relax into quiescence. Throughout that long, lonely afternoon, thunder grumbled and wind whined, but nary a drop of rain added to the wetness saturating the blanket under Magdalena's cheek.

When she'd cried until her throat was raw and her eyes burned, her overwrought emotions calmed. Still, exhausted as she was, sleep was elusive. Even as darkness fell, she still tossed and turned. Finally, she sat up and rubbed her eyes. Joaquin's beloved voice came to her out of the darkness: "It is the duelist with the coolest head and the quickest feet who lives to fight another day."

She'd disobeyed that most important rule, and only Clint's intervention had saved her from the fate her own hotheadedness would have visited upon her. Maudlin self-pity wouldn't help her now. She'd failed utterly, true: She'd not found the will, she'd watched three of her men die, she'd alerted Roberto to her identity, the band had deserted her. And all for nothing.

Of Clint she would not think, for his betrayal was most painful of all. And betrayal it was—of all she'd struggled to become, of all she'd hoped to be for him. What kind of relationship could they have if he didn't respect her right to decide her own destiny? It would be much harder to live with Sean's death on her conscience than it would have been to die, if such God had willed. Why couldn't she make him understand that it was too late to turn back now? Her fate had been foreordained when she took to the road all those months ago. She could only meet it with all her remaining strength, but she could not, and would not, let others live it for her. She'd attempted to bolster the odds in her favor by recruiting her band, and look how that had ended.

No, Clint had only delayed her danger. She wasn't fool enough to think she could walk twice into the lion's den and emerge unscathed, but nor would she enter it defenseless. El Halcon had one advantage over Roberto and Luis—he was beloved by many of the people. If they held Joaquin at the presidio, as she suspected, then perhaps she was not alone, after all. Still, she knew it would take a miracle to save her now. But had not the good Lord granted miracles before? Especially to those who labored on their own behalf?

Prayer is a tool for good, not a weapon for vengeance. The thought came to her as clearly as if Father Franco had made her repeat it in one of her catechisms. Another, more unsettling, memory made her stare blindly into the darkness. She'd been as joyful as a savage when she killed Raul. She'd even wanted to bathe her hands in his blood. God had granted her that opportunity a mere few hours later, but grief had been her lot then rather than joy. Had she failed so miserably not because the battle could not be won but because she'd fought it for the wrong reasons?

It was as if a veil had been drawn from her eyes.

Her single, driving motivation through all she'd done and become had been hatred, immutable hatred. She'd wanted to kill Roberto more than she'd wanted to live the life God had granted her. She *would* have killed him in cold blood, while he was unconscious, if Clint hadn't stopped her. She shuddered in remembrance and rubbed her tingling palms on her breeches.

There was a vast difference between justice and vengeance, as Joaquin had insisted all along, but only now did she see it. Roberto was evil and deserved to be punished for his crimes, but she was no Gabriel to wield a flaming sword over his head. Her heart was not pure enough. By yearning to kill him when he was defenseless she became what she most hated in him: cold, conscienceless, ruthless. Selfish in the purest, most disgusting sense—unknowing, uncaring and unfeeling about anyone save herself.

Magdalena looked up at the sky, and when she saw the stars winking down at her, she felt as if the hovering mass that had smothered her heart had been whisked away. The threatening storm had passed to leave the night purer, more beautiful than ever. Peace calmed her turbulent soul as she stared up at God's bounty.

Life was to be reveled in, not endured. Like all blessings, it must be husbanded and nurtured, not squandered. Clint's sunny soul owed its brightness to his understanding of that basic lesson. Was it too late to let him know that she understood it, finally, too? She groaned in pain every time she remembered Sean's face as he died, but Clint had not knowingly condemned him. Sean would not want her to reject Clint for trying to save her. She suspected Sean, too, would have pushed her out of the way if it had been he closest and Clint behind. She could as easily have lost Clint . . .

A deeper groan escaped her at the thought. No matter that she sent him away. She loved him still and would always love him. Their turbulent relationship had allowed them little time to know one another. Eventually, he'd grow to respect her as much as she respected him. She wanted with all the passion in her soul to share with him the life he'd made her love. If she survived tomorrow, and he still wanted her, she would tell him so.

This time, when she settled back for sleep, her thoughts allowed her to rest. And instead of the dark, troubled nightmares she usually had, she dreamed she was on the crest overlooking El Paraiso, Clint at her side and two children clinging to her skirts. And everywhere, in every direction, there was light . . .

Clint caught up with the Indians several miles up the highway. He whistled loudly, and they reined in. From their disgruntled faces, he could see they'd been arguing among themselves, which probably accounted for their slow pace.

When he drew even, he inclined his head at a small stand of trees off the highway. "I would talk with you, please," he said grimly.

They shrugged and followed him. When all were seated on the lush grass, Clint strode up and down before them, marshaling his thoughts. He began, "Your reaction to finding out El Halcon's true identity is understandable. So, too, did I react. With disbelief, anger and disgust. A woman, I thought, daring to order about a group of strong, able men?"

At their agreeing nods, Clint sighed and spread his hands in helplessness. "But it wasn't long before I was forced to set aside the prejudices that had been instilled in me. For this woman is not as other women. Have any of you seen a woman who can duel so well? Known one bold enough to defy a whole presidio? Can any of you say she hasn't made an able, level-headed leader? In truth, it is her kind woman's heart that has saved you all. Because you have not killed indiscriminately, you have a chance to leave this life with honor. If she vindicates herself, so are you vindicated. When the truth comes out, no one will blame us for the soldiers we killed, for they were acting on orders that would benefit not Mexico, not California, but two greedy men."

When none of them disagreed, Clint made his shrewdest play. "I don't need to tell you that the beliefs we're instilled with from an early age are not always just. As even Charles has come to recognize, you men are not the dull, childish Indians the padres tried to keep you. You are brave, worthy of respect in your own rights. Can you grant Magdalena de Sarria any less? She has literally risked her life to aid your people. Now, when she needs us most, is it right for us to desert her?" Clint briefly described Roberto's treachery.

"So you see, he has little to lose and all to gain by killing her. And he will do so, by fair means or foul, if she goes into Santa Barbara alone. Are we to reward him for his many cruelties and let him go on persecuting your people?"

Pico jumped to his feet and spat on the ground. "The *perro* deserves to die! And I will gladly watch El Halcon kill him." There were rumbles of agreement from the other renegades who had joined with him. Slowly, Benito, Juan and Pablo rose to their feet, as did the latest recruits.

Only Miguel remained sitting, a troubled look on his face. Clint understood how he felt. He had cared for El Halcon more than the others, and Magdalena's deception cut deepest with him. Clint went to him and laid a hand on his shoulder.

"It was not through lack of trust that she didn't reveal herself to you, Miguel. Her very life depended on her anonymity. Knowing who she was could also have endangered you. Besides, you must be honest with yourself. Would you really have obeyed her so readily had you known she was a woman?"

Miguel heaved to his feet. "No, I would not. But such a

*401*

beautiful woman, a lady, how can she live as she does? Don't you want to make her stop?"

Clint smiled wryly. "I tried. But now it's too late. Roberto knows who she is. Her only chance is to prove him for the villain he is. Did you notice the bruises on her face, amigo?"

When Miguel nodded, Clint cogently explained how she'd gotten them—and the other plans Roberto and Luis had made for her. Miguel blanched, then reddened.

He slammed one fist into the other. "That one deserves to be squashed like the spider he is!"

"You are with us, then?"

A definitive nod. "Si."

"Excellent. I suggest you all go to Santa Barbara in groups of two. Mingle with your people and watch. One of you go to Jose Rivas's townhouse and inform him that Magdalena will be coming to the presidio tomorrow. He can rally his own people." Clint's voice grew silky with danger. "If Roberto and Luis want to kill her, they'll have to do it in full sight of the town."

Clint went to his horse and mounted. "I'll join you as soon as I can. Gracias, *compadres! Hasta luego!*" Wheeling his mount, Clint galloped up the highway toward El Paraiso.

The chirping of birds sounding a new day awakened Magdalena. She stretched, blinking at the bright sunlight. How long had she slept? It looked to be far past dawn, when she had intended to rise. Her nose twitched. The luscious scent of chocolate wafted to her nostrils as a long, patrician hand held a tin cup under her nose.

"It's time to rise, my dear."

Magdalena took the cup and sat up. "What are you doing here?"

"Why, acting as guard, of course." Charles nodded his head toward his own pallet, which he'd moved closer to hers. Two pistols sat on the grass within easy reach.

It was a measure of her exhaustion that she'd not even noticed him. Warmth filled her as she realized that even though she'd sent him away, Clint hadn't deserted her. She looked about.

"He's not here, but he'll join you in Santa Barbara," Charles said.

"How does he know Joaquin is held there?"

"Because El Paraiso is virtually deserted. And because he suspects Roberto doesn't want to be tied to your death. The authority behind your execution must be official when it's discovered who you really are." Charles went to his pallet and fetched something. He threw a familiar object at her feet. "Besides, he found this nailed to a tree at the turnoff to El Paraiso."

Her mouth dried with fear when she saw it. She picked up the small gold cross suspended from a fine chain. Joaquin was never without it. They must have had to club him to take it from him. Wrapped about it was a note. She recognized Roberto's bold hand: "Come to the presidio alone, tomorrow at dawn, and we will release him."

That was all, but it was explicit enough. She wrenched off the heavy paper and tore it into bits. She kissed the cross and dropped it in her pocket, then she finished her chocolate and rose to see to her weapons. While she polished the ornate rapier Clint had retrieved, Charles cooked her a hearty breakfast of beef, eggs and tortillas.

Magdalena fell to everything with a will. Charles looked gratified at her obvious enjoyment. "Clint brought the eggs and beef from El Paraiso before going on to Santa Barbara. You'll have a welcoming committee awaiting you, if I know my nephew."

He eyed her tremulous smile with a sigh that might have been one of envy in a lesser man. But Charles Garthwaite was made of sterner stuff. When she'd finished, he asked briskly, "Well, my dear, what is your plan?"

Wiping her mouth on a rag, Magdalena thanked him for the breakfast and began brushing her hair so she could pin it up. "Much was made clear to me in the night, señor."

"Charles, please. If we're to be related, such formality is unnecessary." He admired the blush that tinged her complexion. Even bruised, she was a lovely woman.

Magdalena cleared her throat. "I would have expected you to be appalled at your nephew's interest in me," she said huskily.

"I was not happy when I first suspected your identity, I confess. But you've made a believer of me. If you live, you'll have fine children." His smile was benign, but Magdalena did not disappoint him.

"Could the fact that those children will be half Californio have anything to do with your approval?"

His shrug was unapologetic. "More and more Californios are wedding Americans. The offspring of these alliances will not have the prejudices of their elders."

"Conquer from within, eh?" Magdalena's eyes kindled, but she didn't seem offended.

"My dear, you've a suspicious mind. Now, what are your plans?"

Smiling wryly, Magdalena shook her head at him. She collected her thoughts. "If I can redeem my name without killing Roberto, I will. He is a man who sets great store in appearances. If we do have an audience, then I may be able to anger him into making admissions he might not otherwise make." She inspected the rapier for a speck of dust. Finding none, she rose, strapped on her sheath, and stuck the sword inside.

"Yet you don't go without your weapon."

"I'm not a fool, s . . . . Charles. I'll not die tamely, if die I must." She drew on her hood, put on her hat and pulled the cord tight. Then she flung her cape about her shoulders. The ironic smile she bestowed upon him completed the picture of El Halcon. "Though fate would be unkind indeed to take life from me just as I have learned to treasure it." She went to Fuego and saddled him.

She didn't see Charles go to Reno's belongings, pick up a small book and pocket it. Then he, too, went to saddle the likeliest horse of the few still in camp. Magdalena was mounted before she saw what he was doing.

"No, you should not come. There is great danger, and I'll not have another death on my conscience."

"Well, you'll have to accept my company, regardless, for

**404**

it's sure you'll have my death on your conscience if you don't."

When she cocked her head on one side, he brushed off his hat, straightened his sadly wrinkled suit and smiled at her. "I'm like to die of curiosity." His deep, rich laughter mingled with hers.

As he mounted, he added, "Besides, aren't you curious about Clint? I can tell you much during the ride."

She bowed in her saddle. "Very well, Charles. That is inducement indeed." Her light tone grew heavy as she warned, "But when we reach El Paraiso, I go to the presidio alone."

"We'll see, child. We'll see." Charles wheeled his mount and galloped out of the canyon, leaving Magdalena no recourse but to follow.

Roberto checked his pocket watch yet again, then he resumed his pacing.

Luis, sprawled in the chair he'd pushed back from his desk, shook his head. "You weary me, Roberto. She will come, and we'll have her trapped like the vixen she is. She only delays to make us nervous."

Roberto opened the shutter to stare out into the presidio grounds. The soldiers, too, seemed tense as they stood rigidly at their posts. Magdalena would never leave here alive, yet still he worried. The American was free, and he'd already proved how resourceful he was. The pair of them made wily opponents indeed. Roberto slammed the shutter closed and turned a disgruntled look on his friend.

"Your complacency has already cost us dear. Give the American a chance, you said." Roberto pounded his fist against his thigh. "I will kill him myself when I see him again." When Luis still didn't reply, his tone grew sharper. "Don't you understand that my cousin is a formidable enemy? I have an itch on the back of my neck that warns she will fight to the last. Only when she's dead will we be safe."

"Pshaw! The woman who cowered in the chair before us was hardly formidable. We will soon enough have her so again." The words were scarce out of Luis's mouth when the lookout shouted.

Roberto and Luis rushed to the door. Even across the width of the compound, El Halcon made a striking sight. Her huge stallion shone in the sunlight with a luster of strength his rider matched. Even when she was jerked roughly from her saddle, El Halcon didn't stumble. She straightened her hat and walked gracefully forward, scorning the rough grips that pushed her.

Roberto and Luis drew deep sighs of relief and strolled to meet her, intent upon her rather than the scuffle at the gate. The guards tried to block the well-dressed gringo, but he was followed so closely by Jose and Angelina Rivas and others of the upper class that they had no option but to back off. Short of using their weapons, they had no way to stop the pressing crowd. They were shoved aside, then others filed in, Indians, *vaqueros* . . .

Luis and Roberto met Magdalena in the middle of the grounds. "Welcome, El Halcon," Luis said, sweeping off his hat in mocking deference. "How glad we are to see you again."

Bowing in return, Magdalena replied, "And I you. But this time, your brand of hospitality will be known by all." She made an encompassing gesture with her arm.

For the first time, Luis and Roberto noticed the people still pouring in to line the presidio walls. Luis scowled and called, "Clear the compound, you fools!"

When the soldiers tried to obey, Jose pulled a pistol from his belt and shot it into the air. When all was quiet, his voice rang in the enclosed space. "Why, Luis? Should we not be allowed to witness the trial of El Halcon?"

"Si, si, we stay!" came a shout in a voice Magdalena recognized. Her head reared up. There, leaning against the post outside Luis's headquarters, stood Miguel. And Juan. And Pico. And the others. Magdalena bowed her head, tears misting her eyes, then she nodded slightly in their direction to convey her gratitude. Soon the chant was taken up by all until the air fairly vibrated. The soldiers, nonplussed, looked toward their comandante.

Luis and Roberto exchanged a worried look. Then, tersely, Luis ordered, "Take his sword and bring him into my office."

Magdalena didn't struggle as her weapon was taken away or when she was pushed toward Luis's office. But somehow, when they neared his quarters, the crowd jostled until, despite sharp, repeated orders, they couldn't get through.

With mockery rich in his voice, Jose called, "Let your justice be seen and appreciated, comandante!" Shouts of agreement came from every quarter.

While Luis and Roberto again exchanged an uncertain look, Magdalena watched the small jail. The single guard was as intent on what was happening as the crowd, so when his head suddenly bobbed like a fisherman's lure, then disappeared, Magdalena wasn't surprised to see another, taller head, capped with a wide, shielding sombrero, replace his. She saw the heavy door swing open, then Joaquin stumbled into the light, rubbing at his blinded eyes.

The pair pushed through the crowd until they were standing beside Miguel. Magdalena appraised Joaquin, but, except for a cut on his cheek, he seemed unharmed. He bowed his head and crossed himself as Clint answered his question, and Magdalena knew he'd asked about Sean. Moisture glimmered in his eyes as he looked at her, but then a worried look replaced the grief. He glanced from her to Luis and Roberto, who were still talking in hushed tones. Then, for a timeless instant, Magdalena met the glittering blue eyes that became visible as the sombrero was shoved back.

"Be careful, my love. I am here with you, and here I'll stay," those eyes declared.

She swallowed the lump in her throat and wished fiercely to embrace him before all. She had to look away to contain her emotions. She closed her eyes, said a brief, fervent prayer, then, free of worry for Joaquin, she broke her silence.

"Yes, comandante, share with us your idea of justice," she said clearly.

The crowd hushed their whispering at the way Luis

**407**

stiffened. Magdalena went on, "How you've lied, cheated and murdered for your own gain and for the gain of your partner."

"*Basta!*" Roberto hissed, tightening his grip upon her arm until she winced.

But she ignored him and looked around the ring of watching faces. "I come forward now, fellow Californios, as I should have done long ago. Why, you have wondered, did a man of your kind take to the road? For justice, strange as it may seem . . ."

Luis interrupted, "Must this man pilfer your minds as he's stolen your purses? He'll say anything to save himself." He looked appealingly at the crowd, then went still. Every trace of color left his face.

Automatically, Roberto and Magdalena turned to follow his stare. Some late arrivals were pressing through the crowd, led by a tall, handsome man with black hair and eyes and authoritative mien. Magdalena had never seen Juan Bautista Alvarado, but she deduced from Luis's reaction who he was. Judging from the dust on his short, braided jacket, he'd just arrived in Santa Barbara.

He strode forward. "What is going on here, capitan?"

Luis's welcoming smile was a bit sickly. "We have captured the infamous El Halcon, Excellency, and were going to put him on trial . . ."

Snickers came from the crowd at Luis's notion of "capture." Jose whispered into Alvarado's ear. He frowned severely at Luis.

"You should have imprisoned him and sent a courier to me." He turned to look Magdalena up and down with a scrutiny as minute as her own of him. "So, you came of your own will to save one of your men?"

Magdalena pulled free of Roberto's slack grip and faced Alvarado. She bowed. "Si. I am honored to have you hear my defense." When Roberto bit back a protest she looked at him. "I *am* allowed to defend myself, am I not?"

Under Alvardo's eagle eye, Roberto could do little but shrug. "But this man is a thief and a murderer, Excellency. Nothing he says is to be trusted."

Luis agreed eagerly, "Just last night he and his men killed five of my own troops."

"And I lost three of my men. One of them like a brother to me." Magdalena's voice wavered at the end, then she steadied it and went on. "But they died for the same reason that I became a bandit."

Alvarado leaned forward as eagerly as the rest of the crowd. "Yes? And why is that?"

Magdalena's gaze settled then on Roberto. "Shall I tell them, cousin, or will you?"

His teeth ground together at her mockery, but he stared, stony-faced, straight ahead, refusing to meet her eyes.

"Cousin?" Alvarado repeated. He rubbed his jaw and looked at the short, spare man beside him who wore a priest's cassock and a worried demeanor. "Go on, El Halcon," he said more gently.

"Yes, Excellency, he is my cousin." Whispers darted back and forth among the crowd, growing to murmurs as Magdalena loosened the cord about her neck, took off her hat and tossed it away. The murmurs died when she lifted her hands to her hood. Only crickets and birds chirped as the crowd collectively held its breath.

Composedly, Magdalena took off her hood and turned her face into the light. Gasps, nervous titters and ahs of disbelief were cut short when she made the governor an elegant bow.

"Forgive my attire, Excellency, but I am indeed Magdalena Inez Flanagan de Sarria. Cousin to Roberto de Sarria."

Roberto's eyes darted back and forth, but he saw not one friendly face. Even the soldiers were staring, mouths agape, at the drama.

"Cousin to the man who most foully murdered first my brother, then my grandfather. The lands he lives on are rightfully mine."

"She lies!" Roberto cried. He took a deep breath and forced a reasonable tone. "You must have heard the true story, Excellency. She was found caught in the act, blood on her hands and clothes, holding the very knife that killed my admirable uncle."

"Si, I had his blood on my clothes. From trying to stem his wound and to save the feeble life that still remained in him when I entered the study. I heard the truth from his very lips." Magdalena didn't try to hide her anguish when she droned, "Roberto and Luis, he said. They sent men to kill Carlos, my brother, because they knew he'd not let me marry Roberto. Then, when my grandfather no longer insisted we wed after Carlos died and when he changed his will to leave all to me, Roberto killed him."

"These are the stories of a desperate woman!" Roberto pointed an accusing finger at Magdalena. "This imaginary will. If it exists why have you not come forward before now?"

Magdalena was preparing to answer when Clint and Joaquin walked across the compound to meet them. Upon seeing Clint, Luis ordered, "Seize him!"

Soldiers rushed forward, but Alvarado held up an imperative hand. "*Alto!*" When they obeyed, he turned a minatory look upon Roberto and Luis. "No one will be harmed or imprisoned until I get to the bottom of this." He looked about the surging mass of people and smiled. "Besides, a rat could not get through this crowd."

Clint carefully pulled a short, thick roll of parchment from his jacket and handed it to Alvarado. Magdalena paled, then looked inquiringly at Clint. He nodded slightly, but he missed her glorious smile because he was watching Roberto as the governor read.

"It seems legitimate enough and does indeed leave all to Magdalena de Sarria." The governor rolled the parchment back up and handed it to Clint.

Roberto growled, low and feral, in his throat, but no one but Joaquin seemed to notice, for Clint was saying, "As for Luis's role in this, it's simple." Clint jerked his head, and Miguel brought forward a small wooden chest, lurching under its weight. Clint kicked it open. People strained their necks to look. The lucky few who could see gasped when they glimpsed the dull fire inside.

410

"I can show you where I found this at de Sarria's rancho. They recruited me to help them in their plot to wrest this gold from church ownership." While Clint explained the scheme in more detail, Father Franco stooped to pick up a choice nugget, turning it this way and that into the light.

"I can show you where the find is. It borders the de Sarria property," Clint concluded.

Luis had the look of a hunted man as he blustered, "You'd believe a gringo over me?" But his hand had slipped to the sword at his waist, and slowly, he began backing away, his movements shouting his own guilt.

Alvarado kicked the lid closed in disgust and raised his head to give the order. In a flash, Roberto and Luis had their swords out.

Joaquin and Clint cried together, "Look out, Magdalena!" She turned in time to see two blades arrowing toward her heart. She dove for the ground and rolled. Miguel snatched her rapier from the stunned soldier who'd taken it and threw it to her as she leaped to her feet. She caught it ably and was able to deflect Roberto's lunging thrust.

Before Luis could strike again, he found himself engaged by Clint. Alvarado frowned, hesitating, but now that the odds were even he seemed disinclined to interfere.

Joaquin grabbed his arm. "Please, stop them."

Alvarado was intent on the swordplay. "If this incredible tale is true, then this is the best resolution. If this woman was indeed El Halcon, then she should prevail easily enough. And it will be much simpler if the American dispatches Luis than for me to have to try to explain this tangled web to Mexico and have him punished. They're as likely to make him a national hero just to spite me. No, señor. I'm a strong believer in justice conquering evil. Let us watch for a bit and see how the tide turns."

So Joaquin was forced to watch the battle he'd seen time without number in his nightmares. He could see at a glance what he thought should be apparent to all: that the advantage was decidedly not Magdalena's. He'd taught both Roberto and Magdalena. Magdalena was the most innovative, wily fencer he'd ever schooled, but Roberto was both powerful and cunning. The advantage would go to the one who most wanted to win. And Magdalena was fencing defensively, protecting her person but not threatening Roberto's. Why? What was wrong with her?

Because he couldn't bear to watch, he turned to Clint and Luis. There was more comfort here. Luis's confidence was wavering. His awkward lunges were easily read and handily countered. Clint had thrown off his sombrero, and his hair flashed as bright as the engraving on his rapier when he rotated his wrist, disengaged and stabbed before Luis was ready. Luis managed to bring his weapon up enough to deflect Clint's aim. The swordpoint that would have disemboweled Luis glanced off his upper arm.

Leaping back, Luis wiped the sweat from his forehead. What he saw in the American's eyes chilled his blood. "What have I done to you for you to hate me so?" he panted, angling his sword to block a leftward jab.

Clint had spared a glance at the other battle, and he saw things were not going well for Magdalena. She was backing away, slanting her sword left, right and sideways to block Roberto's furious thrusts, but her ripostes were lackluster. He swallowed the bile of fear and fixed his gaze even more fiercely on one of the men who had forced her into this danger.

"Little, but you have done much to one who means all to me. You'll pay for your despicable acts with your life." And Clint redoubled his efforts, thrusting, slashing, lunging until Luis's parries became weaker and weaker. Finally, Clint saw his opening. He took it without hesitation.

Luis had to swing his blade wide to the left to block an apparent stab at his side, but in the last moment, Clint twitched his wrist. His true aim was apparent to Luis then, but it was too late. Feebly he tried to bring his blade around, but Clint had already slipped through. His swordpoint pierced Luis's breastbone, thrusting through flesh, muscle and bone to a softer, pulsing mass that lurched, then stopped.

Clint drew his sword out and wiped it absently on Luis's

jacket, thinking that the bastard should bleed putrid black to match his evil heart, but the fluid gushing out was the usual red. Clint turned away without a second thought and went to stand beside Joaquin. He didn't even notice the governor's piercing stare, for he was conscious of only one thing.

Joaquin grabbed his arm. "Clint, do something. Cut him down. Help her!"

Though Clint gripped Joaquin's hand with a strength that conveyed his own fear, he didn't move a muscle. He'd learned his lesson well. In sight of all, she had to prevail, fairly. And he loved her too much to deny her that right. Nevertheless, his lips moved in soundless prayer as he watched. God could not be so cruel as to take her now, when they'd won . . .

Roberto's grimace of hatred was matched by the fury behind every thrust, parry and riposte. Clint saw Magdalena's arm tensing to ward off the blows, but the hatred he'd often observed in her eyes was gone. She looked almost . . . mournful, as if she were reluctant to kill him. And that reluctance showed in her fencing. Clint shuddered as she misread a wily feint and almost paid with her life for the mistake. Just in time, she realized her error and arced her blade up barely enough to deflect the furious thrust that would have pierced her heart. There came the ripping sound of tearing silk, and a tiny spot began growing, soaking the dark material at her shoulder, before she stumbled back.

A satisfied grunt escaped Roberto. "So, the fierce El Halcon is a myth. Where is your daring and your skill now, eh?" He ended the taunt with a crafty jab that changed course at the last moment.

This time, Magdalena read the move and parried it easily. She felt her wound throbbing, but perversely, she was glad for its sting. She'd been trying to wear him down, hoping to wound, not kill him. But Roberto was almost as skilled as Carlos had been, and this time there were no buttons on their swords. This time, they played no game. This time, her life would be forfeit if she lost this duel.

She didn't want to kill him, not only because finally she understood the value of life, but also because Roberto was

*413*

her last remaining relative. The same blood flowed in their veins. She'd killed once, gladly, in vengeance and let hatred almost destroy her. Roberto, perhaps, didn't deserve mercy, but her motives were more selfish than altruistic. He still disgusted her, she despised him for what he'd done and she would always mourn her family, but killing Roberto would not bring them back. She didn't want to risk the happiness she finally had a chance for. Besides, she'd won. Clint had found the will and convinced the governor, so Roberto would be punished if she allowed him to live. And that, she knew, Roberto would find far more humiliating than a quick, honorable death.

It seemed he read her mind, for he sneered, "If you think to take me alive, forget it, *puta*. But before I go, I'll take you with me . . . as I did your brother, and your grandfather." He took advantage of her shaken control and slipped under her guard yet again. This thrust was a downward one, however, and his point barely grazed her thigh.

She quickly swiveled sideways. This time, when her eyes met Roberto's, they'd darkened to agates. A distant, muffled cry penetrated her concentration. Vaguely, she recognized Joaquin's voice.

"No, Clint! I can't let her die!" A loud report startled both her and Roberto. Each paused to look. Clint had obviously jerked Joaquin's arm up when he would have fired at Roberto. He snatched the gun away and put his arm about Joaquin's shaking shoulders, though Magdalena could read his own distress in every inch of his tense, muscular frame. When his blue eyes met hers, she quivered as if struck. There was pleading there, and pride, and a love wide enough to fill the ocean.

He said one thing only. "Remember Sean, my love."

She knew something momentous had just occurred between them, but she had no time to think on it, for Roberto engaged her again. Mechanically she parried a fierce jab at her stomach, for she was remembering Sean as he died. How Carlos had looked in death. How loving her grandfather had finally been when he faced his own end. And when

*414*

her eyes focused again, she saw before her the face of the man who had directly or indirectly killed them all.

She saw, too, her own death written in his face. He had taken too much from her; she'd not give him more. The compassion that had stayed her hardened under the rush of memories. This time, when Roberto thrust, she batted his sword aside and riposted with a straight-armed lunge so fierce that only turning slightly aside saved his shoulder.

Magdalena knew nothing, heard nothing then but the soft stomp of their feet on the ground, the singing of twining blades and the beat of her determined heart. Now it was Roberto who backed away and fought defensively. Surprise showed first on his face as he stepped back, parrying her running lunge. Then came slight concern as she read a deceitful feint and parried with a swift upthrust, knocking his blade skyward, then disentangled to aim for his heart. At the last moment, he slammed his blade down. But even that swift reaction was almost too late, for she was ready for the move and disengaged to stab again.

Fear showed in his face now as he read her body motion and backed a step, sucking in his belly to avoid the thrust. He tried to counter quickly with a long-armed feint and swift-footed lunge, but she read him again and blocked the stab, slipping her sword down the length of his, forcing his blade into the ground.

They both panted now, but Magdalena had led a hard, physical life for over two years, and Roberto's only exercise had been riding and an occasional fencing bout with Luis. Roberto's tiredness showed in his sagging blade when he parried a fiendish thrust and riposted sluggishly.

Magdalena blocked the feeble stab with insulting ease, whamming his blade wide and following up with a lunge that pierced his shoulder. He winced and stepped back, countering automatically, but that, too, she parried.

The fear in his face turned to dread, but he didn't go gently. Magdalena, too, was tiring when she finally saw her opening. Her instincts bade her take it, and she lunged, thrusting through his weak guard, reaching for his heart. At the last moment, something, some decency stronger than her hatred, made her pull her arm in. The tip pierced his breastbone, but stopped far short of his heart. His blade sagged downward as he clutched his bleeding chest with his other hand. He wavered, as if he'd fall any moment.

Drawing a deep, relieved breath, Magdalena let her own blade droop as she turned to walk to Clint. Her eyes were fixed on his face, but he was watching behind her.

He screamed, "Look out, Magdalena!"

She sensed movement behind her and whirled. The action threw off Roberto's aim, and she took his point in her side instead of her back. But his last, desperate lunge had left him overextended, and when she reflexively whipped her blade to his throat, he had no defense. He swallowed her swordtip and her name on a final ugly gurgle. His jugular and his windpipe were severed. Bright red, air-filled blood bubbled out. He dropped his sword and fell backward, making awful, wretching sounds in concert with the blood he spit up in mighty gushes. His twitching slowed, then stilled.

Magdalena flung her sword as far as she could send it, clutched her side and fell to one knee. She'd barely touched the ground before Clint was there, pressing his handkerchief to her side, kissing her brow, running his hands over her as if to verify her reality.

"*Te amo, mi vida,* you scared me to within an inch of my life, I'll never let you go," he babbled.

She muffled his words with her fingers. "You stopped Joaquin from killing Roberto, didn't you?"

He nodded uncertainly. "It was the hardest thing I've ever done, but I knew how much you wanted to end this fight yourself. You'd not have been able to live with yourself if Roberto had been killed in such a way, to save you." He held his breath, and her reaction did not disappoint him.

"I love you, Clinton James Browning," she said simply gazing up at him with devotion ablaze in her eyes. She buried her fingers in his tousled hair and pulled his bright head down to hers, her heart singing with such joy that she scarcely felt her wounds.

And in full sight of most of the population of Santa Barbara and the governor of California, Magdalena Inez Flanagan de Sarria, alias El Halcon, proved to all that she was very much a woman. That she loved. That she relished life. And that she scorned convention. Some things, it seemed, would never change . . .

# Chapter 17

"Here old life ends, and here new begins; evil has lost
its power."

**Act I, DON JUAN TENORIO**

Several days later, Magdalena Inez Flanagan de Sarria
Browning dropped her bundle on El Paraiso's precious earth
and knelt to put flowers on each of the four graves. She
stroked the cross on Carlos's mound, marveling yet again
over her grandfather's cunning—and Clint's, for figuring
out the secret. Had abuelo suspected Roberto's true nature
when he hid the will? Or had he put it there as a repentance
for his harshness with Carlos? Magdalena kissed her finger
and touched each cross, tears coming to her eyes, but they
were clean, healthy tears of release, rather than the twisted
grief that had guided her for so long.

She lay back, clasping her arms beneath her head,
delaying the task she'd come up here alone to do. For Clint.
For the four who had died. And for herself. But why, then,
this strange reluctance, if she knew it was right? Magdalena
sighed and twisted the new gold band on her finger.

The governor had, with some persuasion, absolved her

when Clint had made restitution for the money and trinkets they'd stolen. Sean's portion had been given to Father Franco, and they had promised to repay the horses they'd taken out of El Paraiso's bountiful stock.

Alvarado had really been easy to convince, she thought now, with Charles's assistance. He was a compassionate man, and when Charles had given him Reno's book detailing each band member's story—the names scratched out—his stern demeanor had slipped even more. He'd promised Magdalena he would investigate the abuses the Indians were suffering if she would promise never to rob again.

"Besides," he'd added, his dark eyes gleaming, "if I tried to imprison you, I'd be reviled up and down the country, so much have you captured our peoples' admiration." He'd turned then to Charles. "I do it because it is the right thing to do, not because you've swayed me in any way."

Magdalena had turned her head to hide a smile as the pair glared at one another. Charles had insinuated he'd advise his state department to allow the Californios more time to work out their own problems *if* the governor showed the wisdom necessary to bring such a broad, diverse land together. Clint had hustled Charles away before the tiff could deepen into an argument. Charles had left to return home yesterday after the wedding.

Magdalena's smile was both exasperated and fond as she recalled his parting remark. "And when I return in a year, I expect to hold my great-nephew, the first of many." He'd kissed her cheek and serenely begun the long journey back, as convinced of California's destiny as he'd been when he arrived. But at least, she thought, he'd allowed that Californios had a great deal to say about that destiny. He'd carried with him a long letter of instructions to be given to Clint's eldest sister's husband on how affairs were to be managed until Clint could make an extended visit.

Magdalena frowned now, remembering that the subject had caused their only argument since the wedding. And that memory acted as impetus upon her. Clint had done so much for her, and she loved him so. This, she would do for him. She rose, brushed off her skirts, threw the bundle upon the pile of brush she'd erected some distance from the graves, poured lantern oil upon the pile and ignited it. She sighed as she watched the flames lick hungrily at the black velvet and silk . . .

"What are you burning, my love? You shouldn't have snuck off like that and left me napping." Strong arms clasped about her waist.

She leaned back against the broad chest and watched the flames. "I'm burning the last of El Halcon, *querido*."

When the strong frame behind her stiffened, she turned in the circle of Clint's arms. "I want to be your wife and mother of your children. I have my first chance of true happiness, and I won't risk it for anything." She kissed his throat, unaware of the smile in his eyes. "I still think we should go immediately to America. A letter can never settle your affairs there. And who can say? Maybe I'd really like it."

Lifting her arms about his neck, Clint lowered his chin atop her head and rubbed it in the silky mass. "I can visualize how my sisters' friends would react. You'd have them in rebellion in a week and the men would have my hide. No, my love. I can't take you away. Your roots are here. This land is a part of you. The Indians are depending on you for help, and how can you do that in America? Besides, Santa Barbara will be a good place for me to open a new office. I've been wanting to expand for some time. And lastly," Clint lowered his head to nuzzle her small ear, "I've a growing fondness for California fostered by my love for its loveliest daughter. This is a good place to raise our children."

They exchanged yet another kiss, their lips still swollen from the last one, but they could never get enough of one another. Clint's hunger grew quickly, but he tamped it down. Her side was still sore, so he'd curbed his impatience for the past days and coddled her, hoping to aid her healing. He groaned and pushed her away, looking over her head at the dying fire. He kicked dirt over it, then grabbed her hand.

"Come, vixen. I've something to give you."

Magdalena followed him inside to the room he'd insisted on taking until her side healed. She sat on the bed, bouncing luxuriously up and down on its softness, while he fetched a large parcel.

He sat down next to her and put it in her lap, watching her expectantly. The drawn curtains let sunlight fill the room, and it centered on the figure next to her. She watched him, absorbing his hair, eyes, skin and body through every pore. He cleansed her, fulfilled her as nothing in her life ever had. He was light come to earth to ease her darkness. Never again would she accept the night.

It was a strange look to see in eyes that wielded such power, but the fathomless adoration made Clint's heart—and something else—surge with gladness. He shifted and urged hoarsely, "Open it."

She looked down and pulled the string. Her fingers trembled as she drew the garments from the paper: softest doeskin breeches, cream shirt with lace flowing from the bodice, beige boots and a wide, gold-engraved buckle on a supple leather belt. It was the prettiest masculine attire she'd ever seen. She blinked away tears and looked up at the man watching her closely.

"What does this mean?" she asked in a hushed voice.

He took the parcel from her and set it on the floor, then unpinned her hair and ran his fingers through it. "It means, *querida*, that I love you. You'd no need to burn your disguise to please me, for I will always cherish the memory of El Halcon fearlessly leading her band into battle. It took me too long to realize, but it is those qualities that drew me to you first. I was wrong to ask you to stifle them. I want all of you, Magdalena. Every nuance of your personality is precious to me."

Sobbing, she threw her arms about his neck. "Oh Clint, I love you so. I yearn to make you happy . . ."

"You do, Magdalena-Carlotta-El Halcon. Just as you are." He pulled her face against his thumping heart, adding

422

wryly, "Though I hope you heal quickly." He steadied his voice. "There's much I want you to show me. I may not ever surpass your skill with a blade, my dear, but I hope you can teach me to match it."

Magdalena opened his shirt, ignoring the way he stiffened. She kissed one small nipple, smiling when it hardened against her tongue. "Agreed, *querido*, if you, too, will be my teacher."

And there, in the blindingly pure light, Magdalena Inez Flanagan de Sarria Browning celebrated in the most basic way the brilliance of her future. Not a shadow lurked in the room, nor a blot on the heart that surged with life reborn, gifted to her by the magnificent male who, through his love, had made her love herself.